June Love

Karla Hocker

**ZEBRA BOOKS
KENSINGTON PUBLISHING CORP.**

ZEBRA BOOKS are published by

Kensington Publishing Corp.
850 Third Avenue
New York, NY 10022

Copyright © 1995 by Karla Hocker

All rights reserved. No part of this book may be reproduced in any form or by any means without the prior written consent of the Publisher, excepting brief quotes used in reviews.

If you purchased this book without a cover, you should be aware that this book is stolen property. It was reported as "unsold and destroyed" to the Publisher and neither the Author nor the Publisher has received any payment for this "stripped book."

Zebra and the Z logo Reg. U.S. Pat. & TM Off.

First Printing: June, 1995

Printed in the United States of America

A GENTLEMAN'S COURTSHIP

"I think it will be best after all if I take a turn about the terrace."

Thea pushed back her chair, but before she could rise, Stanmore forestalled her by clasping her hands and drawing her to her feet.

"Miss Stone—Thea. I meant what I said. I wish to know you. I shan't press you to tell me anything you'd rather not disclose. But surely there must be more you can share about your life with the Simmons family than that they taught you history and archery?"

"Yes . . . yes, of course. I learned to ride . . . and climb trees . . . and a great many other things." Thea wished he would let go of her hands, and the next instant, that he would not. "But my stay at the vicarage cannot possibly be of interest to you."

"You're wrong." He raised first one, then the other of her hands to his lips. "Thea—little goose. When a man is courting a woman, everything about her is of interest."

ZEBRA REGENCIES
ARE
THE TALK OF THE TON!

A REFORMED RAKE (4499, $3.99)
by Jeanne Savery
After governess Harriet Cole helped her young charge flee to France—and the designs of a despicable suitor, more trouble soon arrived in the person of a London rake. Sir Frederick Carrington insisted on providing safe escort back to England. Harriet deemed Carrington more dangerous than any band of brigands, but secretly relished matching wits with him. But after being taken in his arms for a tender kiss, she found herself wondering—*could* a lady find love with an irresistible rogue?

A SCANDALOUS PROPOSAL (4504, $4.99)
by Teresa DesJardien
After only two weeks into the London season, Lady Pamela Premington has already received her first offer of marriage. If only it hadn't come from the *ton's* most notorious rake, Lord Marchmont. Pamela had already set her sights on the distinguished Lieutenant Penford, who had the heroism and honor that made him the ideal match. Now she had to keep from falling under the spell of the seductive Lord so she could pursue the man more worthy of her love. Or was he?

A LADY'S CHAMPION (4535, $3.99)
by Janice Bennett
Miss Daphne, art mistress of the Selwood Academy for Young Ladies, greeted the notion of ghosts haunting the academy with skepticism. However, to avoid rumors frightening off students, she found herself turning to Mr. Adrian Carstairs, sent by her uncle to be her "protector" against the "ghosts." Although, Daphne would accept no interference in her life, she *would* accept aid in exposing any spectral spirits. What she never expected was for Adrian to expose the secret wishes of her hidden heart . . .

CHARITY'S GAMBIT (4537, $3.99)
by Marcy Stewart
Charity Abercrombie reluctantly embarks on a London season in hopes of making a suitable match. However she cannot forget the mysterious Dominic Castille—and the kiss they shared—when he fell from a tree as she strolled through the woods. Charity does not know that the dark and dashing captain harbors a dangerous secret that will ensnare them both in its web—leaving Charity to risk certain ruin and losing the man she so passionately loves . . .

Available wherever paperbacks are sold, or order direct from the Publisher. Send cover price plus 50¢ per copy for mailing and handling to Penguin USA, P.O. Box 999, c/o Dept. 17109, Bergenfield, NJ 07621. Residents of New York and Tennessee must include sales tax. DO NOT SEND CASH.

One

"I regret, sir. As I've told you before, I have no desire to contract a second marriage."

"Desire? Pshaw! I'm speaking of duty, Stuart. Of obligation!"

Father and son faced each other in the breakfast parlor on the ground floor of Archer Hall's capacious east wing. Rays of morning sun poured through leaded panes in high windows and dispelled the gloomy effect of dark paneling and smothering velvet drapes. From the south lawn outside a window bay as wide as the massive seventeenth-century table was long came the sound of childish squeals and laughter. But if either man took pleasure in the children's delight or in the sunshine, unlooked-for on a first day of February, he did not show it.

Charles Henry Archer, seventh earl Barnet, looked decidedly ill-tempered, bushy gray brows above sunken eyes knitting in a frown, jaw working, color high—a deep crimson that would have provoked his physician, had he been present, to prescribe an immediate bloodletting.

The earl's son and heir, Stuart Seymour Archer, Viscount Stanmore, knew the signs of rising choler only too well and resigned himself to missing yet another meal. He disliked arguments and confrontations. When he was a child, his shrinking from an irate father or tutor had been put down to timidity. But that was a misjudgment of character. Stanmore had never been frightened or intimidated; he had merely, since nature saw fit to endow him with an overgenerous measure of reserve, been rendered acutely uncomfortable by a noisy display of emotion.

Over the years, he had learned to counter bursts of temper with deliberate calm and to absent himself before his head began to throb unbearably. He presented a calm front now, even though it irked to have reminders of duty and obligation thrown at him when his life had been lived in constant awareness of duty to family, to name, and to bloodline.

Ignoring the poached eggs and rashers of bacon on his plate, Stanmore folded his napkin.

"Sir, I did my duty and fulfilled my obligations when I married Charlotte and sired two children."

"Only *one* son. Demme, Stuart!" Lord Barnet's fist smacked on the table and set the silver rattling. "There's measles on the estate and at Ravensbrook. Your cousin Matthew died of the measles!"

"Your fretting is groundless. Matthew was a sickly infant, not a sturdy nine-year-old like Charlie. And both Charlie and Bella have already had the measles."

"There's smallpox! Must I remind you, I lost three sons to that cursed disease?"

And a wife and daughter, Stanmore might have added. But he knew that, although his father might overlook that he once had a daughter, he did not forget or cease to miss his first wife, mother of his children.

Thus, Stanmore rose, saying merely, "I had the household inoculated with Dr. Jenner's vaccine."

"Newfangled, worthless rubbish! It made young Charlie ill!" Barnet shot his son a fierce look. "There's an outbreak now. In St Albans."

"Nigh on twelve miles distant. And we have very little traffic with the town."

"There's the governess! But I've already told her she cannot go there on her day off. Stap me! Four deaths at first report! You must see it's your duty to take a new wife. Have more children. More *sons*." Barnet's powerful voice rose. "Don't walk off when I'm talking to you!"

On his way to the door, Stanmore neither paused nor turned to look at his father. His voice remained low and even. "We've been over these grounds a score of times since Charlotte's death. There's nothing else to be said."

"There's plenty to be said!" Once again Lord Barnet's fist crashed onto the table. "Mansford is expecting you at his Berkshire seat. To look his daughters over."

This did bring Stanmore to a halt. He faced Barnet, who had risen from his chair at the head of the table. They were quite alike in many ways—the same powerful build, although the earl, at sixty-one, showed signs of stooping; the same strong jaw, long, slightly aquiline nose, heavy-lidded dark eyes. But Stanmore's features were clear-cut and chiseled while the puffiness of the older man's face betrayed a tendency to overindulge.

A slight twitch of Stanmore's left eyelid was the only sign that his calm was forced. "I'm barely acquainted with Mansford, sir. And I certainly never expressed an interest in his daughters."

"*I* expressed the interest on your behalf. There's three of his gals, ripe for marriage. One seventeen. And a pair of twins, nineteen. They're related to Somerset on the mother's side."

"And I am turned thirty-two. Nothing—not a connection to the Duke of Somerset or to the King himself—would induce me to contemplate cradle robbing. Even if I were thinking of marriage. And that I most assuredly am not."

"Devil take it, Stuart! Even if you don't measure up to your poor brothers in pluck and backbone, you've never lacked wit."

Stanmore made no reply. There was no point. His "poor brothers" had been resting in their graves these past five-and-twenty years. Nothing he might say or do would convince Barnet that his only surviving offspring, his heir, was not a spineless weakling.

"You've been keeper of the records since you turned sixteen." The earl spoke more quietly, but the belligerent thrust of his head and the tight fists planted on either side of his breakfast plate warned of barely controlled temper. "You of all people must understand the Archers' sacred duty to continue the bloodline."

"The bloodline is being merrily perpetuated on the distaff side. My aunts—" Stanmore hesitated when he saw his father's face turn purple. "Sir, I know you don't care to be reminded, but it was through the female lines in the first place that our claims to royal blood originated."

"Damn your impudence! As if I needed a reminder!"

"Then why ignore Bella's existence? And what about my cousins? Even the title can pass to a female."

Thrusting a chair out of the way, Lord Barnet advanced on his son. "For nigh on two hundred years, bloodline, name, and title have been passed from father to son."

"And thus it will continue. Through your son and my son."

"But if, God forbid, something should happen to young Charles, *you* would be the one to break the tradition!"

Outside the window bay, Stanmore caught a glimpse of his children—Charlie, nine years old; Bella, almost six. They had discarded mufflers and mittens and were chasing each other around a fast disappearing patch of snow in the shade of a venerable oak.

Merry as grigs . . . for the moment. Childhood never lasted long for Archer children, especially if they were male. Already, young Charles James Archer, burning to attend Harrow and Cambridge, was beginning to feel the weight of family tradition.

Archer tradition. Stanmore thought of it as the Archer curse.

"Demme, Stuart! Stop the woolgathering and answer me. Will *you* be the one to break with tradition?"

"If need be, yes."

"Blasphemy!" The already thundering voice rose to a deafening roar. "Do you want to rush me to my grave?"

"Not at all." Stanmore's lid twitched again as pressure began to build in his head, just above the temples. "Wherefore I shall take my leave of you. I would not wish to be the cause of an apoplexy."

"Aye, you'll take your leave! You'll leave for Berkshire in the morning, and there's an end to the discussion."

"I regret, sir, but I'm obliged to post up to London this afternoon. I shall be gone a sennight."

"Demme, you can't! I told Mansford to expect you."

"In that case you will have to inform Lord Mansford that you arranged the visit without consulting me. And now, if you'll excuse me, sir, I must speak with Bella and Charlie."

The earl Barnet's bellow of outrage ringing in his ears, Stanmore did not immediately seek out his children but retired to his own apartments on the second floor of the west wing.

His bedchamber was the southwest corner room in which the three-foot thick outer walls did not meet but formed an open archway into a second chamber situated in the projecting angle-turret. A door opened from the bedchamber to a stairwell enclosed in one of the partial walls—providing the sole access to the muniment room in the very top of the turret.

Up there, surrounded by high shelves, massive chests, several desks, and the musty smell of old parchment and vellum, Stanmore found the quiet he could depend on to subdue the throbbing in his head. An alternative remedy was a wild cross-country ride with the wind tearing at his hair; the only sounds, the fast drumming of hooves and his own harsh breath mingling with that of the horse. But this morning there was no time for a ride.

He sat at his favorite desk, a cylinder-top writing table his paternal grandmother had brought from Paris on one of her numerous visits to her native country. Unlocking and opening the cylinder, Stanmore removed a gilt-edged card from one of the pigeonholes. A dinner invitation from his friend John Markham and John's wife, Lady Felicity, for the morrow, Friday, the second day of February.

On the back of the card John Markham had scrawled a message.

> *Stuart, you rogue! You ignored the previous two invitations. Felicity says I shall have to call you out if you ignore this one because she has planned the dinner specifically to please you. She wants you to meet a guest presently staying with us—but not much longer. Felicity advises you to snatch opportunity by the forelock. I daresay you know what to make of all this. Ah, yes. Our guest is T. E. Stone.*

T. E. Stone was a name that had instantly caught Stanmore's attention when the invitation from Upper Brook Street arrived. T. E. Stone, the historian, whose scholarly theses and dissertations were published by the Society of Antiquaries of London, the Society of Antiquaries of Scotland in Edinburgh, and even by the *Dilettanti* Society.

Hoping to make Mr. Stone's acquaintance well before the dinner party, Stanmore had intended to leave for London within a day or two of receiving the invitation. Unfortunately the earl was suffering a severe attack of gout, which meant that, unless Stanmore remained at Archer Hall to soothe ruffled feathers, all but the staunchest members of the staff would have fled in the sennight he planned to be gone.

Even that morning when he entered the breakfast parlor Stanmore had not yet made up his mind about leaving, since the earl, though recovered, was still in an irascible mood. It was Lord Barnet's carping on a subject Stanmore had considered closed that settled the matter. A bag had been packed several days ago. All that remained to be done was bidding the children good-bye.

Stanmore rose. Bella and Charlie had been clamoring for an archery contest, and as long as the sun was shining there was no reason not to let them have their wish before he left. The days were still short, but the worst stretch of road lay at the beginning of his journey. The distance from Archer Hall to Whetstone and the turnpike was little more than two miles as the crow flies, but the narrow lane joining the two points was rutted and muddied by recent thaws and snaked around fields and coppices, past the ruins of the old Archer farmstead, and past Ravensbrook, John Markham's boyhood home, for a torturous four-and-a-half miles that must be driven at a snail's pace. Once he reached the turnpike, however, he could give the horses their heads.

Then, as soon as he arrived at Barnet House in the Strand, a message to John Markham and Lady Felicity . . . and on the morrow a meeting with the man whose field of expertise was Tudor and Stuart history. T. E. Stone.

Two

"It appears Lord Stanmore has had second thoughts about meeting T. E. Stone."

"Oh, no! I'm sure you're wrong. Stanmore would not change his mind." For the third time in less than five minutes Lady Felicity Markham deserted her companion on the chaise longue and hurried to a window overlooking Upper Brook Street. But, as before, the carriage she heard did not stop at the Markham residence.

She frowned. "I'm beginning to fear some mishap. Stanmore's note clearly indicated he'd be here at six o'clock to insure private, uninterrupted conversation with you before the other dinner guests arrive. I wonder . . . perhaps I should have let him know that he's the only guest expected."

"Besides me."

"I don't count you as a guest. You're almost family."

Distracted, Lady Felicity peeked through the curtains once more. "I wish you hadn't drawn out your stay in Scotland. If you had returned in December when we were at Ravensbrook, you would have accompanied us to Archer Hall for the Boxing Day gathering and the New Year's toast. Lord Barnet does not often offer hospitality to his neighbors, but he does on feast days. More to the point, I've never seen him out of humor on those occasions or reluctant to receive a neighbor's guest."

"Believe me, it wasn't at my instigation that the Highland roads were rendered impassible. On the fifteenth of December my work was done, my trunk packed."

"There he is!" Lady Felicity turned from the window. "Did I not tell you Stanmore is a man of his word?"

"Indeed. And only an hour late."

"Now don't, I beg, let a bit of tardiness set your mind against him."

"It won't. I'm just as eager as Stanmore is—or as you say he is—to have this meeting. In truth, I am *aux anges* over Stanmore's interest in me. His father snubbed me most witheringly when I asked for permission to study the Archer family history."

"But that was three years ago."

"And not on a feast day."

The remark, the gently ironic tone of delivery, went unheeded as the door opened and the Honorable John Markham, his cherubic face enlivened by a boyish grin, mild brown eyes agleam behind gold-rimmed spectacles, ushered his friend Viscount Stanmore into the drawing room.

"Stuart!" cried Lady Felicity and flew across the room to cast herself at Stanmore's broad chest.

He returned the hug.

"A welcome to warm the cockles of my heart." Over her head, artfully coiffed with long guinea-golden curls cascading from a topknot, he directed a quizzing look at Markham. "And well-deserved after your, 'What the deuce kept you?' A fine way to greet a friend."

Keeping a fond eye on his pretty wife, Markham said, "Ingrate. Consider how lightly you got off! I might have instructed the footman not to admit tardy arrivals."

"Indeed." Lady Felicity stepped back. "What made you so dreadfully late, Stuart?"

"Pray accept my apologies. I hope I did not inconvenience you."

"I vow I had quite given you up for dead!"

"I don't believe I'm dead, though after the many mishaps of the day I may very well be my own ghost and not know it."

"How ominous. Did I see you limp? Do tell what happened, Stuart!"

"Barnet House happened."

"Barnet House? Aggravating man! Can you not be more specific?"

Markham said, "My love, aren't you forgetting something?"

"Gracious, yes!"

Lady Felicity's look of dismay toward the far end of the drawing room directed Stanmore's attention to a lady seated on the chaise longue facing the fireplace. He could see only her back, slim and straight; the shoulders a hand's width of creamy skin rising above claret-colored velvet. The back of her head was shapely and elegant, with thick brown hair dressed in a simple twist at the nape of a slender neck.

His gaze on the still figure by the fireplace, he said in a low voice, "It must be earlier than I thought if I am only the second person to arrive. Else, you're keeping country hours and have dined already, and the majority of your guests has left."

"Of course not, silly." Quickly recovered, Lady Felicity gave a gurgle of laughter. "Our guests are all here now."

"And Mr. Stone? I did hope to make his acquaintance."

John Markham blinked owlishly behind the thick lenses of his spectacles and looked inquiringly at his wife.

She placed a hand on Stanmore's arm. "And so you shall, Stuart. Come along. Let me make you known to Miss Thea Stone."

Responding to Lady Felicity's urgent tug on his sleeve, Stanmore accompanied her and Markham across a scatter of luxurious Turkey rugs.

Miss Thea Stone . . . a daughter of the renowned scholar?

She rose and turned, a tall, slender woman; young but not in the first blush of youth, with a frank, appraising stare and a slow, entrancing smile that caught and held his attention. He almost did not see the hand she extended.

"Lord Stanmore." A firm voice, slightly deep for a woman's,

but not unpleasantly so. "I am delighted to make your acquaintance. Your family history is most intriguing."

"You are T. E. Stone."

"Theadora Evalina." Her smile widened. "My compliments, sir. You recovered quickly from the shock—and you were quite astounded, were you not? I saw it in your eyes."

"Far from recovered, I am struck dumb. I have followed your publications in *Archeologia* for several years. It seems impossible—"

"Don't, Stuart!" Lady Felicity cut in. "Pray don't say Thea is too young to be so learned or too pretty to concern herself with stuffy historical matters. You wouldn't be so Gothic, would you?"

"I'm neither Gothic nor would I call history stuffy, my dear. And far be it from me to reprove a lady." Stanmore directed a speaking look at Lady Felicity. "However . . ."

Her limpid gaze was innocent of mischief or wrongdoing. "Why didn't I tell you T. E. Stone is not a man?"

"Precisely. I distinctly recall a conversation we had in . . . October, I believe. Yes, the middle of October. I had come to town for Charlie's birthday gift, and John wanted me to accompany him to Tattersall's. But he was delayed at the bank."

"And you were in alt because the *Dilettanti* Society had published something Thea wrote about Arbella Stuart and the rumor that she bore William Seymour a child."

"Then I'm glad I was kept at the bank," said Markham. "Dash it, Stuart! You're obsessed with family history. I don't recall you boring on about it when we were boys. Why now?"

Lady Felicity would not allow a side issue to intrude. Waving her husband to silence, she said to Stanmore, "And you said you wished you could meet her."

"*Him,* Felicity. I referred to T. E. Stone as a man, and you did not correct me."

Markham said, "Up to your tricks again, my love? I should have known when you insisted I use Miss Stone's professional name on the invitation."

"Tricks, indeed," Stanmore said dryly. He cocked a brow at his hostess. "Assuring me you'd find a way to introduce me to *him*."

"To T. E. Stone. I'm certain I never referred to Thea as *him*."

"Does it matter?" asked Miss Stone, a frosty-green glint in her eyes. She addressed Stanmore. "Surely, sir, if the piece on Lady Arbella piqued your interest, it can make no difference whether the author is man or woman."

"No difference at all," he said. "And I apologize for my bad manners. Miss Stone, it is an honor and a pleasure meeting you."

She inclined her head, a gesture so inherently regal and gracious that for one mad instant Stanmore believed himself in the presence of royalty. Then he saw her eyes, no longer frosty but dancing with laughter.

"I do that well, don't I, Lord Stanmore? Or so my foster father tells me. Only he can never quite make up his mind whether he approves or disapproves of the accomplishment."

Stanmore was not certain how to respond. She appeared to be laughing—not at him but at herself. Though why, he was at a loss to understand. "Indeed, Miss Stone. Am I forgiven my boorishness, then?"

"But of course."

"Thea never carries a grudge," said Lady Felicity. "She says it's a shameful waste of energy that should be put to better use."

"Just something else my foster father told me."

"Indeed," Stanmore said again.

Having come to town in anticipation of meeting *Mr.* T. E. Stone, he found himself floundering in the presence of *Miss* Stone. A first impression of dignity and regal bearing brought to mind Queen Bess as she was portrayed holding a rainbow in her right hand and with the serpent of wisdom entwined on her left arm; but a mere glimpse of Miss Stone's smile allowed one thought only: enchantress.

Theodora Evalina Stone—something about the name struck

him as odd; perhaps the combination of elaborate and plain. Not that it mattered. Theadora Evalina or plain Thea Stone, she could not possibly render the assistance he needed.

Miss Stone gave him a disconcertingly direct look. "Felicity tells me you have questions on *Arbella Stuart—Mystery Unsolved*. It seems to me, sir, that I should be the one asking the questions. Your family is in possession of documents regarding Arbella Stuart which have never been made public."

John Markham said hastily, "If it cannot wait until after dinner, I'm willing to give you an hour to interrogate each other. But only on your solemn oaths to leave the Lady Arbella behind when we sit down to dine."

Lady Felicity added, "And Stuart must promise to tell what horrendous mishaps made him an hour late."

Left alone with Viscount Stanmore, Thea Stone invited him to join her on the chaise longue and offered sherry or Madeira. He declined a drink and after a moment's hesitation said he would prefer to stand by the fire.

She watched him lean against the mantelpiece, a tall man of muscular, well-proportioned build requiring no buckram padding to fill the shoulders of his coat. He did not strike her as bashful, yet he seemed ill at ease.

"You *are* disappointed that I am a female."

He gave her a wary look, which provoked her into adding, "You may speak your mind without fear that I shall burst into tears or lecture on the subject of the rights and abilities of women."

"Miss Stone, I meant it when I said that meeting you is a pleasure and an honor. And I hope that, before I return to Archer Hall, you will permit me to ask a great many questions about your research on Arbella Stuart."

"Of course . . . as I hope you'll answer mine. But you're not being quite frank with me, Lord Stanmore. I can sense disappointment overshadowing your pleasure. I wish you would tell me what it is that bothers you about me."

"You are mistaken, Miss Stone. I find nothing at all disappointing about you. Quite the contrary."

She suspected flattery for the sake of evasion, and was annoyed. But, meeting those unsmiling eyes, she could not doubt his sincerity. Such a strange man.

"Lord Stanmore, I am sensitive to atmosphere and moods. You're hiding it well, but I can feel your disappointment."

"Fey, Miss Stone?"

Despite the slight lift of his dark brows, she did not think he was mocking her. Still, she hesitated to explain the extraordinary sensitivity she experienced at the oddest moments— and, usually, when such perceptiveness was not of the least benefit to her. She did not even know why she had mentioned it at all when, generally, she took pains to hide the peculiarity. Annoyance must have governed her tongue.

He said, "I apologize. That was too personal a question. But I was intrigued. One of my cousins married a MacLeod of Glendale. She vows her mother-in-law, Lady Glendale, is fey."

"It is not unusual among the Scots to find someone with the sight. Where I stayed recently, near Inverness, it was the parson."

"But those with the second sight can see into the future. Lady Glendale, it seems, is able on occasion to see the past."

"And I can see that you're trying to shift my attention from your disappointment."

"You're wrong, Miss Stone."

She frowned, staring at him. Once more, she felt what he felt, a heaviness of heart and mind. If not disappointment, then discouragement perhaps— But the moment of knowing his mind was too brief for certainty.

His questioning look made her realize she was still staring at him. "I beg your pardon, Lord Stanmore. I did not mean to be ill-mannered. The Reverend Simmons—my foster father—would say I was lost in some otherworld."

"An otherworld you will not share?"

"As you won't share your thoughts? Oh, but you're wrong. I will tell you what I saw when I was looking at you. A man who guards his feelings all too well and will deny for politeness' sake that T. E. Stone does not meet his expectations."

His face was expressionless. What a rigid, serious man he was. Not a smile. Not the slightest shift of that wide shoulder pressed against the mantelpiece. No casual propping of a foot on the fender. It seemed impossible that he should be friends with the easygoing Markhams.

"Miss Stone, I cannot allow you to think that the esteem I felt for T. E. Stone has undergone a change since I learned the renowned historian is a young lady. On the contrary. You have my unqualified admiration."

"Thank you." Dryly. "And yet you have reservations."

"None about your scholarship. If you sensed disappointment, it was because I realized that a scheme I conceived must come to naught."

"A scheme involving me. And pray don't think you can deny it. You sent a note last night asking Felicity and Markham to facilitate private conversation with me. Yet, now, you're most reluctant to speak."

"Very well, I shan't deny it—if only to set your mind at rest. I had hoped to engage the services of T. E. Stone. But I can hardly invite a young lady to Archer Hall. Can I?"

For an instant, she was speechless, her heart beating fast. *Archer Hall.* She'd give the last of her jewelry to be allowed into the stronghold of the family claiming descent from Lady Arbella Stuart.

And he balked at inviting a "young lady"!

"Lord Stanmore, I am an historian, a professional chronicler. Most of my working time is spent in other people's homes, their studies and libraries. It is how I earn a living. I've traveled as far as Cornwall, Wales, and Scotland without maid or chaperone."

"Ours is the household of two widowers."

She had known it, of course, but it was not a circumstance she had immediately called to mind or was willing to consider a handicap.

"I can arrange chaperonage. My former governess—"

"No, Miss Stone. Much as I would like to have the benefit of your expertise, I will not hazard a young lady's reputation for the sake of a family chronicle."

She rose. "Pray do not insult me. I am neither young nor a—"

Again, he interrupted. "I doubt you've seen more than four-and-twenty summers."

"Six-and-twenty, this coming June."

"As I said, *young*. And don't, I beg, try to convince me you're not a lady."

"Thea Stone is a lady. T. E. Stone is a woman gainfully employed—that is, as long as she does not offend the august members of the Society of Antiquaries by winning notoriety because of her gender. Thus, since T. E. Stone does not mingle socially, Thea Stone's reputation is quite safe."

Silent, then, they measured each other, Stanmore considering the proud tilt of her head, the hint of hauteur in her eyes, while Miss Stone searched his unsmiling expression for some small sign that he might be about to change his mind.

"Lord Stanmore, three years ago I asked your father if I might see the Archer family records. He all but snapped my nose off."

"He would."

The wry comment made her take a second, sharper look at him. His expression had not changed, and she could not begin to guess whether he approved of his father's response.

A bit stiffly, she said, "I concede Lord Barnet had the right to think me presumptuous."

"Do you, Miss Stone? I wonder why I have the impression that you feel quite the opposite of what you say."

His dark eyes held a spark of humor, as unexpected as it

was disconcerting. More so, since he had read her sentiments all too well.

"But I did not know of this," he said. "Did you call at Archer Hall?"

"I met Lord Barnet at Ravensbrook." She hesitated. To say more might be to rouse unhappy memories for Stanmore.

"My father does not often visit his neighbors." He frowned. "Three years ago, you say? Then it must have been at the ball Lady Ravensbrook gave to show off Felicity, another sterling daughter-in-law added to her already sizeable collection."

She did not know why she still hesitated. After all, he had spoken of the ball first. And the silence was growing awkward.

"Yes, it was at the nuptial ball that I met your father."

Stanmore nodded. The elaborate carving on the mantelpiece was beginning to cut into his shoulder, but he would not move lest Miss Stone get the impression that a mention of the ball made him uncomfortable. He, too, had gone to Ravensbrook that night but had scarcely greeted Lord and Lady Ravensbrook and the newly wed couple when a message had urgently recalled him to Archer Hall. Charlotte had gone into labor prematurely.

Miss Stone's voice, low, apologetic, broke into his thoughts.

"Perhaps I should not have spoken of that night. We heard the next morning about your wife and the infant. Such a tragic double loss."

"And yet I am fortunate, Miss Stone. I have my son and daughter."

He stepped away from the mantel, toward her. "But we are digressing. Frankly, I do not understand why you should wish to see the Archer chronicles. In your essay, *Arabella Stuart—Mystery Unsolved,* you make a convincing argument that Arbella did not bear a child, despite the Archer claim to the contrary."

"And, I hope, just as convincing an argument that there was, indeed, a child. Don't you see? This essay was a companion piece to the one I wrote on Henry, Prince of Wales. Both were commissioned as backdrops to a discussion of sonnets and ballads written during the reign of James I. The *Dilettanti* Society was not interested in stirring up an old controversy; they merely wished to give their members the insight needed to understand certain allusions to the king's cousin, Lady Arbella Stuart."

"I understand perfectly, and I am not about to pull caps with you over the publication. After all, there is no evidence whatsoever to support the ancient rumor."

"But there must be! The Archer chronicles . . . if I could study them—"

His headshake made her say impatiently, "I wish you would listen! I have *reason* to believe there was a child. A son. And with the aid of your family records I would like to prove it."

There was a deep silence while he looked at her strangely.

"Lord Stanmore? That was why you wished to engage T. E. Stone's services, was it not? To prove your family's claim to Stuart and Tudor blood?"

"On the contrary, Miss Stone. I hope to prove our claim is false."

Three

Thea Stone took great pride in her ability to listen attentively and to follow the most convoluted reasoning or argument. For once, though, she must have failed.

"I beg your pardon, Lord Stanmore. Somehow, I misunderstood. I thought for a moment that you said you wished to prove your family's claim *false.*"

"You did not misunderstand, Miss Stone. It is precisely what I said."

She stood facing him and, although fairly tall herself, had to look up to meet his eyes. "But why? Generations of Archers have fought for the right to claim, through Arbella Stuart, descent from James II of Scotland and Henry VII of England."

"And have been ridiculed for their presumption."

"Is that what you fear? Ridicule? Are you afraid I will be like a certain historian of the previous century? That I will, after obtaining permission to examine the Archer records, set out to prove nothing more than that Edward Archer, First Baron Barnet, was a mercenary, offspring of an old Hertfordshire farming and soldiering family?"

"It was never denied. Or that the Archer name can be traced to one Thomas, the archer, a simple bowman in service to Henry II. What previous generations of Archers have tried but failed dismally to establish, as you demonstrated in your essay for the *Dilettanti* Society—"

"I did not—"

Stanmore held up a hand. "Please let me finish. What my

family has failed to prove is that Edward Archer was the man who gave his name to a child born two hundred years ago to Arbella Stuart and William Seymour."

"One hundred ninety-nine years ago, next month."

"I stand corrected. The number of years is, however, quite beside the point."

"Precisely. The point is that you came to town to invite T. E. Stone to Archer Hall, but when T. E. Stone turned out to be a woman, you changed your mind."

"Nonsense!"

The sharpness of his retort caught her by surprise. Before she could say anything, he spoke again.

"I admit I was taken aback when I realized who you are because I saw my plan defeated before I could begin to put it into action. But it was your *youth*, Miss Stone, in combination with your gender that posed the problem."

"Not an insurmountable one."

"Perhaps not. But, then, it hardly matters any longer, does it?"

"Not at all. And you will ask me to examine the Archer chronicles? Capital! When would you like me to come to Archer Hall?"

"I cannot ask you to examine the chronicles."

She stepped back, folding her arms across her chest. "How dense I must be! You admire my scholarship. My problematical youth and gender no longer matter. And I have assured you of my interest in your family history. But you still hesitate to engage my services?"

"Miss Stone." A note of exasperation crept into his voice. "It is *because* of your interest in my family that I cannot do so."

"But why?"

"Archer family history as perceived and recorded by the family, and Archer tradition as it evolved from that history, have been the bane of my life. I want to put a stop to it before my son is crushed by the weight of duty and obligation exacted in the name of tradition. I want to prove that the tale of royal blood is nothing but that: *a tale.* I want to have it settled to my father's satisfaction and to the satisfaction of his aunts and sisters that Arbella Stuart neither bore a child nor placed it in the care of Edward Archer."

He drew a ragged breath. "Miss Stone, how the dickens can you expect me to ask you to Archer Hall when you want to do just the opposite?"

She looked at him curiously. They must have been talking and arguing nigh on half an hour, and in all that time he had shown less emotion than in the past few moments.

"Lord Stanmore, I am a historian. And although I would dearly love to prove that there *was* a child born to Arbella Stuart and William Seymour, and that the child in question was your ancestor, William Seymour Archer, I could not do so if your records don't supply the proof."

"I wonder." All signs of the brief flare of passion had subsided. His voice was cool and even. "Miss Stone, if certain entries in our chronicles proved ambiguous, your interpretation, naturally, would be influenced by your desire to establish the birth of a child."

A heated denial was on the tip of her tongue, but reason and honesty prevailed.

"I should hope you're wrong. However, since my objectivity has never been put to the test, I cannot swear that my opinion will be unbiased if more than one interpretation is possible."

"You're frank, at least."

"I am, generally."

A piece of wood snapping in the hearth drew his attention. He stoked the fire and added another log.

When he turned back to her, Thea said, "I have explored every other known source and found copious references to rumors about Arbella and a child, but nary a word to substantiate the rumors. If there is anything definitive in the Archer chronicles, the matter can be settled once and for all."

He said nothing, only looked at her.

She said, "One way or the other."

"Just so, Miss Stone. I want it resolved one way. You, the other."

"But neither of us, I think, would wish to do so at the sacrifice of truth—if truth is there."

For a moment, his eyes were hooded.

"No, Miss Stone. Not at the sacrifice of truth."

"I knew it. I can promise no more than to do my utmost to remain objective. But that I do promise most solemnly."

She waited. When he did not speak, she said, "Lord Stanmore, will you allow me to explore the Archer chronicles?"

"You deserve a plain yes or no." The dark eyes, keen now and searching, rested on her for a long moment. "But I'm afraid I cannot decide without carefully weighing the consequences. May I give you my answer in a day or so?"

He was wavering, and she was tempted to press for an immediate decision. But patience could work only in her favor. Fellow historians had lost interest in Arbella Stuart and her brief marriage to William Seymour, focusing their attention on King James's eldest son, the tragic Prince Henry. Thus, the acknowledged authority on the Lady Arbella, first cousin to King James and second cousin to Queen Elizabeth, was T. E. Stone. And Thea would wager her birthright that Stanmore knew he needed none other than her to examine the old Archer documents.

"You may have a sennight to decide, Lord Stanmore. Felicity hasn't tired of my company yet, and for a change I'm enjoying my stay in town. I'm in no rush to leave."

He bowed. "Then I am grateful that, unlike most ladies, you enjoy town during the quiet months."

"Unlike poor Felicity." Thea was content, and did not doubt that Stanmore was also, to steer the conversation away from Arbella Stuart. "If Felicity weren't so deeply in love, she'd pester Markham no end to give up his position at the bank, live in the country, and come to town only for the season."

"And John would be happier farming than he is as a banker.

Alas, a younger son's choices are not necessarily his preferences."

What Stanmore did not say, but was understood by both, was that John Markham refused to touch his wife's money for the purchase of a country house and a parcel of land.

"And you, Miss Stone? You don't need the social whirl to keep you entertained in London?"

"Gracious, no! Not that I dislike dinners and dances, mind you. But when a ball turns into a veritable squeeze, as any good hostess would wish, I panic and run."

"Why?"

"Why . . . ?" She faltered. Again, she had disclosed something about herself she did not ordinarily share with a stranger. And again, she did not know why.

She made light of it. "Some childhood memory rearing its ugly head. Memory of an unpleasant crowd . . . a sensation of suffocating. Silly of me, I know."

"You know, yet you cannot help yourself. Let it be a consolation that you're not alone. Most of us, at some point or other, act on old memories."

He started to move about, restless, energetic, his demeanor in accord with his powerful stature for the first time since Thea set eyes on him. But, she noticed, he slightly favored his left foot.

"Felicity was right—I heard her ask if you were limping. And you are, though it's scarcely noticeable. And you've been standing all this time!"

He gave a short, wry laugh. "Even with a limp, standing or walking is better than sitting. Had it been possible, I would have eschewed the use of a carriage this evening. But I was already late."

His laugh, brief though it was, and the humorous gleam in his eyes as he looked at her over his shoulder were encouraging. Perhaps she had been a trifle hasty when she thought him starched, a bit of a dull stick.

"Why, this sounds intriguing, sir. Do you care to tell me what happened?"

"You'll regret asking when you have to listen a second time at dinner. Or do you think Felicity will forget?"

"Not at all. But I shan't regret anything. I'll be too busy prompting you and correcting your tale to be bored."

He stopped, giving her a questioning look.

"I was teasing, Lord Stanmore." Scrupulously honest, she added, "Although, on a rare occasion, it may happen that I interrupt a pompous fool who tries to 'improve' his story with every retelling."

"Then I must make an effort not to be a pompous fool."

Again, she caught a gleam in his eye. If only he wouldn't suppress it so quickly, as if he must, at any price, appear inscrutable.

"And I promise to be on my best behavior, sir. At least until we've had time to get better acquainted."

"Or until I've come to a decision?"

She laughed and shook her head. "Unfair! But I am not easily put to the blush. Or distracted."

"I was afraid not."

"So tell me what happened."

"It's just as I said to Felicity." He set out on another turn about the room. "Barnet House happened."

"The mansion in the Strand? It cannot possibly be responsible for your injury."

"Can it not? But, I daresay, you don't realize how old it is."

"One hundred and fifty years." She sat down, choosing a chair that would allow her to follow his restless prowl around the drawing room. "It was commissioned by William Seymour Archer upon his creation of Earl Barnet in 1660. But he did not live to see completion of the construction."

"You're well informed, Miss Stone."

"Is it true that, for the past sixty-five years, your family scarcely made use of it?"

He kept up his pacing, but his eyes were on her. "My aunts and cousins used to stay occasionally, during the season. But otherwise you're correct. Barnet House stands empty, with only an old couple to take care of some thirty-odd rooms."

"I understand the house has lovely painted ceilings."

"It did have. Neglect and the constant damp from the river have taken their toll. My aunts used to drape the ballroom with crepe to hide the damage. My grandfather—but that's not what you wanted to hear about."

He was silent for a moment, and Thea reviewed her knowledge of Archer family history. Sixty-five years ago, at the time of the second Jacobite rebellion, an Earl Barnet was exiled. The grandfather, Stanmore mentioned.

When Stanmore spoke again, his tone was light, off-hand. "Would you believe that the first thing that happened this morning was the bed collapsing as I was about to rise?"

"Surely you jest?"

"Canopy and all. I feared I was about to smother in shredding velvet and dust."

He had completed a circuit of the room and stood before her, as relaxed as she had seen him only when he spoke with Felicity and John Markham. And Thea, at the dignified age of five-and-twenty, struggled with an unseemly giggle as she pictured him, a look of disgust on his face, and his long, muscular limbs flailing against a shroud of tattered bed hangings.

"How horrid," she managed.

"Indeed. And if you laugh, Miss Stone, I shan't say another word."

"No laughter, I promise! You said it was the first thing that happened, and I must hear what followed."

"When I wanted to ring for assistance, I discovered there was no bell rope. I went downstairs and promptly put a foot through one of the steps. Unfortunately, I hadn't pulled on my boots."

"Did you cut your foot?" No trouble now keeping a straight face. "Brittle wood leaves nasty splinters."

"Dozens of splinters. I had the deuce of a time removing them. And this afternoon when I returned, weary and thirsty, from the execution of sundry commissions with which my children and their exacting governess charged me, I met with the ultimate disaster."

"The one that won't allow you to sit with comfort."

"That is laughter in your voice, Miss Stone. I hear it clearly."

"I vow it's not. It is . . . anticipatory commiseration."

"And well it should be. As I was saying, I was weary and thirsty, and the caretaker assured me that a few bottles of wine remained from my youngest cousin's presentation festivities two years ago. He also made it clear that his arthritis would not allow him to venture into the damp cellars."

She still had not seen him smile, but his tone remained light, and one hand was resting casually in his coat pocket.

She said, "So, naturally, being considerate, you went down yourself."

"Being considerate and in need of refreshment, yes, I went down myself. Stupidly, I gripped the banister in the belief it would prevent my slipping on the rather steep and slimy steps."

"*Stupidly,* you gripped . . . ? Oh, dear. I gather the banister broke?"

"It had, apparently, been unsafe for some time. But since neither the caretaker nor his wife go into the cellars, they had not thought to warn me. I was not halfway down when the handrail and the center support snapped. Left with the choice of toppling over the side with a useless piece of rail in my hand, or letting go and dropping that part of my anatomy meant for the upholstered seat of a chair onto hard stone, I chose the latter."

Thea winced in empathy.

"Yes, the first contact smarted. But it wouldn't have been too bad if, unfortunately, my aim had not been off. Or, perhaps, the soles of my boots were too slick for the sudden change of position. In short, I slid down several steps, a mode of travel that did not agree with me at all."

"A mode of travel, sir, only a very young child may engage in with impunity."

She met his eyes and, since he obviously had not sustained a serious injury or was suffering from embarrassment, allowed herself a smile as her imagination painted a vivid picture of the scene.

To her astonishment, he smiled back. It lasted but a moment, a bright, vivid flash of a grin that brought his features to life and allowed her a glimpse of quite a different man behind the façade of reserve.

Four

When Thea readied herself for bed that night, she had much to think about, not the least of which was her promise to strive for objectivity if she was permitted to examine the Archer chronicles.

She had promised freely and from conviction that nothing could sway her from her word, yet she could not deny that her inclination was directly opposed to Stanmore's. But, then, until she met him, she would not have believed it possible that a member of the Archer family existed who wished to deny his royal blood.

Brush in hand, long brown hair tumbling almost to her waist, Thea went to the writing desk thoughtfully provided by her hostess. Even when on holiday Thea liked to work, and the desk was littered with books and writing paper. She found what she was looking for, a genealogy of the Archers, hidden beneath the blotter.

The brush dropped unheeded to the floor as she drew up a chair and sat down, her eyes already on the uppermost name—Edward Archer. The man to whom the Lady Arbella entrusted her child . . . or so the Archer family had maintained for almost two centuries.

Edward Archer had been a guard in the retinue of the Bishop of Durham, assigned by King James to take Arbella north as punishment for her forbidden marriage to William Seymour. But she claimed illness at Barnet and escaped, however briefly.

And in 1615, after Arbella's death, James had bestowed a barony on Edward Archer.

Why? Others who were with Lady Arbella when she escaped had been sent to the Tower or to Marshalsea prison.

Thea looked at the next name. William Seymour Archer—Edward's adopted son—born March 25, 1611, at Barnet.

Arbella's child. He had to be.

Thea reached for the desk drawer where she kept her strongbox but changed her mind almost immediately. She did not need to see the copy of an entry in her family Bible. She knew it by heart.

God bless the child born March 25, 1611. God have mercy on his mother.

William Seymour Archer, Second Baron Barnet, was later, in 1660, created Earl Barnet by Charles II.

Why?

She skipped to the third earl. In 1701, when the last of Queen Anne's numerous offspring died and the Act of Succession was debated, Henry Stuart Archer claimed hereditary precedence over Sophia of Hanover and her issue. Laughed out of Parliament, he was held up on his way home to Archer Hall and killed by a highwayman.

Political murder, said the Archer family.

And the third earl's great-grandson, Stanmore's grandfather, repeated his ancestor's folly. During the second Jacobite rebellion, while Charles Edward Stuart, the Young Pretender, fought for a lost cause in Scotland, Charles Edward Archer, Sixth Earl Barnet, approached Parliament with a claim to the Scottish and English thrones.

There was an outcry of treason—not universal but strong enough to persuade the seventeen-year-old earl to flee the country. He owed it to Sir Robert Walpole, then a dying man but still influential, that no charge was brought against him and that his mother and sisters did not lose their home by forfeiture to the crown. In November 1760, a month after the death of King George II, Charles Edward Archer at last returned from France with a wife and an eleven-year-old son, the present Earl Barnet, Stanmore's father.

And now Stanmore wanted to prove that the family's claim to royal blood was false. How extraordinarily strange.

Thea was so absorbed in Archer family history that a light knock on the door made her jump. Before she could call out, the door opened and Lady Felicity stepped into the room.

"I knew it!" Looking very fetching in a satin nightgown and wrapper, she fluttered toward Thea. Snatching the Archer family tree from Thea's hand, she thrust it beneath a thick tome of Tudor and Stuart history.

"How often must I tell you that you're not to work at night! Dearest Thea, you need a rest. Come and tell me what you think of Stanmore."

"Sitting up with you and talking into the small hours of morning, I suppose, constitutes a rest?"

"Don't be evasive. But, yes, you'll rest very well if we sit on the bed. Or better yet, if we get under the covers. Aren't you cold, Thea? You didn't put on slippers, and your feet are blue."

In response, Thea hurried to the large four-poster bed where warm bricks awaited her icy toes. Felicity delayed only long enough to pick up Thea's hairbrush before joining her.

"Now, tell me," she commanded as she tossed the brush to Thea with one hand and with the other snatched a portion of the down cover for herself. "Tell me what you think of Stanmore."

Absently, Thea worked on her hair. "I don't know. He is so . . . reserved, so stiff."

"You could not call him stiff at dinner!"

"No, not then. But I noticed that he is always at ease when he's with you and John. It was quite different when we were alone . . . except for a short while, just before you came to fetch us. He unbent then, and even smiled once."

"Will you tell him about yourself?"

Thea's eyes widened. "Why should I?"

"You're going to Archer Hall, are you not?"

"That has not been determined yet," said Thea, looking arch.

"Ah, yes. I heard him suggest another meeting before a decision is made. But, rubbish, Thea! You know you'll end up going."

Archness was replaced by one of Thea's slow smiles. "He doesn't have much choice, does he? Not when he needs an expert to rewrite his family history."

"Then the two of you will be thrown together quite frequently. If I were you, I'd tell him about myself."

"For goodness' sake, Felicity! Thrown together! I'll be *working* at Archer Hall."

"I don't doubt that." Dryly. "When are you not working? But, in case you haven't noticed, Stanmore is quite taken with you."

"Ridiculous!"

"But he is. I know him well, and I haven't seen him look at a woman the way he looks at you."

"I wish you wouldn't speak like a meddling matchmaker."

"Do you dislike him?"

"I neither like nor dislike him. I've only just met him."

"He'd make an excellent husband. For *you,* if you can prove he is, indeed, descended from Arbella Stuart. Although, since he wants to disprove it, we may have a slight problem on our hands. On the other hand, I don't doubt you can charm him into forgetting."

"Felicity, stop it!" Quite suddenly and uncharacteristically cross, Thea had spoken more sharply than intended and immediately embraced her friend. "I'm sorry. You mean well, and I shouldn't have snapped at you. But you know my views on marriage."

Views, Lady Felicity did not share at all. Yet, wisely, she said no more on the subject but bade her guest a good night and went off to quiz her husband about the searching, probing looks Stanmore had given Thea throughout dinner.

Alas, John Markham's chamber was dark, his even breathing

telling Lady Felicity that he was asleep. He did not awaken when she slipped into bed beside him, merely turned a little to wrap an arm around her. And very shortly afterward, Lady Felicity was asleep as well.

Thea, however, lay awake for some time thinking about Felicity's words. Not about Stanmore making an excellent husband for her—that was just the romantic nonsense she expected Felicity to say. But she thought about proving that the Archers of Archer Hall near Barnet were indeed descended from Arbella Stuart.

It seemed she had always wanted to prove that Arbella gave birth to a child. Always . . . since her governess had taken her, a nine-year-old orphan, to the vicarage of Ault Hucknall in Derbyshire, where Miss Simmons had grown up and where her brother, the Reverend Felix Simmons, then held the living.

Thea had been embraced as a sixth daughter by Mrs. Felix Simmons and as a sister by eight lively young Simmonses. The youngsters immediately took charge of the waif their aunt had snatched from the bloodbath and terror of Paris. They coaxed Thea to laugh again, they ousted her nightmares, they tutored her in every sport to be enjoyed in the English countryside. Except for hunting, which was beyond the Reverend Simmons's stipend and the modest independent income he enjoyed from an inheritance.

Everyone had welcomed Thea, but it was the Reverend Simmons himself who derived the deepest satisfaction from her inclusion in his household. He discovered in her the child of his heart who would study with him, debate with him, and, especially, would listen with rapt attention when he spoke on his favorite subject, history. When he learned that, from her own family history, Thea was familiar with the name Arbella Stuart, he regaled the orphaned child with tales of that other orphan, Arbella, who had spent lonely years at her grandmother's house, Hardwick Hall, not far from the vicarage.

Arbella's story had captivated the nine-year-old Thea, and over the years, as she began to see certain parallels between

Arbella's life and her own, her interest had expanded to the point of obsession.

She came to believe with all her heart that Arbella and William Seymour's brief marriage had been blessed with a child—the boy who grew up as William Seymour Archer and became the first Earl Barnet. And now she had met a descendant of that child. But Stuart Seymour Archer, Viscount Stanmore, was determined to prove that there was no link between his family and the Lady Arbella.

It was no great wonder, then, that when Thea fell asleep at last, she dreamed of the Lady Arbella—as she had dreamed many a time since her tenth year, when the Reverend Simmons took her on her first visit to Hardwick Hall.

Thea's chamber was still dark when she awoke and, as was often the case, she needed a moment to determine where she was, and in what century, for in her dreams she felt as if she actually lived in Arbella's time, as if she was a part of Arbella's life.

Reaching for tinderbox and candle, Thea sat up in bed. It might be too early for Felicity and Markham to rise, but it was never too early for T. E. Stone to study her notes on the Archer family.

Stanmore would invite her to Archer Hall. She was certain of it, and she wanted to have memorized the pertinent facts about his ancestors as recorded by outsiders before she studied the records kept by members of his family.

She would also prepare the usual notice for the Foreign Office advising them where she could be reached. She had written countless such notices in the five years she had been supporting herself as a chronicler, had seen the sixth change of Foreign Secretary when the Marquis Wellesley succeeded to the office in December of the previous year—and had long since given up any expectation of a return message.

The Foreign Secretary might still believe that some day she would be needed at home; Thea did not. Yet, since she had given her word, the note would be written, Archer Hall put down as her new direction. Then, in the flurry of activity that always accompanies a departure, she need only date and dispatch it.

Shivering a little in her nightgown and wrapper, she lit the desk lamp, fueled with the scented oil Felicity liked. She thought back on the hour she had spent alone with Stanmore, the brief moment when she had felt what he felt—his disappointment, his hopes of engaging T. E. Stone's services dashed because it would ruin her reputation.

But she had dealt with that misconception, or so she hoped. She had not been able to know his mind again, yet she was certain he would extend a formal invitation. Perhaps later that morning. Surely he'd call to thank Felicity for the dinner.

It was Saturday, the third day of February, 1810. Thea had met Stanmore on February 2, Candlemas Day. Two hundred years to the day Arbella Stuart and William Seymour pledged their troth.

Stanmore did not seek another meeting with Miss Stone until the following Tuesday. Waiting came hard, but no harder than an admission that, despite his assertion to Miss Stone that he must carefully weigh the consequences before making a decision, he had determined as soon as he left Markham House to damn all consequences. Save one. He would safeguard her reputation, no matter how much she protested that it was not at risk.

He would trust her to be objective. He would ask her to Archer Hall.

It was an impulsive decision, which rather took him by surprise since he was of a methodical nature and preferred to plan his moves—even if, as happened all too often, his plans were subsequently overset by his father's capricious humor. Barnet's arbitrariness had made Stanmore competent at dealing with the unexpected; he would know what to do if the results of Miss Stone's examination of the Archer chronicles were not what he wished.

But, having made an impulsive decision, Stanmore was not prepared to act impulsively as well. Thus, he followed his schedule as planned, purchasing new bows, archery gloves, and a supply of arrows for the children, attending an auction at Tattersall's with an eye to possible candidates for a young boy's first horse, visiting his tailor, his boot-maker, and making provisional arrangements for a departure to Archer Hall the following Thursday.

Then, on Tuesday morning, he brought his curricle to a halt in front of Markham House in Upper Brook Street. Handing the reins to the groom, he alighted to call on Miss Stone—intriguing historian of the slow, entrancing smile, the regal bearing, and the occasional frosty glint of green in her eyes.

Assured by a footman that, although Mr. Markham was at the bank and Lady Felicity at some charity meeting or other, Miss Stone was certainly at home, Stanmore told the groom to return in an hour and followed the footman upstairs to a sitting room.

Thea, curled up in a vast wing-backed chair, was searching a biography of King James's elder son, Henry, for references to his cousin Arbella. Since she had told the footman to show Lord Stanmore in at any time he chose to call, she should have been prepared when the door opened. But she dropped the book as she rose to greet the man she had expected, if truth be told, no later than Sunday.

She gave him a searching look but, try as she might, saw not a hint of what decision he had arrived at—if, indeed, he had made a decision.

Stanmore retrieved the volume. Smoothing the pages, he said, "Thomas Birch's *The Life of Henry, Prince of Wales*. I've been searching this age for a copy."

"I found it quite by accident in an obscure little shop in Fetters Lane."

The brief exchange had restored Thea's composure. Accepting the book, she placed it on the pedestal table beside her chair.

"Will you sit down, Lord Stanmore?"

"Indeed. The exercise hardly troubles me at all anymore."

She laughed. It was a low, musical sound he would not mind hearing more often.

"Nevertheless, let me suggest the worn looking leather chair. Markham vows it's the only comfortable seat in the room."

"Thank you." He adjusted the chair so that it faced hers. "There's something I wish to ask you, Miss Stone. On Friday, you said you had *reason* to believe Arbella gave birth to a son at Barnet. Will you tell me what reason that is?"

"An entry in my family Bible. It says, 'God bless the child born March 25, 1611. God have mercy on his mother.' It was—"

"That is all? But it signifies nothing."

"It is the same date your family claims as the natal day of William Seymour Archer, Edward Archer's adopted son. And if you had not been so precipitate with your protest, you would have learned that my ancestress who wrote the words was Dorothea Wortley, daughter of Mary Wortley, who was a waiting gentlewoman to Lady Arbella Stuart."

"Dorothea. And you are Theadora."

"That is quite beside the point. Are you trying to provoke me with your interruptions?"

"I beg your pardon, Miss Stone. There is something about your name—commonly it is Theodora, is it not?"

The question was neither unreasonable nor too personal, yet it took her off stride. Perhaps because Felicity had suggested she tell Stanmore about herself. She had not intended to do so. Had never seen the need to make private disclosures when she hired herself out as a historian. But she might not have a choice this time. Not if, at some later point, she must show Stanmore her family Bible.

He looked puzzled by her silence, and she said, "Yes, Theodora is the more common form of my name, but there has been a Theadora in our family for as long as we've had a Dorothea. Now, shall we concentrate on Dorothea Wortley?"

"By all means, let us do so."

"Dorothea was at Greenwich with her mother and Arbella that summer of 1610 during the celebrations of Henry's investiture as Prince of Wales. She was at the palace when Arbella secretly married William Seymour there on the twenty-second of June. She was at Barnet in March of 1611, when, as rumor had it, Arbella gave birth to a son."

"Tales handed down from generation to generation, Miss Stone? Your family sounds suspiciously like mine."

The gentle mockery in his voice nettled her. She thought of her family's records dating back two hundred years farther than Archer records. Alas, inaccessible to her.

Omitting much, and yet quite truthfully, she said, "My parents died when I was nine. Thus, I have little documentation in my possession, if that is what you mean."

"A pity. Unfortunately, it happens all too often that a female is deprived by entail of possessions that should be considered personal property."

She did not correct his misconception. "I do have the Bible, however. And, before I could read, my father had insisted that I learn by heart the main points of our family tree and history. I can tell you with certainty that Dorothea Wortley was continuously with Arbella from May of 1610 until the escape at Barnet the following year. Later, when Arbella was imprisoned in the Tower, Dorothea occasionally relieved her mother or Mrs. Bradshaw, another of Arbella's waiting women."

"It seems your Dorothea was a kind-hearted soul. Or, perhaps, very young and romantically inclined."

"She was young," Thea admitted. "Turned sixteen the day Lady Arbella married. But you cannot deny that the Lady Arbella inspired devotion and compassion in those who knew her."

"I don't deny it."

"Dorothea had reason to be grateful to Arbella, who invited

her to join her mother so she could celebrate her birthday at court and be in town for the ceremonials honoring the Prince of Wales."

"Yes, that would mean much to a young girl. But to pay for two or three months of pleasure with five years voluntary confinement seems a steep price."

"One year! Only the time Arbella was held at Lambeth, and then during the journey north, which ended at Barnet. Dorothea never spent more than a week at a time in the Tower, and those visits ceased in 1613, when she married."

"But you believe she did not forget Arbella." Again, Stanmore's voice held a lightly mocking note. "You believe that an anonymous blessing invoked years later, refers to Arbella Stuart and a child, whose existence was denied by other contemporaries."

"Not a great many people were in a position to know. Arbella's waiting women—they would not betray her, and admitting the existence of a child would then have been paramount to betrayal. Lady Shrewsbury, Arbella's aunt? She, too, was imprisoned in the Tower for supplying the funds for Arbella's escape. For her, it was politic to deny knowledge of a child—though she never categorically denied that a child was born."

"You're splitting hairs, Miss Stone. And you have nothing on which to base your contention that Dorothea referred to Arbella's child."

"The date. 'God bless the child born March 25, 1611.' On that day Dorothea was with Lady Arbella at Barnet. Why would she later refer to a childbirth unless she had been there to witness it? And she made the entry in our Bible on November 14, 1615, next to the recording of her own son's birth."

"And you conjecture the joyous occasion aroused a desire to commemorate a birth she may have witnessed more than four years earlier? A birth, which must have been accompanied by apprehension and could not even be acknowledged?"

Thea met his skeptical gaze. "It is conjecture, I admit. But not as farfetched as you seem to believe."

"But why the second part of the invocation? 'God have mercy on his mother.' If Arbella indeed bore a son, and keeping in mind King James's unreasonable attitude toward Arbella's marriage, wouldn't your Dorothea have written 'and bless the mother, who saved the child'?"

"In November of 1615, Arbella was dead. Surely, then, it was logical to ask for mercy?"

He looked at her pensively. "Miss Stone, you have not yet learned what decision I made regarding your examination of the Archer records and chronicles. Do you not fear to turn me against you if you show too strong a conviction that there was a child?"

"No. I may wish to search your records for confirmation of my belief while you wish to prove the opposite. But we both wish for truth."

"If truth is there—as you said on Friday."

"You remember." She drew a deep breath. "Are you asking me to Archer Hall, Lord Stanmore?"

"Yes, Miss Stone, I am."

Her heart soared and beat quite madly. She gave him a dazzling smile; indeed, could not have stopped it had she wanted to, but she did not speak lest she shout with joy and forever ruin the reputation of T. E. Stone, sedate and sober scholar.

And for the second time since making Stanmore's acquaintance, she knew the gratification of eliciting a smile in return.

"There can be no doubt I gave you the answer you hoped for."

"No doubt at all, Lord Stanmore. When are we leaving?"

"Just as soon as you have a suitable chaperone. I believe you mentioned an old governess?"

"Miss Simmons, yes."

"Any relation to your foster father, the Reverend Simmons?"

Her eyes widened. "You remember even that?"

"Why should I not? It has only been four days since you mentioned the Reverend Simmons. That is as nothing compared to what you remember from childhood lessons in your family's history."

Accompanied by a breath of frosty air, Lady Felicity blew into the parlor. When she heard that Thea's departure to Archer Hall hinged on the presence of a chaperone, she immediately offered her services until Miss Simmons could make the journey south from Derbyshire.

"I'll be glad not to breathe soot for a little while," said Felicity, stripping off her gloves. "And besides, if I go with you, John will have to come and fetch me back."

"He would, wouldn't he?" Sounding amused, Stanmore offered his chair. "But pray don't try to explain what it signifies. I'd rather not be involved in any of your schemes."

"You never want to be involved in my schemes. How can you be so dreadfully starchy?" Affection and exasperation warred in Felicity's voice. "But I shan't despair yet. See if you won't unbend when you've been around Thea for a while. She will teach you how not to take yourself too seriously."

Thea frowned at Felicity, which did not escape Stanmore's notice.

He gave Thea a speculative look. "Indeed, Miss Stone? Can you do that?"

"I doubt it. Being able to laugh at yourself is not dependent on being taught but on your state of mind."

"We shall see what we shall see," said Felicity, then deftly closed the subject by asking Stanmore to ring for tea and enquiring of Thea how long she would need to pack her trunks.

Five

It had been summer when Thea stayed at Ravensbrook on the occasion of Felicity and John's nuptial ball three years earlier, and any view of Archer Hall, set well back from the country lane shared by both houses, had been obstructed by the rich green foliage and pink and white blooms of a briar hedge and by the lavish crowns of stately oaks and beeches and sweet smelling plane trees. But on the eighth of February, when the hired carriage had passed the ruins of the old Archer farmstead, a distant expanse of brickwork, parapets, and large mullioned windows could be seen from the road through a screen of sparse dry briar stalks.

"It looks like Hatfield House!" exclaimed Thea, bumping her nose against the carriage window as they hit a particularly deep rut. "The south front with its two lovely wings. And there's the clock tower! I vow, it *is* Hatfield House!"

"Archer Hall was patterned after Hatfield," said Stanmore. "But it is smaller, and you will find the interior design slightly different."

"Your turrets rise higher than those at Hatfield."

Felicity looked over Thea's shoulder. "There's Charlie! What a bruising little rider he is! Just like his papa. But he has outgrown his pony. Stuart, why haven't you bought him a horse yet? And Bella—oh, they were having a race, but now she has seen us!"

Thea tore her gaze from the house and searched the park for the two young riders. Stanmore's children. The taller, sturdier of the two was galloping toward the house and soon disappeared around a corner. The other, a slight figure in white breeches and brilliant-red coat, long light-brown hair tumbling about thin shoulders, had stopped and stood in the stirrups to wave excitedly at the carriage.

"You let your daughter ride astride." Thea gave Stanmore an approving look. "How very sensible."

"You're one of few who do not call it scandalous. Alas, you give me credit where none is due. Bella's apparel and style are but a piece of Archer tradition—perhaps the only bit of tradition that can be called sensible. And if you think a moment, Miss Stone, you'll know why every Archer female wears breeches and rides astride."

"Of course! The Lady Arbella escaped dressed like a man."

"She'll fall and break her neck," said Felicity. "Stuart, you must tell Bella not to stand up in the saddle."

"If I speak to anyone," he said rather grimly, "it'll be to Charlie about leaving his sister behind."

The carriage swung right, into a wide graveled drive. The little girl on her pony started toward them, and at the same time the boy came trotting back, a groom riding at his side.

Stanmore's mouth softened and he relaxed against the squabs. Words could not have relayed more succinctly that he was glad he need not reprimand his son.

When the children were abreast the carriageway, they made no attempt to stop their father's coach or to shout at him through the window but rode sedately alongside, Bella smiling and blowing an occasional kiss, and Charlie, after a salute with his crop, trying manfully not to grin from ear to ear.

But as soon as the carriage came to a halt at the sweep of shallow terraced steps rising to the south entrance, the children were off their ponies. Charlie wrenched the carriage door open, and Bella flew into her father's arms before he had quite completed his descent.

"Papa, I would have won the race if you hadn't arrived just

now! But I saw you, and so I stopped. It doesn't mean I lost, does it?"

"Yes, it does," said Charlie. "You lost by default. And you would've lost anyway because I had the lead. Sir, I did not mean to leave Bella behind. I didn't know she had stopped, but I called Jenkins as soon as I reached the stables and saw she wasn't behind me."

"You did just as you ought."

"Yes, sir. And I'm glad she didn't take a toss after all." Charlie's voice deepened—one man speaking confidentially with another. "With girls, you never know what they'll do from one moment to the next, do you? So, perhaps, next time I race with Bella, I shall keep one eye behind me."

"An excellent resolution."

Setting Bella down, Stanmore gravely shook hands with his son, then ruffled his hair, a gesture that made Charlie flush with embarrassment and, at the same time, beam with gratification.

He thrust back his shoulders, unconsciously imitating his father's proud bearing. "I wouldn't believe it, sir, when Jenkins drove up in the curricle yesterday and said you'd be coming in a job-chaise. But you did, by George!" His adult manner left him. "Why, Papa? Was it for a lark? But you don't like that kind of travel, closed in and awfully slow."

"Likes and dislikes are often determined by the company you have, Charlie. And look who kept me company on this trip."

A footman had hurried from the house and was assisting the ladies to alight. Lady Felicity, obviously no stranger to the children, was greeted with enthusiasm; and Thea, when Stanmore made the introductions, with avid curiosity. But only Bella voiced questions.

"Are you one of Lord Mansford's gals? But where's your twin? Or are you the other sister, the one that's scarcely out of leading strings? That's what Cook said to Higgins. But you can't be scarcely out of leading strings, can you? Because then you would be younger than me, wouldn't you, Miss Stone?"

Stanmore looked thunderstruck; Felicity, amused.

Thea preserved a straight face. "No, I am not one of Lord Mansford's gals. Does that disappoint you?"

"I don't think so." Bella wrinkled her brow. "But if you're not one of *them,* Grandpapa will not be pleased to see you."

"That is enough, Bella." Clasping his daughter's shoulder, Stanmore turned her toward the groom waiting patiently with the ponies. "It's time you and Charlie took care of Bess and Cecil."

Thea said, "There's no doubt in my mind after whom Cecil is named. Lord Robert Cecil, chief minister to Queen Elizabeth and King James." She looked at Charlie. "Am I correct?"

"Yes, ma'am."

"But Bess has me in a puzzle. Is she named after the queen, or after Bess of Hardwick, Lady Arbella's grandmother?"

Bella turned around, smiling impishly. "Make a guess, Miss Stone."

"Did you choose the name, Bella?"

The child nodded, looking at Thea expectantly.

"Well, then, if I were you, I'd name her after . . . both. Because the Lady Arbella was the granddaughter of one and cousin to the other."

"Second cousin," Bella corrected, then, walking to her pony, called over her shoulder, "You almost guessed it, Miss Stone! Bess is named after both. But also after me. I'm Arbella Elizabeth."

When Stanmore invited Thea and Felicity into the house, he made no reference to Bella's *faux pas* regarding Lord Mansford's gals or the comment about Lord Barnet's possible displeasure. His voice and face gave no hint of anything amiss, but Thea was acutely aware of Stanmore's irritation. She doubted, though, the feeling was directed at his daughter.

Then she stepped into the great hall, rising past the long first-floor gallery that connected the east and west wings, and she forgot the children, forgot even Felicity and Stanmore in the splendor of Italian marble, graceful columns, and mellow wood—and a sense of familiarity.

At first she thought it was because she had been to Hatfield House. But her memory was reaching farther back, deep into her early childhood . . . when she was four years old, sitting on a cushion at her parents' feet in the great hall of their home. A tall, sullen-looking youth stood beside her. And there was music and singing . . . a juggling act . . . a pantomime. She felt her father's hand stroking her hair. She heard the silvery sound of her mother's voice, asking her if she was tired.

Thea blinked, and she was five-and-twenty once again, standing not in her long lost home but in the great hall of the house whose secrets she wished to uncover.

Excitement bubbled in her. Archer Hall! No matter that Stanmore wanted to prove the opposite, she was certain she would discover that his family was indeed descended from Arbella Stuart.

Impulsively, she turned to him. "I can scarcely believe I'm finally inside Archer Hall. Thank you for asking me! If you'll show me where I may work, I'll get started right away."

He looked at her, and slowly his expression softened. "I'm afraid I haven't determined yet where you will work. Enjoy yourself this afternoon, Miss Stone. Explore the house. It's well worth seeing."

And explore she did, with Felicity, who had seen only a small part of the house when she attended Lord Barnet's receptions. Charlie and Bella acted as guides. Stanmore, Felicity had told Thea over tea and scones served in the small sitting room between their chambers, was closeted with the Earl Barnet for the rest of the afternoon.

The children were knowledgeable guides, explaining the structural design of the building—a squashed U, they called it—with a long central block and two wings protruding south.

The central block, crowned by the ornate clock tower Thea had seen from the carriage, held the great hall, rising two stories high and with a cavernous fireplace directly opposite the entrance. The hall continued behind the fireplace, but only one story high. Above that northern part of the hall were the formal drawing and reception rooms, with the long gallery running alongside and overlooking the great hall.

The two wings boasted yet another story, each floor offering eight chambers, of which two were located in turrets rising from the ground well past the parapeted roof. Another room was located high above the whole structure at the very top of each of the four turrets.

At the east and west sides of the great hall, wide, open stairs with ornately carved banisters swept upward and branched to the long gallery and to the side galleries of the wings. Further stairways were located in the wings proper.

The children knew the age and origin of every piece of furniture, identified every portrait in the galleries—just as Thea, at an even younger age than Bella, had once been able to do in her own home.

Wherever they went, whatever they inspected, Archer Hall presented polished wood, luxurious rugs and carpets, gleaming silver and gold, drapes that had been brushed and showed no signs of fading. If the townhouse on the Strand was falling to rack and ruin, the country seat was not. Archer Hall was well kept and lovingly tended.

Halfway into the second hour of exploration, the children's enthusiasm and Felicity's endurance began to wane.

"I feel as if I had walked ten miles," said Felicity, sinking onto one of the dainty gilded chairs placed strategically in the long gallery.

"We can stop. There isn't much more to see." Charlie leaned against the handsomely carved balustrade and vaguely waved a hand to the right, the other to the left. "Except for the study and other rooms my father and grandfather reserve for their private use."

JUNE LOVE 51

"Nobody," Bella said importantly, "is allowed on the first floor of the east wing unless invited by Grandpapa. He doesn't use the whole floor, but he has locked the rooms where his two wives lived. Charlie and I never got to meet them, because they died a long long time ago."

"He did not have two wives at the same time!" Charlie looked earnestly from Thea to Felicity. "The first one died when Papa was a little boy."

"Smallpox." Bella started a game of hopscotch on the gallery's parquet flooring and hopped and skipped energetically. "Papa's brothers died, too. And Papa's sister. And now Grandpapa won't allow us to leave the estate because there's smallpox in St. Albans."

"Poor dears," said Lady Felicity. "How boring for you."

"Boring?" Charlie snorted. "It's beastly! I cannot even visit Robert at Ravensbrook!"

Felicity looked startled. Robert was one of her husband's numerous nephews and Charlie's boon companion.

She said, "Robert had the measles, but he's better. We had a letter from Robert's papa only yesterday, and he said Robert would return to Harrow in about a sennight."

"And he'll be gone till Easter! That's why I want to see him now. But his mama won't let him ride yet, or go out in the carriage. And Grandpapa won't let me leave Archer Hall."

"Ridiculous! I shall have a word with your grandfather."

"Oh, but you mustn't!" Bella stopped skipping so abruptly that she wobbled and would have fallen if Thea had not clasped one of the thin, flailing arms and steadied the girl. Bella barely paused to thank her. "Please, Lady Felicity! Don't speak to Grandpapa. He'll send you packing. Like Miss Pennymore!"

Charlie said, "Silly! He sent Miss Pennymore packing because she was a governess. But he cannot send Lady Felicity packing. Can he, Miss Stone?"

Thea had no notion to what she owed the honor of being appointed arbiter and felt quite ridiculously touched, but also doubtful of her ability to say the right thing.

"I'm afraid he can, Charlie. Your grandfather is the master of this house and has the right to decide who may or may not reside under his roof. By any gentleman's code of conduct, though, he'd feel obliged to put up with a guest, even if the guest annoyed him."

Charlie nodded. "He also shouldn't have turned off Miss Pennymore while Papa was gone. She was only trying to make him see reason. But Papa will set it to rights. He's with Grandpapa now."

"They were arguing about Lord Mansford's gals earlier," said Bella. "Papa doesn't want them to come here. But it's too late. Grandpapa invited them."

Charlie gave his sister a reproving look. "You're not supposed to be near Grandpapa's rooms either without an invitation. You're lucky Higgins didn't catch you."

"Don't you want to know what Papa said when Grandpapa told him he had already invited Lord Mansford's gals?"

"Why do I get the feeling we ought to end this conversation right here and now?" said Thea, uncomfortable with the drift of the conversation.

Bella gave her an inquiring look; Felicity was drooping in her chair; but Charlie responded.

"Because it's none of our business, ma'am. And because Bella shouldn't have eavesdropped in the first place. But she always does."

He flashed a grin, and Thea could not help but think that the father ought to take lessons from the son.

"I like listening at doors," said Bella without a sign of embarrassment or contrition.

"Well, you shouldn't do it, pet." Felicity yawned delicately. "What about our tour? Have we truly explored everything?"

"Why don't you rest awhile," suggested Thea, who had begun to suspect during her three-week stay at Markham House that her lively friend might be in a certain delicate condition. However, nothing had been said to her, and she could be mistaken—or, perhaps, Felicity was not yet sure herself.

"I would still like to see the chapel, but you needn't come, Felicity. We can explore it again another day."

"What chapel?" asked Charlie, and Bella gazed at Thea in astonishment.

Felicity caught Thea's eye, and anything Thea might have wanted to say remained unsaid. Instead, she begged the children's pardon and told them she must have mistakenly credited Archer Hall with a chapel that belonged to some other house.

Feeling absolved from further duty to their guests, the children ran off to find a less exacting amusement than playing guide.

"And now," said Thea, shepherding Felicity firmly in the direction of their own rooms on the first floor of the west wing, "will you kindly explain those extraordinary grimaces you made when I mentioned a chapel?"

"I don't doubt I looked as dumbfounded and openmouthed as the children. But grimaces? Really, Thea!"

Thea teased, "You looked as horrified as if you had caught me opening Pandora's box."

Laughing, Felicity entered the corridor leading to their chambers. "No wonder Charlie hurried his little sister off. But you exaggerate. I merely gave you a warning look since the children, apparently, are not supposed to know about the chapel."

"Then I am not mistaken that there is one?"

"No. In truth, though, I had forgotten. I heard it mentioned only once, and that was ages ago, when John's parents invited me for a weekend so they might judge my suitability as a bride for their youngest son."

"But where is the chapel, and what was said about it?"

Felicity frowned. "I believe it's merely a room somewhere in this wing, locked and the entrance disguised. Lord Barnet has threatened the staff with instant dismissal if they so much as breathe the word chapel."

"Why?"

"On account of some mysterious mishap years and years ago."

"What sort of mishap?"

"I'm not sure. A young girl, a maid, I believe, was hurt in the chapel. Or, perhaps, she died there. I seem to recall talk of the chapel being in disrepair. Also, it has ghosts or some such thing." Felicity stopped in front of her chamber. "I truly don't remember anything specific."

Thea looked at her in disbelief.

"I vow I'm speaking the truth, Thea! Do you think I had eyes or ears for anything but John during that weekend? I was expecting his proposal, you little goose!"

"I suppose that explains an incredible lack of interest in such titillating talk."

"It does." Felicity opened her door. "And what's more, some day you'll believe me."

She shut the door before Thea could make a retort but, a moment later, opened it again. Thea had already reached her own door past their sitting room, but that did not stop Felicity from voicing the thought that had popped into her head.

"Rumor has it that Mansford wants to settle his daughters. And since Lord Barnet has been pressing Stuart this past twelvemonth to take another wife, it is entirely possible that Barnet sent for the young ladies so Stuart can look them over."

"Mansford's gals, as Bella calls them? Do you know them?"

"They were in town last year for the season—the Misses Sylvia, Sibyl, and Serena Forrester. Ordinarily, I wouldn't expect Lord Barnet to consider the daughters of a mere viscount eligible to marry into the Archer family. However, they are connected to the Duke of Somerset on the mother's side, which rather changes the situation, don't you think?"

"What situation?"

"Their eligibility. Although the present Duke of Somerset is not a direct descendant of your Lady Arbella's husband, the duke and William Seymour have a common ancestor in the Protector Somerset. And that would make a marriage between

Stanmore and one of the Misses Forrester highly desirable in Barnet's eyes, would it not?"

But Thea had paid little attention. *"Visitors,"* she said with distaste. "I hope you're wrong! This is the one time I don't wish to be confined to the study or some far off room for the better part of my stay. I must have access to the galleries, at least. If I cannot view the portraits because of visitors, how will I put a face to each of the men and women who contributed to the chronicles?"

Felicity suppressed exasperation. Work! And the reputation of T. E. Stone, who never mingled. That was all Thea could think of.

"It will be difficult," she said, summoning a suitably commiserating look. Then, using a different tack, she added, "And most likely Stanmore will be obliged to squire the ladies about and won't be available when you have questions or a need to consult with him."

Thea's eyes kindled. "That will be unacceptable. I can see that I shall have to have a word with him."

"Do!" Felicity said cordially. "But privately, lest you provoke Lord Barnet."

Lowering her voice, she stepped closer to Thea. "I have not personally seen Barnet in a rage, but John told me he is the most cantankerous and irascible man he ever met. When provoked, he would rant and shout at Stuart, even in front of John!"

"Naturally I shall seek a private interview with Stanmore. My dealings are with him, not with the Earl Barnet."

Six

Thea counted on having a private word with Stanmore before the day was over. Her prospects looked good at dinner time. Lord Barnet did not appear—another attack of gout, said Stanmore. Instead, nine-year-old Charles James Archer, scrubbed and combed and, like his father, wearing a dark blue coat and champagne-colored pantaloons, took a seat at the dining table. With his son for company, surely Stanmore would not be long sitting over his port after dinner and would be free to give Thea a few moments of his time.

The table in the family dining room seated twelve. Four places were laid, two to the right and two to the left of Lord Barnet's empty chair at the head of the table. Dishes were set out, and Stanmore told the butler that he would ring when they required further service.

Charlie, sitting beside Thea, was clearly proud. "Bella had to eat with Nurse since Miss Pennymore isn't here anymore. But Papa said I'm old enough to help him entertain his lady guests."

"I am very grateful to you and your father," said Thea. "Without you, I would have felt quite lonely on this side of the table."

Gratified, the boy sat a little straighter. "But since we're informal, you may also converse across the table with Papa and Lady Felicity."

"Thank you, Charlie."

Privileged by her husband's long friendship with Stanmore,

Felicity said, "It's a pity about Miss Pennymore. What are you doing about a new governess, Stuart? And Charlie should have a tutor, whether he remains here or attends Harrow in the fall."

Beside Thea, the boy grew still, holding his breath.

Thea looked across the table at Stanmore. Briefly, their eyes met, and with a start she realized that she knew his mind once more. She felt what he felt—pain and anger, and determination.

Stanmore's voice, however, betrayed none of his feelings. "I shall try to persuade Miss Pennymore to return to us. And I've engaged a tutor. He'll start on the first of March."

"Only for the summer! Right, sir?" Charlie's voice was hoarse with tension. "I'll be going to school come autumn, won't I?"

"It is not settled, Charlie."

"Because of Grandpapa! It's not fair! *You* are my father. *You* ought to say that I may go to Harrow."

Again, Thea felt Stanmore's pain.

He spoke gently. "Charlie, if I said no, would you abide by my decision?"

The boy was silent and looked about to cry.

"You would, wouldn't you? Even if you felt hurt. Or if you were angry. You would do as I tell you because I am your father."

Charlie nodded.

"And your grandfather is *my* father. I cannot ignore his wishes. For over a hundred years Archer children have received their education at home."

"The first four earls went to Oxford. William Seymour, too, went to Oxford. He even was chancellor of Magdalen College. If I didn't want to go to Cambridge later with Robert, would Grandpapa let me go to Oxford?"

"Your grandfather fears that, away from home, you will not be looked after as you should be. I will try to reassure him and convince him that nothing horrid is going to happen to you if you attend Harrow. But it will take time, Charlie."

Picking up his fork, Charlie stabbed at a sliver of braised duck. But he did not eat. The fork dropped with a clatter.

He choked out, "Grandpapa isn't worried about *me*. He's worried about *the heir*. Please, sir. May I be excused?"

Silence fell, thick with the absence of even the slightest clink of glass or silverware. Stanmore was looking at his son, and only a twitch of his left eyelid betrayed that he was not as calm as he appeared. Felicity had blanched, stricken that she should have stirred up such controversy between father and son, and with a look appealed to Thea for help.

The plea was not in vain. Thea said, "A stranger has no place in a family dispute, and I know I should not have listened or, at least, I should pretend I did not. Alas, I have no shame, and I don't even wish myself small enough to crawl into a mouse hole. On the contrary, I am going to do the unforgivable. I am going to meddle."

Thea's voice with its rich, smooth tones always commanded attention, and this night was no exception. All eyes turned to her.

Charlie said, "I have aunts who are meddlers. And I don't like them."

"Now there's a gauntlet flung down," said Stanmore. "I wonder, Miss Stone. Will you pick it up?"

"But of course." She smiled at the flushing boy. "Not until strangers have tested each other's mettle can affinity or liking develop between them."

Charlie's eyes lit in understanding. "Like Robert and me the first time Papa took me to Ravensbrook to play. Robert had to draw my cork, and I had to give him a shiner before we liked each other."

"Yes. But I hope you don't feel it necessary to invite me to a bout of fisticuffs. I prefer to prove my mettle by less physical means."

"That's because you're a lady. But don't worry, Miss Stone. I couldn't fight you even if I wanted to, because a gentleman doesn't hit a lady."

"You relieve my mind."

A choke of laughter was heard from Felicity, but otherwise she remained unusually silent and only toyed with her food.

Reaching for his wine glass, Stanmore asked, "And how were you planning to meddle in our affairs, Miss Stone?"

She frowned. "Come to think of it, meddling is too strong a word. Mainly, I wanted to offer a distraction."

"You succeeded."

During their earlier meetings, a sudden switch to wryness had taken her off stride. But no longer.

She matched her tone to his. "Thank you, Lord Stanmore. What a nice compliment."

"I knew you'd appreciate it."

"What are you talking about?" demanded Charlie. "Papa, did you pay a compliment? It did not sound like one to me."

Stanmore looked at Thea.

"I think it was a compliment," she said, serving the boy a wedge of game pie, which, she hoped, would tempt him to eat a little. "And pray don't disillusion me, Charlie. Your father asked me to Archer Hall against his better judgment, and if I could think that he saw fit to pay me a compliment, I would feel ever so much more at ease."

Charlie gave her a hard look. "You're bamming, Miss Stone. Aren't you?"

"Perhaps a little. But, listen. I wanted to tell you about *my* tutor."

"Girls don't have tutors."

"I did. He is my governess's brother and also my foster father. Because of his scholarship and teaching abilities, I am fluent in several languages, have a fair grasp of the sciences, and—"

"French? Italian?" Charlie's mind was fixed on languages. "What about Latin? Greek?"

"Yes, indeed. I also speak Spanish and German."

"Then you must be as learned as the Lady Arbella. She also had tutors besides having several governesses. But there wasn't much else for her to do. She was in disgrace because her parents married against the queen's wishes. And also, there was a chance that she would become queen after Elizabeth. That's why her grandmother had her educated so well. Because Arbella was of royal blood. Are you, Miss Stone?"

"Did your papa tell you that I am a historian? That my specialties are the Tudor and Stuart reigns, and that I have a personal interest in the Lady Arbella?"

"He said you want to look at our chronicles. Is that what a historian does?"

"Yes. And if I had gone to school—which I wanted to do since all my foster brothers did, and even my sisters attended a young ladies academy for a few years. But I would not have learned Latin, the language used in many of the old documents."

"That's because you were a girl. Girls learn drawing and singing and dancing at school. Boys always learn Latin."

This was irrefutable, and Thea wondered if, for further distraction, she would need to enlarge on her thorough grounding in philosophy and other subject matters discussed by the Reverend Simmons.

"Papa had a tutor." Charlie's voice held no enthusiasm. "And that's why he's a great deal cleverer than Robert's father, who was at Harrow and Cambridge. At least, that's what Robert's father says. He says at school he learned not much more than getting into scrapes. And Robert is getting into scrapes, too—when he isn't home, being sick."

The boy sounded so wistful that Thea deemed it wise to introduce a different topic, which she did by asking Stanmore whether he had related his misadventures at Barnet House to his son.

Since he had not but was quite willing to do so, the meal was concluded on a satisfactorily light note. Charlie was sent off to bed, and while the rapid clatter of his feet could still be heard in the distance, Felicity excused herself, claiming fatigue.

"Are you unwell? Shall I go with you?" Thea asked with quick concern.

A look very much like annoyance crossed Felicity's face but was gone in an instant, and Thea could not be certain that it had been there.

"Dearest Thea! You are worse than John. I promise you, I'm merely tired. Let me have a good night's rest, and tomorrow I shall be right as rain."

In a rustle of silk, Felicity swept to the dining room door, which Stanmore opened for her. She paused to give Thea a saucy look over her shoulder. "Besides, you must have a hundred thousand questions to ask Stuart, and I wager in a few moments neither one of you will miss my presence."

"How true," Thea countered. "And if you hoped for a polite disclaimer or an appeal to change your mind, you're out of luck. So, go and catch your beauty sleep, child. Leave the evening hours to adults, who have serious business to discuss."

"What serious business?" asked Stanmore when Felicity had disappeared, chuckling.

"I should let you enjoy your port before I trouble you. If you'll point me to a sitting room, where I may wait?"

"No need to wait. We can talk now. There's a fire in the library, and a decanter of port as well, should I feel in need of fortification."

"Excellent. Let us go there at once."

"Afraid I'll change my mind, Miss Stone?"

She merely smiled and preceded him into the short passage that led into the north hall, thence into the brightly lit great hall. She trod on steadily, thinking of the distance to the library—one hundred and twenty feet from east wing to west wing—and that he might, indeed, change his mind along the way if he recalled that her chaperone had retired. Yet she could not help but stop for a moment to gaze at the multitude of wall sconces and the enormous chandeliers suspended from the two-story ceiling.

"How many candles you must use!"

"Yes." Dryly. "We make a great many beeswax candles ourselves and still buy more by the hundred. Miss Stone, if you do not wish to acknowledge apprehension that I will change my mind about a talk, at least tell me what this serious business is that we must discuss tonight. Have *you* changed your mind about staying?"

"Oh, no!" she said, horrified at the mere thought of not staying on, and resumed a brisk pace toward the library. "Nothing like that! I am eager to see where I shall be working—if at all possible, I should like it to be a room on the first floor so I may have quick access to the galleries."

"You're fond of gentle exercise, Miss Stone?"

"Lud, no! When I exercise, I do so vigorously. But you must know that is not why I want to be near the galleries. I believe you're teasing me, sir."

"I am. Must I apologize?"

She cast a quick look at his face. "You're teasing again. Capital! But I wish you weren't quite so parsimonious with your smile or so vigilant about hiding any suspect twinkle in your eye. You make it difficult to know when you're funning."

"Trying to teach me to unbend, Miss Stone?"

This time the gleam of amusement was unmistakable. Contrarily, this made her wish he would not be quite so agreeable. And if she replied in a like vein, it would only prolong the banter, which, she had to admit, she enjoyed more than a little. However, she was not at Archer Hall for her enjoyment—not *that* kind of enjoyment, anyway.

Firmly, she switched the conversation back to her concerns. "About my office, Lord Stanmore. I'd like it to be near the family portraits so I can review them when I wish and put faces to the names of your chroniclers."

"But, surely, you don't plan to examine the life of every one of my ancestors? That is two hundred years of records. And the answer we seek must be—if it is anywhere—in the very first volume of the chronicles."

"But you mentioned ambiguity in the entries. Most likely,

it was too dangerous at the time to keep a precise record of the events. Documents may have been hidden and the hiding place passed on by word of mouth. You will not credit how often this is done! Then, at some later point—in your family, perhaps, when the third earl was killed by a highwayman—surviving family members suddenly realize the danger of losing a secret document forever. And someone makes an entry somewhere in the chronicles, where another generation can find it."

He looked as if he wished to contradict her. But he said, "As your Dorothea did in your family Bible."

"Precisely."

A sudden thought struck her—the outrageous fee he had agreed to pay her by the week—and brought her to a halt at the foot of the flight of wide steps sweeping gracefully upward from the great hall to the galleries.

"Lord Stanmore . . . perhaps you fear it will render my work too dear if I spend time studying the full history of your family?"

"Do you feel it will help if you have the whole picture?"

"But of course. I would not have suggested it otherwise."

"In that case," he said gravely, "do as you wish. If necessary, we shall keep the great hall dark and pay you out of the candle money."

She searched his face—not a muscle quivered. But his eyes—no, she could not be mistaken. There was laughter dancing in his eyes.

"Indeed, sir! Thank you!" Giving him an arch look, she sketched a curtsy. "You have now contrived to make me feel an avaricious harpy."

"A gainfully employed woman, I believe, was how you called yourself but a few days ago."

"I see I must be very careful about what I say to you. You have a prodigious memory."

"Trained like yours, by reciting family history. But, in truth,

I do not find it difficult to recall previous conversations with you."

They still stood at the foot of the stairway and something, perhaps a sound, perhaps a feeling of being watched, made her glance upward. The movement of her head caused Stanmore to look up, too. If there was anything else he had wanted to say to Thea, it remained unspoken when a slight, elderly man in the somber attire of a gentleman's gentleman started downward.

"Yes, Higgins? I hope nothing is amiss with my father?"

"His lordship is as well as can be expected," Higgins said primly, stopping a few steps above them. "He wishes to see you, my lord. Immediately. On a matter of grave importance."

Stanmore's hesitation was almost imperceptible. "Tell my father I shall be there directly."

He waited until Higgins had retreated up the stairs and traversed some distance down the long gallery toward the east wing.

"I apologize, Miss Stone. I fear we must postpone further talk to the morrow."

She hid disappointment. "It is my habit to start work at eight o'clock. Where shall I meet you?"

"I'll send for you."

"Good night, then, Lord Stanmore."

Stepping close, he took the hand she offered and held it. "I have not thanked you for your 'meddling' at dinner."

"And it is quite unnecessary that you do so. A diversion was needed, and I provided it. That's all there is to it."

"Don't belittle your effort." His voice became strained. "I find it rather difficult just now to deal with Charlie. Unfortunately, it is true that my father's concerns are for *the heir* rather than for the boy himself, and I understand how Charlie feels—I felt it myself as a child."

Thea wanted to say, I know! I felt your pain, your anger. But I also felt determination, did I not? To make changes for Charlie's sake.

Perhaps, if Stanmore had not still held her hand, she might have spoken her thoughts aloud. But she had not realized how distracting the clasping of hands could be. His grip was warm, firm but not crushing, and she was vividly aware of his touch. Surely he could not be so oblivious of her hand in his that he had forgotten to let go?

He said, "I understand my son's resentment all too well, but I know I should not permit him to voice it."

With some difficulty she collected her thoughts. "Why? He was among friends."

"You think it right that a child should question his father's and grandfather's decisions?"

"Within reason. And Charlie did not overstep the bounds of propriety. He did not shout or drum his heels as many a child his age would have done in a tantrum."

"No, he did not, did he?" Stanmore looked pensive. "He asked to be excused when it seemed he was about to lose the struggle for composure."

The warmth flowing from his hand to hers was beginning to tingle and spread up her arm. The sensation was not unpleasant but strangely disturbing. Disquieting. She tugged gently.

He looked at their clasped hands and slowly let go. "Your hand is burning hot. My apologies, Miss Stone. I made you uncomfortable. I should have paid attention sooner."

"Your thoughts were on Charlie."

And hers were awhirl. She was both relieved and sorry that he had let go. If she was also a little piqued that his holding on had been mere oversight, she did not admit this—even to herself. Moreover, the tingling warmth, though less pronounced, had not subsided and was spreading throughout her body. She felt as if she was standing rather too close to the vast fireplace of the great hall and that its monstrous hearth contained, instead of a token mound of small logs, the thick tree trunks for which it was designed.

Stanmore said, "Charlie was embarrassed by his outburst. I

wanted to give him permission to leave the table in order to spare him further humiliation."

"You wanted to, but did not." It helped to be thinking of something else; the feeling of warmth receded. "You believed you must tell him no, that he must stay and suffer the consequences of his outburst. But you needed time to steel yourself against his pain. And then I stepped in and announced my intention to meddle, and it was too late for you to refuse his request. Never mind that he also forgot he wanted to be excused."

"How could you know what I felt? What I was about to tell my son? Fey again, Miss Stone? You begin to frighten me."

She studied him. "You're puzzled. But I doubt you're frightened. And let me assure you, it does not happen often that I precisely know another's thoughts—as if they were spoken aloud. In all the years I've been aware of my peculiarity, only once was I able to 'read' or 'hear,' or whatever you wish to call it, a direct thought concerning me personally. And then only, I believe, because I was—"

She broke off. In danger of my life, she had been about to say. Wooed with glib promises while the messenger from her former home reached for the dagger hidden inside his coat.

There was something about Stanmore that invited confidences. Not even Felicity had she told about the occasional bouts of extraordinary perceptiveness; the childish fear of a crowd.

"Because you were what, Miss Stone?" Stanmore's eyes were keen. "Or will you not tell me?"

"I don't know. Perhaps I will. But not now. It is too long a tale, and you must attend your father."

Seven

And she had not even asked him about the chapel.

What a strange thought to wake up to in the middle of the night.

Thea stared into the darkness surrounding her. She had been dreaming again. Unlike her usual dreams about Arbella, which were brief scenes of various episodes in Arbella's life, this dream had been a sequence of tableaux, the settings and characters changing quicker almost than the eye could perceive them. She remembered nothing specific. Not a backdrop or a face.

Yet she *knew* Arbella had been present. Also King James and his queen, Anne of Denmark. And Henry, Prince of Wales, who had been friend as well as cousin to Arbella. Thea could almost believe she had dreamed of the grand masque the queen gave in Henry's honor, and in which Arbella participated as a river nymph, her last appearance at a court ceremonial. But Thea could not be certain. Not when the tableaux changed so quickly that it was impossible to distinguish the ladies' costumes.

But even if the dream was different from others, it did not explain why it would awaken her to regrets that she had neglected to ask Stanmore about the chapel, which was not, after all, a matter of urgency or priority.

As she was drifting off to sleep again, she remembered another snatch of dream, one totally void of the Lady Arbella's presence. The central figure had been Thea herself, and even though the circumstances were as indistinct as the tableaux, she remembered a vivid sensation of warmth spreading throughout her body. The same strangely disquieting warmth she had felt when Stanmore clasped her hand. But even though she retained an impression of a man beside her, holding her hand, and a deep voice whispering her name, she could no more tell who the man in her dream was than where they stood or what he said besides "Thea."

Rueful, but at the same time laughing a little at herself, Thea decided that she was experiencing the first alarming signs of extended maidenhood. Not only had she been distracted and perturbed by the reality of a man's quite innocuous hand clasp, but she was also dreaming about it.

It was time, high time, she immersed herself in work and gave her unconscious mind a new direction.

Punctually at eight the following morning, a knock fell on Thea's door. A footman, she assumed, to take her to Stanmore. But it was Stanmore himself who had come to show her to the muniment room, located in the uppermost part of the turret gracing the southwest corner of the west wing.

As they started up the stairs to the second floor, Stanmore said, "One moment, Miss Stone," and reached out to adjust her shawl, which was drooping dangerously low on one side.

Again, she was vividly aware of his touch. She felt the warmth of his hands on her shoulders and upper arms and found it delightful. She knew a mad instant of wanting to lean back against him. Truly, she must be mad! And imaginative, too, to think that the sensation aroused was a different kind of warmth than the disquieting yet not unpleasant burning she had experienced the night before.

Else—and she feared this was worse—she was now accustomed to his touch, even desirous of it, for no longer did she find it disturbing.

Resuming her ascent, she thanked him and hoped that the

breathless note in her voice would be attributed to the climb. But she had been trained since earliest childhood to combat discomfiture and shyness, and before she reached the top of the stairs, she was quite composed again.

On the second floor they encountered footmen, arms piled high with loads of male attire which they were carrying into a chamber facing the central stairway of the wing. Stanmore took Thea to a corner room with two large windows and, at the angle of south and west walls, an archway into the turret room, bright and cheery by benefit of four windows.

Everywhere in the main chamber were signs of hasty packing, armoire and chests gaping open, a silver-backed hairbrush and a strop lying on the carpet by the four-poster bed. A man in riding dress was trying to shut a wide drawer without disturbing a stack of snowy cravats draped over one arm. At their entrance, he straightened, a veritable giant of approximately Stanmore's age.

"About done, my lord." A quick grin lit a craggy, weathered face tanned to the same deep brown as the man's close-cropped hair. "Just need to check that those oafs who call themselves footmen haven't forgot half your possessions in the drawers."

Thea looked curiously around the room, the furnishings as they must have been when Archer Hall was built almost two hundred years ago—solid and massive, and with some very fine carving typical of the period. Unless she had misunderstood the big man, this was Stanmore's room. But he was moving out.

"Miss Stone, this is Silas Wilkins. If I told you that he is my valet, you would most likely not believe me. And, in truth, he is much more than that."

"I'm his lordship's factotum, ma'am." Another grin flashed. "Generally, I require to be addressed as Wilkins. But since you'll be helping his lordship with the chronicles—and he needs a mighty bit of help there—Silas will do."

"Thank you." She had to crane her neck to meet Silas's eyes, for he was a head taller than even Stanmore was. "I must warn you though, I cannot promise that my assistance will bring Lord Stanmore the results he hopes for."

"Ma'am, that won't do. You *must* promise. If we cannot believe that there'll be a satisfactory end to the matter, then we'll have nothing to fortify us against the rumpus the lad's father is kicking up."

Fascinated, Thea watched Silas Wilkins stride off—one of the staff but dressed like a country gentleman and with the confidence of a squire. It had taken her a moment to figure out that "the lad" was not Charlie but Stanmore. But who was included in the "we" when Silas explained the need for her promise? The other servants? Perhaps, he was referring only to himself and Stanmore. Or, she thought, amused, he was using the royal "we."

He turned in the doorway for a sketchy bow before disappearing from sight, whistling as he went.

Meeting Stanmore's quizzical gaze, Thea raised a brow. "Would I be wide of the mark if I suggested that you and Silas grew up together?"

"You'd be hitting dead center, Miss Stone. And there's no point in telling him to mind his manners or his tongue. He wouldn't give a straw."

"Because he knows you will not dismiss him?"

Stanmore approached a narrow door to the left of the archway into the turret room. "I owe him a debt of gratitude I can never repay."

She thought she heard a sudden tetchy note. "You have no need to justify Silas Wilkins to me."

"Is that what you think I am doing? No, Miss Stone. And neither, if I gave the impression, am I irritated by your remark. After all, I invited your comments."

"So I believed. But I could have been mistaken."

"If I sounded angry—" His mouth tightened, and for a moment he said no more.

He looked at her. "Silas has always done as he pleases, and because he will turn up in unexpected places at unexpected times, he was able to save my children from drowning. It has been four years, but still the mere thought of it—their narrow escape—I find it impossible to speak of the incident without breaking into a cold sweat of terror."

"Oh, indeed!" Goosebumps puckered her skin. Four years ago, the children had been two and five. Somebody must have been grossly negligent to let them wander off near a body of water. "I am sorry I made you think of it."

"You couldn't have known."

He turned and opened the door. "I wanted to explain so you would feel kindly disposed toward Silas. I regard him as a friend, and since I've appointed him your assistant, to fetch and carry whatever documentation you may require from the chests or shelves, you'll be seeing quite a bit of him."

She thought his concern for both Silas and her strange but rather touching. "Thank you, Lord Stanmore. And you may rest assured that you have no need to worry about my acceptance of Silas."

Moving closer, Thea saw that the archway into the turret was at least three foot deep and that the door Stanmore held open led to a landing in the thick wall and an enclosed stairwell rising past and above the archway.

"The only access to the muniment room," said Stanmore.

She stepped into the wall cavity. Lanterns were affixed to the brick on either side, just above the banisters, and to the paneling overhead. The lanterns were not lit, but sufficient light penetrated from the downstairs chamber and from above to make mounting the stairs safe.

Picking up her skirts, Thea climbed swiftly. The angle was almost that of a steep ladder, but the steps were comfortably spaced and deep enough for a secure foothold. At the top of the stairs was a long, rectangular opening, a hatch without a cover but with a waist-high balustrade on all four sides and a gate opening into a spacious chamber. The muniment room. As in the turret room below, high windows admitted light from all four sides.

At a glance, she took in the shelves filled with ledgers, leather-bound histories, and even some ancient scrolls. There were chests and coffers of various size and build, and four writing desks, two of which she judged to have come from France. But the feature that caught and held her attention was a carved lectern in the corner between the north and east windows. On its slanted top, beneath a glass cover, lay a book.

She walked toward the lectern. The book was large, not as thick as some she had encountered, but by no means could it be called slim. It was bound in dark blue morocco, tooled in a gold and red design, which, on closer inspection, proved to be minuscule bows and arrows.

"The first volume of the Archer chronicles," said Stanmore. "The glass cover was commissioned by my grandfather upon his return from France. Until then, the book was kept in a wooden chest in the respective title holder's chamber in the east wing."

A memory stirred. Softly, Thea said, "And guarded with his life."

"Why does that make you sad and smile at the same time?"

She had not realized that her feelings showed. Indeed, she was certain they would not have been obvious to the casual observer. It was disconcerting to learn Stanmore was watching her so closely that he noticed even the slightest change of expression.

She kept her eyes on the book beneath the glass case, and her voice light. "I remembered that my father used to sleep with a strongbox beneath his bed and a pistol on the night stand."

"As I said yesterday, Miss Stone, your family sounds suspiciously like mine. Do you mean to tell me what it was that your father guarded with his life? Or will you keep all your family secrets to yourself while I bare mine for your inspection?"

"And even *pay* me for my curiosity."

"Do you not think that entitles me to at least *some* gratification of my interest in you?"

She looked up, then. "But you know all there is to know about me."

"About the professional side of you. I would, however, like to know your personal history."

She was startled into saying, "I can think of no reason why you should take an interest in me."

"Can you not?"

His expression gave nothing away, and his mind was closed to her. As she should have known it would be when a little knowledge could be of benefit to her!

Idle curiosity seemed out of character. Could he be taken with her, as Felicity suspected? But that was nonsense.

Or was it? Lud! What a complication that would be.

The large, airy tower room suddenly seemed too close and confining. Turning, she looked out the window facing north—the direction from which Miss Simmons would arrive in a day or two, for Thea had sent for her former governess by express the day Stanmore issued his invitation.

"My apologies, Miss Stone. I should not have pestered you with personal questions."

The reminder that her mentor and confidante, brisk, tart, and utterly matter-of-fact, would arrive shortly had a bracing effect on Thea. Of course Stanmore was not taken with her. Vespera Simmons would say 'twas a flight of fancy that made her think it. Stanmore was merely curious—as any man would be when he spent the greater part of his life in the country, with nothing but the familiar faces and concerns of neighbors to serve as a distraction.

Composed once more, she faced Stanmore.

"I must apologize. There's no reason why I should not tell you a little about myself. My excuse must be that I was taken by surprise. No one else who engaged my services showed the slightest interest in my family. Except for Felicity, of course. She questioned me unmercifully when her father asked me to Bellesmere Court to bring order to the Ruthven records." Thea

hesitated, then said in a rush, "Go ahead. Ask me what you like."

He looked amused. "A broad invitation. Shall I take you up on it?"

She knew then that he would never press her for answers she'd be unwilling to give, and relaxed.

He said, "I assumed you and Felicity were childhood friends. But a childhood friend has no need to question unmercifully. I take it that you did not meet until Lord Bellesmere commissioned you?"

"Yes, five years ago. It was my first truly significant commission."

"But are you and Felicity not also distantly related? Or, perhaps, I should say you are connected."

"Felicity told you?"

"No."

Appropriating the chair from the Louis XIV desk she had admired earlier, he placed it near the window for her.

She declined to sit.

"Then how do you know of my connection to Felicity's family?" she asked. "Don't misunderstand. I don't object to your knowing, but I am curious. It is not something that is generally known. Even Lord Bellesmere wouldn't have been aware of it if Miss Simmons had not written to him."

"Is it not obvious? Felicity's family, the Ruthvens of Bellesmere Court, are descendants of an illegitimate son of the Master of Ruthven, who was killed, along with his father, the Third Earl of Gowrie, in the bizarre incident referred to as the Gowrie Conspiracy. And Mary Wortley, Lady Arbella's waiting woman and mother of your ancestress Dorothea Wortley, was also a Ruthven. Second cousin to that same Earl of Gowrie I just referred to, was she not?"

"So I gave it away myself when I spoke of Dorothea. La, sir! I was prepared to find you as familiar with Arbella's history as I am. But that you also studied the background of her attendants! Lord Stanmore, I am impressed!"

"Are you?" His voice was smooth, but his eyes held a challenge. "Then why not treat me as an equal?"

Her breath caught as, for an instant, she mistook his meaning. But it was impossible. He did not know that in rank she was superior to him. What he meant, of course, was that they were kindred spirits, colleagues in historical interest, and that therefore she might address him without the title.

Still, the request was surprising since the Archers were notoriously high in the instep. But then, Stanmore had surprised her more than once already.

"Certainly, Stanmore." How easily his name tripped off her tongue without the prefix—betraying that, in her mind, he had been Stanmore all along. "I find that nothing is quite such a bore as having to use a person's title with every word I utter."

He looked startled, then, suddenly, laughed. "What a facer to my ego! You grant my request to avoid boredom."

"When you hoped I'd be flattered?"

"No." Serious. "I hoped to be friends with you."

"Then I beg your pardon. Shall I call you Lord Stanmore again?"

"No, Miss Stone. I still hope to be friends. I hope we *are* friends?"

"Yes . . . yes, of course."

"And, I think, you can better teach me when and how to laugh at myself if we're less formal."

She smiled and shook her head. "I have no such intention. Surely you know that Felicity was only funning?"

"Was she? I did not think so."

"No matter. You have no need to be taught to laugh at yourself. You did that splendidly just now. If only you would show your feelings more often."

"That would be very much against my nature."

"I can believe that. I've never met a man more reserved than you."

"But so are you, Miss Stone. Reserved. You may be livelier

than I am, and smile and laugh more readily, but you do not share your innermost thoughts."

He stood at least three paces from her, but she took an involuntary step backward as if, by distancing herself, she could stop him from seeing that which she did not want to be seen.

Quite tartly, she said, "My innermost thoughts are on the Archer chronicles. And instead of talking about ourselves we should discuss my schedule and work space."

For a moment longer, he looked at her. Then he nodded. "The cylinder-top writing table holds my personal correspondence, but you still have three desks from which to choose your own."

"I am to work *here?*"

"Is the muniment room not the ideal place to examine our chronicles?"

"Is that why you moved out of your chamber? To give me the use of this room?"

"You cannot wish to pass through my bedchamber every morning. Or to wait for Silas to fetch volume after volume to a room off the gallery just so you can be near the portraits."

"Ordinarily, I'd be delighted to work here, high above the bustle of daily life. But, Stanmore! You're expecting visitors. If my office were near the portraits it would be easier for me to retreat when someone approaches while I'm viewing your ancestors."

He frowned. "Miss Stone, I do not wish you to retreat and hide yourself. In this house, you are a valued guest."

"Thank you. But I explained that T. E. Stone does not mingle socially."

"Then you must be Miss Thea Stone for the few days Lady Mansford and her daughters will be staying here."

"Impossible. I cannot work *and* be Thea Stone."

"You can take a holiday. Or, if you prefer, you can work and pretend it's vulgar curiosity that draws Miss Stone to the Archer records."

She gave him a repressive look. "I *prefer* not to mingle."

They stood facing each other as if in confrontation over some weighty life or death matter. And in a manner of speaking it was to T. E. Stone, whose livelihood could so easily be jeopardized. It occurred to Miss Thea Stone, however, that they must look quite ridiculous.

She started to laugh. "If your children were to see you with that formidable frown—"

He cut in. "Or you, as you were but a moment ago, with a glint of ice in your eyes and your arms akimbo."

She looked pointedly at her arms, which had remained decorously at her sides throughout the exchange.

"Metaphorically speaking, Miss Stone." He bowed. "It is all settled, then. The muniment room is yours. Explore at your leisure. I shan't bother you for a while."

"How overbearing you are." Her smile took the sting out of the words. "But, surely, you're not leaving? I may have questions."

"Questions must wait. This afternoon, at three o'clock or, perhaps, a little sooner if I can arrange it, will you ride with me to the old farmstead ruins? Edward Archer's sister lived there. Lizzy Archer. According to the chronicles, she was the wet nurse of Arbella's child."

"The wet nurse! Oh, indeed! I should very much like to see the place. I had no idea—a wet nurse was never mentioned—but, of course, an infant would have needed one."

"Until later then, Miss Stone."

"Yes, until later. And, Stanmore . . ." She smiled. "Thank you ever so much."

Leaving to perform various and sundry duties, Stanmore carried with him, indelibly etched in his mind, Thea Stone's slow, entrancing smile and the glow of anticipation in her eyes.

Eight

Alas, due to the capriciousness of the weather, the ride to the old Archer farmstead had to be indefinitely postponed.

After establishing Thea in the muniment room and holding a brief consultation with the bailiff, Stanmore had driven to St. Albans to persuade Miss Pennymore to return to Archer Hall. The governess declined, stating unequivocally that she preferred to assist her uncle, a physician, in tending the rising number of smallpox victims rather than expose herself once more to Lord Barnet's irascible temper.

Before Stanmore was halfway home, the pale February sun disappeared behind a wall of threatening clouds, and by the time he left the curricle in the stableyard, he was drenched. The dirt lane to the farmstead ruins he planned to visit with Thea was but a winding riband of mud.

The wider lane to Ravensbrook was in no better shape. Felicity, who had left that morning to call on her husband's parents, would not have returned to Archer Hall but for her duties as chaperone. She might not be above using a small ruse now and then to further what she considered a perfect match, but she would not risk Thea's reputation by leaving her alone overnight in the household of two widowers.

Thus, an hour before dinner, when all hope of more clement weather had faded, Felicity and the Earl of Ravensbrook, along with a groom, set out on horseback despite Lady Ravensbrook's remonstrations. There was just enough turf, shriveled and dead though it was, next to the muddy lane to give the horses a foothold. But what would have been a brisk twenty-minute ride on a fine day took thrice that time on a sodden night, and it did not help that Felicity's lantern went out because the stable boy had neglected to replenish the oil.

The rain did not cease the following day, or the day after. It was still raining a week later, when Miss Simmons should have long been at Archer Hall and Lady Mansford and her daughters were expected to arrive, but did not.

Thea thought it a pity that Miss Simmons was caught in the rains and might be marooned in some drafty inn with damp sheets, but she did not worry unduly. She was fully occupied with the Archer chronicles—and Vespera Simmons knew how to take care of herself.

As to Lady Mansford and the Misses Forrester, no one but Lord Barnet regretted their absence, and he did not hesitate to blame his son. Stanmore should have gone to Berkshire instead of haring off to London!

He also blamed Stanmore for the condition of his gouty leg, which kept him confined to his chambers. This latest attack of gout, Barnet insisted, was brought on when his heir invited "a ferreting female calling herself a historian" without consulting him—an attitude that strengthened Stanmore's resolve not to disclose the true purpose of the historian's visit until Miss Stone confirmed that the Archer family history was a sham.

Lord Barnet declared he had no interest in Miss Stone and no desire to set eyes on her. But the one time he requested Lady Felicity's presence in the hallowed precincts of the east wing's first floor to take a dish of tea with him—Barnet substituted claret for the tea—he catechized her thoroughly on Miss Stone's credentials.

Sporadically, a groom fought his way to Barnet, where the Edinburgh and Holyhead roads converged. There was little or no private carriage travel, but the stagecoaches and mails were running, if lamentably behind schedule. The coachmen reported rain from Finchley Common in the south to Norman

Cross in the north, with the gravel washing away and ruts so deep that it was a wonder any coach made it through at all.

But the coaches were running, which meant that Miss Simmons, if she had started on her journey from Derbyshire by stage, should have arrived at Barnet. On his next foray into town, the groom made inquiries at the inns, but Miss Simmons was not there. He did, however, return with a letter for Lord Barnet from Viscount Mansford, who did not wish to see his wife and daughters exposed to the hazards of mired roads and, as he had learned, smallpox in St. Albans. Mansford suggested that a more propitious time for a visit would be early April, before his ladies went to London for the season.

Thea did not mind the rain. It bothered her as little as snow and ice would have bothered her since she hardly noticed anything that happened outside the muniment room. This was not unusual while she was in the first phase of her work, the reading of every available bit of documentation. Felicity, who had witnessed Thea's distraction when she was working on the Ruthven records, was unconcerned and said as much to Stanmore when Thea fell silent in the middle of a conversation.

He had hoped to draw Miss Stone out a little and get to know her, but another man could have been no greater rival for her attention than his family's past. He tried to keep her focused on her companions with an introduction of three-handed whist after dinner, only to see her put down the cards and stare off into space.

Stanmore was not a man to admit defeat without a fight. When conversation and cards did not work, he tried music. From Felicity he knew that Miss Stone enjoyed performing on the pianoforte. Alas! When preoccupied, she could not be depended upon to finish a piece. Or, if they sang, her lovely contralto voice would begin to drift and finally be silent altogether, leaving Stanmore and Felicity to carry on as best they could.

Finally, Stanmore resigned himself to the fact that, whenever Miss Stone's eyes held a faraway look, he need not bother to address her. She might be physically present, but her mind would be two hundred years in the past.

One particularly dismal night, when fog and a softly keening wind added a mournful note to the rain, Stanmore begged to be excused after dinner since work awaited him in the estate office. Felicity decided to retire early, and Thea said absently that she would, too.

Thus, as soon as the meal was taken, Stanmore accompanied the ladies across the great hall. "I truly am sorry I must desert you this early. But my bailiff left me a list of complaints and requests from tenants to look over, which I must not postpone."

"No, indeed," said Felicity. "The rain is much gentler now, but I don't doubt that last week's storms damaged some roofs. Just think how miserable the poor dears must be. Even their beds may be soaking wet!"

"No doubt," Stanmore said drily, "if I were a slum landlord. But Purvis deals with such emergencies immediately. The complaints and requests I am speaking of concern a long-standing feud among four families sharing a piece of grazing land. Purvis thinks it is time I intervened."

"Oh." For a few moments, Felicity continued in pensive silence. "I daresay a bailiff is essential in the management of an estate . . . if he is a very good bailiff like Purvis and can be trusted to do what is right?"

Thea had not been paying close attention to her companions but heard Felicity's tentative question. "What is this, Felicity? Why this interest in a bailiff? I thought you told me that you and Markham would be settled in town for quite a few years yet."

"Pish! You shouldn't comment when you haven't been listening properly. Stanmore and I were discussing *his* bailiff."

They had reached the gallery stairs, where they would part—Stanmore to go to the estate office on the ground floor of the west wing; Thea and Felicity to mount the graceful flight of open steps to the first floor.

Indeed, Felicity seemed eager to retire and started up the stairs immediately.

But Thea hesitated. She was aware of a feeling of disquiet that had not been there a moment earlier, a restlessness she could not explain . . . something tugging at her mind, demanding some kind of action. But she knew not what.

Stanmore said, "Felicity tells me I should pay no heed to your distraction—that it will last only as long as you're absorbing the contents of the chronicles. But I know what high expectations you had, and I wonder whether your preoccupation is due to disappointment. Miss Stone, the chronicles are not what you expected, are they?"

She faced him, and there was not a hint of preoccupation or distraction in the look she turned on him.

"No, they're not. I find them troubling, and your question leads me to believe you expected this. Stanmore, the chronicles were not begun until six years *after* the birth of the child and Arbella's flight from Barnet. The first entry is dated March 25, 1617, and it states merely that the construction of Archer Hall was completed and that William Seymour Archer turned six years old that day. The earlier years—"

She broke off, aware of the tingling warmth she had experienced once before—on her first night at Archer Hall. Then, too, she and Stanmore had been standing at the foot of the stairway. He had held her hand. Only this time she could not blame the sensation on Stanmore's touch. He stood close but not too close, one hand resting lightly on the lion's head atop the newel post, the other loosely at his side.

He said, "Yes, Miss Stone. The earlier years, the events most pertinent to my family history, are merely a retrospective summary without supporting documentation. And, no doubt, you think I should have warned you. Indeed, I lived in daily expectation of having my ears boxed for not doing so. Yet you never said a word."

"But then, neither did you." Thea wished she carried a fan; the warmth, the disquiet of her mind, played havoc with her concentration. "But was my silence not a most effective punishment?"

"A threat hanging over my head—like the sword of Damocles."

"Then I am satisfied and shall consider the score evened."

Coming back down the stairs, Felicity said, "What score? What on earth are you talking about?"

"Stanmore's omissions."

Thea turned to him once more. Perhaps she imagined it, but she thought he also looked rather heated.

"Stanmore, you must have known that I expected the chronicles to begin when Edward Archer received the infant from Arbella's arms—or at least shortly afterward. The later entries, dated and recorded in journal form, have a ring of authenticity, a force of persuasion. But that summary—written so long after the fact—must always be subject to question."

If he had still wondered whether she would be able to maintain objectivity, she must now have put his doubts to rest. But she should have known that he would neither give a sigh of relief nor some other overt sign of satisfaction.

He said, "Indeed, I knew you would be troubled. I read those passages as a boy of six or seven and accepted them as irrefutable fact. But three years ago, I studied the material again, and I was troubled, too."

Three years ago, his wife died. Thea knew nothing about his marriage and could only wonder whether it had been the pain of losing wife and a child that drove him to the muniment room and its cache of old records. As long as she had been at Archer Hall, she had not heard him—or the children—speak of Charlotte Archer, Viscountess Stanmore. A very beautiful woman, if the portrait in the gallery was a true likeness. But the artist had portrayed her as haughty and cold.

Felicity said, "Stuart, that was not well done of you. If you knew Thea would be disappointed in the chronicles, you should have warned her. She made no secret of it that she wishes to prove your family's claim true."

"And Miss Stone is aware that I intend to do the opposite. I could alert her to other troublesome points, but I shan't do so."

Thea was beginning to feel light-headed but forced a smile. "I believe Stanmore does not want to appear to be influencing me."

"To stay objective will be challenge enough for you without the added burden of knowing my admittedly biased point of view. Good night, ladies. Rest well."

He turned abruptly and strode toward the hallway opening off the great hall behind the wide sweep of stairs. He had his back to Thea, but she was sure he tugged hard at his collar and cravat—as if he was choking or feeling too warm.

Something in her protested against his leaving. The strange warmth engulfing her seemed to diminish as the distance between them widened, and she found herself reaching out as if to hold him back.

"Thea? Are you coming with me?"

She dropped her arm and hastily joined Felicity on the stairs.

"Good," said Felicity. "You look better. I suppose it was annoyance that made you look flushed when you spoke with Stuart. For a moment I feared you had a fever. Perhaps the measles! The children's nurse said that the gardener's son is down with them."

Indeed, Thea felt better. Even the light-headedness was gone. But she wasted no time marveling.

"The measles! Felicity, have *you* had them?"

"Oh, yes."

Pausing on the first-floor gallery, dimly lit by domed lamps in wall brackets, Felicity smiled serenely. "You've guessed, have you not? Dearest Thea, don't be angry that I did not tell you. I've always envied you your secret, and it was so delicious to have one of my own—even if for just a little while."

"Don't be silly. Of course I'm not angry, but I am surprised that Markham let you go with me."

"He wasn't happy to see me leave, but he thought it would do me good to escape the London fog for a little while."

"Did he," Thea said drily. She took Felicity's arm and steered her toward their chambers. "But who is to say he was wrong? At least, the fog here is washed clean by the rain."

Felicity giggled.

A few moments later they parted, Felicity to write her husband, and Thea to study the notes she had taken earlier that day in the muniment room, where, every morning, Silas Wilkins mended her pens, dusted the desk and the next two volumes of the chronicles if she was about to be done with the previous set he had fetched from the shelves.

That night, Thea found it difficult to concentrate on the notes as her mind returned again and again to the strange experience at the foot of the gallery stairs. Twice now it had happened—whatever "it" was—but much more pronounced this second time.

For some reason she felt she ought to know what those eerie sensations portended; but she did not, though she could now smile at her earlier fear that they were the reaction of a no-longer-young maiden to an agreeable and not unhandsome gentleman. She knew it was not that. By no means could she claim indifference, but she was *not* reduced to light-headed giddiness when Stanmore was near.

Which was just as well.

But if it wasn't an unwise attraction that made her feel so strange, then it must be something else. She looked at the clock on the mantel, but the light from her writing desk did not reach that far. And the time did not really matter anyway.

Thea rose and with swift, purposeful steps left her room. The small domed bracket lights in the hallway and on the side gallery still glowed softly. The great hall below was dark, the candles in the chandeliers snuffed. However, at the foot of the gallery stairs a pedestal lamp shed a pool of light near the spot where Thea had stood earlier.

Without hesitation, she stepped on that spot, judging her position by imagining Stanmore standing by the newel post with his hand on the lion's head.

She waited, but nothing happened. No warmth. No odd sensation of restlessness as if she ought to be going somewhere, doing something. No light-headedness.

After a while, she moved around a little in case she had misjudged her position after all. But to no avail. She stared into the darkness of the great hall, almost two hundred years old, already an anachronism when it was built since most functions of the great hall had by then been relegated to smaller, individual rooms.

She remained downstairs for ten, perhaps fifteen, minutes with no purpose but to absorb the atmosphere of the place. The Lady Arbella Stuart could not possibly have been inside Archer Hall; it wasn't built until after her death. But she had been nearby, and a number of Thea's dreams about Arbella had occurred while staying near or after visiting a place where Arbella had stayed. And Thea had already dreamed once, on her first night at Archer Hall. Surely she could expect to dream again.

The dream, when it came, was not a new dream. But never before had the images crystallized to such sharpness.

The Lady Arbella in doublet, hose, and riding boots, a cloak around her shoulders and a short sword at her side, was standing in a narrow, unadorned chamber. Slightly behind her, two women—one veiled, the other hooded but showing the partial profile of a young girl no older than sixteen or seventeen. And facing Arbella, his back to a brick hearth swept bare of kindling and ashes, a man dressed like a farmer in breeches and smock and holding an infant in swaddling clothes.

Arbella stepped forward to receive the child in her arms.

She kissed it, then turned, handing the infant to the young girl behind her, and quickly left.

And Thea awoke, tears wet on her face from the pain and sorrow she had felt in that plain, whitewashed room. She did not doubt that what she felt was Arbella's pain and sorrow at parting from her child.

The narrow room must be part of the old Archer farmstead Stanmore had promised to show her, for Arbella's male disguise placed the dream scene on the third day of June, 1611, the day Arbella escaped from the Bishop of Durham's men at Barnet. Her steward had procured a horse, and she rode to London, thence fled by boat to Lee, where a French vessel awaited her.

Had they sailed immediately, Arbella would have escaped safely to Calais. But she insisted on waiting for William Seymour, whose escape from the Tower had been arranged simultaneously. But Seymour was delayed, and when Arbella finally agreed to set sail, her ship floundered in adverse winds. Hours later, Seymour found a different vessel and, because of the weather, sailed to Holland instead of France.

He was safe, but Arbella was captured and sent to the Tower William Seymour had just fled. There she died without seeing husband or child again.

As Thea lay in the dark thinking about her dream and Arbella's tragic life, she recalled yet another dreamlike image. She had no idea whether it was something she dreamed that same night or some previous night—or whether it was totally a figment of her imagination.

The image showed the same narrow chamber with the brick fireplace and wood mantel where Arbella had bidden farewell to her child. Even the child was there, no longer an infant. Perhaps a year old, he was sitting on a braided rug on the hearth stone. And nearby stood a young couple gazing at each other, their hands entwined.

The young lady appeared to be the girl in the other dream, but Thea could not be certain. Again she saw only a partial profile even though the girl did not wear a hooded cloak this time. She had long brown hair, quite straight and falling to her waist, which looked incredibly tiny above billowing skirts.

Thea saw the young man more clearly. He looked much like King James's son, Henry, as portrayed in a miniature painted shortly before his death. The hooded eyes reminded her of Stanmore, but that was not surprising since both men shared Tudor ancestors. Henry's nose was larger, his mouth fuller than Stanmore's, his hair lighter and almost touching the ruff of his doublet.

What the scene signified, Thea did not know. If the young man was indeed Henry, Prince of Wales, and the child on the hearth Arbella's son, then contemporary sources were wrong about Henry having withdrawn his friendship from Arbella after her marriage. Thea had never yet dreamed what was not afterward proven true, and if Henry had seen the child before the winter of 1615, when Edward Archer first made it known at James's court that he was raising Arbella's son, then Henry had obviously shared the secret. But Henry died in November of 1612. Rumor had it that he was poisoned by order of King James.

But the girl with Henry . . . the way he gazed at her seemed to indicate they were lovers. The only romance contemporaries had noted—and others had hotly denied—was Henry's brief enslavement by Frances Howard, the child bride who had set the court by its ear, had later divorced her husband, married Robert Carr, Viscount Rochester, and was convicted of murdering Rochester's friend, who opposed her divorce and remarriage.

It was rather confusing, to say the least. Also, no gentleman visitor to see the child was mentioned in the first volume of the chronicles. Only two ladies.

At the end of the second week of rain, the groom brought mail for Thea and Felicity.

Thea's letter was from Miss Simmons, who wrote that she had booked a seat on the stage immediately upon receipt of Thea's express. She had meant to leave within two days. Alas, the day before her scheduled departure, Mrs. Felix Simmons had taken a fall down the attic stairs and broken an arm and an ankle. Miss Simmons had been so busy looking after her sister-in-law and the bustling vicarage household that she had not had time to write sooner. She still intended to join her dear Thea but could not possibly do so for another week or two, and she hoped this would not inconvenience Lady Felicity.

"Not at all," Felicity assured Thea, even though her own letter from Markham had been a plea to bring her visit to an end and to let him know when he might fetch her.

"Are you sure? Markham will wonder—"

Felicity interrupted. "John cannot be aware that the lanes to Barnet and Whetstone are swamps. If he knew, he would not ask me to travel just now. And Ravensbrook has promised to help me with a surprise for John, but even though we have no more than one or two gentle showers a day, we cannot possibly take the carriage out just at present. So, you see, it'll suit me very well to be staying on."

They were both in the muniment room, which Thea scarcely left during the day except to eat or for a quick look at the portraits. If she had been less preoccupied with the chronicles—two hundred years of Archer past contained in some twenty-odd volumes—Felicity's airy tone and her smile when she spoke of a surprise for John would certainly have caught her attention. But Thea noticed nothing, except the six volumes that still needed to be read.

"Good," she said absently. "I only hope you won't become bored."

Felicity, who was beginning to feel a trifle worn from assisting Stanmore with the education and entertainment of his children in the absence of a governess, raised a brow. But Thea did not notice that either. She had jotted down a reminder to write her foster mother and Miss Simmons after dinner and was already reading again.

Thea finished the last volume of the chronicles late in the afternoon of Thursday, March 1, the day the rains stopped altogether—the same day the tutor arrived at the Green Man in Barnet and was told to leave his trunks at the coaching inn until the lane to Archer Hall could be negotiated by wagon or cart. Usually it gave her a feeling of exhilaration to know that the first phase of her work was completed, but this time she had to acknowledge mixed emotions.

Pensive, she closed the morocco-bound book on the last entry, a brief statement that Charlotte Archer, Viscountess Stanmore died in childbirth on the first day of August, 1807. The child was stillborn. There was no mention of the infant's gender. There were no further entries at all.

Looking up, she saw Stanmore seated at the cylinder-top writing table, not more than five or six feet from the mahogany desk she had chosen.

"Stanmore! I did not hear you come in."

Nine

He rose, giving her a quizzical look. "Are you returned to our century then, Miss Stone? May I address you, or will you still look straight through me as if I were but a ghost of the past?"

"If that is what I did, I apologize. But, surely, you exaggerate."

"Do I?" Using the tinderbox from his desk, he lit the lamp on hers. "I spoke to you when I entered an hour ago. You looked at me, yet you say you did not hear me. You certainly made no reply when I asked if you would care for some refreshment. What's more, this wasn't the first or only time you gave me the cut direct these past weeks."

"I promise it shan't happen again." She smiled. "Now that I shall need your help, you may be certain I'll notice you."

"How long it has been since I saw that smile! I believe the last time was when I asked you to ride with me to the farmstead ruins."

This startled her. "I did not know you counted my smiles. And, surely, I must have smiled many times since then."

"Preoccupied smiles. Cursory smiles. Polite smiles. But not a smile from the heart."

"Nonsense!" she said, uncomfortable with the turn the conversation had taken. "Speaking of the farmstead ruins, when can you show them to me?"

"If the sun cooperates, in two or three days. But I warn you, only the walls of the downstairs rooms are still standing."

"That should be sufficient."

"Sufficient for what, Miss Stone?"

"To picture what the house was like when Arbella saw it the day she made her escape from Barnet. It says in the chronicles, 'The most gracious Lady Arbella stepped across the threshold of Edward Archer's abode on the afternoon of the 3rd June, 1611, and blessed and bade farewell to the child she delivered unto the said Edward Archer's care on the 25th March.' "

He looked amused. "I had no idea you meant to memorize our chronicles. But I doubt Edward's abode refers to the farmhouse. Only Lizzy Archer lived there. Edward had his own cottage."

She remembered the room in her dream, long and narrow, whitewashed walls, the fireplace opposite the door through which Arbella had left.

"But the chronicles don't mention a cottage."

"Don't they?" He frowned. "Then the information must be in Lizzy's household accounts or the Archer Hall ledgers. Or both. I've read everything so often that I can no longer distinguish where I found which particular bit of information."

"Since I've read only the chronicles, I cannot be mistaken. There's a reference to Lizzy suckling Lady Arbella's son along with her own, but nothing about a cottage. Surely she kept both infants with her at the farmhouse?" Pushing back her chair, Thea moved cramped shoulders and neck. "I shall have a look at the old accounts. Where do you keep them?"

"In the sea chest beneath the west window."

His long-legged stride took him swiftly to a weathered oak chest with brass handles and hammered brass corners on the opposite side of the room, where the setting sun reflected yellow-orange in the window panes.

He raised the lid. "These are the accounts for the Archer farm from 1604 when, apparently, Lizzy took the reins, to 1650 when she died. Also the accounts for Archer Hall from December of 1615, when the first building materials were purchased, to about 1700. Later Archer Hall ledgers are kept on these shelves to my left."

Thea rose but did not join him at the chest. "I wonder why Lizzy had the farm and Edward the cottage."

"Perhaps because he was never home until he left the Bishop of Durham's service? Edward was a soldier and could hardly work the land while he traveled with his master."

"Lizzy had a child. Was she married?"

"There's no mention of a husband or her married name in the farm accounts."

Thea glanced at the first volume of the chronicles on the lectern in the corner behind her desk, then looked down at a stack of notations she had made while reading. She had no need to refer to them, but the sight of the terse comments in her own hand helped fight a quite unprofessional reluctance to voice what was on her mind.

She said, "You want to prove your family's claim false. But have you considered that it could be worse than a mere boastful false claim?"

"I not only considered it, I'm convinced it is what happened." Leaving the chest open, Stanmore crossed the room again. "Edward Archer used his sister's son to swindle King James."

Deep inside, Thea knew Edward Archer's claim was no swindle. But, no matter that her heart rebelled, the rational, questioning scholar in her could not be silenced.

"It is a possibility, just as it is still possible that Edward Archer indeed raised Arbella's child. I certainly understand now why you spoke of ambiguity in the entries. That summary of the first six years of the child christened William Seymour Archer is a historian's nightmare. I will find it as difficult to prove that Edward was a mountebank as proving he was a savior."

"You still believe he was the latter?"

Standing behind her chair, she met his gaze fully. "I have

not relinquished my belief that Arbella had a child. I doubt I will—unless I find proof positive to the contrary."

"And I hope for evidence to help *my* cause, but if I cannot have that I shall settle for a list of persuasive arguments to show my family—my father—that there is at least a possibility our chronicles are a sham."

"Is that why your father is kicking up a rumpus, as Silas called it? I believe it was that first morning, when you were about to show me this room."

"My father does not yet know that I've turned heretic. But the gout is plaguing him worse than ever before, and when he's in pain he needs no other reason to kick up a rumpus."

She smiled. "He especially does not need a visit from a ferreting female."

"You were not meant to hear that. I apologize." His brow knitted. "Who told you? But, I suppose, I need not ask. It was Bella."

"Does it matter? I took it as a compliment. There's a Bow Street runner, called the Little Ferret because he is most adept at ferreting out the hiding-holes of thieves and cutthroats. If I am half as successful at ferreting out the truth of your ancestry, I shall count myself fortunate."

His expression softened. "You're very kind, Miss Stone."

"Not at all. Stanmore, I had hoped to find documentation here at Archer Hall, perhaps a letter signed by Arbella, that would prove the child's status. There is no mention of anything of that nature in the chronicles. And, surely, if you had such a document in your possession, you would have said so at the time you showed me the first volume?"

"If we had such a document—any document at all—I would not have begun to doubt what generations of Archers regarded as indubitable."

"Yes, I was naively optimistic." Absently, she toyed with a pen that needed mending. "Your most convincing argument in favor of a swindle will always be the lack of documentation."

"True. But it puzzles me that Edward—and whether he was

swindler or savior is in this instance immaterial—was able to convince King James without documentation that the child was Arbella's. Yet he must have done so. I cannot think of any other reason for James to bestow on Edward the title of Baron Barnet, a large tract of land adjoining the Archer farmstead, and a purse that enabled him to build Archer Hall."

"Perhaps Edward did have proof. Perhaps he surrendered whatever documentation he had in return for the title and purse."

"The title, a bribe to keep silent? But in that case—" Stanmore paused, his eyes narrowing. "It would point to the claim being true, would it not?"

"It could. Or it could mean Edward was as adept at forging as he was at swindling." Thea put down the pen. "But there is one circumstance we have not yet considered. You said he convinced King James. But did he? It is stated in the chronicles that he went to Greenwich Palace and met with the queen."

"I am aware of it, and I thought Edward shrewd. It was no secret that James never forgave his cousin for having eaten of the forbidden tree, as he phrased it, when she married William Seymour. But Anne of Denmark always had a fondness for Arbella and intervened several times on her behalf with the king."

"But even if Anne believed every word Edward Archer told her, she still had to approach James about the reward."

Stanmore leaned against the desk. "If Anne wanted to ensure that the child would be reared with all the benefits of a nobleman's son, who is to say she did not spin James a yarn about Edward Archer? I doubt she was above intrigue, and James certainly had a penchant for creating nobles."

"For which he generally expected payment."

"But he also made grants of money and land. Although," Stanmore conceded, "that was mostly to the Scots who had accompanied him to England."

Stanmore stood lost in thought, and Thea crossed to the western window. She opened it and leaned out, enjoying the brisk air, free of even the slightest hint of rain. It was dusk, changing to dark, and from the height of the muniment room she could see the last faint pink glow of sunset beyond the park.

She thought of King James's wife, Anne, whom Edward Archer had sought out rather than the king himself. She thought again of the dream image she'd had of Henry, Prince of Wales, in the whitewashed room that might have been Edward Archer's cottage.

Stanmore said, "All that discussion led us nowhere. But you enjoyed it, did you not? Arguing point and counterpoint?"

"Yes, it is what makes the past come alive."

"And I feel lost. I no longer see which argument will help me and which won't."

Thea closed the window. "Some arguments will suit both your and my purposes."

"That is why I need a clearheaded historical scholar to help me. But enough of this for today. Miss Stone, you did not come down to luncheon."

"Silas brought lunch to me."

She returned to her desk, where Stanmore was about to snuff the light. "Don't, please! I want to stay a bit longer. We need not raise any more questions or arguments to add to the confusion, but I should like to make a list of what is pure, undisputed fact. If you have other things to do, you need not stay. You may trust me to continue the exploration of your family's past without bias."

"I trust you implicitly."

She acknowledged his assurance with an inclination of her head.

He said, "I have not seen you do that since you pardoned my boorish behavior the day we met. Such a simple gesture, yet so gracious. So regal. The queen could not have done better."

For an instant, she faltered. Then she laughed. "Which queen? And careful how you answer. There are some queens to whom I'd rather not be compared."

"Elizabeth, of course. She was by far the most regal of our queens since the Middle Ages."

Thea inclined her head once more in just the manner she had been taught from childhood.

"Thank you, good sir." She sat down. "The compliment is appreciated even though it's wasted on a useless—well, almost useless—accomplishment. It does, on occasion, serve its purpose with the members of the Society of Antiquaries. Now, back to Arbella and Edward Archer."

"Even Queen Elizabeth would, on occasion, listen to Lord Cecil when he bade her set aside duty for a while and indulge in relaxation. As I am bidding you now."

"And I," she said, giving him a saucy look, "hope that my regal air will serve its purpose with a gentleman who should know better than try to distract the clearheaded historian he commissioned at a very steep fee. Do you know how much we have yet to discuss?"

A smile lurked in his eyes. "But since I pay the fee, I may determine the rules and conditions of your employment. And I now order you to forget about the chronicles and come with me in search of refreshments."

"Presently. Stanmore, Arbella died September 25, 1615. And immediately, rumors started about a child born during her imprisonment at Barnet."

"Yes. I believe it was the rumors that gave Edward the notion to use his sister's son and claim he was Arbella's."

"Indeed. Edward's timing and the fact that he was at Barnet at the crucial time are points in your favor." Thea made a notation, then looked at Stanmore again. "However, we are not dealing with conjectures just at present. We are considering historical facts."

"I beg your pardon. I forgot."

Stanmore drew up a chair. "Then, speaking of rumors—which are fact—we must add that there was talk also of Arbella being poisoned by orders of King James."

"Yes, the same was said when James's son, Henry, died."

"The physicians attending the prince were certain Henry died of a fever contracted while swimming in the Thames. And the members of the College of Physicians who examined Arbella's body testified she had starved herself, which was confirmed by Arbella's attendants."

"Starvation, a broken heart, and a broken spirit. How sad," Thea said softly but immediately shook off her somber mood. "Stanmore, you are indeed very well informed."

"I had three years to study every detail pertaining to Arbella's life and time. I know that, justified or not, King James never lost the fear that Arbella—or her issue—would be used to depose him. William Seymour also ranked in the succession through his grandmother, Katherine Grey. Any child born to Arbella and Seymour would have been a threat to James, which is why he immediately separated the pair when the marriage was discovered."

"In that, I cannot blame him. He had been the instrument to force his mother's abdication when he was but an infant. Yes, I think we can say with certainty that James feared the existence of a child born to Arbella and Seymour. As late as 1618, Arbella's aunt was called up before the Star Chamber and examined about a child, but Lady Shrewsbury never obliged the king with an outright denial."

"Edward certainly took a risk when he made his claim." A quick smile transformed Stanmore's lean face. "But that takes us back to conjecture."

Thea murmured absently in agreement while she skimmed her notes. "Arbella's son, William Seymour Archer, was given the title of Earl Barnet in 1660 by James's grandson, Charles II. Stanmore, do you have the royal decrees on the creation of Edward's and William Seymour Archer's peerages?"

He showed her the vellum scrolls wrapped in baize and stored in a strongbox.

"*Tomorrow* you may peruse them at your leisure. But you'll find no cause or reason given for creating Edward and William peers."

"Neither do the state papers give cause or reason. I searched them."

"The more you probe into my family's history, the more questions you'll raise. Believe me, there are no facts, no documents to support the claim that my family is descended from Arbella Stuart. Come, Miss Stone. Are you ready to leave?"

She made no move to rise. "There is one indisputable fact. Neither the first nor the second Earl Barnet made a public claim of royal descent. It was Henry Stuart Archer, Third Earl Barnet, who came forward when the Act of 1701 vested the succession in the nearest Protestant descendants of the Stuarts."

"And then no one believed that his claim had merit. My rash forebear was laughed out of Parliament."

"And fatally shot on his way home."

"By a highwayman. *You* don't have to be told how commonplace highway robbery was in those days."

"No," said Thea. "But his son was convinced that the highwayman was but a tool of those who feared the Archer claim did have merit and wanted Henry Stuart Archer dead and the documentation he carried destroyed."

"If there ever was documentation, it is not identified or listed in any of the estate books. Not even a cryptic notation like the entry in your family Bible. There is only that one chronicle entry in 1701 bemoaning the loss of some unspecified papers." Stanmore shrugged. "And my family have stubbornly fought to prove their claim of royal descent ever since."

"Until now."

"Yes, until now. My father is fanatic about bloodline and tradition, as was his father before him. I want the nonsense stopped."

Stanmore's jaw hardened. When he spoke again, his voice was as harsh as Thea had heard it when they first met and he called family history and tradition the bane of his life.

"I want Charlie to attend Harrow and Cambridge if that is his wish. I want to see him free of duties and responsibilities that may not be to any purpose at all. I want both my children to marry as they please and *when* they please. It is unconscionable to thrust a youth of twenty or younger into marriage to ensure the succession."

From the genealogy Thea knew that all Archer males married young. Stanmore had been nineteen. At twenty-two, he was a father.

A corner of his mouth turned down deprecatingly. "But I cannot simply tell my father be damned and go to hell."

She was beginning to understand him well enough to know that, indeed, he could not. It was not in his character to do so. But neither was it in his character to give in. He would fight in his own quiet but determined way.

In the process, he might destroy her dream.

Ten

As Thea had once half jokingly said to Felicity, Stanmore needed her to rewrite his family history. If she begged off at this point, he would be left to sort through the tangle unassisted since, for the moment at least, she had no rival among her colleagues in knowledge of or interest in the history of the Lady Arbella Stuart. Even general interest in the tragic lady—or any Stuart—had waned when the third George acceded to the throne, and the House of Hanover at last gained widespread acceptance.

But Thea would not beg off. She had argued with Stanmore to give her the commission. She had committed herself to evaluate the chronicles and had promised to find the truth—if truth was there.

"Miss Stone, if I made you uncomfortable with my outburst, I apologize."

"Outburst? For goodness sake, Stanmore! Don't be so severe on yourself. I took no offense. 'Twould be a sad state of affairs if we weren't permitted to speak with some passion on matters dear to our hearts."

He relaxed. "Then, with your leave, I shall now express with passion a matter previously introduced but ignored by you. Miss Stone, I command you to put aside your pens and notes and leave with me this instant."

"I will in just a moment. Stanmore, I take it you wish to prove that Edward Archer used his sister's illegitimate child to extort money and privileges from the crown?"

"A question nicely calculated to take my mind off leaving. You're a master at getting your way, are you not?"

She did not deny it but said, "It would be in *your* best interest if you gave up dictating when I must or must not work."

"Would it?" His tone was wry. "Well, then, Miss Stone, if it can indeed be proven, it will settle matters very nicely for me. But you would be grievously disappointed, would you not?"

"Yes. I still hope to prove that Arbella's love for William Seymour was blessed with a child."

"How strangely you phrase it. Arbella's love for William. Do you not believe that he loved her, too?"

"I think he liked her well enough, that he was flattered to have been chosen by her. But love her? No, I don't think he loved her as she loved him."

"He named a daughter after her in his second marriage."

"That must have been to appease his conscience! *His* escape was successful, while Arbella was caught. And when he returned home after her death, he was forgiven. All his dignities were restored!"

"Infamous."

"Mock if you must, but I had thought better of you. Stanmore, you will agree that if he had loved her, he would have returned instantly and removed her from the Tower. He knew it could be done! *He* had escaped from there!"

Stanmore smiled. "Yes, it would be sad indeed if we were never to speak with passion. Miss Stone, you are a romantic."

"And that amuses you?"

"It pleases me."

There was a tender note in his voice. Or had she imagined it?

To cover confusion, she said, "How is it that so often we end up speaking about me when we should keep our focus on your concerns? I think I should next look at those household accounts you spoke of. Will you please fetch me the volume covering the year 1611?"

His smile deepened, but he made no comment. He lit a candle, then turned to do her bidding. Lifting a volume from the chest, he glanced at the date before taking it to her.

He snuffed the candle. "Lizzy's accounts are diaries as much as farm records. They make interesting reading, though her penmanship leaves much to be desired."

Thea opened the book randomly. Awkwardly formed letters made her squint at the text that seemed to be a recipe for curing the ague and childbed fever, and which Lizzy had seen fit to insert between expenditures for the shoeing of two horses and the thatching of a barn roof.

She looked up at Stanmore. "Interesting, indeed. Unfortunately, you're also correct about the penmanship."

"It is especially difficult reading by lamp light." Reaching over her shoulder, he firmly closed the ledger.

She raised a brow. "Now, who's getting his way?"

"Your eyes look tired. I should have made you stop reading as soon as I got here."

"When I was near the end of the chronicles? You might have had your nose snapped off, but you would not have succeeded in tearing me away."

"Perhaps not. But I shall succeed now, if I have to carry you from the room."

"And get stuck in the stairwell? I thank you! No doubt you mean well, but I think it will be best for both of us if I leave voluntarily."

"You're wrong. One of us would like it better if carrying you were necessary."

He had a knack that afternoon for taking her off stride, but, perceiving the gleam in his eye, she rallied instantly.

"Oh, I see what you are about! Having once insisted that I am of tender age and unable to fend for myself in a widower's household, you now wish to prove it. You expect me to blush and lower my gaze. But I am not a green girl to be put out of countenance with an outrageous suggestion."

The gleam intensified. He reached out and touched her cheek. "But you *are* blushing."

"Nonsense." She felt the heat rise in her face, and started to laugh. "I was not! I'm sure of it. Not until you called my bluff. I am beginning to think that you're an incorrigible flirt."

"If that is what you want to believe, I shall not disabuse you. Not for a while."

His tone was as light as it had been previously, but Thea deemed it wise to put a stop to the banter. She rose and took a few steps toward the lectern, where the lamp light would not be full on her still warm face.

She said, "It's odd about the chronicles—the opening summary and the entries immediately following it. Style and penmanship are those of a well educated man. This in itself might not have given me pause if the style had not also deviated so vastly from that employed by later chroniclers."

Turning, she found that he had followed her. "Did you not think it peculiar that the early entries were written from a point of view indicating a totally disinterested observer? Then, when William took over the duties of chronicler, he adopted the personal style of a diarist."

"On the twenty-fifth of March, 1622, his sixteenth birthday. That, too, became an Archer tradition, the heir being the record keeper until his son in turn takes over at sixteen."

Thea had an excellent memory for names and dates, and a quick review confirmed Stanmore's words.

"I should have seen that it was so! With one exception. Your grandfather, the sixth earl, was only seven years old when his father died, and the chronicles were maintained by his mother. But never mind that. What I should like to know is who wrote the summary of the first six years and made the entries until William took over? I feel it cannot have been Edward. He was a soldier, son of a yeoman farmer. Although both he and Lizzy would have had some education—and Lizzy's efforts bear me out—it would hardly have been equal to the elegant phraseology applied in the summary."

"Again I must refer you to the accounts. The Archer Hall ledgers, this time. When the house was completed, Edward engaged the services of a chaplain and a bailiff. The bailiff kept the ledgers; we have his signature. The chaplain, we must surmise, began the Archer chronicles. The handwriting is the same as that in some volumes of sermons."

"The chapel! I meant to ask you about it. But I have so many questions, I hardly know where to start."

"I am at your service, Miss Stone. But for the rest of the day—and there isn't much left—I want you to forget about Archer history. When I last saw Felicity and the children—and the tutor, whom you have yet to meet—they were planning a picnic and an archery contest in the gallery since the grounds are still too wet. Come, we'll join them."

If he meant to distract her, he had succeeded. Her eyes sparkled. "An archery contest! I have not held a bow this age!"

"You're fond of archery?"

"Exceedingly. It is the one sport that allows me to defeat all eight of my foster siblings, and they're excellent marksmen. They taught me."

"Then let us be off. I have waited long for a partner to compete with me against my children."

He held out a hand. The light was dim where they stood, but she had seen his hand often enough to know that it was shapely, with long fingers and square, carefully buffed nails.

Thea remembered all too well how his touch had affected her on previous occasions, but she could no more reject the gesture of invitation than she could forget who she was. Without further ado, she clasped the offered hand.

Not until the following morning when Silas Wilkins had dusted and placed on her desk several more of the household accounts, was Thea struck by the enormity of the task before her.

When she closed the last volume of the chronicles on the

previous day, Stanmore had been there. In the effort of battling a growing tendency to respond to his lighter side, in the sheer pleasure of the subsequent archery contest, she had not truly allowed herself to dwell on the questions that had accumulated in her mind while she read.

Perhaps her concern would have surfaced during another talk with Stanmore later that night. But there had been no opportunity. Shortly before dinner, Mr. Justin Markham, the fourth of Lord Ravensbrook's five sons, brought young Robert, whose departure to Harrow had been postponed again and again by his anxious Mama. Now that the rains had stopped, Mrs. Justin Markham had agreed that he was to leave the following Monday, and Robert wanted Charlie to come to Ravensbrook until Sunday.

Charlie thought it a capital scheme. Not only would he have a visit with his friend, but he would also get to ride through the mire, a treat he had been denied for all of the three rainy weeks.

Robert and his father stayed for dinner, then took Charlie off with them. Stanmore excused himself and the tutor, Benjamin Locke, a shy young man, who looked as if a gust of wind could knock him over. They had received orders to wait on Lord Barnet and were not seen again that night.

Now, seated at her desk, and with the morning sun warming her back, Thea suddenly felt daunted, inadequate to dealing with the challenge of keeping her promise that she would remain unbiased when, at the same time and despite an insidious whisper of doubt, she wanted to prove the birth of Arbella's child.

But a thread of doubt was there, and for the first time since she had immersed herself in Arbella Stuart's history, Thea had to remind herself that—no matter how questionable the chronicles, no matter what she would find in the accounts—she *knew* that Arbella had borne a child and given it into the care of Edward Archer.

Her knowledge was not based on anything concrete or of a

nature that she would care to share with the august members of the Society of Antiquaries. At best, they would laugh at her; at worst, they would never again allow her to contribute to their publications if she so much as hinted at her source.

Her certainty stemmed from dreams.

The dreams had started soon after Thea's first visit to Hardwick Hall, where Arbella spent so many years, first in the old house, then in the magnificent new Hall built by her grandmother, Bess of Hardwick. The Reverend Felix Simmons, to whom Thea divulged her dreams, dismissed them at first as the outgrowth of an overactive imagination. But eventually he had to admit that this could not be so.

Thea was only ten and by no means an expert on Arbella Stuart's history. The Reverend Simmons had told her about Arbella's early years, which, he believed, would most interest the young Thea. Yet her dreams concerned later episodes of Arbella's life at King James's court, before Reverend Simmons had ever brought them to Thea's attention or she read about them in the various histories they had begun to study and compare.

'Twas extraordinary, said the Reverend Simmons. Baffling. How was it possible that Thea dreamed about events when no one had told her that they happened? Perhaps, he suggested, Dorothea Wortley kept a journal and Thea was privy to the information it contained. But Thea was certain that she had been told and made to recite only that Dorothea was with her mother and Lady Arbella from May of 1610 until June of 1611, and thereafter paid occasional visits to Arbella in the Tower.

If the dreams perturbed the Reverend Simmons, he never gave an indication of it to Thea. When, in her thirteenth year, Thea wondered whether she was a witch or sorceress, he nipped apprehension in the bud by introducing her to cultures and religions that cherished those endowed with her gifts. He explained that there were many things man's mind could not fathom and were therefore called supernatural, but that did not mean they were evil or undesirable. It all depended on how the gifted person chose to use his talents.

And so, to her, the dreams became a commonplace occurrence to be accepted—like the brief spells of extraordinary perceptiveness. But even though she accepted, she did not share the peculiarities in her personality with anyone save for the Reverend Simmons and, of course, Miss Vespera Simmons, her governess, only link to the past. Until Stanmore entered her life. Thea had been in his company less than an hour before she had mentioned one of her gifts. But not the dreams.

And since that strange experience at the foot of the gallery stairs, she had repeatedly dreamed about Arbella bidding farewell to her child, and about Prince Henry in Edward Archer's cottage. Somehow, she must find evidence that those dreams were but mirrors of what had actually happened in the past.

She thought of the Scottish Lady Glendale, whom Stanmore had mentioned during their first meeting. He said she could see the past, and Thea wished she could meet the lady.

"Beg pardon, ma'am." Bearing a tray, Silas Wilkins had quietly returned to the muniment room. "His lordship said you must have some tea at least, since you did not go down to breakfast."

"Thank you, Silas. Do you know if Lord Stanmore will be joining me this morning?"

"Not for a while, that's for sure." Silas poured. For a man his size he was amazingly deft in his movements. "My lord Barnet sent for him."

"Again!"

The exclamation had slipped out before Thea could consider the impropriety of it. Silas was grinning. Of course, he would. He did not know the meaning of self-consciousness.

"The lad may come up afterwards, though. The study and the muniment room are the places he'd often be after a session with my lord Barnet. Especially the muniment room, because it's quiet . . . isolated. Of course, he could feel different now that you're here."

"I hope not." She had become accustomed to Silas's bluntness and his occasional references to Stanmore as "the lad." "I'd hate to think that I deprived Lord Stanmore of a refuge."

"Likely he won't mind at all. Seems he has taken a fancy to you, ma'am. Now, if there's nothing else I can do for you, I'll be off to the stables." Again his wide grin flashed. "After three weeks trotting in a circle in the barn, two of his lordship's mounts need my weight to remind them a rider is for carrying, not for tossing."

"Be careful," she said absently, her mind still focused on Silas's assumption that Stanmore had taken a fancy to her. Felicity had suggested the same three weeks earlier.

Thea stared off into space, scarcely aware of the large man's departure until she heard the gate to the stairwell click shut. She would like to believe that Felicity and Silas were wrong, and for a while she had been quite successful at duping herself. But it would not do. Facts must at last be faced.

She might be inexperienced in dalliance or courtship, but she was not so naive that she had not noticed that the warmth Stanmore showed her was quite different from the warmth he showed Felicity. For a while she had been able to pretend it was playfulness. But deep inside, she must have known—*had* known—that playfulness or flirtation was as alien to Stanmore's nature as telling his father be damned.

In truth, if there was playfulness, it had all been on her part. Had she not disliked his reserve and tried to draw him out? And when he responded with warmth and threatened to overset her composure, her concern had been only that he should not notice when it would have been wise to respond with coldness.

What a bumblebroth! She had no one to blame but herself, since a gesture from her at the very start would have sufficed to keep him at a distance. Perhaps there was still time to hint him away. His attentions had not yet become marked—

But of course they had, if even Silas noticed.

A bumblebroth, indeed! If only she had behaved differently from the onset . . . if only she weren't so reluctant now to change the situation.

For a while longer, Thea sat motionless, sunk in gloomy thoughts. But, finally, having made up her mind to be on guard and give Stanmore no encouragement whatsoever, she reached for the cup of tea Silas had poured. The tea was cold, but she drank it anyway and poured another cup, tepid, but a welcome boost to flagging spirits.

Thea examined the stack of old household accounts on her desk. Three volumes of Lizzy Archer's accounts covering the years 1609 to 1618; and the four oldest of the Archer Hall ledgers, which started in December of 1615 and were considerably larger and thicker than Lizzy's books.

She picked one of Lizzy's slim volumes, bound in plain brown leather that had not aged well at all. The paper was yellowed and brittle, the writing faded, and Lizzy's penmanship had not improved since the previous afternoon. But besides laboriously entering expenditures and profits from harvests, market sales, and the like, Lizzy had also commented on the weather, on births and slaughtering of farm animals, on fairs, visitors, and other events of daily life.

Thea searched for Lizzy Archer's entries in March of 1611 . . . the month Lizzy's brother was at Barnet with the Bishop of Durham, who, on orders of King James, was taking the Lady Arbella north, where she would live confined in the bishop's care and custody while her husband, William Seymour, remained imprisoned in the Tower.

The bishop's retinue with Arbella, her waiting women, gentleman usher, steward, private physician—all devoted to her—had arrived at Barnet on the twenty-first of March and could proceed no farther since Arbella was too weak and ill. She had been unwell since she learned she was to be removed from Lambeth, where she had been able to send letters to her beloved husband in the Tower and enjoy stolen visits from him. But King James believed her illness feigned, and when he received the bishop's message from Barnet that Arbella could not go on, he sent his own physician to report on the case.

Dr. Hammond arrived at Barnet on the twenty-sixth of

March and confirmed Arbella's weakened condition. If she indeed gave birth to a child, unbeknown to King James, then the birth must have taken place before the royal physician examined her—although it was not unlikely that the examination consisted of nothing more than the feeling of Arbella's pulse. Still, one must assume a physician could tell whether a woman was with child.

Edward Archer had claimed that Lady Arbella spoke with him on the twenty-second of March, after she learned that he had a sister living nearby—Lizzy Archer, who had a four-month-old son. On the twenty-fifth, Edward had received from the Lady Arbella's arms a newborn child.

And if Lizzy, suckling her own child, was wet nurse to Arbella's son—as mentioned at the beginning of the chronicles—then, surely, some small entry in the farmstead accounts would support the fact.

Thea thought of Stanmore . . . he must have looked for a reference to a second infant in Lizzy's accounts. But he had said nothing when he handed her the volume. In fact, he did not touch on any specifics of his family's history until she raised a question.

She felt sure it was delicacy of principle that stopped him from voicing his views on anything regarding his family history that she might not yet be aware of. He did not want to appear to be pushing his interpretation before she had formed her own opinion.

It was not difficult to see Stanmore as a descendant not only of the Lady Arbella Stuart but also of William Seymour, later Earl of Hertford and Duke of Somerset, whom Arbella had loved because he was so different from the courtiers of her time. William was serious, a scholar like Arbella herself, and not often seen at King James's court or at Anne of Denmark's frivolous pursuits at Somerset House and Greenwich Palace.

Although Thea could not forgive Seymour for failing Arbella in the escape they had so carefully planned—he from the Tower, and she from Barnet, where she had been granted a month's respite to regain her strength—Thea realized that Seymour's weakness must be attributed to youth. He was only twenty-three when he married Arbella and, from all accounts, quite unsuited to the plots and intrigues that had surrounded Lady Arbella Stuart for most of her thirty-five years.

All in all, William Seymour had been an honorable man and, after his return to England, rose to high position at Oxford and at court and distinguished himself in the Civil War in support of the royalist cause. He had been one of the four lords who petitioned the Commons to be allowed to suffer death in the place of King Charles I.

Stanmore, too, was honorable, not given to frivolous pursuits. His serious, reserved manner hid a will of iron. Thea had caught glimpses of it and was certain that, if he found himself in Seymour's situation, he *would* succeed in freeing his wife from the Tower, or Newgate, or wherever she might be held captive.

And Thea was certain that, no matter what truth—if any—about his antecedents would come to light, Stanmore would set his children free from the restricting bonds of Archer tradition.

Resolutely, Thea started to read Lizzy Archer's entries in March of 1611. The sooner it could be proven that, despite their shortcomings, the Archer chronicles did not lie, the better for Stanmore. He would need time to prepare his father that, royal blood or not, Charlie must go to Harrow in September.

Eleven

Stanmore strode into the sitting room off Lord Barnet's bedchamber but came to an abrupt halt at some distance from his father, ensconced in an armchair by the fireplace, a decanter and glass at his elbow. The gouty leg was swaddled in shawls and rested on a cushioned stool. Despite the heat from a roaring fire Barnet was wrapped in layers of tartan rugs.

"Pardon my bluntness, sir, but you don't look well at all. I wish you'd let me send for Dr. Sellers."

"Rubbish! There's nothing wrong with me but a touch of the gout. And I told you what you can do to give me a boost. Get rid of that female who's prying into our affairs! *You* invited her. *You* show her the door."

"Miss Stone will stay until she has finished what she set out to do."

"Aye! And what did she set out to do?" The earl's color deepened. "You know what happened when your grandfather allowed that fellow from the Society of Antiquaries to examine our records! The bounder called them a hum!"

"Then you'll be pleased to know that Miss Stone would like nothing better than to prove that Lady Arbella did, indeed, give her son into the care of Edward Archer."

"Bah! You were taken in! No doubt she knows precisely how to blandish and cajole."

Miss Stone and cajolery were such a paradox that Stanmore could not help but smile.

"What did I say? Why are you grinning?"

"You do Miss Stone an injustice, sir. I almost did not ask her to Archer Hall because of her conviction that our claim is true."

"Now you're talking rubbish! You make no sense at all."

Stanmore had hesitated to provoke an outburst of fury and recriminations while the outcome of Miss Stone's examination of the chronicles was still in doubt. Nothing had been resolved, but further delay would not do.

"Sir, it is I who wants to prove our claim false."

Barnet stared. He picked up the brandy glass and downed the contents.

"The devil you say! Are you mad?"

"If not believing in the sacrosanctity of lineage and tradition constitutes madness, yes, then I am mad."

"Confound it!"

Barnet smacked a fist against the arm of his chair. For several minutes nothing could be heard in the room but a stream of invectives, accusations of treachery and unfilial disrespect, and occasional reminders of duty and responsibility to future generations of Archers.

Stanmore did not try to interrupt or to justify himself but stood, to all appearances at ease, with one hand in a pocket of his coat as he listened with great patience even while the familiar throbbing started behind his temples and forehead.

At last Barnet ran out of words and breath and sank back in his chair. He was panting and his color was high, but the heat of fury had died in his eyes now that he had vented his spleen.

Stanmore stepped closer and, bracing himself against the heat from the fireplace, adjusted a rug that threatened to slide to the hearth of black marble.

"Leave it be!" Barnet said querulously. "And don't stand there, blocking me from the warmth."

"I'll move gladly. I don't see how you can bear it. Hell can be no hotter than this blaze." Stanmore raised a quizzing brow.

"Preparing, sir? For the day the gates of hell will open to you?"

A bark of dry laughter was cut off abruptly. Barnet stared at his son. "A joke? From you? What the deuce is going on?"

"I am unbending, sir."

"Don't speak in riddles. What do you mean, you're unbending? Is this another of your mad starts?"

"Perhaps. Father, will you receive Miss Stone?"

"Why the devil should I do that?" Barnet glowered, but his voice had not risen above the moderate roar he always employed when demanding an explanation.

"She has been in the house three weeks. You have received Lady Felicity but not her friend, Miss Stone."

"Always thought it a demmed shame that Lady Felicity was already married when you put off the black gloves. Bar sinister or not, she's a Ruthven with a pedigree as long as ours."

"Longer. And Miss Stone is connected to the Ruthvens through Lady Arbella's waiting woman Mary Wortley, who was second cousin to the third Earl of Gowrie."

"Miss Stone! Why the devil are you trying to impress me with Miss Stone's antecedents?"

Wondering whether full disclosure would be too much for his father's constitution and bring on an apoplexy, Stanmore turned a little to face the full-length portrait of a woman on the wall space next to the door leading into his father's bed chamber. It was an awkward spot for the exquisite painting. But it was where Barnet, from his chair, could see the portrait of his first wife, Stanmore's mother.

Stanmore had been seven years old when his mother, his sister, and three brothers succumbed to the smallpox. He remembered his mother's gaiety, her tenderness—and he remembered his father, no less temperamental than he was now, but easily soothed by his wife.

A young boy's impressions may be faulty, but Stanmore was convinced that if his father ever loved anyone, he had loved his first wife. It was that conviction that had always helped him bear with Barnet's irascibility even if it could not prevent the physical discomfort occasioned by arguments and confrontations.

Gruffly, Barnet said, "Your mother was a beautiful woman. Lively. Kind. Loyal. A devoted, loving wife and mother."

"Everything that Charlotte was not."

"Your wife had beauty."

Stanmore looked at his father, but the older man's gaze was fixed on the portrait.

"Yes, Charlotte had physical charms. But they did not make her a beautiful person."

"And, I suppose, because I picked the gal, you blame me for your disastrous marriage?"

"Blame? Yes, I suppose I did for a while. But during that last year with Charlotte and since her death, I have had more than enough time to think on the situation. You, sir, were as much a victim of Archer tradition as I was."

"*Victim!* What rubbish—what balderdash are you spouting now?" Barnet was spluttering. "It was *your* fault Charlotte acted as she did. I told you not to give a filly like her too much rein! I warned you she'd kick over the traces!"

Stanmore made no reply. There was nothing he could say to make his father admit, or even understand, that there had never been any hope of a successful marriage for him and Charlotte. And there was no point in dragging up Barnet's second marriage, which had hardly been more pleasant than Stanmore's first.

Barnet said, "Now that you're older and wiser, you'll know how to handle a woman. And Mansford's gals are of a different stamp. Very strictly reared, I understand."

"As I've told you before, sir, I have no interest in Lord Mansford's daughters or in any young woman you may plan to throw my way. When I marry again, *I* will choose the lady."

"*When* you marry again? Before you hared off to London you wouldn't even consider the possibility of a marriage. Now you say *when* you marry?" Barnet scowled at his son. "Stap me! There's something deucedly odd going on with you."

"Odd, sir? Did you not impress upon me it was my duty to take a wife?"

"I didn't say *you* should do the choosing. Demme, Stuart! You have no more notion of what you need in a wife than you have of what you owe the family. And don't think we've said the last about that dumbfool notion to disprove the family claims. We have not! But I'm not up to any more argumentation."

"I can see you're not." Stanmore hesitated. Despite the earlier outburst, he thought his father was subdued, which was as unusual as it was worrisome. He wanted to suggest again that Dr. Sellers be sent for but knew it would be to no avail.

"Go! Leave me be! I want to rest."

"Very well. But you sent for me. Higgins said it was important."

"Higgins is a fool."

"True, but not such a fool that he would summon me without your leave."

"If I wanted you earlier, I now find no pleasure in your company."

Barnet sounded so much like a petulant child that Stanmore took another, closer look at him.

"I think it's your own company you're tired of. Why don't you come down to luncheon today? You have your cane, and I'll gladly lend you a shoulder to lean on. And if it still proves too much for your leg, we can carry you down in a chair."

"The deuce you will! Do you want me to play the fool or have your visitors think I'm at my last prayers?"

"Hardly. You're but one-and-sixty. Until this latest attack of gout you were confined to a chair no more than two or three days at a time and have kept flesh and muscle in good condition." Stanmore looked at the brandy decanter. "And you know how to put an end to your misery now."

"Damn your impudence! Will you preach at me?" Barnet

attempted to swing his gouty leg off the footstool—but subsided with a groan.

Once more Stanmore braved the heat from the fireplace to save a rug from slipping onto the hearth. He received no thanks, but when he turned to leave, Barnet stopped him.

"Come back later. Have luncheon with me. I want to discuss a horse for young Charles. He's getting too big for a pony."

"I'm taking care of it. I met Eversleigh at Tattersall's when I was in town. He has a four-year-old, trained by himself. An anxious parent—or even a grandfather—won't need to worry about a child riding him, but he's spirited enough to please a young boy."

Barnet did not, in general, take kindly to being forestalled, but his interest was piqued, as always when talk turned to horseflesh.

"From Eversleigh's Irish stud?"

"Yes. He's planning to take a dozen hunters up to Tattersall's the middle of the month and will stop here to let Charlie try out the four-year-old."

"I should be up and about by then."

"If you're not, I *will* have you carried out in a chair."

Barnet's face relaxed, but he would not permit himself to smile.

"We don't have to discuss the horse, then. In that case, I suppose, you'll be thinking there's no need for you to take luncheon with me?"

"There's every need, sir. I've not yet said the last about Miss Stone."

When Stanmore stepped out of his father's sitting room and closed the door, he saw a dainty streak of pink rounding the newel post at the top of the stairway, then disappear downward.

He did not call out lest his father hear but set off in pursuit, reaching the ground floor in time to see the door to the breakfast parlor close. He increased his speed and, a few moments later, entered the room.

"Bella!"

The skirt of her pink wool gown hitched to her knees, his daughter was about to climb out one of the windows in the south bay. Hearing her name, she obligingly closed the window again and faced her father.

Wide blue eyes looked serenely up at him. "Good morning, Papa. Will I have a horse, too?"

"Not until you're older. And before you ask how much older, let me tell you that at the moment I am interested only in the topic of eavesdropping. Bella, have you forgotten everything I said about listening at doors the last time you were caught?"

"Not everything, Papa. And if I promise to pay more attention this time, may I have a kitten when Charlie gets his horse?"

It was tempting to use the kitten as a bribe to scotch her distressing habit. But bribery smacked of dishonor, and Stanmore could not bring himself to apply it to his daughter. Yet something must be done.

He had sent notices advertising the governess position to the London papers, but had so far received only one reply. It could not hurt to wait another week, but then he must set up appointments and go to London to interview applicants, whether he'd find only one or a dozen interested in the post. Felicity was being very kind, devoting her time to his children, but she was looking a bit drawn lately. Markham would not thank him if his wife returned worn to the bone.

"May I go now, Papa?"

"Bella, why are you not with Lady Felicity? She was planning special games to play with you after your lessons."

"I *am* with Lady Felicity. And with Mr. Locke, too. Since he doesn't have Charlie, he gave me lessons. Now we're playing hide and go seek, and it's Lady Felicity's turn to seek."

"I see."

The nursery and schoolroom were located on the second

floor of the west wing, at the opposite end from Stanmore's original chamber, and he was certain neither Felicity nor the tutor expected the game to extend to the east wing, and especially not to the floor occupied by Barnet. Indeed, Stanmore feared the talk with his daughter must be an extensive one.

He drew out a dining chair and lifted Bella on his knee.

By the time Stanmore considered his paternal duty done—whether Bella paid attention or not was a different question—the bailiff had already been waiting half an hour for him. Regretfully, Stanmore postponed a visit to the muniment room.

Mr. Purvis kept him in the estate office close on two hours, and scarcely had the bailiff left when, hard on his knock, Silas Wilkins entered.

"Princess lost a shoe. I'll take her to the smithy, shall I?"

Closing the ledger Purvis had left for his inspection, Stanmore gave a nod of assent. Silas and the blacksmith's daughter were planning to marry in June, and it was not unusual that Silas played stable lad if the duties involved would take him to the smithy. What was unusual, however, was his seeking out Stanmore to report his leaving.

"Just make sure Miss Stone has everything she needs."

"Ah, lad! That's why I'm telling you that I'll be off. I thought maybe you'd like to check on Miss Stone yourself."

Stanmore gave him a wry look. "Am I that obvious?"

"You are to me." Silas grinned. "But then, I've known you from the cradle."

"Some day I'll cure you of saying that," said Stanmore, but he was smiling, too. Silas, a month older than he, had indeed known him from the cradle since, thirty-two years ago, Silas's mother was wet nurse at Archer Hall and the two cradles stood side by side.

"I shan't be able to join Miss Stone until the afternoon. I'm promised to my father for luncheon." Checking his pocket watch, Stanmore rose. "And if I don't go to the apiary now and look at the new hives, I'll be in the suds not only with the beekeeper but also with Purvis, who designed the wretched hives."

"Much you care about being in the suds! Why don't you admit you don't want to hurt their feelings. And hurt they'd be if they knew you detest bees. But never mind, lad! I left Miss Stone with a Stack of those old books from the chest, and I doubt she'll be wanting for anything."

Silas half turned to leave. "Except, maybe, your company. She was asking after you when I took her tea up. Seems to me she was wishful to see you."

"Then I can only hope Miss Stone does not change her mind in the meantime."

"She doesn't seem to be the giddy type, changing her mind every time she turns around."

Stanmore stepped around the desk. "Since you're going to the smithy, why don't you ride into Barnet afterwards and find Dr. Sellers. Ask him to stop by. And if he can be persuaded not to let on that I sent for him, my father may even submit to an examination."

"I'll do that." Silas held the door for Stanmore. "And you don't be too proud this time to wear one of the beekeeper's veils."

"Never fear. I have no desire to get stung on my neck and nose again."

After luncheon, Thea had not long returned to her desk in the muniment room when Stanmore joined her. She thought he looked a little pale and tense when he came to stand beside her chair. It was no secret that he had taken lunch with his father, and she wondered if Lord Barnet was still kicking up a rumpus.

"You should be out on the terrace with Felicity and Bella," Stanmore said. "You'll give yourself a headache if you do nothing but read all day."

"La! How do you expect me to learn about the past, except by reading? And it never gives me a headache."

"But your eyes get tired. I saw that yesterday."

"It was much later in the day then. Don't worry, Stanmore. My eyes are fine."

The tight look about his mouth left. "Yes, they're very fine eyes. Beautiful eyes. I noticed them immediately when we first met. Right after your smile."

There was such warmth in his gaze that she could have no doubts about his sincerity. But, no matter how delightful it would be to have him continue in that vein, this was precisely the kind of attention she must discourage.

"Pray don't digress." Giving him her most severe and repressive look, she opened one of Lizzy Archer's account books. "I'm afraid I have bad news for you. Look at this. July of 1626."

"I am looking, Miss Stone." But his eyes were on her.

"Lizzy's son, John, was fifteen years old that summer. He was killed by lightning."

"I used to think your hair is brown. But now, in the sunlight, I see a gleam of russet here and there."

It seemed prudent to ignore him, but it was difficult to keep her attention on events almost two hundred years ago when she wanted to smile and encourage him to go on.

"Stanmore, read what Lizzy wrote on her son's death. Read about the lawn shirt and velvet coat she commissioned for John's burial. Read about her grief. Her pain."

"I did read it, Miss Stone, and it occurred to me that it could all have been part of the deception."

She should be glad he had finally turned his mind to serious matters, but all she could do was wonder what else he had noticed about her.

She said, "Lizzy's style is that of a simple but forthright and honest woman. I cannot see her as a deceiver. She lost her son and grieved, poor dear. Why should she write about his death if he was alive at Archer Hall as William Seymour

Archer, the baron's adopted son? Why would she mention John at all in her accounts if she gave him to her brother so he could claim the child was Arbella's? And Lizzy did mention John, when he needed shoes. Once, she ordered a new saddle for his cob. There were expenses for broadcloth, fustian, shirt linen, et cetera, indicating she sewed his clothing—except for the shirt and coat he wore to his grave."

"You argue the case well, Miss Stone."

"Thank you."

He leaned a little closer. "You have shadows beneath your eyes. I fear you don't get enough rest."

"Nonsense. I woke up once or twice from a dream. That is all."

He kept looking at her.

She glanced down at Lizzy's account book and determinedly switched the conversation back to the early seventeenth century.

"I take it we are agreed that Lizzy's son died. And, as we know from the chronicles, that Edward's adopted son, William, was alive at Archer Hall. I am sorry, Stanmore. For your sake, I had hoped we could prove that Lizzy's son was used to dupe King James."

"You hoped for my sake . . . yes, I believe you did."

"You sound as if I had offered a sacrifice."

"Did you not? Your wish and mine must always present a conflict."

"I don't deny it." Leaning back in her chair, she met his gaze squarely. "Neither could I deny that swindle was a distinct possibility. I admit that my feelings were sadly at odds while I searched for an answer."

"Perhaps now you can understand why, at first, I felt I could not ask you to undertake this commission."

"But no longer. You said you trust me! You must know that I would not, despite personal leanings, keep it from you if I discovered something that would prove your suspicions."

"I do know it." His voice was gentle. "But you will find

yourself torn, your peace quite cut up, the longer you study the chronicles and supporting records and accounts."

"My peace cut up! Stanmore, that is putting it too strong!"

Moving a book from the corner of her desk, he perched on the vacated spot.

"You've been at Archer Hall three weeks. I doubt you learned much about me during that time; you were so very deeply immersed in the past. But I had opportunity aplenty to study you. Unobserved."

"I'm not sure I appreciate being studied, especially when I'm unaware of it."

"That proves my point. When you're deeply into research, you notice nothing around you. Miss Stone, you're a woman with a calling, with a passion for what she is doing."

She regarded him warily. He was smiling and, perched on the desk, he was disturbingly close.

"I am very interested in history," she admitted cautiously.

"Interested in history in the general sense. Yes, I would agree to that. But you're *enthralled* by the history of Arbella Stuart. Why, Miss Stone?"

She wanted to deny it but could not.

Briskly, she said, "We digress again. Stanmore, this won't do."

"Why not? I wish to know you. Not T. E. Stone, the historian; but Thea Stone, the woman."

"And I told you that first and foremost I am a historian."

A gleam lit in his eye. "I certainly had proof of that."

"I think it will be best after all if I take a turn about the terrace."

She pushed back her chair, but before she could rise, Stanmore forestalled her by clasping her hands and drawing her to her feet.

"Miss Stone . . . Thea. I meant what I said. I wish to know you. I shan't press you to tell me anything you'd rather not disclose. But surely there must be more you can share about your life with the Simmons family than that they taught you history and archery?"

"Yes . . . yes of course. I learned to ride . . . and climb trees . . . and a great many other things." Thea wished he would let go of her hands, and the next instant, that he would not. "But my stay at the vicarage cannot possibly be of interest to you."

"You're wrong." He raised first one, then the other of her hands to his lips. "Thea—little goose. When a man is courting a woman, everything about her is of interest."

Twelve

Courting.

A rush of joy made Thea's heart leap. She could still feel the fleeting touch of his lips against her fingers, could hear the tender note in his voice when he called her Thea—little goose.

She had never expected to be called a little goose by a gentleman, and she must be quite mad not to take exception. But Stanmore had made it an endearment, and it warmed her heart.

He was watching her. "You're not indifferent! Thank heavens! I had not meant to speak so soon for fear of rushing you. But I could not help it."

Common sense returned with chilling suddenness.

"Stanmore, please!" She disengaged her hands. "You mustn't speak like that . . . of courting. You don't know me. Not truly."

"I am very much aware of it. Did I not say I want to know you?"

Her much-praised calm was slipping. "Must you quibble? You understood what I meant . . . that you don't know who I am."

"I felt there was some mystery about you."

"My name is not Thea Stone."

He did not bat an eye but once more possessed himself of her hands.

"That does not surprise me either. I always thought there was something odd about your name. Only I did hope that

Thea—Theadora Evalina—was your true baptismal name because it's the name that comes to mind when I think of you."

"It is." She tried to reclaim her hands but gave in without a struggle when he held fast. For a few moments she would allow herself to believe that courtship was possible.

"I am Theadora Evalina von Hochstein."

"That is not so different. It is still Stone—a *high* stone. You see, I've not forgotten my German, though it has been many years since I was in the schoolroom."

She looked at him suspiciously. "You're laughing at me!"

"I'm trying to put you at ease. My dear Thea, I have long suspected that you must be what I have heard delicately referred to as a love child?"

She gasped.

"It wasn't all that difficult to guess. Fostered in a vicarage—the vicar's sister, your governess—it all fits the pattern. Were you given your father's last name, or your mother's?"

"My father's." Her voice was choked. She tried to look outraged, but the laughter bubbling in her made it a vain attempt.

He frowned. "I've got it wrong?"

"All wrong. Lud, Stanmore! What an imagination you have. Will you say next that the governess is my mother?"

He was about to speak when Bella's voice, shrill and breathless, could be heard from below.

"Papa! Where are you? Papa! Papa!"

With a look of apology, Stanmore let go of Thea and strode toward the stairwell, where Bella, long hair flying about her face, was coming into view.

"Papa, be quick! It's Grandpapa! He fell!"

Opening the gate in the balustrade, Stanmore scooped up his daughter.

"Where, Bella?"

"In the great hall."

"Leave Bella with me," said Thea, hurrying toward them.

"Thank you."

He thrust the girl into Thea's arms and was gone in the blink of an eye.

Bella squirmed. "I want to go, too!"

Still listening to the fading footsteps, Thea replied absently. "We'll both go. But you must hold my hand and not leave my side. If your grandfather is hurt, we don't want to get in the way."

"Higgins says he broke his neck!"

Thea let it pass. The earl's valet was not noted for sound judgment, and Bella looked more excited than alarmed. Obviously, the child had no concept of the consequences of a broken neck and was merely parroting Higgins's alarums; but it was time to pay full attention to her. Later, when someone else had charge of Bella, Thea could indulge in daydreams of the girl's father.

"Where in the great hall was your grandfather when he fell?"

"The east wing side. He was coming down the gallery stairway. Higgins says Grandpapa wanted to practice since he meant to eat dinner downstairs."

"The stairs! I thought—"

Bella's wide-eyed gaze silenced her. Thea had believed Lord Barnet slipped on the marble tile of the great hall, which would have been bad enough for a gentleman laid up with the gout for several weeks. But a fall down the stairs . . . Higgins might not have exaggerated after all, in which case Bella's presence— or even Thea's—in the great hall would be anything but desirable.

"Let's go, Miss Stone!"

Thea now regretted her absentminded assent, but it took no more than a glance at Bella's face, the firm little chin, the set mouth, to convince her that it would not do to say they weren't going after all. Clearly, the situation demanded what Vespera Simmons would call a bit of gentle manipulation.

Deliberately slow, Thea led Bella from the muniment room. She slowed her steps even more when they reached the first floor and Bella tugged her in the direction of the gallery stairs, which would offer an immediate and unimpeded view of the opposite side of the great hall where Lord Barnet had fallen.

"You're dawdling, Miss Stone. Can't you walk any faster?"

"In truth, I don't know what we ought to do. If your grandfather is hurt, we'll be in the way, for I haven't the slightest notion how to deal with injuries. Do *you* know how to set a leg or bandage an arm?"

"No. But Silas does. He was just coming in when Grandpapa fell, and he sent me to fetch Papa because Higgins was wailing and wringing his hands."

The efficient Silas. Thea should have known he'd take matters into his capable hands.

The girl tugged again. "Hurry, Miss Stone!"

"Wait, Bella. Since neither one of us would be of any use to your grandfather, it could only be said that we had come to gawk."

This, finally, gave the child food for thought. She ceased pulling Thea's arm and at last, when they stepped from the hallway into the side gallery, came to a halt. The gallery was deep enough that they could not yet see the great hall below, but they did hear the murmur of voices.

"We'll wait here, if you like," Bella offered. "Otherwise, if Grandpapa saw you, he'd call you a gapeseed. You would not like that, would you?"

"I would not," Thea said gravely.

For a moment, they listened to the voices below.

"I cannot hear what they're saying." Bella tilted her head and listened again. "That is Dr. Sellers! I wonder how he knew that Grandpapa would need him?"

Thea had no answer to that but posed a question of her own. "Your father mentioned that you were on the terrace with Lady Felicity. How did you come to be inside when your grandfather fell?"

"I was giving Mr. Locke a tour of the house because Lord

and Lady Ravensbrook fetched Lady Felicity in the carriage. They went to look at—"

Thea was not destined to hear what Felicity and her husband's parents planned to look at. Silas Wilkins was coming up the grand staircase, and Bella ran to meet him.

"Did you mend Grandpapa, Silas? Where's Papa? How did Dr. Sellers know he would be needed?"

He caught her, swinging her high. "Your grandfather will be fine. He did not break any bones, but he'll be needing to spend a few days in bed. Your papa is with him. And Dr. Sellers is here because I let him know earlier today that your grandfather seemed poorly. And now that I've answered all your questions, Miss Butterfly, I'll take you to Nurse."

Ignoring the child's protest, he lifted her onto one broad shoulder.

"Miss Stone, if you'll go to the east wing, his lordship will meet you presently outside my lord Barnet's rooms."

"Thank you, Silas."

Thea watched the large man break into a trot, which had Bella squealing with glee in no time at all. Then Thea walked past the long line of Archer portraits toward the first floor of the east wing, where no one went without an invitation.

She had been raised to know her mind, yet she wavered in indecision. She wanted to see Stanmore, and she did not. She wanted to believe that courtship was possible, although she knew she had no right to encourage or receive his addresses.

There was no time to ponder the situation. Stanmore was waiting for her just inside the hallway leading off the side gallery.

"Thea, I apologize. I would have come to you, but I want to speak with the physician again before he leaves."

"How is your father?"

"Bruised and shaken and quite dazed. Dr. Sellers found neither broken bones nor a concussion, but he's considering cupping since my father's pulse is too rapid and his color too high."

"A barbaric treatment. I pity your father."

"Thea, I want to thank you for keeping Bella away. It cannot have been easy."

"I'm afraid I made use of subterfuge."

"At times that is the way to handle the little minx." He sounded preoccupied, but his eyes were keen as they searched her face.

She feared what he could see and what he would say. This was not the time or the place to speak of courtship or reasons why it must not be.

Hoping to divert him, she put a hand to her cheek. "Do I have an ink smudge?"

"No. I was thinking about our conversation—before Bella called me—and I was trying to gauge your feelings. At the time, I believed you were stifling laughter. But as soon as I left I was beset by doubt."

She was relieved. Her feelings on any subject other than courtship were easily explained.

"Are you, perchance, referring to your calling me a love child?"

"Dash it, Thea! Again you look as if you're about to burst out laughing. And all the while Silas and Dr. Sellers examined my father for broken bones, I could think of nothing but that I offended you, only to find your eyes dancing again!"

"I am shameless, I admit. And I daresay I should be offended, if not on my account, then on my father's. But what I remember of him and what Miss Simmons told me, leads me to believe that he would have considered it a famous joke and laughed loudest of all."

Once more he searched her face. "Good. You mean it. Now I won't have to spend precious time apologizing when we continue our conversation, which will have to wait, unfortunately, until my father—"

She interrupted him. "Yes, of course it must wait. In truth, I'm glad of the respite . . . though not of the cause. I need time to think."

"I did rush you." He gave her a quizzical look. "At my age, though, I cannot afford to dawdle."

"Your age! Unless your genealogy is wrong, you are but thirty-two."

"If you studied the genealogy, you must also be aware that the fifth earl died at age thirty-two. The third earl was forty-eight when he departed this world. My grandfather, at sixty-two, attained the ripest age of any Archer these past two hundred years."

There was nothing she could say in refutation. Archer men married young and, in most instances, were indeed buried young.

"But it is nonsense to believe that the pattern will continue," she protested.

"Of course it is nonsense. Though I will not hesitate to use the argument in blackmail. Thea, I believe I fell in love the moment I saw you in Felicity's drawing room."

It thrilled and at the same time troubled her deeply to hear him speak of love. She must not listen to such talk.

Or might she listen and deal with the consequences later?

She had never been so undecided. She was certain only that she must not start explaining now, when at any moment one of the doors would open and the physician would join Stanmore to share his prognosis. Her story was not a simple one and would brook no interruptions. Especially since, suddenly, she was inclined to side with Felicity against her foster father and the view on marriage he had instilled in her.

"Thea, did you hear me?" Stanmore traced a frown line on her forehead with a fingertip. "I said I fell in love the moment I saw you."

She forced a smile. "What exaggeration. For the longest time, while you and Felicity and Markham stayed near the door, you saw only my back."

"A beautiful back, slim and straight. Your hair—even confined in a twist at the nape of your neck it showed off its richness of texture and color. And your shoulders, a hand's width of creamy skin above claret-colored velvet."

"Stanmore! For heaven's sake, stop."

"No, you cannot make me stop. If you were indifferent—but you're not. I cannot be wrong about that—I saw it in your eyes. Yet you are reluctant to receive my addresses."

"I will explain. But there's no time now."

Stanmore cast a look over his shoulder. The doors in the hallway remained closed, but there was no telling when Higgins or Dr. Sellers would call him to his father's bedside.

He turned back to Thea. "Later, when my father is settled, you shall tell me what your reasons are, and one by one, I will diffuse them. I promise you, there is nothing in your past, your present, or your future that will make me change my mind about you."

She knew a moment of pure happiness before, once again, the chill of reality set in.

"You're wrong, Stanmore."

She cocked her head, listening, certain she had heard the sound of a door opening. But when she looked past Stanmore, all the doors in the hallway behind him were closed.

Without warning, a spell of light-headedness dimmed her vision, but the sensation passed in an instant. On the left-hand side, the third door was now open, and she saw a massive four-poster bed in that third chamber, a gray-haired, beetle-browed man all but buried beneath a mountain of quilts and tartan rugs. Charles Henry Archer, Sixth Earl Barnet, whose portrait showing him as a much younger man hung in the long gallery.

Barnet's color was high, a strange, mottled red. A bruise ornamented the side of a jutting chin. Dark eyes—which might have been Stanmore's eyes if they weren't so bloodshot—glared in impotent outrage at someone Thea did not know, a youngish, lanky man in boots and breeches, a baggy shooting jacket imperfectly disguising his bony frame.

The stranger paid no heed to Barnet's glower until he had

finished buckling a scarred black leather bag sitting at the foot of the bed. Then he gave the invalid's shoulder an encouraging squeeze and spoke a few soothing words. Picking up his bag, he nodded to Higgins, waiting to usher him out of the chamber.

Thea blinked as once more light-headedness washed over her. She was aware of an arm around her waist, of her head resting against a hard chest.

"Thea, what happened? If your eyes were not wide open, I'd think you fainted."

The anxiety in Stanmore's voice startled her. For heaven's sake! She'd only had a bit of a dizzy spell.

She disengaged herself. "I was light-headed, that's all. But your father! Stanmore, did you hear? The physician said he has the measles!"

"Dr. Sellers?" Stanmore looked perplexed. "Thea, he's still with my father. And he said nothing about measles earlier."

"Yes, he did. I heard and saw . . ."

She stared past Stanmore at the firmly closed third door on the left. Stanmore followed her gaze, and as they both watched, the door opened and out came a lanky man in boots, breeches, and baggy shooting jacket. He stopped just outside the door. Drawing a watch from the bulging pocket of his jacket, he spoke to Higgins, who had followed him.

Thea could scarcely make out what the physician said to the valet, and that was strange since she had heard him clearly when he spoke to Lord Barnet. Then she realized that even with the door wide open, she could not, from where she and Stanmore stood, see into the chamber. She could not see the four-poster bed, or the scowling gray-haired man beneath the mountain of quilts and tartan rugs.

Higgins returned to the sickroom and shut the door. Dr. Sellers approached Thea and Stanmore, and once more she noticed the bony frame beneath the disreputable jacket as the physician bowed to her before addressing Stanmore.

"You'll never credit this, my lord. Your father has contracted the measles. He's running a fever, and that's why he got dizzy on the stairs. Now, I know Master Charles and Miss Bella will be all right. They've had the measles. But what about you?"

Stanmore was no longer paying attention to the physician. He was looking at Thea.

And Thea, feeling unequal to the task of trying to explain the inexplicable, picked up her skirts in one hand, secured her shawl with the other, and fled toward the long gallery, escape route to the opposite wing.

Thea slowed to a decorous walk long before she reached the muniment room. Her proud forebears would turn in their graves if they knew how thoroughly she had lost the legendary von Hochstein composure. A woman of five-and-twenty running like a hoyden. Worse, like a coward.

Sitting down at her desk, she tried to concentrate on the Archer Hall ledgers, but for once her mind refused to concern itself with matters two hundred years in the past. She needed to resolve the present. She owed Stanmore an explanation—several explanations.

He must be told why he could not pursue his courtship. And that, all of a sudden, seemed easier than explaining what she could not explain: the strange incident in the hallway outside his father's room. Never before had she been able to see into a closed chamber or hear what was spoken there.

But this was not the first instance here at Archer Hall of "never before." There was the difference in dreams since her arrival. The strange experience at the foot of the gallery stairs. And again she had no explanation—except that never before had she concentrated so hard on the past or on the fate of one family.

Thea was not frightened—she had merely been taken by surprise when Dr. Sellers came out of Barnet's chamber and she realized that she heard and saw something she could not possibly have heard or seen. It had not helped to find Stanmore's eyes on her at the moment of revelation. But now she felt excited. The experience in the east wing must be considered a blessing, an extension of the gift of perceptiveness.

The Reverend Simmons had always maintained that such a gift must be accepted as is. But this past winter she had met Angus Comyn, the white-haired, gentle parson in a small Inverness-shire town. Parson Comyn had the sight, and he told her that the gift must be likened to a talent. If it was exercised frequently, it could be honed like a craft. If it was neglected, it could wither.

And again Lady Glendale came to mind, a MacLeod who could see the past. Or so Stanmore had said.

Stanmore . . . he had called her a little goose and told her that, when a man was courting a woman, everything about her was of interest.

Abruptly, Thea left her desk and started to pace. She felt disoriented, as she did after some of her more vivid dreams when she could not immediately tell where she was, or in what century. But this time, she could not blame a dream. The confusion was caused solely by her state of mind, her inability to judge what she wanted to do. Or, rather, what she ought to do.

Lud! What she wouldn't give for a brisk cross-country ride to clear her mind!

She grimaced wryly, remembering that not too long ago she had offered the last of her jewelry for an invitation to Archer Hall. And her birthright for something or other she could not recall. She seemed to have bartered all her possessions away—at least in her imagination—and now there was nothing left to exchange for a horse.

Moving from window to window, she gazed at the slowly drying landscape. Near the house, patches of snowdrops and crocuses dotted the lawn. Rhododendron and lilac shrubs along the drive, and the plane trees in the courtyard formed by the wings, showed the faintest hint of green.

The grounds at Hochstein would also be showing the promise of spring. But Hochstein now belonged to a cousin, and she doubted she'd ever see it again. Yet the Foreign Secretary wanted her to be prepared. When she saw him in January, he said the wind of change was blowing across the Continent.

It was imperative that she think clearly and come to a decision. Theadora Evalina von Hochstein must never be ruled by her heart alone.

Stanmore had left her in no doubt that he was about to make a formal proposal of marriage, no matter what she told him about herself. But he was wrong. There was one formidable obstacle that made a proposal impossible.

Thirteen

In the end, there was more than one obstacle to Stanmore's proposal, and even though this second one could not be termed formidable, it was immediate.

Two hours after Dr. Sellers left Archer Hall, the Ravensbrook carriage pulled up at the north front. The earl and countess accompanied Felicity into the house and sent a footman to fetch Stanmore from his father's bedside and Thea from the muniment room.

Stanmore was the first to arrive in the north hall where Felicity and Lady Ravensbrook, still in their wraps and cloaks, were seated by a fire just lit in one of the twin fireplaces. Lord Ravensbrook, in his greatcoat, was pacing the length of the Axminster carpet spread on the marble tile and stopped only now and again to finger an ancient crossbow or a longbow of the archery collection.

Stanmore's offer of refreshments was declined, and as soon as Thea joined them and had greeted the couple whose hospitality she had enjoyed three years earlier, Lady Ravensbrook, without roundaboutation, stated the purpose of their intrusion.

"We met Dr. Sellers and have decided to take Felicity back to Ravensbrook with us. She assured us she has had the measles, but in her situation she shouldn't be staying in a household stricken with an infectious illness. I'm sure you'll agree with us, Stanmore, that Felicity must take special precautions."

Stanmore's initial puzzlement changed to understanding. He smiled at Felicity. "You're making me a godfather at last?"

"Yes. Isn't it famous?"

"Then pack your trunks. And speedily, I beg. John will call me out if you fall ill here."

"No, he won't." Impishly, Felicity showed off her dimples. "He knows you're the better shot and the better swordsman."

Lady Ravensbrook frowned, but the earl chuckled and called his daughter-in-law a minx.

He turned to Thea. "We cannot dictate what you must do, my dear. But we'd like you to come with us as well."

"Thank you. How very kind you are. But, truly, there's no need. I've had the measles."

"So has Felicity," said Lady Ravensbrook. "But I cannot feel sanguine about her staying here. And since she is your chaperone . . ." She delicately allowed the words to trail.

Stanmore said, "Of course Miss Stone will accompany Felicity. At least until her official chaperone arrives."

Thea did not want to leave even for a short while, but with every eye upon her, she did not argue. Perhaps it was the hand of fate arranging this. Perhaps, away from Stanmore and Archer Hall for a few days, she could see more clearly—not what she wished, but what she ought to do.

"I shan't be a burden to you for long," she said to Lady Ravensbrook. "Miss Simmons should be here early next week. But I wonder, would Felicity not be better off if she returned to town? You, too, have the measles at Ravensbrook."

"Not any more," said Felicity.

The countess nodded her beturbaned head. "We haven't had a fresh case since Robert came down with the measles, and I doubt there's anyone left who hasn't had them yet. But here at Archer Hall the sickness is only just beginning."

"Most of the tenants' children were ill at the same time you had the measles at Ravensbrook," said Stanmore. "And the gardener's son got them during the rains. But how my father caught the measles is as yet a mystery. He swears he had them as a youth. And even if he hasn't had them, he was confined to his chambers for almost a month and hasn't been near any of the tenants."

Felicity, about to leave to supervise her packing, turned back.

"I meant to tell you, Stuart. When we saw Dr. Sellers, he had just been to the Applejohn farm. One of the daughters is under-housemaid here, and your housekeeper sent her home about a week ago. It seems the girl breaks out in a rash every time she helps with the laundry. Only this time it wasn't a rash. It was measles. But the Applejohns didn't know it until Dr. Sellers told them today."

"Hurry now, Felicity." Ravensbrook's impatience showed in the increased tempo of his pacing. "Pack only what you need for tonight. Your trunks can be sent tomorrow."

Felicity and Thea complied, only to find, when they hastened back to the north hall with a bandbox each, that the countess had removed her sable-trimmed cloak and the earl his caped greatcoat and were taking wine with Stanmore by the now merrily crackling fire.

Stanmore set his glass on a table. "Miss Stone, will you give me a moment of your time before you leave?"

Relieving her of the bandbox, which was quite heavy for its size, he drew Thea aside and walked with her toward the second fireplace, where the afternoon shadows were not dispelled by leaping flames in the hearth.

"What did you pack?" As he thrust the bandbox on a high-backed settle, he caught Thea's self-conscious look. "Half a dozen volumes of the Archer Hall ledgers?"

"One volume—the first. I didn't think you'd mind."

"I don't. Thea, I will come and see you at Ravensbrook. Tomorrow, if I can."

"If you can . . . please do. Now that I have given you my name, I must tell you all of my story. As soon as possible."

"So serious." He looked at her keenly. "Some time ago I assured you I'd never press you with questions you may not be prepared to answer. I meant it, Thea. And remember what

I said earlier today. Whatever you disclose to me, it won't change how I feel about you."

Softly, she said, "Nothing in my past, my present, or my future . . ."

She smiled at him, and as always his heartbeat accelerated as he savored the enchantment of that smile. Then he saw the shimmer of tears in her eyes.

"Thea!" He possessed himself of her hands. "What have I done—what have I said to make you cry?"

"I'm not crying. I am . . . touched. You suspect I have a scandalous past, do you not? And yet you say it would not change your feelings for me."

"A scandalous past! No, I don't suspect that at all. Merely that there may have been an instance when someone took advantage of your innocence. Thea, you are by far too trusting even now, and I'll never understand why your foster father permitted you to leave his protection. He is either an unworldly or a very foolish man."

She wanted to protest but, seeing Lady Ravensbrook gather cloak and muff, let the subject drop. Even a defense of Reverend Simmons must wait until they could have uninterrupted time.

"I must go." She removed her hands from his clasp. "Stanmore, it's none of my business, but should not Bella come with us? Charlie is already at Ravensbrook . . . and she has no governess . . ."

"If it's measles you fear, both children have had them. But do you not hear that screech? Silas persists in calling her Miss Butterfly, but she makes enough racket to put a dozen peacocks to shame."

And indeed, the high-pitched cry, "Here I am! Wait for me!" burst into the hall while the child herself was still somewhere in the west wing.

"Lady Ravensbrook extended the invitation," said Stanmore. "Both children will stay until Monday morning when Robert leaves for Harrow."

"I will return with them, at least for the day. I intend to continue working, and I refuse to have all my belongings packed and carried to Ravensbrook when Vespera may arrive at any moment. Stanmore, I have two trunks to be filled with nothing but notes and reference works! And most of the material is up in the muniment room."

Bella came running into the hall, stopped to view the two separate parties near the two fireplaces, then headed straight for Lord and Lady Ravensbrook and Felicity.

Stanmore said hurriedly, "Thea, this morning I told my father that I plan to disclaim any connection to Arbella Stuart. Unfortunately, he places the blame at your door even though I explained that you wish nothing more than to prove Arbella did give her son into Edward Archer's care."

She saw Lord Ravensbrook drumming his fingers against a tooled-leather quiver, displayed beside a bowman's protective leather jerkin and knew she ought to cut short her talk with Stanmore. But she must know the worst.

"Stanmore, does your father forbid me the house? Is that why you're pressing me to stay at Ravensbrook?"

"He planned to come down to dinner tonight so he could meet and question you."

"Poor man. Now he must wait until he's better."

"He has a mild case of measles but is sick enough to be more cantankerous than ever. If you're here, he may send for you. And though I've ordered the staff to do nothing unless it's approved by me, Higgins may just be fool enough to fetch you to my father's bedside."

"I don't mind that, I assure you. Only I'd rather not be summarily dismissed when I haven't even studied the ledgers. Who knows? I may discover that a secret compartment was built in a wall to hide important papers. And then there's Barnet House in the Strand. It is almost as old as Archer Hall and will have its own secrets."

"The town house! I doubt—" Stanmore broke off when Ravensbrook started toward them.

But the nursery maid arrived with Bella's portmanteau, and Ravensbrook turned about to follow the maid, Felicity, and Bella to the carriage.

Stanmore picked up Thea's bandbox. "At luncheon, I told my father that I mean to persuade you to marry me."

She paled. "I wish you had not done so."

They could say no more, since Lady Ravensbrook swept down on them and with practiced ease steered Thea after her husband and daughter-in-law, leaving Stanmore to follow with the bandbox.

As he was about to hand Thea into the carriage, she whispered fiercely, "You should not have spoken to your father. See me as soon as possible. I beg you!"

On Saturday, all of Felicity's trunks and one of Thea's arrived at Ravensbrook. Stanmore, however, did not call, a circumstance that added to the turmoil in Thea's heart and mind.

She had spent the night alternately pacing and standing at the window staring out into the night. She was drawn to Stanmore, no doubt about it. She would even go so far as to admit that she was a little in love with him.

More than a little.

But it did not matter. She had no right to fall in love. She had no right to encourage him.

Unless . . . but, no. A von Hochstein never went back on her word.

And yet, so much had changed in the five years since she gave her word. The Treaty of Tilsit made Tsar Alexander an ally of the Emperor Napoleon. Mr. Pitt was no longer the Prime Minister and Lord Mulgrave no longer the Foreign Secretary.

After a rapid succession of administrations, it was now Mr. Perceval who led the government, and the Marquis Wellesley who sat in the Foreign Office. But they did not take a different view of her situation.

In '06, Hochstein and other German states had joined the Confederation of the Rhine and placed themselves under French rule. But there was unrest in the states; loyalties among the ruling families were divided. With encouragement, Lord Wellesley had told her in January, the German states would break with France. Thea was to serve as the encourager for Hochstein.

The wind of change . . . she did not mind fulfilling her political obligations, but she wanted to be released from personal commitment. Surely she could free herself without loss of honor. Surely . . .

Back and forth she argued. By morning she forced a decision, for she knew, if she met Stanmore undecided, she would only make matters worse.

During that endless day of waiting for him, she changed her mind a hundred times or more, then suffered through another sleepless night of weighing what she wished to do and what she ought to do. Sunday morning, heartsore, she had come full circle to her original decision to tell Stanmore her story and make him understand that he must not pursue his courtship.

And this time, whether Stanmore called or not, she would not waver.

On Sunday afternoon Lady Ravensbrook and Felicity were stitching on a tapestry in the countess's sitting room, and Thea was trying, though with little success, to study the ledger she had brought from Archer Hall. Three times, she had read the entries from December of 1615, when the first building materials were purchased, to March of 1617, when Archer Hall was completed. But the only item her mind had retained was payment to the carpenter, J. Fletcher, in January of 1617, for a dozen oak pews—which reminded her that she had still not asked Stanmore to show her the chapel.

"Thea!" Felicity's voice held a note of reproof. "Stop the

woolgathering. Mother Markham suggested that you join us here by the fire. That window has always been drafty."

Thea's apology was cut short by the butler's entrance.

Oxton approached the countess and, conveying disapproval in stance and voice, announced, "Lord Stanmore is requesting a *private* interview with Miss Stone."

If Lady Ravensbrook was surprised that Stanmore's call was not a neighborly visit, she was too well-bred to betray it.

She turned to Thea. "My dear, will you see him?"

"Yes, of course."

Now that the moment of confrontation had come, she was quite calm. Setting the ledger on a table, she rose. "Oxton, where is Lord Stanmore?"

"I took the liberty of asking him to wait in the blue salon until I could ascertain that you're at home to callers."

Lady Ravensbrook raised a brow. "Lord Stanmore is a friend, Oxton, not an importuning stranger. But never mind now. Show Miss Stone to the blue salon."

Thea followed the butler's stately progress to a room at the back of the ground floor. Obviously, the blue salon was not generally used by the family. No agricultural tract lay forgotten on a table, no dish was set out with Lady Ravensbrook's favorite comfits, and no fire was laid in the grate. But the afternoon sun shone golden through a window, and Stanmore was there.

Dressed for riding, he stood by the window, not looking out but facing the door. He started toward her the moment she entered, his long, quick stride making nothing of the distance between them.

"I planned to see you yesterday." He bowed over her hand. "It was the longest day to live through."

She turned to the butler still hovering in the doorway. "Thank you, Oxton. That will be all."

He bowed and stepped back, leaving the door open a good thirty inches.

"You may shut the door, Oxton. I have something of import

to discuss with Lord Stanmore and don't wish to be interrupted. If we require anything, I shall ring."

Oxton might disapprove, but he knew the tone of authority. He closed the door with the proper degree of respect and firmness.

As puzzled as he was amused, Stanmore was watching Thea.

"I'm not sure any longer that it is merely an accomplishment when you take on that regal air. Who are you, Thea? A fairy princess from some strange, enchanted land?"

She did not smile. "I am the Princess Theadora Evalina von Hochstein."

His amusement faded. "You're in earnest. A princess. From which court? Not the Prussian, I think. From one of the new, French-ruled kingdoms . . . Bavaria? Saxony?"

"No. Hochstein is a principality, a tiny, arrow-shaped land extending from the northeast tip of Bohemia into Saxony. Shall we sit down? Though my tale is not a long one, it cannot be told in two or three words."

He stepped close, his expression as impenetrable as the day they met. But Thea felt his tension.

"First tell me this, Thea! Is it because your rank is above mine that you're reluctant to receive my addresses?"

He was offering an easy way out. She had only to say yes, and he would not approach her again. She would not be required to explain the tangled web his courtship made of her life.

But she could not add insult to injury.

"No, Stanmore. That has nothing to do with it."

A glow ignited in the dark eyes, and before she knew what he was about, he caught her in his arms and kissed her. His mouth was firm and demanding. His arms tightened around her as if he feared she would pull away. Yet it never occurred to her to deny him the kiss. The moment their lips touched, she had no thought but that this was meant to be.

She felt no shyness; only fulfillment. She knew no doubts; only certainty that this was right. There was no hesitancy on her part. The feel of his arms, the taste of his mouth, everything about the embrace was familiar and so welcome that it seemed impossible this was their first kiss.

Stanmore loosened his hold. "Thea, we are meant for each other. Did you not feel it?"

No matter how difficult, how painful, the Princess Theadora Evalina von Hochstein must not be ruled by her heart.

She stepped away from him.

"What I felt was an inevitability . . . of our meeting . . . and of the kiss . . . perhaps of our falling in love. If love it is that we're feeling?"

"It is love, Thea. What else would it be?"

"I don't know. But, Stanmore, I do know we are *not* meant for each other."

He was undaunted. The kiss had told him what he needed to know.

"I love you, Thea Stone. I love you, Theadora Evalina von Hochstein. And if you haven't yet recognized your feelings for me, I am content to wait until you do."

Everything he said made her task more difficult, more painful. Yet she could not bring herself to use bluntness and be done. Against better judgment, she was waiting, hoping for a miracle, an argument that would convince her she could have a marriage of her choice after all.

"Thea, I *know* you're not indifferent to me."

"There is a bond I cannot deny. A force that draws me to you."

"That is love."

"Or merely attraction. It is not impossible to confuse the two. But the argument is futile. Stanmore, you mustn't pursue your courtship of me."

"Thea, my love. My little goose. You may as well try to convince Bella she mustn't listen at doors any more."

He did not touch her, but his eyes held her captive. "I am courting you because I love you. Because I want to marry you."

She could scarcely breathe for the coil of pain in her chest.

"Stanmore, I am married."

Fourteen

Stanmore stood thunderstruck. He did not ask her to repeat what she said. He could not doubt what he had heard. The words still echoed in his mind, loudly, cruelly.

I am married.

He felt numb, but he knew that pain was not far away. Thea had betrayed him, just as Charlotte had done, though in quite a different manner.

Thea. Miss Stone. Married.

He became aware of her, still standing but a few paces away. She looked her most regal, back straight, head held proudly; yet she had never seemed more vulnerable. He saw her eyes and knew that she was suffering. But he could not comfort her. Not now, as numbness wore off and devastation set in.

She did not speak but turned slowly and walked to a sofa upholstered in the same shade of royal blue that covered every chair in the room and was repeated in the gold-corded window hangings. Her posture lost none of its poise and dignity when she sat down, insteps and ankles decorously covered by the folds of her gown, one hand resting lightly upon the other in her lap. For some reason, the picture she presented made him think of Lady Jane Grey awaiting her execution.

It was an analogy that gave him pause and spawned yet another analogous thought. He had judged and condemned Thea without a hearing . . . as King James had judged and condemned his cousin Arbella. But James merely adhered to the divine right—which had since been abolished and, in any case, could never have been Stanmore's justification.

He wasn't aware of making a conscious decision to join Thea, yet found himself walking toward the sofa. She moved a little to make room for him, and when he sat down beside her, they were half facing each other.

She spoke first. "Shall I ring for wine? Or brandy? The ride must have chilled you."

"No!" His voice was too harsh compared to her quiet tones. He made an effort to moderate it.

"Thea, if I understood correctly, you've been traveling and working on family histories for the past five years. When did you marry? Where is your husband? And who the deuce is your husband?"

"He is Count Sergei Tushenko. We were married on the twenty-second of June, 1788. My fourth birthday. Tushenko was fifteen."

Again she had rendered him speechless, and when he found his voice, he could only think to say, "On the twenty-second of June, 1610, Arbella married William Seymour."

He considered it an inane remark, but it elicited the ghost of a smile from Thea.

"The wedding day is but one of many things Arbella and I have in common. Of course, it would have been better yet if the twenty-second of June had also been her birthday. But I share that with my ancestress Dorothea Wortley."

Stanmore recovered his wits. "Thea, you cannot possibly have been married when you were four years old."

"Can I not? Margaret Tudor was twelve when she married James IV of Scotland."

"But that was a royal marriage, three hundred years ago. She had reached the age of consent . . ." His protest lacked conviction. In truth, he did not know how marriages were arranged on the Continent.

Thea said, "My father was the ruler of Hochstein. I was his firstborn child. My mother conceived again, but it was too soon after my birth. She miscarried and was unable to bear more children. Hochstein is not governed by Salic law; thus, I am—was the Hereditary Princess von Hochstein."

He raked his hair with hands that wanted to close around the throat of a man he had never seen, never even heard of until a moment ago . . . hands that wanted to shake Thea until she confessed she made up the tale of Count Sergei Tushenko.

"I'm trying to understand . . . but I cannot. When you insisted that you must tell me your story, I thought you might have been taken advantage of, or that there had been some youthful indiscretion . . . an attempt to elope, perhaps. But marriage! I know early marriages are arranged among royalty for dynastic reasons. But, dash it! You were an infant!"

"There was trouble brewing at Hochstein—a cousin plotting to usurp the throne. And when the Empress Catherine of Russia offered the son of one of her favorites as a husband for me, my father accepted in the belief that a tie to the Russian court would deter Cousin Friedrich."

Stanmore's concern was not with a cousin, only with Thea. "But the marriage—it cannot have been a marriage! A betrothal—"

"The vows were made *per verba de presenti,* and whether you call it betrothal or marriage, it is a legally binding contract."

It boggled the mind. He remembered Bella on her fourth birthday . . . a baby despite her efforts to emulate her seven-year-old brother.

"Sanctified by the Church?"

"That it wasn't. Since it was stipulated that we—Tushenko and I—would each live at our own home until I reached maturity, the vows were to have been solemnized at that time."

"When you were orphaned—I believe you said you were nine years old?"

"Yes."

"Why did Miss Simmons bring you to England, to her brother's house? Surely, if you had no close relations, the proper place for you would then have been with the family of your—" His tongue refused to form the word husband. "Your betrothed?"

"Forgive me." Thea rose. "I'm too restless to sit still."

He rose as well. "You need not answer," he said, his voice strained. "I have not forgotten that I promised not to press you."

"I *want* to tell you. But I am unaccustomed to speaking about that part of my life, except with Vespera Simmons, who has been with me from my second year on. When we arrived in England, she explained my situation at the Foreign Office and, of course, to the Reverend Simmons and his family. Other than that, there's only Felicity's family who were told the truth."

He nodded. He did not want to be cool and stiff toward her as if he did not give a straw one way or the other, but the reserve that had peeled off layer by layer during the past month, was firmly back in place.

Thea's eyes were on him. She reached out and gently touched his face, then turned and started to pace.

Stanmore stood motionless, wondering why she had chosen that very moment to touch him. She must have read his mind and determined to show him that reserve, once broken down, could not be rebuilt without some cracks. Had she stayed close but an instant longer, he would have shaken her.

Or swept her into his arms and damned the consequences.

Stopping at the window, she faced him. "It was impossible for Vespera Simmons to take me to St. Petersburg when my parents died."

"Why?"

"We were in France at the time."

He frowned. "That would have been in '93 or '94 . . . the Reign of Terror."

"My parents died on the fourteenth of October, 1793."

He did not know what to say, whether to go to her, or stay where he was, distanced by half the room's length.

Then she spoke again, a note of hesitancy in her rich voice attesting that she was not as unmoved as she seemed.

"We had been staying at court . . . there was a connection on my mother's side to Marie Antoinette. But we weren't with the royal family when they were captured at Varennes. By then, we had leased a small house in the Faubourg St. Martin. After the execution of the king, someone betrayed us. We were taken to the Conciergerie . . . and we saw Marie Antoinette again when she was moved from the Temple. Two days before she was executed . . . my parents went to the scaffold."

The afternoon sun sparked russet lights in Thea's hair. For an instant, he saw the lights as drops of blood.

This time he did not wonder what he ought to do. He went to her.

"Thea, I am sorry—about your parents, that you were in Paris during the bloodbath."

"It was a long time ago, and although I'll never forget, the sharpness of the horror has worn off."

"How did you and Miss Simmons escape?"

"Robespierre—he was still powerful then. He arranged that we were taken in by a tavern keeper. It wasn't unusual. Children of the aristocracy, if they were not killed, were frequently placed in service. The miracle was that Vespera was allowed to stay with me."

"Were you at least sent out of Paris?"

"No. The tavern was near the Place de la Révolution. Robespierre considered it simplest and safest. On the fourth of December—fourteenth *frimaire* of the Year II—he released an Englishman condemned as a spy in return for his promise to take us to England. The man kept his word."

"The Place de la Révolution—that was where the guillotine stood, was it not? And you were there. In a tavern. No wonder you don't like a noisy crowd."

Her eyes widened. "You remember that?"

"I remember every word you ever spoke to me."

"Stanmore—"

She had been composed, almost unnaturally so, throughout their talk. Now she faltered and turned abruptly.

"I am so very sorry. I wish—"

She did not say what she wished, but there was a stillness in the way she held her head, a rigidity of shoulders and back, betraying emotions held tightly in check.

He wanted to touch her, soothe her, but she said without turning around, "Please don't."

But she needed him, and he scarcely hesitated before wrapping his arms around her from behind and drawing her against his chest.

She neither struggled nor relaxed against him but stood quite still, as if patiently waiting for him to let go of her. But he could not. He loved her. No matter how wrong she had been when she kept her marriage a secret, he could not allow her to shoulder the blame for his falling in love.

He did not know her full story, did not know how she felt about Count Tushenko, the man she called her husband, but he was certain that Thea was as unlike Charlotte as archery was different from swordplay and would never deliberately betray anyone. And at the back of his mind an insinuating thought took hold—the thought of making the impossible possible.

Beneath his right wrist, he felt the beat of her heart. Painfully fast—like his own.

"Thea. Dearest Thea. Won't you please turn around?"

"For the love of God!" Her voice was unsteady. "Must you make everything so much more difficult?"

"As difficult as possible. Thea, don't blame yourself because I fell in love with you."

Her breath caught. "And you call *me* fey!"

"There's nothing fey about this. 'Tis the bond of love that allows us to know the other's mind. You knew that I wanted to hold you. And I sense remorse tearing at you. But believe me, there's nothing you could have done or said that would have changed the course of my fate."

"You're wrong. If I had been more reserved—"

"No. Reserve might have served the purpose when I was a callow youth. Though I boldly jumped the highest fence, the widest ditch, a cold word or a repressive look from a lady could unnerve me then. But I am no longer nineteen. I am two-and-thirty."

Slowly, she turned in his arms.

"Stanmore—at nineteen, you were already married."

"Yes."

For a moment they looked at each other. He had been nineteen and Charlotte, Thea knew from the genealogy, twenty-four.

Stanmore said, "Never fear that I nursed a broken heart. Neither Charlotte nor I pretended to love the other. If we deserve pity, it was for the emptiness in our lives. And even though I love my children, an emptiness remained—until I met you."

She looked stricken. "How I wish I could turn back the time! I should have called myself *Mrs*. Stone."

"I would still have fallen in love with you."

"No! You would not have allowed your attentions to become fixed on *Mrs*. Stone. Stanmore, it simply did not occur to me. I never dwelled on my married status but, naturally, I was aware of it. And, I suppose, if I thought of it at all, I considered myself unapproachable as well as immune."

"Immune?" If she had not been so distraught, he would have smiled at her choice of word. "Was there no sprig of fashion, no aspiring beau in Derbyshire for whom you conceived a tendre?"

"No," she said, considering the question quite seriously. "And it isn't as if I was kept from society. On the contrary. My foster parents are well connected and I was included in any invitation they received."

He drew her closer. "And none of the young men fell passionately in love with you? I cannot believe that."

"If they did, they hid their passion well. More likely, though, I was too much of a bluestocking to suit their tastes. Stanmore—" Leaning back against his arms, she looked at him gravely. "Please believe that I never intended to deceive. I've been thoughtless, I admit. But I've been Miss Stone since I put up my hair. And the more time passed the less I considered Sergei Tushenko and the marriage."

He could not have wished for sweeter words. Indeed! He would fight to make the impossible possible. And he would succeed.

He felt a rush of excitement, not unlike the thrill of a steeplechase, but he put the years of practice at presenting an outward calm to good use.

"There were times when I wished I did not have to think of Charlotte, but since I could not avoid seeing her occasionally, I found it impossible to ignore her existence."

"I have not seen Tushenko since the wedding festivities at Castle Hochstein twenty-two years ago."

Sweet words indeed, sending hope soaring high. He drew her close again, caressing her back, her shoulders, the nape of her neck.

"Then the marriage can be annulled. It may even be invalid. I seem to recall a law that a contract of matrimony involving a minor is invalid unless the vows are repeated when the party or parties reach the age of consent. At least, it would be invalid here in England."

"The vows were repeated."

Gently, she freed herself from his embrace. "It was arranged by the Foreign Office when I was sixteen. I was personally present, and Count Tushenko was represented by the Russian ambassador."

This was a hurdle he had not anticipated. He did not know anything about Hochstein, had never heard of the principality until Thea mentioned it, but if the Russian court and the English government took an interest in the matrimonial affairs of Hochstein's princess—exiled princess—then it would not be a simple matter to extricate her from the tangle.

His heart sank. It might be beyond his power.

"But the marriage has not been consummated," he persisted. "It was stipulated by the Foreign Secretary and the Russian ambassador that Tushenko would come to England in June of '05, when I turned twenty-one."

"But he didn't." Fiercely. "Or did he, Thea? Is he in England now?"

"No. But it doesn't change the situation."

He wanted to hold her again, and kiss her to prove how much the situation was changed, but her troubled expression warned him to proceed with caution.

"Thea, any marriage not consummated can be annulled— even if it was sanctified by the Church. And yours was not."

"I gave my word to Lord Mulgrave—he was the Foreign Secretary then—that I would not petition for annulment."

"Why, Thea? Why is the Foreign Office interfering in your personal life? And why do you permit them to do so? Why does Tushenko? He is ten, eleven years older than you. Did he not object to the stipulation that you must be twenty-one before he could claim you as his bride?"

Once again, she started to pace, moving away from him.

"I don't know how Tushenko felt. But if I had returned to Hochstein before I turned twenty-one, the Council would have appointed a regent. And that suited neither the English Foreign Secretary nor the Russian ambassador, who had precise instructions from the Emperor Paul."

The thought occurred to Stanmore that the life of a ruling Princess von Hochstein would be governed by obligation and responsibilities, by customs and tradition, just as his life was.

Had been. He could not say when or how it happened, but he no longer felt that the only way to escape Archer tradition was to prove the tale of royal descent a fabrication.

And Thea was obviously not a ruling princess . . .

But she was speaking to him, and he had best pay attention.

"Tushenko was supposed to leave a troop of his men in Saxony while he fetched me from London. Then, with his men and with the aid of the Elector of Saxony, he was to wrest Hochstein from Cousin Friedrich."

"Wait! Something is missing in this fantastic tale. I gather that sometime between your preposterous marriage and your parents' death in Paris, you lost Hochstein. To that same Cousin Friedrich who was plotting against your father at the time of your marriage?"

"Yes."

Thea reached the door and turned. Daylight had begun to fade, and at a distance he could no longer read her expression.

Silence stretched between them. Before it became awkward, he said, "Tell me how your father lost Hochstein. And when."

She started to move again, toward the fireplace this time, as if determined to keep her distance from him.

"Friedrich von Waldfrieden attacked that winter after the marriage ceremony. He had mercenaries. My father had only the men employed about the castle and a handful of guardsmen."

"Hochstein did not have an army?"

He thought he heard her laugh, but it was the softest of sounds and ceased almost as soon as it began.

"The men of Hochstein are farmers and miners and silversmiths. They've always rallied around their ruler when they feared their livelihood threatened, but otherwise they like to go their own way. And that particular winter was so severe, battles might have been fought in the village squares and no one would have stuck a nose out of doors."

She stopped by the fireplace. "Mind, most of what I can tell you I learned from Vespera Simmons. What little memory I retained of that time has blended with what she told me and what I heard from my parents in Paris."

"I understand. But if you had no help from the Hochsteiners, how did you escape?"

"On the second day of siege, my great-grandmother, the Baroness von Waldfrieden, arrived. She lives not far from Castle Hochstein, but in Saxony. I don't know how she learned of Friedrich's perfidy, but she's his grandmother as well as my father's, and everyone, Friedrich included, loves and at the same time stands in awe of her."

"Present tense? She is still alive?"

"I hope so." Thea leaned against the mantelpiece. "We correspond, but since Saxony and other German states are now under French rule, there is no easy way to communicate. Messages to and from the Continent have taken as long as seven months. Grandmother Augusta wrote in June of last year, remembering my birthday, but the letter didn't arrive at the vicarage until January. So, until the next letter, I can only pray that she's alive and well."

"How old is she?"

"She is ninety-two, though I doubt she'd admit this. Vespera says that even twenty years ago, Grandmother Augusta refused to answer questions about her age."

"And she helped you escape from Friedrich?"

This time, there was no mistaking the sound of a soft laugh.

"According to Vespera, Grandmother Augusta arrived in a sled drawn by six horses. She got out, brandishing her cane, and told Cousin Friedrich if he must disgrace the family by acting like a robber baron, he might do so and live to regret it. But she wasn't about to stand by while one of her grandsons murdered the other. And she ordered him to let everyone in the castle go."

"He complied? That is incredible."

"Perhaps. But she is the matriarch of the powerful von Waldfrieden family of Saxony. She had three children, a daughter, who was my father's mother, and two sons, the younger of which was Friedrich's father. Augusta's grandson by the elder of her sons is the titular head of the family, but it is Augusta who rules. And so Friedrich let us go. In Grandmother Augusta's sled."

"It seems the past century bred strong women," he said absently, his mind teeming with more questions. "My great-aunts are a bit like your great-grandmother—not in position, but in character. They're the ladies Charlie called meddlers."

"Your grandfather's sisters? From the way Charlie referred to them, I did not make the connection." The change of topic animated Thea. She pushed away from the cold marble of the mantelpiece. "It says in the chronicles of 1745 that your grandfather's sisters hid in the chapel—"

"Thea," he interrupted. "Where is your—where is Tushenko now?"

For a moment she was silent.

"At Hochstein. In '05, on the twenty-second of June, the day his vows and mine were supposed to have been solemnized, he married Friedrich's daughter."

Fifteen

"The devil you say!"

For Stanmore, this was strong language in the presence of a lady, especially since he had already invoked the deuce when he demanded to know the identity of Thea's husband. But initial incredulity was outweighed by exasperation and a strong sense of ill-usage, and for once he was uninhibited by dislike for an open display of emotion. Without hesitation he followed the dictates of his lacerated feelings.

He left his position by the window and, at the same time, Thea started toward him from the fireplace. They met near the sofa, and immediately he caught her by the shoulders.

"Thea, how could you! First dealing me a blow with the news of this *marriage,* as you call it. Then you all but convince me that annulment will be nigh impossible. And after all that, you casually drop that the curst fellow has a wife!"

"*I* am his wife."

"Dash it! You're not married at all. You're free!"

Thea's breath caught as he towered above her, his dark eyes ablaze. His grip was hard, proprietary, and he had about him an air of passions unleashed that made her stare in wonder.

"You're free!" he repeated. "Free to marry me."

"Stanmore, I am not!"

His mouth descended on hers, effectively cutting off further protest. She did not fight him. She could not. Could no more refuse this second kiss than she could the first.

And when he would have released her, she wound her arms

*A*llow us to proposition you in a most provocative way.

GET 4 REGENCY ROMANCE NOVELS *FREE*

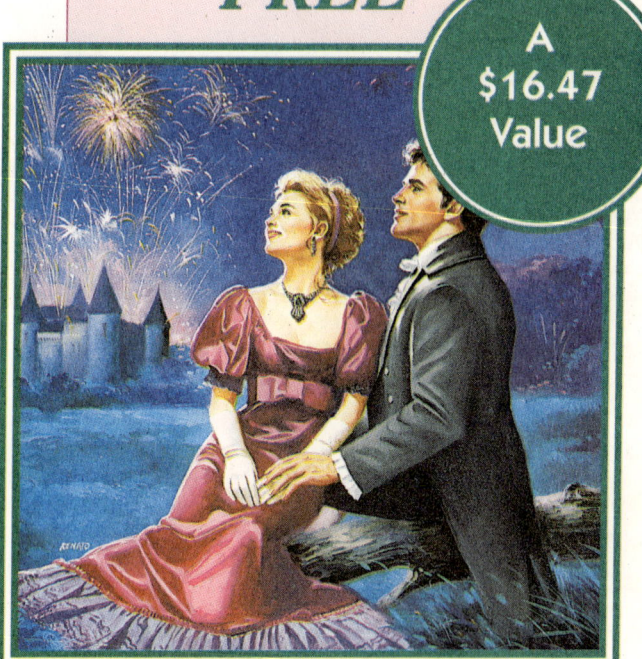

A $16.47 Value

NO OBLIGATION TO BUY ANYTHING, EVER.

PRESENTING AN IRRESISTIBLE OFFERING ON YOUR KIND OF ROMANCE.

Receive 4 Zebra Regency Romance Novels (A $16.47 value) *Free*

Journey back to the romantic Regent Era with the world's finest romance authors. Zebra Regency Romance novels place you amongst the English *ton* of a distant past with witty dialogue, and stories of courtship so real, you feel that you're living them!

Experience it all through 4 FREE Zebra Regency Romance novels...yours just for the asking. When you join *the only book club dedicated to Regency Romance readers,* additional Regency Romances can be yours to preview FREE each month, with no obligation to buy anything, ever.

Regency Subscribers Get First-Class Savings.

After your initial package of 4 FREE books, you'll begin to receive monthly shipments of new Zebra Regency titles. These all new novels will be delivered direct to your home as soon as they are published...sometimes even before the bookstores get them! Each monthly shipment of 4 books will be yours to examine for 10 days. Then, if you decide to keep the books, you'll pay the preferred subscriber's price of just $3.30 per title. That's $13.20 for all 4 books...a savings of over $3 off the publisher's price! What's more, $13.20 is your total price...there's no additional charge for shipping and handling.

No Minimum Purchase, a Generous Return Privilege, and FREE Home Delivery!

We're so sure that you'll appreciate the money-saving convenience of home delivery that we guarantee your complete satisfaction. You may return any shipment...for any reason...within 10 days and pay nothing that month. And if you want us to stop sending books, just say the word. There is no minimum number of books you must buy.

Say Yes to 4 Free Books!

COMPLETE AND RETURN THE ORDER CARD TO RECEIVE THIS $16.47 VALUE. ABSOLUTELY FREE.

(If the certificate is missing below, write to: Zebra Home Subscription Service, Inc., 120 Brighton Road, P.O. Box 5214, Clifton, New Jersey 07015-5214

4 FREE BOOKS

Yes! Please send me 4 Zebra Regency Romances without cost or obligation. I understand that each month thereafter I will be able to preview 4 new Regency Romances FREE for 10 days. Then, if I should decide to keep them, I will pay the money-saving preferred subscriber's price of just $13.20 for all 4…that's a savings of over $3 off the publisher's price with no additional charge for shipping and handling. I may return any shipment within 10 days and owe nothing, and I may cancel this subscription at any time. My 4 FREE books will be mine to keep in any case.

Name _____

Address _____ Apt. _____

City _____ State _____ Zip _____

Telephone ( ) _____

Signature _____
(If under 18, parent or guardian must sign.)

RF0695

Terms and prices subject to change. Orders subject to acceptance by Zebra Home Subscription Service, Inc.

GET 4 REGENCY ROMANCES FREE

A $16.47 value.
FREE!
No obligation to buy anything, ever.

ZEBRA HOME SUBSCRIPTION SERVICE, INC.

120 BRIGHTON ROAD
P.O. BOX 5214
CLIFTON, NEW JERSEY 07015-5214

AFFIX STAMP HERE

around his neck and drew him close again. She was aware that her behavior was improper, unprincipled, but it did not matter. It mattered only that they should go on touching, holding, cherishing . . .

Lest she lose him . . . and his love . . . as had happened in days of yore.

"Thea—"

His breath coming in ragged gasps, he looked at her. There was still a blaze of light in his eyes, but it was the light of love—and it returned Thea to bleak reality. Yet during that instant when she was suspended between enchantment and reality, she recalled the fear of losing him and his love.

As in days of yore.

How extraordinarily strange . . . she could not possibly have lost Stanmore's love in days far in the past.

She shivered, and knew not why.

Stanmore demanded, "Now, if you dare, tell me again that you're not certain whether you love me. After that kiss, tell me!"

And she could not.

"There!" He drew her close. "I knew I could not be mistaken."

Tightening her arms around his neck, she said fiercely, "I am pledged to Tushenko. Don't you understand? His marriage to Erika is invalid. Erika is not his wife, and any children born—"

"Rubbish. Tushenko must have arranged for annulment himself."

She shook her head. "Grandmother Augusta would have heard of it and let me know."

"Then *you* must petition for annulment."

"I cannot."

"Don't be stubborn, Thea." No less exasperated than before, he yet strove for a light, teasing note. "Why do you want to condemn innocent children to bastardy? Or your cousin, Erika, to living a life of sin?"

"You're being flippant." She gave him an incredulous look. "How can you!"

"I'm trying to make you see sense. You don't want the man, do you?"

Secure within the circle of his arms, she knew she wanted no man but him.

"Stanmore, please understand. What I want has nothing to say in the matter. When I learned—several months after the fact—that Tushenko had taken Erika to wife, I fully intended to have my marriage annulled. But the Foreign Secretary—"

He cut in. "Leave me to deal with the Foreign Office. *You* must write your foster father and ask him whether we must petition an ecclesiastical court."

"If it were as simple as that! Even if I were at liberty to have the marriage set aside, I would have to petition—"

Again Thea was interrupted, but this time the culprit was not Stanmore. After the briefest of knocks, Lady Ravensbrook entered, followed by Bella, Charlie, and Robert Markham, a tow-headed youngster of Charlie's age.

"You're hugging," said Bella, watching with interest as her father released Miss Stone.

The boys said nothing. Crimson faced, they shuffled their feet.

Lady Ravensbrook smiled. "We've come to fetch you from this cold room. You must be quite chilled by now. And I see that Oxton neglected to have someone draw the curtains and light the lamps. Pray accept my apologies."

Her tone and manner could not have been more gracious, but neither Thea nor Stanmore were in any doubt that Lady Ravensbrook would not leave them alone another moment.

Stanmore bowed. "*I* must apologize. I should not have kept Miss Stone so long."

He accepted an invitation to join the rest of the Markham family in the drawing room but stayed only long enough to listen to the children's enthusiastic if somewhat incoherent account of the gamekeeper's spaniel, accidentally shut into the larder while his master conferred with Lord Ravensbrook; to exchange a word with the earl and three of his sons; and to express his gratitude to Lady Ravensbrook and Robert's mother for the hospitality shown Bella and Charlie.

Taking his leave of Thea, he said, "I shan't be able to call tomorrow. But perhaps on Tuesday morning you will ride with me?"

Knowing herself the cynosure of all eyes, Thea inclined her head. "Thank you. That would be delightful."

A sudden smile lit his face. "I have the perfect mount for you. Her name is Princess."

Princess . . . had he made it up?

Thea was an excellent horsewoman, and there was nothing she would have liked better than to ride out with Stanmore. But she was certain Lady Ravensbrook would insist on a groom accompanying them, making it impossible to continue their talk.

And talk they must, for it was obvious that Stanmore did not take her marriage to Sergei Tushenko seriously.

She could not blame him; deep in her heart she had never quite believed in the marriage either—vows spoken almost twenty-two years ago by her father on her behalf and repeated by a dreamy sixteen-year-old, who saw less significance in a ritual that placed the Russian ambassador as the groom's representative at her side than in the parallel between herself and the Lady Arbella Stuart. They were both married on the twenty-second of June, though almost two centuries apart, and both were separated from a husband through political intrigue.

But Stanmore must be made to understand that because of the Tushenko family's close connection to the court of St. Petersburg she could not ask for an annulment of her marriage. She had promised—and a von Hochstein did not go back on her word.

Shortly after dinner, she excused herself and withdrew to

her bedchamber. She lit a candle on the night table, thereby leaving most of the room in darkness, but that was fine with her. Light was distracting when she was in desperate need to collect her wits. She must see Stanmore before that ride on Tuesday morning, and when she did, she must be composed.

She stood at the window and looked out into the night, as she had done most of Friday night and on Saturday. Surely it wasn't impossible to recapture the calm, the sense of destiny, that had allowed her to face Stanmore in the afternoon.

But that was before she had been embraced and kissed. Before she knew without a doubt that her feelings for him were love. Before she understood how very empty her life would be without him.

As empty as it had been when she lost him . . . in days of yore.

Thea shivered. There it was again, the strange thought that had no foundation in reality. She had indeed suffered loss in the past. But none concerning Stanmore. And she had learned to hide her pain.

When she was quite young, dogs had mauled her kitten. Her father told her that the Princess von Hochstein might cry in the privacy of her chamber but never in the castle yard. Tears were a sign of weakness, he said. And later, at the Conciergerie, when the sight of human misery or a rat bite made her cry, he had commanded her to smile. A von Hochstein, he said, did not give in to physical or mental anguish.

Rudolph von Hochstein had followed that dictum when his name was called on the fourteenth of October, 1793. When his wife's name was called next, he had blanched and started to shake. But Alwina, gentle yet strong, took his hand and smiled at him. Drawing strength from his wife's fortitude, Rudolph reminded Vespera Simmons of her promise to care for his daughter, then he and Alwina stood with their arms around Thea until guards prodded them toward the door.

And Thea, because she knew it was what her parents expected, had held her head high with a smile firmly in place—

until she no longer heard the rattle of the tumbril through the barred windows. Then she screamed, and immediately Vespera Simmons was there to hold and to rock her. There were no words of comfort. Thea knew as well as anyone in the Conciergerie that no one who was taken away in the tumbril was ever seen again.

For a moment, Thea pressed palms and forehead against the cold glass of the bedroom window at Ravensbrook—quite a different feel from the bars at the Conciergerie. Neither she nor Stanmore were in any danger of being carted away in a tumbril, but their separation once her work at Archer Hall was done would be as final as the separation from her parents in the Reign of Terror.

As a nine-year-old she had been brave as long as her parents could see her. Surely, at twenty-five, she could be strong for a week or two. She had never before neglected her work for any reason, and she was not about to make an exception, especially not when Stanmore would find it difficult to interest another historian in Arbella Stuart's case.

If she could return to Archer Hall soon, she might be done in a sennight. Then a few days at Barnet House in London . . . and Stanmore need not even accompany her.

But her heart rebelled. This was not what she wanted. She was in love. Not with the man chosen by her father and the Empress of Russia, both long dead. She loved Stanmore.

She had not sought love, but neither, apparently, had she guarded against it. And now it was too late to shield her heart. To be near him, to be his wife, had become more important than anything. More important than proving that Arbella Stuart had borne a child. And much more important than to be installed, at some point when governments deemed it politic, as the rightful ruler of Hochstein.

She had lived in England sixteen years. Whether Vespera Simmons and her brother intended it or not, she had been raised an Englishwoman. When she thought of home, she did not think of Castle Hochstein, which her own memories and

Vespera Simmons's descriptions had turned into a beautiful picture she carried in her mind and could view or ignore as she wished.

Home meant the vicarage in Ault Hucknall with its creaking stairs, its rambling, narrow corridors, drafty doors and windows, and the untidy, overgrown garden where she had romped with her foster siblings. It meant the warm kitchen, where Mrs. Simmons had acquainted her daughters and Thea with the functions of chopping block and cleaver, of ovens and spits and the old-fashioned wood stove. Home meant the quiet book-lined study where Vespera and the Reverend Felix Simmons had taught her.

And yet, the Foreign Secretary and the Russian ambassador—and also, alas, Thea's foster father—insisted that her destiny lay in Hochstein. At the side of Count Sergei Tushenko, her husband.

Her destiny. Her fate.

Suddenly, in the dark, Thea inclined her head in the manner Stanmore had called regal and gracious. And then she laughed at herself as she had done countless times before. The princess without a country; without a people.

But the relief that laughter brought was transient. She had scarcely drawn breath before she was pulled again into the maelstrom of doubt and indecision.

Perhaps, if she had laughed five years ago when Lord Mulgrave at the Foreign Office held forth on birthright and destiny . . . alas, her sense of humor failed her at that crucial point, and she had made a fatal decision.

All night Thea paced or stood by the window, her heart and mind in turmoil. The candle on the night table guttered and went out, but she did not light a new one. The dark suited her mood.

When morning dawned, she was calm once more. If, with the loss of Hochstein as a child, she had incidentally gained the right to shape her own destiny, then she had given that right away with a promise five years ago. Her situation now was no different than it would have been if she still lived in the castle with her parents as her father's heir . . . the next ruler of Hochstein.

Composed but with little interest in her appearance, she took off the gown she had worn all night and as soon as a maid had brought water, performed her ablutions and dressed. It was only when she picked up a hair brush that she caught a glimpse of herself in the mirror. The blanched and drawn face was that of a stranger.

Aghast, she stared at the image. She could not possibly go to Archer Hall looking like tragedy personified.

She pinched her cheeks but gained only some odd-looking marks. A vigorous scrub with cold water proved more beneficial, and when she had dressed her hair in a top knot and coaxed thick strands to fall softly curling to her shoulders, she felt she might be able to face Stanmore—after she had practiced a smile.

A tap on the door made her whirl. She forced a smile an instant before Felicity peeked into the room.

"Good! You're up." Still in nightgown and wrapper, Felicity entered. As she approached Thea, she started to frown. "You look different."

"My hair. Do you like it?"

"You know I do. It's how you wore it at my wedding ball. But that's not what I mean. You're smiling, but there's a look in your eyes . . . I don't even know how to describe it."

"Never mind then."

Afraid that her eyes betrayed her misery, Thea turned from Felicity and went to the night table to fetch the Archer Hall ledger. But, the ledger wasn't there.

"Felicity, when is the carriage coming for the children? I mean to go with them to Archer Hall."

"At eight, I should think. When Robert leaves. Thea—what happened yesterday? You were a long time with Stuart."

Thea sighed inaudibly. She could play the game of pretending not to understand. But she was not in a playful mood, and in the end Felicity's perseverance would wear her down anyway. And at least she had been spared an interrogation the previous evening, while she was in an agony of indecision.

Slowly, she faced her friend again. "As you suggested weeks ago, I told Stanmore about myself."

"Then he proposed!" Felicity turned pink with excitement.

"No! Nothing like that."

How quick she was with a denial even if she would never forget what he said . . . that he was courting her because he loved her. Because he wanted to marry her.

Felicity narrowed her eyes. "If Stuart did not propose or didn't at least give you to understand that he was about to do so, why then did you tell him about yourself? Or did you not mention that preposterous marriage?"

"I did. Felicity, we shall talk tonight. I must go if I don't want to miss the carriage."

"Rubbish! It's barely seven. Thea, what is it that you're not telling me?"

"There is nothing else to tell."

"When will you go to the Foreign Office? You'll see, now that you have Stuart on your side, you'll be out of that tangle in no time at all."

Thea felt cornered by Felicity's expectant look. If told the true state of affairs, Felicity would give her no peace but would argue and cajole and—not for the first time—call her a pawn in the struggle for dominion on the Continent. And Thea did not think she could face an argument now.

Pulling her bandbox from beneath a chair and searching it, she said, "I cannot find the ledger I brought from Archer Hall. I thought I might have packed it, but I did not. Did I leave it downstairs?"

"A pox on the ledger!" Felicity pushed the bandbox back under the chair. "What I want to know is, when will you and Stuart marry?"

Thea's calm snapped. "On the twenty-second of June!"

Felicity's mouth dropped. "But Thea! Surely not on that

date! Oh, I knew I should have followed you upstairs last night! But Mother Markham wanted me to go with her to the nursery and look at John's baby things. I shall speak with Stuart. He cannot have agreed—"

"Felicity, stop!"

Horrified by what she had done, and not understanding how she could have been so foolish, or how such a contrary retort even entered her mind, Thea searched for words.

"Lud! I don't know what possessed me—some evil spirit prompting me—"

The bedroom door flew open and into the chamber tumbled Bella, landing on hands and knees. Thea and Felicity stared, then moved as one, hurrying to the child. But before they reached her, Bella had scrambled to her feet.

"I'm sorry I intruded." She turned large reproachful eyes on Felicity. "You must not have shut the door properly. And now I've hurt my hand."

"Let me see."

Striving for calm, Thea stood by while Felicity gently examined the small hand held out to her. When she touched the wrist, Bella winced.

Felicity said, "You may have a sprain. I'll wrap it for you, but when you get home you must show it to Nurse. She'll rub a liniment on it, and that'll make you feel better."

"Silas will do it. He uses goose fat." Bella wrinkled her nose. "It smells nasty."

"If a nasty smell is all the punishment you'll suffer for eavesdropping, you may count yourself lucky." Felicity drew the child close. "You were listening at the door, were you not?"

Smiling her imp's smile, Bella turned to Thea.

"Now I know why you hugged Papa. Because you're going to marry him!"

Sixteen

In the muniment room at Archer Hall, Thea sat motionless at her desk. She had found the missing ledger before she left Ravensbrook in Lady Ravensbrook's sitting room, where she had set it down when Oxton announced Stanmore, but the book lay unopened before her.

Footsteps on the stairs sent her heart racing—until she heard the soft whistle. A moment later, Silas Wilkins emerged from the stairwell. As on most mornings, he was dressed for riding.

He flashed a cheerful grin. "So you're going to be a June bride, like my Elspeth. My felicitations, ma'am. You couldn't have picked a better man than our lad."

She made a strangled sound that could have been a sob or a choke of laughter and put her head on the desk, her face hidden in the crook of her arm.

Silas, apparently, did not doubt that he had heard a sob, for almost immediately she felt the comforting touch of a large hand on her shoulder.

"There now." His voice was low and soothing. "If it's the megrim's you're feeling, that's not unusual. Or so I'm told by my Elspeth. Though she puts it down to a long betrothal. Four years it's been for us, but you and the lad cannot have been pledged for more than a day. So why are you blue-deviled?"

Thea raised her head and saw Silas occupying the corner of her desk where Stanmore had perched the afternoon he told her that he was courting her only three days ago, yet it seemed like three months.

"You're mistaken, Silas. Lord Stanmore and I have no plans to get married."

"Trying to keep it a secret, Miss Stone? In that case you shouldn't have told our little Miss Butterfly."

"I was afraid you heard it from Bella. But it was a misunderstanding. I explained . . ."

Thea fell silent. She had indeed tried to explain to the child—and to Felicity—that she had blurted out the date in a moment of aberration from her usual good sense. But she had known even then that Bella did not understand. Or did not want to understand. And Felicity had looked quite maddeningly knowing and smug. But at least she had promised not to badger Thea any longer on the subject of marriage.

"I made a mistake, Silas."

He rose. Gone was his amiable smile. "Then, perhaps, you'll have the goodness to explain to me as well."

Her eyes widened. Even in his capacity as Stanmore's friend, Silas was overstepping himself.

"I believe it will be best if Lord Stanmore explains it to you."

"If you're playing fast and loose with the lad's affections, you'll have me to reckon with."

Quietly, she said, "Don't be insolent."

For a moment they measured each other, Silas scowling and looking precisely the kind of dangerous mammoth one would not wish to encounter alone, and Thea returning his belligerent stare with calm authority.

Silas's eyes fell.

"I'm worried," he said gruffly. "He's in love, and no doubt about it. And when a man falls in love for the first time when he's past thirty, he falls hard."

"Apology accepted."

He gave her a look of surprise and grudging admiration. " 'Twas indeed meant as an apology, but not many would have taken it as such."

"I'm not blind to your concern for him, but all I am prepared to tell you is that I made a grievous, stupid mistake when I mentioned a wedding date. It was meant for Lady Felicity's ear alone—" She made a moue of distaste. "It was a result of losing my calm. There is no excuse for it."

He started for the stairwell but turned back after a few steps, no longer angry, just the old familiar Silas with his amiable, open look and an air of assurance.

"I could've sworn—and I'm still ready to wager my blunt—that you're just as taken with him as he's with you."

She said nothing.

Silas searched her face. "And so you are."

"Silas, I have work to do." She opened the ledger at random.

"Meaning no disrespect, but why no wedding date? We all know he rode out yesterday to ask you. Couldn't help but knowing, could we? Not with my lord Barnet shouting and a'carrying on as if the lad meant to marry another like the Lady Charlotte. And *she* was chosen by my lord Barnet himself."

"Meaning no disrespect, Silas, but I wish to be left alone."

"Shouldn't be alone when the blue devils are eating at you. Talk to me, lass. Don't order me from the room." His eyes were kind. "You caught me off guard with that haughty look once, but I doubt I'll dance to your tune a second time. So you may as well make the most of my company now. Later you can see to it that I'm dismissed."

"Without a reference." She gave him a quirky smile.

"That's better."

For a long moment, silence reigned.

Thea closed the ledger. "Where is Lord Stanmore now?"

"He'll have gone to the apiary. Seems some of the bees have taken it into their heads to swarm when they shouldn't."

She recalled Stanmore's teasing to pay her out of the candle money. She had only half believed him when he said that candles were made at Archer Hall.

Silas asked, "Do you want me to fetch him?"

"No—there's no need. I'll be here all day. Silas, will you tell me something?"

"For instance?"

"What happened four years ago?"

It was his turn to be silent.

"Lord Stanmore said you saved his children from drowning . . . but who would have been so careless and let them wander off? The pond is quite far from the house, and Bella was only two."

Brow knitted in a deep frown, Silas strode to the east window. He stood there, all but blocking the light with his large frame as he looked out over the grounds toward the pond in the distance.

"If you know that much, I suppose you may as well hear the rest. For I doubt Stanmore would bring it up." Silas turned. "The children were with their mother that morning. She had taken them to the gazebo by the pond."

"A gazebo? I did not know there was one. And I can see the pond clearly from up here."

"Aye, until the trees leaf out. But even if you went down to the pond, you wouldn't find the gazebo now. Stanmore had it torn down. And he had the pond cleared of the water lilies, foolish, useless things Lady Charlotte insisted on having."

Once more, he looked out the window, then, with a firm tread, returned to Thea. She waved him to a chair, but he declined with a shake of his head.

"Lady Charlotte used the gazebo as a trysting place. And she used the children to hide her treachery from Stanmore. From us all. No one caught on until the accident."

Thea felt cold as she listened to Silas's expressionless voice.

"Seems she was letting the little ones play in one of the rowboats tied up near the foot bridge. But one day Bella started to cry. Charlie somehow got her out of the boat, and they appeared at the gazebo and called for their mama at an inopportune moment. And so the next time she met her lover, she set them adrift."

"Impossible!" Thea's voice shook. "She couldn't have! They were babies!"

"She'd do anything to get her way. There were two more boats, and no doubt she meant to row out later and fetch them. But Bella reached for a butterfly on one of those damned lilies. And the boat capsized."

Thea's hands clenched. No wonder Stanmore could not bear to recall the incident. "Thank God you were nearby!"

Silas nodded soberly. "Charlie wouldn't talk until he saw his father—Stanmore had been summoned by my lord Barnet's aunts, and it took several hours to fetch him back. But when I heard all that happened before I got to the pond—upon my oath! I would have strangled the woman if she hadn't run away to her parents by then."

And by the look on his face, Thea knew that he would indeed have done so.

Silas thrust his hands into his coat pockets. "Charlie could swim and got hold of the boat and hung on, just as he'd been taught. But Bella was trapped by the water lilies. Charlie tried to rescue her, but he couldn't hold the boat and his sister at the same time. So he let go of the boat."

"They must have cried out! Didn't their mother or her lover hear them?"

"They did. When I got there, *she* was lying in a swoon on the foot bridge, but her paramour had gone in after the children. The pond is deep, though not very large. But when you're my size, hardly anything seems large. And the Frenchman couldn't swim. *He* would have done more good if he had taken the time to untie one of the other boats. But he didn't. He made matters worse for the children with his thrashing and kicking."

Thea rubbed her arms. Something in Silas's voice made her shiver.

He circled the desk once, the sound of his boots loud and angry in the quiet room.

"I didn't have time to untie a boat, but I'm a strong swimmer. I plucked Bella out of the lilies and told Charlie to hang on to my neck. He was quite tuckered out by then, poor little lad. I shoved the boat to the Frenchman and got the children out of the water."

Silas frowned at the cluttered surface of Thea's desk. She was sure he did not see the jumble of books, or the blotter with the spatter of ink stains, but was reliving the scene at the pond four years ago.

"It was summer," he said. "But with the pond being deep, and shaded most of the day, the water is always cold. Both children looked blue when I had them on the bank. I held Bella upside down and slapped her back. Startled her so much, she coughed up the water she'd swallowed. And, bless her, by the time I wrapped her and Charlie in my coat, she was right as rain."

"And the Frenchman?"

Once more his footsteps were the only sounds as he took a turn about the room.

He faced her. "Dead by the time I got to him. Seems he wasn't able to reach the boat."

Thea did not realize she had held her breath until the pressure in her chest forced her to exhale. She met Silas's gaze, clear and guileless as a child's.

He said, "Now I've told you all I'm prepared to tell. If there's anything else you want to know, you must ask his lordship."

She was still looking at him, and his gaze did not waver.

"Thank you, Silas."

He nodded. "Do you feel better now? It always helps when you can take your mind off your own troubles for a while, doesn't it?"

"Yes," she said, surprised that it was indeed so. She did feel better—and if it was a question of occupying the mind, hers would be busy for some time to come, wondering about Silas and the Frenchman.

He pointed to the ledger in front of her. "If you're done with that one, I'll put it up for you."

"No, I have barely started." She remembered the payment in January, 1617, for a dozen oak pews, and gave Silas a considering look. "There is something you could do, though. You could tell me, or better yet show me, where the chapel is."

He raised a brow. "Are you asking me because Stanmore told you to leave it be?"

"Of course not. I've mentioned the chapel to him, but there simply hasn't been time to see it yet."

Silas cocked his head, listening. "Then you can see it now. With *him*."

His hearing, apparently, was keener than hers. But now she heard it, too—the firm yet light step that was Stanmore's.

A moment later, his dark head appeared at the top of the stairwell, and then he pushed through the gate and came striding toward her, his face alight with joy.

"Thea! They told me you were here, but I scarcely dared hope it was true. And," he added without conviction, "you shouldn't be."

And all she could do was smile at him.

"I'll be off," said Silas. "Miss Stone is wishful of seeing the chapel, and I daresay you'd rather show her yourself. Eh, lad?"

He received no reply and departed, whistling softly.

Stanmore held out his hand to Thea. Without hesitation, without so much as a single thought, or even a partial thought, for the agonies of her third sleepless night and the painful decision she had wrought at dawn, she accepted his hand and allowed him to draw her to her feet.

The next moment they were in each other's arms. The kiss was promise, avowal of love. It was remembrance and discovery. It was a flame lit in days of yore, burning bright, never to darken.

Still embracing, they gazed at each other, secure in their

love. No words were needed. Their hearts and souls reflected in their eyes.

Time stood still in the muniment room, but nowhere else. The sun moved imperceptibly, and one of the rays hit the glass dome atop the lectern. It bounced off in a bright flash of light that even the lovers could not miss.

They turned their heads, and although they immediately sought each other's eyes again, the spell woven by love and innate knowledge of the other's heart was broken. Once more, words became important.

"Thea, promise me—"

"Don't ask for promises." Still feeling the glow of pure happiness, she smiled at him. "If Bella said—"

"*Bella!* I believe we are at cross-purposes, my dear. I haven't seen the little minx this morning, nor, much as I adore her, do I intend to see her until I've spent considerably more time with you. But if she has been naughty again, I promise to take her to task. Later."

"You misunderstand. If reprimand is due, it is due me."

"Indeed?" His hands caressed her back. "But even for you, it must wait till later. There are more important things I want to address now."

"Just don't make me promise anything. I am too happy—what a poor word that is! I am too blissfully happy to know what I would be promising. And is it not strange to be happy when I know my work here will be done in a matter of days and I shan't see you again?"

"In your heart you know we belong together. You know I won't let you go."

"We have no choice. I am bound by my word."

"To what purpose? So that you can some day return to Hochstein and demand that Tushenko leave this other woman . . . this Erika . . . and take you as his wife?" His arms tightened around her. "Thea, you cannot possibly want that."

"I have an obligation, a responsibility, to Hochstein." The

words sounded pompous and hollow in her ears. And they were hollow, for even as she spoke them, she clung to him wanting never to let go.

"This is nonsense, Thea. Your parents took you away when you were four years old. Any obligation you had to Hochstein by accident of your birth ceased when your father's people did not lift a finger against Friedrich. And when Tushenko took your cousin to wife, did they cry shame? Did the clergy of Hochstein raise a protest against bigamy?"

"They believe I am dead. As does Tushenko."

"Dead! How very convenient."

She gave him a wry look. "And how *conveniently* I forget that I have no right to delight in the feel of your arms."

"That is not at all the same thing."

"Is it not? Lud! When I'm with you, I no longer know what is right or wrong. I came to tell you that annulment is impossible, and instead I cling to you and kiss you."

"Thea—" His voice was husky. "Do you love me?"

She looked into the dark, compelling eyes. "I love you."

She wanted to say more, warn him that love did not change the situation, but his mouth claimed hers in a kiss that made her blood race and pushed all thought of caution to the back of her mind.

Breathless, he said, "Then nothing is impossible. We'll petition the courts and parliament and the archbishop and—"

"The archbishop cannot help. Hochstein is Catholic."

If she sought to nonplus him, she did not succeed. He smiled.

"A Catholic German princess, raised in France and England—in an English parsonage, no less. What an eclectic upbringing you've had. But never mind. If your foster father and our courts cannot help, we'll write the pope."

"Stanmore, he's a prisoner. Besides, it's the Hochstein Council to whom I must apply. And that is quite impossible—"

He silenced her by brushing a fingertip against her mouth. "Don't say it's impossible. For now, just promise to think about it. I'll be going to London early next week to interview governesses. Come with me, Thea. See Lord Wellesley. You gave your word five years ago. Much has happened on the Continent since then."

"There's a wind of change blowing. That's what Lord Wellesley said in January. He seemed to think I'd be needed in Hochstein at any moment. But so did his predecessors."

"See! And you're still in England."

She stepped out of the shelter of his arms. "What is happening to me? I no longer know my own mind."

"You know your heart."

She did not answer.

"But you still feel bound by obligation and responsibility. Thea, think what would happen if you were to return to Hochstein and claim Tushenko as your husband."

She turned abruptly and went to the window where, earlier, Silas had looked out to the pond. In the painful examination of her conscience she had not considered the personal aspects of her commitment. Her wifely duties.

Perhaps that was not so very astonishing. She did not know the man to whom she had been pledged, had no recollection even of the fifteen-year-old boy who accepted her hand in the audience chamber of Castle Hochstein.

Or did she? She recalled the flash of memory when she stepped into Archer Hall's great hall for the first time. She had remembered sitting on a cushion at her parents' feet in the great hall of her old home. There had been music and singing . . . a juggling act . . . a pantomime. And at her side, a tall, sullen-looking youth . . .

Stanmore said, "I know what havoc an arranged marriage can wreak in two people's lives. I married to oblige my father. It was my duty to ensure the continuation of the name and, as was tradition, he had already chosen my bride. Charlotte had been engaged to be married at seventeen but was jilted when her father made imprudent investments. She accepted me to escape penury. There was no love in our marriage. Only misery."

Thea did not move from her position at the window. From a distance the pond looked gray. Dark gray with streaks of silver where sunlight, dipping through still bare branches of tall beeches and massive oaks, touched the water. 'Twould make a cool, shady retreat on a sweltering summer day. Now it was cold, unwelcoming.

She turned, sensing Stanmore's presence close behind her even though she had not heard him move.

"Thea—" He did not touch her, but his voice was a caress. "I've found love at last. You're mine. I won't give you up."

With a tremulous smile she took a step toward him, straight into his arms. She could not speak, could only show him her love by holding him close.

Then, sudden apprehension—startling and chilling in its intensity.

"You're mine. I won't give you up."

'Twas a vow made to her in the past. By her lover.

A month later, he was buried . . . taking their love into the grave.

Seventeen

"Thea, what is it?"

She became aware of Stanmore's concerned look.

"The vow . . . the words you used . . ."

She fell silent. The moment of apprehension had passed. Like a hazy dream, forgotten upon waking, the cause of her uneasiness had left only the vaguest of impressions. She knew she had been apprehensive, but could not think why.

Stanmore said, "If I frightened you, I am sorry. 'Twas not my intent."

"No. I'm being foolish. And that is nothing new these past days. If I once took pride in my calm good sense, I must now claim superiority in foolishness."

"If that refers to loving me, then be as foolish as you like."

He cupped her face in his hands. "But must love turn you pale as a ghost? You look paper-white, as you did outside my father's room when you felt light-headed. Or so you said."

He stepped back. "Thea, what happened that day? How did you know about the measles before Dr. Sellers made his report?"

She hesitated, but only briefly. She trusted him. Trusted him not to laugh or call her a sorceress.

"I *saw* the physician and your father inside the room. Higgins, too. And I *heard* Dr. Sellers speak to your father."

He looked at her and shook his head. " 'Tis impossible."

She did not argue.

"Or is it?" He, too, turned a little paler. "Do you have what the Scots call the sight?"

"The sight—" She thought of Angus Comyn, the Scottish parson, who admitted to having the sight.

"I don't know, Stanmore. Whatever it is, I did not have it until I came to Archer Hall. I know I have peculiar . . . gifts. I told you about a sensitivity to moods and atmosphere. Not that I can draw on it at will—indeed, I considered it the weaker of my gifts. But I wonder. Perhaps I misunderstood the purpose of that sensitivity."

"You said gifts. Plural."

"The other gift is dreams. But that is all I claim. An occasional extraordinary perceptiveness, and the ability to see in dreams what happened in the past. Anything else I experienced here has never happened to me before. There's something about Archer Hall—"

He held up a hand. "Wait. The dreams. What about them? Will you explain?"

"I will try."

"Please sit down. You still look on the brink of a swoon."

She sat at her desk, turning the chair so she faced Stanmore, who pulled up a second chair. Having once decided to take him into her confidence, she did not yield to last-moment doubts. Concise and to the point, she described the dreams she'd had since her first visit to Hardwick Hall as a ten-year-old.

Dreams concerning Arbella Stuart as a favorite at James's new court . . . Arbella's gradual fall from grace as she demanded marriage, and rumors circulated again, as in Elizabeth's reign, about Catholic plots to crown her Queen of England and Scotland . . . her secret marriage to William Seymour . . . confinement at Lambeth with stolen visits from Seymour, rowing up the Thames from the Tower . . . Arbella weak and ill and miserable at Barnet . . . bidding farewell to her child.

And the last dream with Arbella's son sitting by the hearth

in a whitewashed room, and the young couple gazing at each other.

Stanmore stared at her.

"You don't believe me." She smiled ruefully. "I hoped you would, since you seemed to believe that your cousin's mother-in-law has the gift to see the past."

"No, you misunderstood. I was intrigued. That's why I mentioned Lady Glendale to you. Now I'm not sure what to believe. But I'm beginning to understand why you're enthralled by Arbella's history."

For a moment he sat lost in thought, and she did not disturb him.

"Thea . . . you said that when you dream, you feel as if you lived the dream? As if you were a part of the past?"

"Yes, although I don't think it was the case right at first. But during that June when I turned sixteen and my foster father and Vespera Simmons took me to London to meet with the Foreign Secretary and Tushenko's representative, we also explored the sites where Arbella had stayed or visited. I cannot help but think that walking where she had walked, standing where she had stood, made the difference."

"But that also applies to Hardwick Hall."

"I never dreamed about the time Arbella lived at Hardwick Hall, though. That was where she had pined for London and court life during Elizabeth's reign. The dreams showed Arbella after James's accession."

"Everything has changed. The palaces—Whitehall and Greenwich, Richmond, Somerset House—were all at one time or another rebuilt."

"But the grounds are the same, and very often the outer structure. I also visited the Tower. The rooms where Arbella was confined—in the Bell Tower, and in the Lieutenant's Lodgings—those have not changed."

He had listened intently and now leaned forward. "Thea, you are still convinced that my forebear, William Seymour Archer, was Arbella's son. Are you not?"

"More than ever after reading the chronicles. Despite the fact that they were not begun until after Arbella's death."

"But what about that last dream? The visit from a young couple when the boy was older? No such visit is mentioned in the chronicles."

"I know."

She rose and went to the lectern with the first volume of the chronicles beneath its glass cover. She did not remove the book; only looked at it.

She said, "In here are references to 'an esteemed young lady who was promised anonymity' and who visited the child repeatedly for the first two years. Once, this visitor brought another lady with her. And this second woman, 'highborn and attended by four servants,' returned frequently until Archer Hall was built."

Thea turned. "I do wish the two women had been named."

"Could the girl in your dream be the 'esteemed young lady who was promised anonymity'?"

"Reason tells me that it must be so." She smiled. "Or do you think the secret would have been preserved if more than one young lady visited the Archer farmstead or Edward Archer's cottage? Supposing, of course, that the child was indeed Arbella's."

He came toward her. " 'Your ancestress, Dorothea Wortley, was young."

"And devoted to Arbella." She hesitated. "Dorothea married in the spring of 1613 and left for Hochstein. That would explain why the young lady in the chronicles visited only during the first two years of the child's life. And I'm sure the girl in the dream when Arbella kissed her son good-bye was Dorothea. There was no one else that young among Arbella's companions."

"There was certainly no young man in Arbella's entourage. The stewart, the gentleman usher, the personal physician, none of them was young."

"The young man in that last dream looked like Henry, Prince of Wales."

Stanmore raised a brow. "Henry withdrew his friendship after Arbella's escape. And he died in November of 1612, when the child was barely eighteen months old."

"The child in the dream was no older than that, perhaps younger. But you're right. It makes no sense for Henry to have been in the Archer farmhouse or in Edward's cottage with Dorothea."

"If it were possible for you to visit the cottage, do you think it would inspire you to sense, or see, or dream more about the past?"

"Perhaps. That is why I said I may have mistaken the purpose of my sensitivity. Since coming here—" Her eyes widened. "Are you saying the cottage still stands?"

"I believe Silas said you want to see the chapel." His smile showed a trace of his daughter's impishness. "Come, I'll show it to you."

A tremor of excitement ran through her. "The cottage and the chapel are one and the same!"

"You'll find the reference at the beginning of that ledger on your desk. At Edward Archer's insistence, the architect designed Archer Hall's west wing around the cottage."

"But I read the entries through March of 1617 just yesterday at Ravensbrook. I remember only a payment for a dozen oak pews."

"Your prodigious memory has let you down. The information is there, on one of the first few pages. Could it be—" A gleam lit in his eyes, but he said no more.

He did not need to. She knew, better than he, that her mind had been filled with thoughts of him and daydreams of a love that must not be.

"The ledger," he said, "also gives a description of Edward's cottage before it was transformed into a chapel. And since the transformation consisted of nothing more than the substitution of pews for settle, table, and bed, and the addition of an altar in front of the fireplace, you won't have any difficulty imagining what the room looked like when Edward Archer lived there."

"I saw the cottage in my dreams."

Again she thought of Angus Comyn and how he had explained his gift, the sight.

"Stanmore, let us go to the chapel. At once. Someone I met this past winter in Inverness-shire explained the sight to me as an aura . . . the effluvia of events to come, pouring from living beings as well as inanimate objects. I started to dream after visiting Hardwick Hall. Surely then it is logical that there are also effluvia of past events. And my mind is susceptible to those emanations!"

He raised a quizzing brow. "You speak of logic in the same breath as the sight and dreams?"

"Don't . . . please don't jest about it."

"No. But, Thea—neither would it be wise to let dreams become an obsession."

"I fear you caution me too late. I feel too close to Arbella, her fate, not to wish to force more dreams."

"Your fate need not be to lose your love, like Arbella." His eyes held her captive. "There is no King James to forbid our marriage."

"Must we argue my marriage again?" She kept her voice light. "You once said you hoped we would be friends. Now I say let us be friends. At least for the week or so that I will need to complete a study of the ledgers."

He did not reply but frowned at her in an absent manner. Not for the first time, she wished that she could command perceptiveness at will and know his mind. But all she was aware of was her own mounting anxiety as she waited for his answer.

"Thea—if you expect friendship to mean that I will stop loving you, then, no, it cannot be. I am determined to win you."

Heady words, making her heart race. But reason prevailed.

She shook her head. "You shall not wear me down with arguments. If that is your aim, I cannot stay to complete my work."

"You misunderstand. I do promise not to argue. 'Tis courtship I will not give up."

She turned away, facing the lectern. "This is madness."

"Madness would be to let you go. Thea, I am two-and-thirty and have found love at last. I won't give you up."

"And I am going on six-and-twenty. I'm not a green girl—"

He interrupted. "You're five-and-twenty. Still in the spring of life."

"But not so green that I cannot see the pitfalls in the course of action you propose."

She heard him step closer but had no time to turn before he closed his arms around her, drawing her against him. It felt so right, so natural, that she made no move to pull away but rested the back of her head against his shoulder.

"I love you, Thea. I shan't let you come to harm. That, too, I promise."

But the harm was done. She had fallen in love.

Wanting to stay where she was, held in his arms, she yet pulled away. "Shall we go, then? To the chapel?"

"Historian, first and foremost." He gave her a quizzical smile. "You did warn me, did you not?"

"I did. But I fear that this morning I neglected my duties sadly. Now I'm determined that I must, at least, see Edward's cottage."

"Very well. I shan't argue, and I shan't press you."

He retrieved her shawl from the chair at her desk. "You will need this. The chapel hasn't been used in twenty years."

"And I wish you would tell me why. And also why Bella and Charlie don't know about it. Felicity mentioned rumors of ghosts and an accident but knew nothing specific."

"The tale of ghosts was started by a maid when she tripped and fell after she scared herself witless by imagining voices in the locked chapel. My father soon put a stop to that nonsense. But it's not the reason why the chapel hasn't been used."

"Nor would ghosts have to be kept from Charlie and Bella. What happened twenty years ago? Or mustn't I be told?"

"I'll tell you what I know. But only three people could say what truly happened that day. And all three were killed in the chapel."

She gave him a startled look. Nothing she had read about the Archer family had prepared her for this.

Opening the gate to the stairwell, Stanmore preceded Thea down the steep, narrow steps. "Some day Charlie and Bella will have to be told. But when? And how much must I tell them?"

"Vespera Simmons always says that children are not the delicate creatures parents believe them to be."

"Your Miss Simmons sounds like a sensible lady. Perhaps she will advise me when she arrives."

"I hope it is soon."

He stopped and turned so abruptly that she all but fell into his arms.

Catching her, he held her close. "I'm of a mind to fetch her myself so I can have you back at Archer Hall for good."

Thea permitted herself to relax against him. A moment's delight. An instant of pretense that love was all that mattered. Surely that was not so very wrong.

It was Stanmore who ended the embrace. He assisted her down the last steps, and they emerged from the stairwell in the wall into the room that used to be his bedchamber.

He said, "Twenty years ago, my father's brother occupied these rooms. He was considerably younger than my father, who was forty-one then. Francis Archer was only twenty-two. My grandfather was alive, as was my father's second wife. We also had a chaplain, Dr. Henley. A widower with a sixteen-year-old daughter."

"And Francis fell in love with Dr. Henley's daughter?" Thea hazarded.

"He wanted to marry Serena Henley. My grandfather forbade the match."

"Why? Your uncle was not the heir. And a chaplain's daughter is not precisely ineligible."

"Miss Henley was not a suitable bride for an Archer. Every Archer male, younger son or elder, must marry as if he were the heir. Since you're familiar with our genealogy you know that we never had an abundance of males who survived past childhood. I am the youngest of four sons, yet I will inherit."

They proceeded to the main staircase of the west wing.

"Francis and Serena met secretly. One day, my grandfather discovered them. In the chapel."

Thea shivered. Three people died there. . . .

Stanmore offered his arm, and she took it. The stairs were wide enough for three or four abreast, and she felt in need of support as images formed in her mind.

Three people died. Stanmore did not need to name them. She knew they were his grandfather, his uncle, and Miss Serena Henley.

In her mind, Thea saw a stark white room, oak pews, a square table draped with altar cloth and bearing a cross. Behind the altar table, a fireplace with a crude wood mantel, and on either side a collection of guns, pistols, and swords affixed to the wall.

Between altar and fireplace, Thea saw a young girl in a white muslin gown over a billowing skirt of lavender satin clinging to a young man's arm. She saw the sword in the young man's hand, saw him trying to shake the girl off at the approach of another, older man, whose iron-gray hair was tied in a queue and lightly powdered.

Thea heard Stanmore saying, "We don't know precisely what happened. A footman started toward the chapel when he heard my grandfather shout. But he hesitated when he realized the shouts were invectives directed at Serena Henley and that Francis was there as well, just as furious as his father.

Thea saw the young man, Francis, thrust Serena aside. The

girl stumbled against the altar, caught her balance and, just as the older man snatched a sword off the wall and Francis, face contorted with rage, raised his own weapon against his father, flung herself between the two men.

And the bodice of Serena's white gown turned crimson around the point of Francis Archer's sword.

Stanmore said, "The footman was still in the great hall when he heard Serena scream. He took fright and ran to fetch my father from the east wing. I was with him and followed to the chapel. My grandfather and uncle were both dead, clearly by each other's hand. Serena was breathing but unconscious. She died before her father and a physician could be sent for."

Thea saw no more of what happened in the chapel twenty years earlier. She was suddenly aware of an odd warmth stealing over her, the same inexplicable burning sensation that had twice overcome her at the foot of the gallery stairs.

She realized that they had reached the ground floor of the west wing. In front of them was the hallway pointing north from the stairway. On their right was the corridor leading into the great hall and to the gallery stairs—not a great distance from where they stood now.

They entered the north hallway with the estate office on their left, and on the right, the study, conscientiously pointed out by Charlie and Bella during the tour of Archer Hall but not shown. It was one of their father's private rooms, they had explained.

Stanmore stopped at the study door.

"Archer pride and Archer tradition were the cause of the tragedy," he said with the touch of bitterness that always colored his voice when he spoke of family tradition. "Serena Henley was not of a noble line, and my grandfather was obsessed with the idea that Archer blood—synonymous with Stuart and Tudor blood—must remain untainted. He killed a young woman and his own son rather than see them married and beget children unworthy of the Archer name."

"No, you're wrong!" The sensation of warmth was distracting, but she could not let the misconception stand. "Your grandfather did not kill Serena. Francis did. He did not mean to do it. He raised his sword against his father, but Serena stepped between them."

Stanmore had been about to open the study door. He turned, frowning.

"I saw them, Stanmore."

As on a previous occasion, she was aware of a disquiet, a restlessness, something drawing her, urging her to do something, though she did not have the slightest notion what that something should be. She wanted to run—not from whatever force it was that tugged at her, but toward it, and that seemed to be inside the study.

It might have been a rather frightening feeling, that irresistible draw, but Stanmore's presence, the solid strength of his arm beneath her hand, kept fear at bay. For reassurance, she clutched the cloth of his coat sleeve.

"Thea, your hand is burning hot."

"I'm sorry." She loosened her grip. "Where is the chapel? Are the swords and pistols still there, beside the fireplace?"

He looked at her strangely.

"The weapons are there. My stepmother and Dr. Henley urged my father to have them taken down. But he would not break with tradition. But, Thea—that custom, the placing of a favorite gun and sword in the chapel when an Earl Barnet dies, is not written anywhere."

"No, and I wondered why weapons were kept in a chapel. It struck me as odd. But then, the chapel itself, hidden away, is rather odd."

Again he frowned at her, and she noticed that he looked hot and uncomfortable.

"I'm not sure we should see the chapel now. Thea, you look flushed with fever. Could you have caught the measles?"

"Nonsense. But you—"

Suddenly, Silas's voice filled the hallway as he appeared from the direction of the great hall.

"I figured I'd catch you hereabouts. There's a lady arrived

for you, Miss Stone. And since that fool of a footman made her wait while he's looking who knows where for you, I thought I'd point her in the right direction."

Thea's breath caught. The woman coming toward her was a most welcome and familiar sight with her warm smile, flame-red hair still untouched by gray piled beneath a wide-brimmed black hat, and trim figure shown to advantage in a pomona-green traveling gown and black spencer.

"Vespera!"

And as she flew toward her dear friend and confidante, the strange warmth, the force tugging at her mind and will, were gone. Instantly, without a trace that they had ever been.

Eighteen

When hugs had been exchanged and Stanmore introduced, Thea took her former governess to the chamber previously occupied by Felicity. Declining the services of a maid, Vespera Simmons started to unpack her trunk and two large portmanteaux while delivering the many loving messages sent to Thea by the Simmons family.

Of Thea's eight foster siblings all but Miles, the youngest, were married and lived close enough to visit the vicarage frequently if not daily. As their children outgrew infancy, the vicarage garden and the attics once more became highly favored playgrounds. But even when inclement weather made visiting impossible, the vicarage was never quiet since Mrs. Simmons had opened her heart and home to girls who found themselves with child and disowned by their families.

"I might have been here sooner," said Vespera, shaking out a gown in her favorite shade, moss-green, before hanging it in the armoire. "Unfortunately, five of the seven girls staying with us at present are of good birth and, therefore, incapable of performing the simplest chore without supervision."

"You should not have come at all." Thea looked up from the portmanteau she had opened. "I have missed you and wished for your arrival, but Mother Simmons needs you more than I do."

"Mary's wrist and ankle are mending nicely, and under ordinary circumstances I wouldn't have hesitated to leave a week ago."

Thea had been about to set a stack of handkerchieves into a drawer. She turned sharply.

"Something else happened. What is it? Father Simmons is ill! Is that it?"

"Felix did have a touch of bronchitis. But he, too, is well on the mend." Vespera took the handkerchieves from Thea, put them away, and briskly shut the drawer.

She met Thea's anxious look. "Miles came home last Monday."

Captain Miles Simmons, closest to Thea in age, was serving in Portugal, in the 52nd regiment of General Craufurd's Light Division. He was not due a furlough for another eight months.

Thea's mouth was dry. "How badly is he hurt?"

"He'll live. Lost a hand, though, in one of those minor skirmishes he was always writing about. Then, in hospital in Lisbon, they had some kind of fever epidemic. He looks like a scarecrow, but he says he's in fine fettle. They sent him home to be fattened. And, of course, to learn to shoot and to wield his saber with the left hand."

"He'll do it, too." Thea's smile was shaky, but a few deep breaths restored her composure. "You've always had a knack for conveying bad news in such a manner that my worst fears were allayed by the time you stopped speaking. But his right hand! Vespera, I'm going home. Miles will need—"

"Whatever he needs, he's already receiving more than his share. Mary is fussing over him like a mother hen. And when Mary is resting, one of your sisters takes over."

"But none of them can stay for long. They have their own families."

"Gussy is staying. Her husband will be in Ireland for a month, and she moved herself and the children into the vicarage the day before Miles arrived. She couldn't have timed her visit better had she tried. The others take turns. And, of course, Mary's girls do what they can. It's amazing to see how our wounded hero inspires eagerness to perform simple chores previously spurned."

Having removed the last garment, Vespera closed the trunk lid.

Thea said, "You should have written."

"Naturally I would have done so if I'd had any doubts about leaving. However, Gussy has proven herself astonishingly deft at changing bandages and I'm not needed at all. And neither are you."

Thea gave a little choke of laughter. "Lud, it's good to have you here! I don't know what I missed more—your companionship, or the sting of your tongue."

"And now you have both." Vespera smiled. "Miles sends his love. But he says if you show up at the vicarage before he has mastered the art of being left-handed, he'll never challenge you to a shooting or fencing match again. Or to an archery contest. Tell me, do the Archers serve luncheon?"

"In about half an hour. But if Miles believes he can put me off with a threat, he is a looby. I'll wait if you think I should, but when I've finished here in a week or two, I'll be in Ault Hucknall."

"You may miss him, then. He's supposed to see a London physician soon and report at the Horse Guards. He plans to break the journey at Barnet and visit you here. Now tell me, Thea—no, wait!"

Vespera went to the dresser and opened the capacious tapestry bag she carried in lieu of a reticule when traveling.

"First let me give you this. From Lord Wellesley. Why did you not inform him where you'd be staying?"

"But I did." Accepting the letter, Thea broke the seal. "I wrote the notice when I merely suspected that I might be invited to Archer Hall just so I could be sure I wouldn't forget in the hustle of packing."

"Did you post it, though?"

"Dearest Vespera! What else would I do with a letter placed prominently on my desk for that very purpose?"

"You've been known to use letters as markers in books."

"I gave up that habit years ago."

Thea skimmed the message written in the Foreign Secretary's own hand, then read it again. Slowly, she sank onto the chaise longue at the foot of the bed.

"What is it?" A pair of shoes in her hand, Vespera gave Thea a sharp look. "Something happened at Hochstein, did it?"

"Cousin Friedrich is dead."

"Indeed! Good riddance, I say. What else does Wellesley write?"

"Erika declined to succeed her father. Her son is the new Prince von Hochstein."

"The one named after your great-grandmother?"

"You need not frown. Augusta von Waldfrieden is Erika's great-grandmother, too."

"I'm frowning because that child is only three years old."

"The Council appointed his father as regent."

"Tushenko as regent. *Well!*" Vespera looked at the shoes in her hand. "I suppose that means we have to pack a bag and post up to London immediately. Just when I thought I would not have to see the inside of a carriage for a while!"

"Lord Wellesley does want to see me, but not until the thirteenth . . . Tuesday, next week."

"In that case—" The shoes disappeared in the armoire to be lined up with a pair of slippers and a pair of half boots.

Thea folded the letter into a narrow strip. "Cousin Friedrich's death does not change *my* situation. I cannot fathom why Lord Wellesley is asking for a meeting."

"You *cannot?* For goodness' sake, Thea! Did you not read the papers?"

"I've had more important reading to do. Vespera—" A note of excitement crept into Thea's voice. "There's a room here at Archer Hall—the chapel, which was a cottage two hundred years ago. Arbella Stuart's son spent the first six years of his life there, and Arbella herself visited once."

"A cottage incorporated into the house? Well, I've heard stranger things." Retrieving a set of hair brushes from the tapestry bag, Vespera placed them on the dresser. "But, for the moment, pray take your mind off past history. Thea, I cannot believe you did not read the papers. At least *The Times!* It is not like you to show so little interest."

"Nothing in the papers could have been half as intriguing as the Archer chronicles." Thea smiled. "Besides, I knew I could rely on you to enlighten me."

Vespera poured water into the wash basin. "I assume you know that Napoleon made Tsar Alexander an offer for the hand of his sister? After all, that happened last November."

"Certainly. I read the news before I left Scotland. And when I arrived in London, the latest *on-dit* was that Napoleon also considered the Archduchess Marie-Louise as empress of France. But no matter whom he chooses, I doubt his second marriage will be any more valid than Tushenko's to Erika. Unless he can—"

"Napoleon has chosen." Having washed her hands, Vespera dried them briskly. "Early last month he withdrew his offer for the Grand Duchess Catherine. As it turns out, the tsar had already made his refusal known a day or two earlier, but that is neither here nor there. The point is that, valid or not, there will be a marriage between France and Austria."

Thea was silent, tucking the folded note from the Marquis Wellesley into her sleeve.

"Thea, don't you see? A rift between France and Russia provides an opportunity for a new alliance between Russia and England."

"Then it is to be hoped that Russia will prove more steadfast an ally than she was in the past."

Vespera looked pensively at Thea. "Tushenko is Russian. He is—or was, until he left St. Petersburg—a close friend of the tsar. The thought occurred to me that Lord Wellesley means to ask you to go to Hochstein."

The same had occurred to Thea. She had tried to dismiss the notion, but Vespera's words made that impossible.

"There's no point in speculating," she said quietly. "I shall know soon enough."

With a sharp look at her former pupil, Vespera Simmons sat down beside her.

"You will, indeed." She gave Thea a quick hug. "And now, I think, it is high time that you tell me why you look as if you hadn't slept in days."

Thea did not even consider prevarication. She had never been able to deceive the woman who had known her from her second year.

"Because I am in the worst tangle imaginable."

"Indeed."

"Vespera, I have fallen in love!"

Stanmore had just finished eating a hurried luncheon of bread, cold meats, and ale when Thea and Vespera Simmons entered the dining room.

He rose, noting with quick concern that Thea looked pale. But, perhaps, she only appeared pale beside Miss Simmons's flamboyant coloring. Earlier, in the muniment room, Thea had looked fine. Or did she? He had seen her eyes after their kiss, her smile, and had exulted in the love she no longer tried to deny. If there were also shadows beneath her eyes, quite possibly he did not notice.

He said, "I apologize that I did not wait for you and the baked sole Cook prepared for luncheon. Unfortunately, I must leave immediately."

Thea gave him a questioning look.

Vespera Simmons said, "I am sorry to hear it. I was looking forward to getting acquainted."

"As was I. But I assure you, the opportunity is merely postponed, not eliminated."

He seated the ladies, then alerted the kitchen with a tug of the tasseled cord dangling above the table near the earl's empty place.

"My great-aunts sent for my father. Since he's in no shape for the two-hour ride to Rothamstead, I shall have to go."

"They are well, I hope," said Thea.

She was seated to his left, looking up at him, and he wanted to bend down and steal a kiss. But he could scarcely do so under Miss Simmons's watchful eye.

"Physically, they are stout. Amazingly so at eighty-five and eighty-seven. But they have their little foibles. This time, they're convinced someone is prowling about the house at night. Anne fears ravishment. Elizabeth, that she will be murdered in her bed."

"The poor dears. You must go immediately and put their fears to rest." Thea smiled, adding softly, "Godspeed, Stanmore."

The smile said much more than Godspeed. It enchanted him as it did the first time he saw it, and if Vespera added her good wishes to Thea's, he did not hear them. Only Thea existed for him at that moment, and the look they shared.

At last a tart voice brought him to his senses.

"You will hardly prosper in your quest if you do not leave," said Vespera Simmons.

He bowed and was surprised to see her look at him quite kindly. Once more, as upon their introduction, he had to acknowledge that, indeed, the lady was not what he had expected.

He turned to Thea. "I've asked Silas to show you the chapel. He will come for you when you've eaten."

"It can wait until you return."

"I don't know when that will be. The last time Elizabeth and Anne sent a summons, they detained my father a sennight to search for the thief of a necklace they later remembered having given to one of my cousins."

"A sennight!" Thea's face registered consternation. "By then it will be time to go to London."

"You've decided to accompany me. Capital!"

Two footmen entered bearing trays, and Thea watched with a pensive frown as they set out several covered dishes and an apple and raisin compote, from which came a delicious aroma of cinnamon and cloves.

At last, she looked at Stanmore. "I must be in London next week, Tuesday. Vespera brought a message from Lord Wellesley."

This startled him, but he recovered instantly. "And I intend to be with you when you see Wellesley. If I have to bring my aunts to Archer Hall for safety or for peace of mind, I shall leave Rothamstead no later than Sunday."

He turned and strode off. A footman sprang to open the door, but before Stanmore could exit, Bella came skipping into the dining room.

"Papa, I've been looking for you! May I go with you to see Aunt Anne and Aunt Elizabeth?"

"Not this time. I'm riding, and I want to be back as quick as I can."

Bella hung her head.

Despite his hurry to be gone, Stanmore picked up his daughter for a kiss. "There'll be another time. We'll go in the carriage and have a picnic in Aunt Anne's summer house."

She wound her arms around his neck. "Since I may not go now, I don't suppose you can bring me a kitten instead? James—he's the footman Aunt Elizabeth sent with the letter, and he says their gardener found three kittens in the potting shed."

"I'm sorry, Bella. I'm not carrying a kitten on horseback."

He stepped aside to allow the footmen to leave the room, then set Bella down. "I must be off. Give Charlie another hug for me."

"Papa, if I may not go with you, and if I cannot have a kitten, may I be a bridesmaid then? Charlie says I'm too young. But I'm not, am I?"

"I haven't a notion how old a bridesmaid must be. But I do know that, before you can be a bridesmaid, we must have a wedding." He looked at Thea, planning his next words for her as much as for his daughter. "And as long as a certain lady labors under a misguided sense of commitment, I see no wedding in the near future."

"But yes, Papa! We're having a wedding! In June."

"Silas's wedding? Then you must speak to him and Elspeth."

He saw that Thea had turned paler than before, but before he could express concern, his daughter spoke again.

"*Your* wedding, Papa. Miss Stone said she'll marry you on the twenty-second of June."

"Bella—" Thea's voice was strained. "I explained it was a mistake."

"It was not a mistake! I *heard* you. And so did Lady Felicity. You were telling *her!*"

Stanmore looked speculatively from his daughter to Thea. Vespera Simmons, he noted, was watching him.

"Miss Simmons, permit me to introduce my daughter. Perhaps you would answer Bella's questions about bridesmaids while I speak with Thea."

"You may have five minutes. No longer, or luncheon will be cold. And mind you don't add to Thea's distress."

Without waiting for a reply, Vespera Simmons held out a hand to Bella. "Come, child. You and I shall have some of this delicious apple compote while we get acquainted. How is it that you're not at your lessons?"

Thea and Stanmore left the dining room as Bella explained that she did not have a governess, and her brother was doing Latin and needed all of the tutor's attention, and Mr. Locke had sent her to Nurse.

"And, of course," said Stanmore, closing the door, "there will be a perfectly reasonable explanation why she is *not* with Nurse."

Thea said nothing but allowed him to take her elbow and steer her toward the north hall, which opened onto the courtyard with the stables adjoining it.

In a tone he might have employed to discuss a mildly interesting play or news item, Stanmore said, "And she will also have a sound excuse why she was listening at doors again. Though she cannot have been paying proper attention this time."

"She *did* pay attention. Lud, Stanmore! I don't know what possessed me. There was Felicity, interrogating me about our meeting and not believing that you hadn't proposed and that we weren't planning marriage. And asking *when* we'd get married—"

Thea fell silent. Stealing a sidelong look at him, she encountered his quizzical one.

"Poor Thea. So you've set a wedding date to put an end to Felicity's badgering and supplied me with two witnesses that you did. You won't find it easy now to put me off."

"You treat this as a joke. How can you? And to think that I used to consider you stiff and formal!"

"Felicity was certain you'd teach me to unbend. It seems she was correct."

He stopped just inside the north hall. Outside, in the courtyard, the groom would be waiting with his horse, but he could not leave Thea distressed. Facing her, he caught her hands. They were cold, and he raised them, warming them with his breath.

"I suppose you thought of me as a bit of a dull stick?"

Looking self-conscious, she lowered her eyes.

"Pleading guilty, Thea?"

With a little choke of laughter, she said, "Lud, yes. But I only considered you a dull stick that first half hour when Felicity and Markham left us to discuss the Lady Arbella. Thereafter I never made the mistake again."

He traced the curve of her mouth with a fingertip. "That is better. I was afraid I'd never again see your smile or the laughter dancing in your eyes. But now I can leave, taking your smile with me."

Immediately she was serious again. "How can I laugh when I've made such a mull of everything? Bella does not understand that what I said was not what I meant. That some evil spirit whispered into my ear."

"Evil? No, that cannot be. If it was a spirit, it was a mischievous one. A helpful if misguided imp."

"I know that gleam in your eye! Stanmore, I do not understand you any more. How can you be amused when Felicity and Bella—heavens! I shouldn't be surprised if Bella already told Charlie and Mr. Locke and Nurse, for she did tell Silas! Lud! What a tangle!"

He gathered her into his arms. "Thea, my love. It doesn't matter whom Bella told. I wish you would believe me when I say that you're mine. I shall not let you go."

"Oh, yes, you will. Immediately." Her smile was strained. "Five minutes are up, and you ought to be on your way."

"Then I'll bid you adieu. *Au revoir.* We'll see Wellesley together. And we'll be married. On the twenty-second of June, like Arbella and Seymour."

Nineteen

Stanmore's vow was still on Thea's mind an hour later when, after they had paid a brief visit to the school room, Silas Wilkins collected her and Vespera for the promised visit to the chapel.

We'll be married . . . on the twenty-second of June . . . like Arbella and Seymour.

But Stanmore was wrong. Thea knew as surely as if it had been spelled out that the summons from the Foreign Office presaged her departure to Hochstein.

Once before, the week prior to her twenty-first birthday when she was in London awaiting Tushenko's arrival, she had known that same certainty pertaining to something about to happen to her. Acting upon that certainty had saved her life.

"Thea? Don't tell me you're no longer interested in seeing the chapel."

Vespera's dry voice had frequently served to catch Thea's wandering attention. This time was no exception.

"Of course I'm interested, and well you know it. But I was woolgathering and hadn't noticed where we are."

They were on the ground floor of the west wing. Vespera was entering the study, and Silas held the door for Thea, still in the hallway where she and Stanmore had stood that morning when Vespera arrived. Thea lingered a few moments. But there was no eerie sensation of warmth or burning, no disquiet, no strange restlessness urging her on.

She had been quite certain it was the chapel drawing her

with such irresistible force that its power was made manifest in a sensation of heat. She still believed this was the case, especially since Silas had confirmed that they would enter the chapel through the study, and she was disappointed that nothing was happening to her. Yet, at the same time, she was relieved, for she could not deny that Stanmore's presence had been vastly reassuring. Without him, the morning's experience might have been unnerving.

On the other hand, without him, she had never felt that strange warmth, that tug on her mind and will. Never without him . . . the descendant of Arbella Stuart.

Pensive, she entered the study.

Silas followed, closing the door. "You see how ill-proportioned this room is, ladies? It's thirty foot long but only ten foot deep. That's because behind this room is another one. The chapel you've wanted to see."

"Edward Archer's cottage," said Thea, looking around the study, an oak-paneled room Stanmore had chosen for his private use.

It was sparsely furnished—shelves stocked with books bound in red vellum, a desk and chair at one end, and a credenza, sofa, oval table, and two chairs with carved backs and arms on the opposite side, where a tall window overlooked the courtyard of the north front.

"Vespera, you remember the story of Edward Archer, the foster father of Arbella Stuart's son, don't you?"

"Oh, yes." Dryly. "I never have any trouble remembering when something is told me a dozen times."

Thea laughed. "If I had a vengeful nature I'd treat you to a lecture my governess once gave me on the evils of exaggeration."

"Then I'm glad your governess nipped any vengeful tendencies in the bud. Silas, are you going to show us the chapel?"

"Presently. You'll be interested to know that the chapel is thirty foot by fifteen." Silas was enjoying himself as guide.

"You can enter from here or from the great hall. The door on this side was always there, but it was modified so it could be activated by a hidden mechanism. The door opening from the great hall, also disguised by wainscoting, used to be a tiny square of a window."

Thea recalled what she had seen in her dreams. "There must have been a door once at one of the narrow ends, opposite the fireplace."

"That'll be on the left as we enter the chapel. The lintel and the jambs show clearly through the whitewash." He approached the length of paneled wall facing them. "Miss Stone, will you look at the frieze dividing the wainscoting? This is why you need me and couldn't just come and see the chapel on your own."

Reaching out, he deftly twisted one of the bosses on the frieze, then gave a push with the flat of his hand. Noiselessly, a portion of the wall swung inward to reveal a dark cavity.

"Sorry. I forgot the lamp." With a sheepish look, Silas went to the desk. "I've always wondered if Edward Archer was a Catholic. He could've had the north door made into a window to brighten up the place, but, apparently, he told the builder to design the house so that the chapel was hidden away with no window showing that there was another room."

"I'd hardly call it hidden," said Vespera. "Anyone seeing this study must wonder about the odd shape. What I want to know is how this could have been kept from the children. Or did I misunderstand earlier? Did you not say that they haven't been told of the chapel because of some foolish order given by the earl Barnet?"

"It's foolish all right," said Silas, searching through various drawers. "But it's not up to me to countermand it, and that's why I couldn't allow Bella to tag along."

"Bella seems to be a most inquisitive young lady. And though I could be wrong about the boy since we exchanged little more than a how-do-you-do, he did not strike me as a dullard who wouldn't notice that the study should be twice as deep as it is."

"Our Charlie is as bright as they come. Bella, too." Silas had lit a lamp and gathered it and a handful of tapers. "But for as long as they can remember, the study has been one of their father's private rooms. Even our Miss Butterfly, though she wouldn't hesitate to put her ear to the door if she believed she'd hear something interesting, would not enter unless invited."

Thea had ignored the exchange as she stood at the open door and stared into the chapel. Sufficient light penetrated from the study to show her a strip of flagged floor and the side view of one row of pews.

Not waiting for Silas and the lamp, she stepped inside, opening her mind and senses to the essence of the ancient room—Edward Archer's cottage, where Arbella briefly held the son she would never see again.

And still Thea felt nothing, save for a tickle of dust as Vespera swept past her. She was not displeased but felt confirmed in her suspicion that without Stanmore she could not perceive the power that burned without pain and tugged at her mind.

While Silas lit several candles in wall brackets, he recounted for Vespera Simmons's benefit the tragic story of the three people killed in the chapel. Charles Edward Archer, Sixth Earl Barnet, who had spent twenty-five years in exile after proclaiming his right to the English and Scottish thrones at the time his namesake, Charles Edward Stuart, fanned the flames of the second Jacobite rebellion. Francis Archer, his younger son, who had fallen in love with a lady deemed unsuitable for a man of royal descent. And Serena Henley, who did not want her lover guilty of patricide.

As Silas spoke, Thea looked toward the altar and the fireplace behind it, a collection of guns, pistols, and swords affixed to the wall on either side of the crude wood mantel. She imagined the two men, father and son, facing each other, sword in hand. And Serena . . .

Serena lay on the flagstones between the two men, the bodice of her gown stained crimson.

Francis Archer's eyes burned with hatred as he confronted his father across the still form of his beloved. "I curse you and the Archer name. I curse the blood you value so highly. The blood that's naught but a bastard's blood!"

He lunged, and steel clashed with steel.

"Thea!"

She gave a start. From one instant to the next, the image of the two men and of the girl lying on the flagstones was gone. There was only Silas, burning taper in one hand and reaching with the other to adjust a sword to the left of the fireplace.

"You're shaking." Vespera looked at her with concern. "Exhaustion, I think. Too many sleepless nights."

"Yes," Thea said absently, still looking toward the altar and fireplace and wondering if imagination had carried her away, or whether she had truly seen and heard—

The blood that's naught but a bastard's blood.

It made no sense. And yet—the scene had looked so real, much more so than the images that had formed in her mind earlier that day when Stanmore told her what he knew about Francis and Serena. Earlier, she had not been aware of hearing as well as seeing.

She sank into a pew and leaned her head against the hard wood. So solid. So constant. Oak pews that had survived for two centuries. The walls, the floor, the fireplace, were even older.

If she was able to see the past, should she not have seen Arbella? Instead, she saw a more recent past. But a past that also had its secrets, for Stanmore had not known that it was Francis and not Charles Edward who caused Serena's death.

But she wanted to know about Arbella Stuart. Surely, if nothing else, the visit to the chapel—Edward Archer's cottage—would serve to stimulate dreams. She had not dreamed at Ravensbrook. But, then, she had scarcely slept the three nights she spent there.

For the rest of the afternoon Thea poured over the oldest of the Archer Hall ledgers in the muniment room. In a sennight she would see the Foreign Secretary, and she was sure she wouldn't be returning to Archer Hall.

She was satisfied that Stanmore's ancestor, William Seymour Archer, was Arbella Stuart and William Seymour's son. But she could not feel that she had done the work Stanmore engaged her to do until the ledgers were examined, and also the documents in the strongbox, even though Stanmore had assured her that they shed no light on the conferment of a title on Edward Archer and, later, on his adopted son, William Seymour Archer.

When she joined Vespera for dinner, she had learned nothing new. Her eyes felt gritty, her head as if it were filled with cotton wool, and it was beyond her power to stifle yawns.

"If you don't mind," said Vespera when the footmen had withdrawn after setting out the first course, "I should like to retire as soon as we've eaten."

"I'm sorry." Guiltily, Thea fought against yet another yawn. "I shall be better when I've eaten."

"*You* may be. But not I. Have you not wondered how I contrived to arrive on a Monday morning?"

Thea had not. She had scarcely had a moment to appreciate that Vespera arrived at all.

"You traveled on a *Sunday!*"

"Felix came close to an apoplexy, I assure you. But it was Friday before I was convinced that Miles did not need me, and I could not be sure of a seat on the stage. So I hired the innkeeper's carriage but had to wait till Saturday afternoon. Old Lady Webster had already bespoken it and would not oblige me when I asked her to give it up."

"But, Vespera! If it's the carriage I'm thinking of, it's as old as Methuselah. I was sure it couldn't travel the distance without breaking down."

"It did break down. At Norman Cross." Vespera helped herself to a serving of spit-roasted chicken. "That is why I did not arrive with the cock's first crow, as I had planned."

"Oh! Did you lose a wheel? Were you badly jolted?"

"An axle broke. But it could have been worse," Vespera said cheerfully. "It could have broken miles away from town. Or in a place where the cartwright wasn't accustomed to travelers demanding repairs at odd hours of the night."

"Indeed," Thea said dryly. "You have almost convinced me that your travel was blessed with the greatest of good fortune."

Vespera's eyes danced with laughter. "It was. You see, the axle broke right in the yard of a coaching inn where the driver meant to change horses. Although no chamber was available, I was allowed to wait in a private parlor that wasn't needed until breakfast."

"A parlor—how tame!" Thea teased. "Don't say you would not have preferred the tap room!"

"It might have been less noisy than the parlor facing the courtyard."

Thea gave her former governess an affectionate look. "No wonder that you're tired. You should have rested this afternoon."

"I would have—if I were ninety-nine instead of forty-nine. But I do admit that after spending several hours in Bella and Charlie's company this afternoon, I almost did not make it down to dinner."

"Did they give you a tour of Archer Hall?"

"That, too. But mostly we talked. The tutor is a nice young man, but shy, and does not know how to draw the children out."

Thea smiled. "Something *you* do to admiration."

Vespera did not rise to the bait. She only nodded absently, a slight frown marring a brow that was otherwise without a wrinkle, and devoted herself to her dinner.

The second course was served, and Vespera rallied, asking about Lady Felicity and John Markham, whom she had met several times. Sharing Felicity's good news, Thea remembered that she had not yet discovered what surprise Felicity was planning for Markham.

"What could she be scheming? She said Lord Ravensbrook was helping her, and they had to wait for the roads to dry before they could pursue the matter further. I know they—including Lady Ravensbrook—have driven out at least once."

"She's looking for a country house," Vespera said promptly. "Lady Felicity never liked London, except during the season. And now that she's expecting, she'll want to live in the country."

"She'd go to Ravensbrook, like the wives of Markham's brothers."

"Lady Felicity was an only child. She's accustomed to a certain amount of privacy which she may not find at Ravensbrook."

Thea offered a platter of asparagus. "It's beyond Markham's means to maintain two residences, and he cannot give up the town house as long as he works at the bank."

"Lady Felicity can afford the purchase and maintenance of *several* houses."

"Markham is a man of principles. It would not suit him to be supported by his wife."

Vespera sipped her wine.

"You look . . . disapproving," said Thea.

"I was wondering if it would suit Markham better to see his wife unhappy when she must raise her children in London."

"Of course not."

"So he would be unhappy, too, because his wife is unhappy?" Vespera shook her head. "I trust he has more sense than to give up happiness and, ultimately, love for the sake of a *principle.*"

Thea met the older woman's gaze across the table.

"Principles must be upheld, even at great sacrifice . . . isn't that what you and Father Simmons taught me?"

"Indeed. But I hope I also taught you that there are good principles and foolish ones. And that, if a sacrifice is called for, it can only be at your own expense and not cause pain to another as well."

Subtly, the purpose of the conversation seemed to have changed. Thea was not sure that she wished to pursue the topic further and felt relieved that the footmen returned to serve dessert.

Immediately after sampling the gooseberry tart, Thea and Vespera rose and left the east wing. As they approached their rooms, a maid came out of Thea's chamber.

She curtsied. "It's all unpacked, Miss Stone. Sorry it took so long. But after Jenkins fetched your trunk, no one thought to carry it up until half an hour ago."

"Gracious! I had quite forgotten that I had a trunk at Ravensbrook. Thank you, Betty."

"His lordship didn't forget. Good night, miss."

"I was looking forward to getting acquainted with Stanmore," said Vespera as Betty hurried off. "I hope he'll return before we must leave for London."

"He will."

Thea smiled to herself. If he had to bring the great-aunts to Archer Hall, he'd return by Sunday. And he had sent for her trunk . . . because he wanted her back at Archer Hall now that Vespera was here.

Vespera gave her former pupil a sharp look, but all she said was, "Go to bed. You're asleep on your feet."

Thea hugged her. "I'm glad you're here. Good night, dear friend."

"Sleep well."

After a step or two toward her own door, Vespera looked back. "Thea—do you have dreams here at Archer Hall?"

"Yes, indeed."

"That is what I thought. But you did not mention dreams

in your letter, and I wondered if—Thea, do you remember the night after Felix and I took you to Greenwich, and how distressed you were about the dreams you had?"

Thea frowned. "That was ten years ago. I don't recall—oh!"

"You do remember."

Thea gave a little choke of laughter. "I had not thought of it in ages. It was the first time that a dream appeared so real, I believed I was the girl who served Arbella and Seymour a morning meal. After the marriage, before he left her bed. I was perturbed because I . . . the girl . . . was quite sympathetic with Arbella's look of marital bliss. And I—the girl—had very specific thoughts that betrayed a carnal knowledge *I* should not have had."

"And now you're near Barnet where Arbella—whether she was with child or not—very clearly exhibited the first signs of deep melancholia. I worried that, if you dreamed, your sympathy for her would give you pain. Felix worried, too. Which is why he said nothing in the end when I insisted on traveling Sunday."

Touched, Thea embraced her friend once more. "I promise you, it does not make me apprehensive when I seem to live the dreams. I did feel Arbella's pain when she parted from her child, but I believe it is through Dorothea's eyes that I see the past, and she was not a melancholic person."

"Let us hope not."

"Of course she wasn't! She married the Hereditary Prince von Hochstein and lived happily ever after."

Smiling but with a frown still clouding her eyes, Vespera pushed Thea toward her bedroom door. "Then I shall wish you sweet dreams."

Twenty

It was dusk when she slipped from the palace by one of the straggling wings and hurried to the river. She was late for her tryst, but she was young—turning sixteen on the morrow—and she had dispensed with the farthingale under her gown and could run like a deer.

She smelled the Thames, the familiar foul stench, before she heard the soft smacks of the water breaking against the bank. She liked the sounds. They were pleasant and clean. But she could do without the sight of the river and the smell, always more noisome in the summer months.

Slowing her pace as she approached the mooring where he would fasten his boat, she walked to the water stairs, her eyes carefully averted from the river lest she catch sight of the gray-brown murkiness and the flotsam of refuse and dead rats and dogs.

He should have been there, waiting for her. But there was no one on the bit of parapet where he usually sat and dreamed of conquests, of a daring crusade against the popish House of Habsburg—if only the king were not so set on conciliation. She did not think that another of the endless celebratory jousts had been planned for that day at St. James's or Whitehall; more likely, he was at the shipyards watching the carpenters at work on his beloved *Prince Royal* and had lost track of time.

Disappointed, she turned her back on the river. She could not often steal away; her mother was too observant. But this night, her mother was preoccupied, preparing the Lady Arbella's apartments for—

Hands covered her eyes from behind. She could not quite suppress a startled cry, although 'twas not fear that made her heart beat faster, and when she heard his soft laugh, she wanted to scold him for playing a childish trick on her. But that would make him haughty and distant. Precious time would go to waste, time they could better spend kissing . . .

His mouth brushed her shoulders, the nape of her neck, easily accessible since, along with the farthingale, she had also removed the stiff neck ruff. She pushed his hands from her eyes and turned slowly.

"Thea—"

His voice, the way he said her name, sent her pulse racing. And when he kissed her, she forgot time, forgot the noxious fumes from the river, forgot even the danger of being seen with him.

The sound of playful shrieks, of giggling and good-natured cursing a little farther down the waterfront, nearer the gate house, drove them apart. Thus it happened every time they met here at Greenwich Palace. Whether they walked in the fountain court or in the gardens, in the park or on the river's bank, others of the queen's court would sooner or later follow suit.

"Come away with me," he urged. "We'll row to Woolwich and find a tavern and pretend to be ordinary folk."

She laughed softly. "As if you could ever be ordinary! And in Woolwich of all places, where your face is familiar from your many visits to the Prince Royal. Will she be completed soon, to be launched?"

"Do not try to distract me." He drew her into the shelter of the chapel wall. "Thea, give me leave to speak to my father and to yours."

"No!" She started to tremble. "The king would see me in the Tower before he'd receive me as a daughter. And not only I would suffer his wrath, but my mother as well."

"Then what are we to do? I love you, Thea! I want to marry you."

"I love you, Henry."

He caught her in his arms, and immediately her trembling ceased. In the short six weeks they had known each other, his kiss had changed from a boy's diffident offering to a man's ardent demand. And so had her response changed from innocent acceptance to fiery reciprocation. Their kiss was promise, avowal of love; their love, a flame burning bright, never to darken.

Again they were disturbed, this time by men's shouts and snatches of song coming from the river.

Clutching the soft fabric of his doublet, she pressed against him, her head resting on his chest, as they listened to the singing and an occasional splash of oars. She felt the beat of his heart, strong and steady—as was he, this most favorite and favored son of England.

His stature was that of a man, with wide shoulders and strong limbs, yet he was only four months older than she. But he was Henry, Prince of Wales, future King of England, Scotland, and Ireland, and his father was beginning to look about for a suitable bride for him. A bride, it was rumored, who would serve to bring about conciliation with the Catholic courts of Europe.

King James would not consider Dorothea Wortley suitable. She was not of a position to conciliate anyone. Her father was Baron Wortley of Wortley, of old Saxon stock, and that was very well. But her mother was a Ruthven. Only through the queen's intercession was Mary Wortley permitted to remain in the Lady Arbella's service and accompany her to court; only by the queen's grace had Dorothea been invited to spend a few months with her mother in Lady Arbella's household.

Mary Wortley's cousin, John Ruthven, Third Earl of Gowrie, had together with his brother, the Master of Ruthven, conspired to imprison King James at Gowrie House in Perth. That was but ten years ago. Gowrie and the Master of Ruthven were *killed, but James had also pursued family members not implicated in the plot. William Ruthven escaped abroad; Patrick had not been so fortunate and was still imprisoned in the Tower.*

But the conspiracy was not all that instilled in the king an implacable hatred of the Ruthvens. As a youth, no older than Prince Henry was now, King James had been seized and humiliated by the Earl of Mar and the First Earl of Gowrie in the Raid of Ruthven. And that First Earl of Gowrie had been the custodian of Mary, Queen of Scots, and shortly before James's birth had pointed his sword at Mary's womb during the murder of Riccio, her suspected lover.

No, indeed. King James would not consider Dorothea Wortley a suitable bride for his son, no matter how much Thea and Henry loved each other.

"It is quiet now," Henry said softly. "And also dark enough to hide us from curious eyes. Come with me. If you don't want to go to Woolwich, we'll row for pleasure. The river is peaceful at night. You will enjoy it, and at midnight, I shall bring you back."

"I love you, Henry. But I do not share your love of the river. It is ugly and filthy, and how you can bathe and swim in it—" She shuddered.

"You make it difficult for me to give you a surprise. At midnight your birthday begins, does it not?"

"You remember!" She touched his cheek, still soft as a boy's. "Tell me about the surprise. What is it?"

"If I told, it would not be a surprise."

"But I am curious. Please, Henry. Tell me."

He hesitated, then withdrew something from the pouch on his belt. As he held it out to her, Thea could see only a white cloth wrapping. Whatever the wrapped item was, it was smaller than the palm of his hand.

"Take it, Thea. 'Tis my ruby ring. I had a T and an H engraved on it. And tomorrow's date, 22 June, 1610. I planned

to give it to you at midnight and pledge you my love and troth."

Tears stung her eyes, and she could not speak. She loved him—more than life. He could not marry without his father's permission, but the pledge of his love was all she desired.

She closed his hand over the wrapped ring. "Let me go now, but come to my chamber at midnight. My mother and Mrs. Bradshaw will be attending the Lady Arbella. No one will disturb us when we pledge our love and troth."

"Thea—"

"Shh."

Winding her arms around his neck, she drew his head close and kissed him. And she knew that to possess his love was worth the loss of freedom or even life—if they were found out.

Archer Hall was always quiet at night, which was not surprising since it was so very large and only a handful of people occupied the main floors. Except at mealtimes, when the ground floor came into use, the earl and his valet resided in lonely splendor in the east wing. By comparison, the west wing was crowded. Thea and Vespera had chambers on the first floor; Stanmore, the children and their nurse, and Mr. Locke, on the second floor.

But any noise occasioned by the children's activities on the floor above was absorbed by thick walls, and when Thea was torn from deep slumber by an annoying clatter and an insistent, loud voice, she did not question that the noise originated in her own chamber.

She recognized the voice as Vespera's and reluctantly opened her eyes, only to squeeze them shut against a flood of bright light.

"Thea, sit up! I saw that you're awake, so don't pretend sleep."

"Was it necessary to light every lamp and candle?" Squinting, Thea raised her head when the clatter started again. "What are you doing? Why are you up in the middle of the night?"

"It is noon. The light you see is a particularly fine March sun. And I have brought you what I shall charitably call a late breakfast."

Vespera appeared by the bed to sweep a bow and motion in the direction of the windows where a table from the adjoining sitting room was set, and tempting smells escaped from silver chafing dishes.

Thea did not protest when Vespera bundled her into a wrapper and ordered her, as if she were a child again, to wash her hands and brush her teeth. She was too benumbed by the fact that it was noon and not the middle of the night to say anything before she had drunk two cups of tea. By then, Vespera was well into the telling of how Lord Barnet had sent for Thea, but when the maid could not rouse her, had asked Vespera to the east wing.

"But he has the measles." Thea's mind had cleared, though she did not feel refreshed after her long sleep. And the dream—*had* there been a dream? She did not remember; could think only of Barnet's summons. "Stanmore ordered that no one was to be admitted to his father's chambers."

"Stanmore isn't here. You can hardly expect the staff to ignore Lord Barnet's wishes. He says that yesterday already he was feeling perfectly stout, and that the physician is a quack."

"But why did he want to see me—or you?"

"Apparently that prim little man, Lord Barnet's valet, overheard Nurse and the housekeeper debating whether Bella made up the tale of a June wedding."

"Lud!" Tea spilled on the lace tablecloth as Thea thrust her cup onto the saucer. "I made a mistake. A foolish, stupid mistake! I admitted it! Why will no one believe me?"

"Not even the unwitting groom, it seems. At least, I did not hear Stanmore correcting his daughter when she announced the good fortune in store for him."

"I shall have to see Lord Barnet." Thea went to the armoire

and pulled out the first gown she saw. "He'll be furious, and I won't have him blame Stanmore."

"As a matter of fact, Lord Barnet is quite pleased."

Thea spun. "Impossible."

"He did seem put out at first," Vespera admitted. "But then I told him who you are."

The gown slipped from Thea's fingers.

"He got my dander up," said Vespera. "I could not bear to listen to him abuse you as a scheming wench."

Thea said nothing but sat down again and poured herself a fresh cup of tea.

Vespera nudged the sugar bowl closer to Thea. "Lord Barnet has invited us both to take dinner with him tonight. At seven."

Again Thea said nothing. She added sugar to her tea and stirred vigorously. Suddenly she started to laugh. It was a shaky laugh, but a laugh nevertheless.

"Lud, Vespera. What a tangle! And the worst part is, I don't want to get out of it. Not at this end."

At six-thirty that evening Thea put the finishing touches to her toilette. She had once more dressed her hair so it fell in waves from a top knot to her shoulders, a style that softened the shadows beneath her eyes which neither fourteen hours of sleep nor a ramble through the Archer Hall park had erased.

Her gown was of ruby-red silk with a wide, square neckline and puffed sleeves. There were no frills or flounces to distract from the simple elegance of design or from the exquisitely worked lace of the stole Thea planned to carry.

Usually, with this gown, she wore her mother's diamond collar, but it seemed too ostentatious for the occasion. A string of pearls, the only other piece of neckwear left from the small stock of jewelry her mother had taken from Castle Hochstein, was unsuitable because of its length. There was a gold bracelet set with opals, which would hardly do. And three rings. Her mother's diamond ring, her father's signet ring, and a ruby he had occasionally worn on his little finger.

It was when Thea took the ruby ring from the jewelry case and the light from the lamp on the dressing table caught the stone that she remembered the dream.

The dream in which she had walked by the river—no, not she. Even though it had felt as if she was the girl in the dream, it had been another Thea. Thea Wortley. Dorothea.

Her ancestress had stolen away from Greenwich Palace to meet secretly with young Henry, Prince of Wales. And had been promised a ring, engraved with the initials T and H. Thea and Henry.

Thea sat at the dressing table and stared with unseeing eyes, at the ring in her hand. She did not have to examine the wide band. She knew the initials were there, entwined and embellished. She had offered the ring to the Englishman who helped her and Vespera escape from France, but he declined, asking if he might have the silver cross she had worn on a riband around her neck.

And thus she still had the ruby. She had always assumed that the entwined initials stood for Theodor—not an uncommon name among her ancestors—and for Hochstein, and that the "v," the abbreviation for "von," was lost in the elaborate embellishments.

But if the initials stood for Thea and Henry . . .

In the dream, Henry had also mentioned a date, the twenty-second of June, 1610. Thea was not aware of a date on the ring. It was not impossible, however, that the finely etched leaf arabesques on either side of the initials hid the date from the naked eye.

The twenty-second of June, 1610. The day Dorothea turned sixteen. The day Henry and Dorothea pledged their love.

Also the day Arbella Stuart secretly married William Seymour in her chamber at Greenwich Palace at some time between three and four in the morning. The minister performing the ceremony had been the Dean of Rochester's son, and among the witnesses were Lady Arbella's waiting ladies, her steward, her gentleman usher, and Seymour's friend, Edward Rodney.

Mary Wortley had been one of the waiting ladies. She would have been with Lady Arbella at midnight, when Dorothea planned to admit Henry to her chamber to pledge their love and troth.

Thea's hands shook just a little as she slipped the ruby ring onto the middle finger of her left hand.

On her first night at Archer Hall she'd had a dream—a snatch of a dream—that seemed unrelated to Arbella's history, because Thea had believed herself to have been the central figure. The circumstances had been indistinct, but she had retained an impression of a man beside her, holding her hand, and a deep voice whispering her name.

She had assumed the dream was of herself and Stanmore. But, perhaps, it had been Dorothea and Henry. Thea and Henry. Perhaps then, as in the dream of the past night, there had been no separation of identity between the Thea of 1610 and the Thea of 1810.

Thea and Henry. There had been a dream of a young couple gazing into each other's eyes in Edward Archer's cottage . . . and a child, about one year of age, playing on the hearth stone.

And there had been a dream of the Lady Arbella bidding farewell to an infant in Edward's cottage, then placing it in the arms of the younger of two women accompanying her. Thea had awoken from the dream with tears wet on her face. She had believed it was Arbella's pain and sadness that made her cry . . .

Twenty-one

Despite Vespera's assurance that the earl was eager to meet her, Thea did not expect to be received with any warmth. Too well did she remember his cold snub at Felicity's nuptial ball and his designating her a ferreting female shortly after her arrival at Archer Hall. Though she had chosen to accept the epithet as a compliment, *he* had not meant it as one. She was therefore pleasantly surprised by Lord Barnet's gruff but unquestionably cordial manner when he greeted her and Vespera in one of the turret rooms on the first floor of the east wing.

A round table, covered with snowy damask under a lace cloth, stood near the south window and was set with exquisite china and crystal and gleaming silver. Dinner was served immediately. Apologizing for the haste, Barnet explained that since he had no intention of following Dr. Sellers's recommendation to feed off invalid's fare, he strictly adhered to another of the physician's orders, namely to eat the last meal of the day before eight o'clock.

Since this was Thea's first encounter with Barnet—save for the brief and less than pleasant meeting three years ago and the premonitory glimpse she caught of him the day he had a fall down the stairs—she could not tell whether the ruddiness of his complexion was a sign of continued ill health. The bruise on his chin was scarcely noticeable, and he did not look as if he had the measles. But then, if he had suffered a very mild form of the illness, the rash of the eruptive stage would also have been very mild and of a brief duration. Barnet seemed well, and he certainly was in good humor.

Throughout dinner, Higgins, the valet, stood by the earl's chair while Thea and Vespera each had a footman to serve them and to fill their glasses, a striking departure from the informality in the family dining room below. Barnet was an attentive host to both ladies, but, Thea was quick to note, inclined to let his gaze linger on Vespera, who was in exceptionally high good looks that evening and not averse to encourage the earl's bluff heartiness.

As Thea watched him, she had no difficulty seeing a family likeness to Stanmore. But the likeness was only in physical appearance. Stanmore would not slap the flat of his hand on the table for emphasis of a point made. Neither was he prone to burst into boisterous laughter, or to scowl suddenly at an unexpected retort. Indeed, while Stanmore's and Charlie's natures seemed quite alike, Barnet's and Stanmore's could not be more opposed.

After dinner, Barnet invited Thea and Vespera to join him by the fireplace and take wine with him.

Catching Vespera's eye, Thea nodded.

"We'd be delighted," said Vespera. "I'm rather partial to a glass of port now and again."

Rising, Barnet nodded approvingly. "Good woman. 'Tis naught but newfangled rubbish that ladies must leave the table. Besides, I'm wanting a word with Miss Stone."

"I have a feeling," said Thea, "I ought to have a fortifying dose of brandy instead of port."

Barnet shot her a keen look, then gave a bark of laughter. "Can't pull the wool over my eyes, Miss Stone. If you want me to think you lack in pluck, you shouldn't try to outstare me."

"I'll be sure to remember. Next time."

"I don't doubt you will." Moving stiffly, Barnet ushered the ladies to chairs by the fire. "Higgins, bring the book, and then don't bother me until I ring for you."

The book was an *Almanach de Gotha.*

Barnet waited until the valet and the footmen had left, then opened the book to a marked page. He handed the tome to Thea.

"That is your family?"

The entry on the von Hochsteins was a long one, as she had known it would be. She glanced only at the last few names. Prince Theodor von Hochstein, her grandfather. His wife, Giesela, née von Waldfrieden. Their son, Rudolph, Hereditary Prince von Hochstein.

"It's an old edition," said Barnet.

"Yes, so I see. It does not show my father's marriage or his accession to the throne. Or my birth."

Raising his glass, Barnet sniffed the bouquet of his port before drinking.

He asked, "Can you prove you're the Princess von Hochstein, as Miss Simmons claims, and not some imposter?"

"No. Nor do I wish to prove it." Closing the *Almanach de Gotha,* Thea set it on the table between her chair and Barnet's. "Here in England, I am Thea Stone, historian. My other identity can be of interest only in the country of my birth."

"My son wishes to marry you."

A lump of pain formed in her chest. "It cannot be."

"Why not?" Bushy gray brows met in a scowl. "Stanmore told me you're satisfied that William Seymour Archer was the child of Arbella Stuart and William Seymour. In which case my son would be the perfect match for you—if you *are* the Princess von Hochstein."

She did not miss the challenging note, but she ignored it. If Barnet believed he could draw her into an argument about her birth or her and Stanmore's suitability, he would learn his mistake.

"Lord Barnet, I was indeed convinced that Lady Arbella bore a son, whom she placed in the care of Edward Archer. I came here in the hopes of finding proof."

Francis Archer's words echoed in her mind . . . *blood that was naught but a bastard's blood.*

"And?" Barnet drummed his fingers impatiently. "You've studied the chronicles, have you not? And the accounts?"

"Unfortunately, none of your records were of help. And in the meantime—"

She fell silent. While she had not hesitated to speak to Stanmore of the dreams and glimpses of the past, she could not, would not, do so to his father.

"In the meantime," Barnet said testily, "you've been listening to Stanmore and his nonsense that it's all a hum! And you were gullible enough to believe him."

"You're wrong, Lord Barnet."

"The deuce I am! If I were, you wouldn't think yourself too good for him!"

"Sir!" Vespera Simmons, seated opposite the earl, gave him a cool look. "You forget yourself."

His color rose, perhaps from temper, perhaps from embarrassment. "Your pardon, ma'am."

The apology was directed at Vespera, and Thea half expected her former governess to dole out a second reprimand. Instead, she rewarded the offender with a nod.

"You've been ill," said Vespera. "I daresay that accounts for your testiness."

"Does it? Or is it the deuced orneriness of the young that accounts for it?"

"Are you referring to your son, Lord Barnet?" Vespera smiled. "I found him most obliging."

"Aye!" Barnet's voice bit. "Never loses his temper but somehow or other always gets his way. Only this time, it seems, *his* way will get him nowhere."

Thea's presence was forgotten, but she was content to have it so. She had much to think about . . . a dream involving a youthful couple, who vowed to pledge their love in the girl's chamber while, only a few doors away, the Lady Arbella Stuart prepared to enter secretly into a forbidden marriage.

Thea's dreams had always proven true. But this one—perhaps it was too farfetched. Yet, she held other fragments of knowledge that might, if regarded from the right perspective, fit the puzzle.

Thus Thea occupied herself with speculation while half listening as the earl, much calmer now, told Vespera Simmons about the three perfectly suitable and willing young ladies he had selected, and whom Stanmore had refused, sight unseen.

"Said he'd choose a wife himself. And what came of it?" Stretching his long legs toward the fire, Barnet shot Thea a fierce look. "The one he chooses won't have him!"

Thea twirled the stem of her wine glass. For an instant, the port glowed bloodred in the firelight.

Like the stain on the bodice of Serena Henley's white gown.

She set the glass down. "Lord Barnet, did your brother confide in you? Did he say anything to you about the Archer bloodline?"

For a moment, silence reigned.

"Why the interest in my brother, Miss Stone? Francis has been dead for twenty years."

"It says in the chronicles that he died in a hunting accident. And your father, of a stroke when he heard the news. You were the keeper of the chronicles at the time. You know the deaths were not caused by a hunting accident or a stroke."

The earl's ruddiness faded.

Vespera said, "Thea, my dear. Surely an event of two decades ago can have no bearing on the question whether or not the Archers are descended from Arbella Stuart."

Thea still looked at the earl.

He stared at the flames in the hearth. "Perhaps, it does, ma'am. Miss Stone will have heard from my son that my father and brother killed each other because Francis insisted on marrying the chaplain's daughter."

He turned to Vespera. "What Stanmore does not know—and I fail to see how Miss Stone can have gotten wind of it—is that my father and Francis quarreled earlier that day when

Francis insisted that our line is descended from a bastard child."

"Does it matter?" asked Vespera.

Heat stained Barnet's blanched face.

"Does it—" He caught himself and moderated his tone. "Miss Simmons, I took you for a sensible woman. How can you ask?"

"I ask *because* I am sensible. Whether or not you can prove legitimate descent, or descent from Arbella Stuart, or from Abraham himself, you are and will remain the Earl Barnet with a son and a grandson to succeed you."

He opened his mouth but closed it again without saying a word.

"Many of our great families are descended from bastard children," Vespera continued calmly.

Barnet shook his head. "The Archers are not a bastard line. We have the chronicles. We have the story by word of mouth, passed on from generation to generation. Twice an Earl Barnet addressed Parliament and declared his place in the Stuart line of succession."

"Sir." Thea waited until he turned to her. "Allow me to point out that you recorded the deaths of your father and brother to suit *your* notion of what is right and proper for future generations to read. The same may have been done in the past."

"Perhaps," said Vespera, "you planned to tell Stanmore the truth at some later time? That Francis quarreled with his father over the legitimacy of the bloodline?"

"No."

The uncompromising sound was echoed by the snap of a log as flames split it in two.

"No," Barnet repeated. "Strife on the subject of descent wrought disaster once. I had no intention to tell anyone. I hoped to prevent a recurrence. Alas! My own son—"

"Your son," Thea said sharply, "would never turn against you."

Warmth stole into her face under Barnet's scrutiny.

He said, "Stuart has the Archer looks, but in character he is like his mother. She was gentle and loving and awakened what chivalrous instincts I possessed. In my son, the gentleness repulsed me. I wanted him to be like his older brothers. Rugged. Boisterous. Not afraid to engage in a bit of rough and tumble."

"Prepared to let his temper rule him in a family quarrel?" The sudden flare of her own temper brought Thea to her feet. "As Francis did?"

Stiffly, Barnet started to rise as well.

"Please don't get up." Already, she regretted the outburst. "And forgive me. I shouldn't have spoken as I did."

"No need to apologize." Barnet's voice was harsh. "There was more truth in your words than I care to admit."

"Then, if you'll excuse me, sir, I should like to retire."

"One moment, Miss Stone. Why won't you marry my son?"

Twenty-two

Again, Thea's chest tightened with pain. Why, indeed? Every one of her reasons—Hochstein, Tushenko, a promise to the Foreign Secretary—seemed without value when measured against love. Her love for Stanmore. And his love for her.

Barnet said, "Stuart must marry again. Must have more children. More sons. I lost three, and he has only young Charles."

Vespera raised a brow. "And Bella."

"Aye. But that's not the same as more sons. Besides, a daughter isn't immune to illness either. Or a wife. I lost both in the same smallpox epidemic that killed the boys. Twenty-five years ago." He stared at his hands. "Only Stuart survived."

"Why did you not remarry?" asked Vespera. "You could have had more sons yourself."

"My second wife was barren." He looked up and caught Thea's eyes on him. "Which is why Stanmore must marry again."

"Good night, Lord Barnet. It was kind of you to ask me to dine."

The ever ready scowl darkened his face. "Go, then! But don't think you've heard the last about marrying my son. I'm not snubbed quite that easily."

She curtsied. "Unlike a certain young woman three years ago, who asked your permission to look at the chronicles?"

"So! That was you, was it? I suspected as much, since it

would be unlikely that there are two females calling themselves historians."

"Two ferreting females, sir?" She gave him an arch look. "Indeed, that would have been most unlikely."

Dark eyes, like Stanmore's, glinted under thick, gray brows. "I'll say this in your favor: you don't seem to take offence or behave vaporish."

"How can I, when it is a most complimentary description?"

He nodded. "I'm beginning to see what or, more precisely, *who* brought about the change in my son."

Giving Thea no opportunity for a retort, he addressed Vespera Simmons. "And you, ma'am? Must you retire as well?"

"Not unless you wish for solitude."

"Do you play piquet?"

"I do."

"In that case, I certainly don't wish for solitude. I've had a month of it, and I'm tired of my own company."

As Thea turned to leave, he said, "Miss Stone, you did not let me finish when I spoke of Stuart earlier. I was going to add that I may have done him a great wrong when I called him spineless in the past."

"Not *may have*, sir." She stood quite still, not looking at him but facing the archway into the adjoining sitting room. "You very definitely did."

She sensed Vespera's disapproval, but she did not apologize. And she did not think that Barnet expected it. She approached the archway and, when she reached it, turned. The earl was watching her.

"Sir, did your brother have reason to suspect that your family is of an illegitimate line?"

She thought he would not answer, for he bent and took a pack of cards from the shelf beneath the table at his side. But something made her wait.

Finally, he spoke, and the testiness in his voice might have been directed equally at himself and at Thea. "I don't know, Miss Stone. I did not linger outside the estate office when I realized my father and brother were arguing once again. Later, I wished I had."

Vespera said, "Perhaps your brother was lashing out in anger. Considering the legendary Archer pride, descent from a bastard was probably the most hurtful thing he could say to your father."

"Perhaps."

An image flashed through Thea's mind, of a man tapping the walls of the chambers beneath the muniment room. The chambers Stanmore had vacated when she arrived. The chambers once occupied by Francis Archer.

Before she could formulate a question, Barnet said, "For a while, after the tragedy, I wondered if Francis had found something . . . documents we believed lost. I searched his rooms here and in London. Demme! I searched every single room of both houses for a secret compartment."

"London?" Thea's eyes narrowed. "Barnet House wasn't closed up twenty years ago?"

"My father's sisters stayed in town that spring of '90. Anne's eldest daughter was to be presented at court. And Francis was required to play escort."

"Sir, do you recall which chamber Francis occupied at Barnet House?"

"The room known in the family as the 'succession chamber.' "

"As in succession to the throne?"

"Aye. 'Twas in 1701, before the Act of Succession passed, that the third earl addressed Parliament with a claim to the throne. He stayed in that room the night before he was laughed out of town."

"And was killed on his way back to Archer Hall."

"Aye, Miss Stone. According to his son, that was when a number of documents disappeared. I thought that mayhap Francis had found something."

"And did he?"

"No." Looking fierce, Barnet hit the arm of his chair with

a fist. "My father and Francis wouldn't have died the way they did if the lost documents had been there. If Francis had found them, he would have known for certain that the Archers are descended from Lady Arbella Stuart's son. He wouldn't have jabbered about a bastard line!"

Thea nodded and left, her mind spinning. A bastard's blood. Thea and Henry. Henry, who had contracted a fever after bathing in the Thames, and died in November of 1612, at eighteen years of age. And Thea . . . Dorothea Wortley, who had married the Hereditary Prince von Hochstein in the spring of 1613, and in 1615, at the birth of her son, made an entry in the Hochstein family Bible to commemorate an earlier birth.

God bless the child born March 25, 1611. God have mercy on his mother.

As Thea closed the door to Lord Barnet's sitting room behind her, she heard the approach of light yet firm steps from the gallery. Heart pounding, she listened. It couldn't be . . . or could it? He had been gone a day and a half.

She hurried toward the sound. From different sides, they reached the corner of gallery and corridor simultaneously.

"Thea—"

His voice, the way he said her name, sent her pulse racing. And when he caught her in his arms and kissed her, she forgot resolve, forgot obligation and duty to Hochstein, forgot that her love must be denied.

Stanmore loosened his hold and looked at her. "I love you, Thea."

A look and three short words were all that was required to cure forgetfulness.

Tears blurred her vision, softening his face, making it appear younger all of a sudden, unshaped as yet by life . . . Prince Henry's face, as the other Thea must have seen it two centuries ago. The other Thea, who had loved unwisely.

She blinked and met Stanmore's quizzical gaze.

"I know," he said. "I promised not to press you. And I

shan't. But I'll gladly leave once more if I can have another kiss when I return."

Somehow, she summoned a smile. Somehow, she kept her voice light. "Impossible. You cannot leave again. We have work to do. Unless you did not catch the prowler who disturbed the ladies at Rothamstead?"

He grimaced. "And what a prowler! Armed to the teeth with pistols, a mace, and a rusty old broadsword."

"You apprehended him?" As she gripped his hand, she thought she saw him wince. "He did not hurt you, did he?"

"He was more likely to hurt himself. Thea, 'twas my aunts' ancient butler. He believes it is 1745, my grandfather exiled, and the king's soldiers coming to arrest Anne and Elizabeth."

"Poor man! What did you do with him?"

"I brought him with me. For the present, he's in Silas's care. But I had best inform my father." Stanmore cocked a brow. "I am told you and Miss Simmons were honored with an invitation to dinner. How does it come about that I meet you in the corridor?"

"Lord Barnet is playing cards with Vespera; so I left. Stanmore, can you not see your father tomorrow? I have so much to tell you. And I want you to go with me to the chapel. Immediately."

He searched her face. "What happened, Thea?"

"Let me tell you on the way to the chapel."

"Very well. But first you must change into a warm gown or, at least, fetch a thicker shawl than that gossamer confection you've draped around your shoulders."

She did feel cold outside Barnet's warm rooms, but if what she suspected came true, if Stanmore's presence would indeed summon the strange power that burned without pain and tugged at her mind, then she would not need a warm shawl. But until speculation was proven true, it was simpler to fetch a shawl than to explain and, possibly, argue.

As they walked the length of the gallery, Thea described her experience in the chapel, the brief scene she had envisioned of Francis and his father. She told Stanmore that Lord Barnet had heard part of a quarrel, Francis insisting that theirs was an illegitimate line. Finally, she summarized the dream about Prince Henry and Dorothea Wortley.

"So, you see," she concluded her report. "You may be correct after all, that your family is not descended from Arbella Stuart."

He did not reply immediately, but when they reached her chamber and he opened the door for her, he asked, "Have you told my father what you told me?"

Her eyes widened. "Share the dream with a stranger? Confess that I *see* things? Of course not!"

He lightly touched her face. "Go and change. And prepare yourself to confess to me why you must visit the chapel again at this time of night."

There was no help for it then. When she had donned a warm gown and spencer and rejoined him, she described the strange sensations she had experienced in the corridor outside the study and at the foot of the east gallery stairs, not far from that part of the great hall which adjoined the chapel.

"But only when I was with you, Stanmore."

"I felt it." He took her hand and clasped it firmly as they descended to the ground floor. "Not the tug on the mind, the urging to do something. But the warmth and *your* disquiet. I found it eerie . . . disturbing."

"I did, too. The pull of that power was quite strong the morning we stood outside your study. It was difficult to concentrate on anything else. Then Silas arrived with Vespera, and the strange sensation was gone."

They entered the north hallway of the ground floor, with the estate office on the left and the study on the right.

Stanmore drew in his breath sharply.

"Do you feel it, too?" she asked.

"Yes." Tightening his grip on her hand, he stopped. "Is this what you meant when you spoke of effluvia of past events pouring from certain sites?"

She did not reply but drew him toward the study door, opened it, and stepped into the dark room.

Not wanting to let go of her, Stanmore plucked a lamp from its bracket by the door. "Careful, Thea. I can scarcely see where we're going."

Slowing her step, she said in a soft, breathless voice, "I used to think it was Arbella who drew me. I was so wrapped up in her life, I never realized that the more logical explanation was Dorothea."

"Logical," he muttered. "What can possibly be logical about this?"

The heat was so intense that sweat ought to be pouring down his face in streams, but he felt none. What he did feel was a sense of eagerness and anticipation coming from Thea, and a strong pull on his hand as she led him toward the paneled wall.

He held the lamp high. The light caught the broad frieze which separated the wainscoting into two tiers at shoulder height. The ornamental bosses on the frieze were clearly visible.

He was reluctant to let go of her hand to twist the boss. "Did Silas explain how to open the chapel door? Can you do it, Thea?"

"I watched him, but I don't recall which of the bosses will unlatch the door." She turned to him, her face flushed, her eyes fever bright. "Hurry, Stanmore! Open it up. I must go inside."

He hesitated.

"Stanmore? You're not frightened, are you?"

"Frightened? Yes, I suppose I am, though I don't know why. I've been in the chapel. I know there's no danger of walls or ceiling crumbling. But, dash it!" He lowered the lamp. "For some reason I don't want us to go inside."

"I must go."

"Why? What drives you, Thea?"

"I don't know." She gave him a helpless look. "You once

said to me that I am a woman with a calling. That I am enthralled."

She felt the powerful force drawing her, felt its heat. "I must go, Stanmore. Alone, if necessary."

She would have removed her hand from his clasp, but he held fast.

"That frightens me even more. No, my dear Thea. I will not let you go alone."

He raised the lamp in his left hand, and with his right hand guided hers to one of the bosses. "Twist."

She did, and Stanmore pressed his left arm and shoulder against the panel, which started to swivel inward. A surge of relief swept over Thea. Relief that he had not denied her access to the chapel. Relief that he was coming with her.

She turned her head to give him a smile, and as she did so, her gaze fell on his arm pushing against the door panel. The lace ruffle of his shirt sleeve had fallen back, and the lamp light revealed an angry red welt on the inside of his wrist.

"You're hurt! The aunts' butler—"

"It's only a bee sting. Don't fret, Thea."

Escaping his clasp, she took a step forward to relieve him of the lamp and to open the door panel all the way. But she never carried out her intention. As her foot crossed the threshold, she received a jolt as if struck by lightning.

"Lud!"

She blinked her eyes in the brightness that suddenly surrounded her—as if someone had lit every candle, torch, and lamp in the chapel. But the light did not come from lamps or candles. It was sunshine streaming through a window directly opposite her and through an open door to her left.

A trestle table with benches stood in front of her, a low bedstead in the corner by the open door, and to her right was a fireplace surmounted by a crude wood mantel.

"Stanmore, how strange!"

She turned and beheld a sight even stranger. There was no sign of Stanmore. No sign of the study or any part of Archer

Hall. Only a bit of yard outside the chapel door, with chickens scratching in the dirt, a meadow beyond the yard, and beyond that, the golden stubble of harvested fields.

A rutted lane led to a farmhouse barely visible in the distance, and down the lane, toward her, came a man wearing a smock and breeches. As he drew close, Thea recognized him from a dream. He was the man who had handed Lady Arbella the swaddled infant in Edward Archer's cottage.

Again he carried a child—riding his shoulder, this time, a sturdy little fellow gowned in lace-trimmed blue velvet and crowing with glee.

"Run, horse! Run, Father Edward!"

Twenty-three

"You're early, Mistress Thea. I did not expect you ere the sun is lower."

He neither bowed nor smiled, but the gray eyes in the weathered face looked at her kindly while she stared at the child on his shoulder. The little boy squirmed and tried to hide his face in the man's gray-blond hair.

"He does not remember you, mistress. It's been too long since last you graced us with your company."

"Yes. Over three months."

Thea took a deep breath to calm the pounding of her heart. She was not frightened—at least, she did not think that fear was part of the emotions teeming in her. Excitement, yes. And a sense of satisfaction that, finally, she had discovered where the strange and powerful force had tried to lead her: to Dorothea Wortley, her ancestress.

Her mind seemed to consist of two parts—that of Thea Stone, and that of Thea Wortley. The one noted with a historian's detachment that she carried a riding whip and gauntlets in her hand and wore hose and boots beneath the full skirt of her gown—a gown unlike any she had ever worn, with an open ruff that brushed against the back of her head when she moved, and with sleeves that were puffed and slashed and closed around the wrists with stiff, lace-edged cuffs.

The other Thea was carrying on the conversation with Edward Archer and struggled not to show hurt at young William's inability to recognize her.

"He has grown," she said. "And he has learned more words. He called you Father Edward."

"If it please ye, Mistress Thea, will you step inside? 'Tis far too warm for an October day."

"And William in velvet!"

"Lizzy would not let him go lest fittingly gowned for the occasion."

"Pray give him to me. He'll hurt his head on the lintel if he stays on your shoulder."

Edward Archer swung the boy down, and as she received the warm little body in her arms, she was filled with such tenderness that tears stung her eyes.

"Lady," said William, nuzzling her neck and ear. "Smells good."

Won over by the scent of lavender, the boy raised no objections when she carried him into the cottage. He babbled happily of chicklings and kittens, of Father Edward and John and Lizzy, and was content to be held in her arms when she sat down at the trestle table. Neither did he take offense that she remained silent, which was just as well since she could not utter a single word. She ached with longing for this child, whom she could see so rarely.

Edward Archer set two pewter cups on the table, then brought two jugs.

"Dandelion and gooseberry wine. I'll be off to the stables. I don't doubt your horse would like some oats."

She smiled her gratitude.

"Mistress Thea—" He hesitated. "What is the news of Lady Arbella?"

"Not good. She pines away."

"Is there hope of release, or—" He leaned close and, even though no one was around, lowered his voice to a whisper. "Or escape?"

She shook her head. "Though there is talk of the latter, I doubt it'll come to pass. After Seymour's escape last summer,

Lieutenant Waad will not again be caught unawares. And the King is—"

The clatter of hooves silenced her and drew her eyes to the second door, the open door revealing a part of the sunbathed stable yard. Time seemed to stand still, but at last she heard the familiar firm tread, the scuff of boots on cobbles. And she heard his voice before she saw him.

"Edward! Prithee, take my horse and care for it."

Neither slow nor hurried, Edward Archer moved to obey the summons.

She rose from the bench. Her pulse raced, and she clutched the child so fiercely that he began to squirm. Through the open door, she watched the two men meet, Edward bowing, then continuing toward the stables.

And Henry was coming to her, his long stride quickly covering the distance to the cottage. She had last seen him five weeks ago, in early September, shortly after the royal family's return from Woodstock. He had been glowing with health and vigor; now he was pale. Five weeks ago, he had been strong in limb and body; now he looked thin, despite the padding of his doublet and full, puffed sleeves.

"Down!" demanded young William, struggling in her arms.

She put him down and watched him strut—not an easy feat in petticoats—toward the fireplace where a number of carved farm animals sheltered in the empty grate. William squatted on the hearth stone and engrossed himself in play.

"Thea."

Henry's voice, the way he said her name, had not changed in the two and a half years since they first met. It still held the power to rouse her blood and make her forget the hopelessness of their love. Encircled in his arms, brought alive by his kiss, she once more allowed herself to believe that in the end love would conquer obstacles and opposition.

"I love you, Thea. I vow we'll be together soon."

"My love is yours. Forever."

But as she gazed at him, a deep chill came over her heart and soul. The chill of fear.

"Henry, they say you're ailing."

His brow darkened. "Faith, and who is 'they'? Can I not suffer an ache of the head without all the kingdom knowing it?"

This easy irritation was unusual for him and worried her as much as his pallor.

She touched his cheek and felt his skin, dry and brittle. "What ails you? Has Dr. Hammond prescribed for you?"

"Aye, he physicked me. But let us speak of more important matters. Thea, I had occasion to approach my mother privately."

"Yes?" She squeezed his hand. "What did she say? Pray do not tease me with silence!"

"She expressed desire to see the child."

"God's reward upon her! Oh, Henry! I can scarce believe it. When does she wish to see him? I can slip away—mayhap tomorrow. Will you come as well?"

He smiled. "You're like a child yourself when you are pleased. But, Thea, I must remain at court. My sister's betrothed is looked for any day."

"But the Queen? She will be able to leave?"

"She'll send for you. Perhaps on the morrow, perhaps the day after. She does not like the match for Elizabeth. I suspect she may be pleased to be absent when Frederick of Palatine arrives."

"Henry—" She drew him toward the fireplace. "You have not spoken to William. Come and see how he has grown since June."

"How can I speak with him when he does not speak to me?"

Again, she heard a touch of irritation in his voice. But, a moment later, he caressed the child's soft curls and smiled at him.

"Faith! But you have grown. I recognize you not. Are you

the same William who hid under the table when I was here last?"

Distinctly, the child said, "Fine lord."

Henry laughed. He reached into his purse and withdrew a miniature ship.

He handed it to William. " 'Tis a replica of the *Prince Royal*."

Chubby hands turned the gift over and over.

Thea knelt. "It is a ship, William. It carries men across the water."

"Ship," repeated William and set it down beside his carved animals.

Henry went to the trestle table. Pouring from one of the jugs, he said, "He needs tutoring. Edward must speak to the vicar at Barnet."

"William is not yet two!"

"I had tutors before I was two."

She kissed the child, who was already at play again, then rose and joined Henry at the table.

Quietly, she said, "The circumstances of your childhood were different."

"His childhood could be different as well."

"No!" Instinctively, she clutched her left hand, where Henry's ruby ring graced the middle finger. "If the King knew what we have done, William and I would be in the Tower. And my mother, too."

"That may have been true two years ago. But I am eighteen now." His eyes had a feverish look. "The age, Sir Walter Raleigh once told me, the ancients held worthiest for going to war. I can protect you now, Thea! And your family. I have followers—strong, faithful men who will support me in any battle I wish to fight. Even if it is to oppose my father."

"Henry! Dearest!" She cupped his face with trembling hands. "Do not act rashly, I pray thee! If we can win your mother's support—"

He was seized by a sudden, violent shiver.

"Henry, you *are* ill! I vow 'tis your bathing in the Thames and your walking on the river's bank at night that gives you chills and fever."

He embraced her. " 'Tis but a fit of an ague, Thea. Let me be off now, and I shall drink more of Dr. Hammond's draught. Then I shall be better. I must be better. There's much to prepare for my sister's nuptials."

"I will ride with you."

"And will you not fear to be seen with me?"

"I shall disregard fear—but you must promise not to approach your father until we have further speech."

They looked at each other; she, with a plea in her eyes; he, with a touch of arrogance in his.

At last, he said, "I promise not to broach the matter until Elizabeth is wed."

With that she was content. If ever there would come a propitious time to approach the King about his son's marriage to Dorothea Wortley, it must be after Princess Elizabeth had joined hands with the Elector of Palatine, a union desired with equal eagerness by King James and Henry.

"I will see that the horses are saddled." Once more, Henry took her into his arms. "But kiss me first. I hunger for you—perhaps that is why I am ill. You starve me before you grant me another taste of you."

She wrapped her arms around his neck. "Don't I suffer hunger, too? You are my love and my life. Without you—"

His mouth claimed hers, silencing her. Their kiss was promise, avowal of love. Their love, a flame burning bright, never to darken.

When he tore himself away, he was paler than before. "Bid the child farewell if you want to ride with me part of the way."

"Henry—"

"You're mine, Thea, I won't give you up. I shall proclaim you my wife, and William, my son." Turning, he strode toward the door to the stable yard. "After Elizabeth's marriage."

But he will not live to see his sister marry.

The thought jarred. As earlier, when she first saw Henry's pallor, she was struck by a chill of fear.

"Henry!"

She started after him, but a distressed cry from the child made her turn to the fireplace.

"Ship." William's mouth trembled. "Broken!"

She hurried to the small figure of woe and was already stretching out her arms for him, when he flung the wooden ship. It hit the flagstones in front of her. She tried to avoid it, but the edge of her booted foot slipped on it, and the toy was catapulted into the grate.

And she, still with arms outstretched and stumbling a few involuntary steps forward, caught the mantel—but nevertheless hit the wooden ledge with her forehead. Pain exploded behind her eyes and brow. The sunny cottage was suddenly, instantly, pitch dark.

But she must not swoon.

As if through a thick fog, she heard little William's plaintive cry, "Lady!"

She must not swoon. Must bid her son farewell and ride with Henry, who was ill.

"Thea!"

She must not swoon.

Twenty-four

"Thea!"

She must not swoon. Henry was calling her. The horses were saddled.

Strong arms cradled her head and shoulders. "My love! Dearest Thea! For goodness' sake, say something!"

Stanmore's voice. Stanmore's arms. So strong and reassuring.

But she could not see him. She blinked, and blinked again. The darkness remained.

She stirred, feeling through the thickness of her skirts hard, cold stone beneath her.

"Where are we, Stanmore?"

"Thank God! I feared—Thea, are you all right?"

His arms tightened around her, and a kiss landed half on her eye, half on her cheek. It felt nice, but—

"Stanmore, can you do no better?"

This surprised a relieved choke of laughter out of him. "I apologize. My aim was never good in the dark."

"But why are we in the dark?" She thought of the cottage. "And *where* are we?"

"Where but in the chapel? Don't you remember that you opened the secret door?"

She wanted to point out that was a long time ago, but changed her mind. "Why the dark? We had a lamp."

"I dropped it when you swooned."

She raised her head, and caught her breath at a stab of pain behind her eyes.

"What is it, Thea?"

"I did not swoon."

"You did. And I caught you, but I dropped the lamp. The glass dome shattered. I suppose we must be grateful that the flame was extinguished."

"When was that?"

"But a few moments ago, though I confess it seemed like aeons with you unconscious. Thea, do you think you can stand if I help you up? I'm afraid my knees rebel against the hardness of the floor."

She ignored this. "Stanmore, was I with you all the time?"

"All of what time?"

"After you dropped the lamp. After I swooned, as you call it."

He was quiet, but in the dark she felt his eyes on her.

"So I *was* here," she said.

"Thea, let me take you to your room."

"Wait. I must tell you something, and the dark suits me well."

"Then let us sit in a pew."

"I shan't object. The stones are very cold."

Having discovered a pew almost immediately behind them, he settled her within the shelter of his arms. For a moment, she was content just to sit and to savor his nearness, his strength, his warmth. And to allow herself to believe in the power of love.

'Twas no more than the other Thea had done when Henry kissed her. The other Thea had allowed herself to believe that love would conquer obstacles and opposition.

But love was vanquished. Thea Wortley and Prince Henry met in the cottage in October. Early October, 1612, since Frederick of Palatine was expected but had not yet arrived. And on the sixth of November, Henry died.

"Thea, why did you ask whether you were with me after you swooned?"

"Would you believe me if I told you that I did not swoon

but that I stumbled into the past? That, instead of the chapel, I entered Edward Archer's cottage of two hundred years ago?"

"Are you saying that is what you did?"

"Yes."

She could not see his face in the dark, but his very stillness told of an inner struggle.

"Tell me then," he said.

When she had finished, he was quiet for so long that she began to fear having put him to sleep with her tale.

"Stanmore? What do you think?"

"I think you swooned and dreamed of that visit to the cottage."

"It did not feel like a dream. And that is not what I asked you. Don't you think this confirms absolutely that William Seymour Archer was Dorothea and Henry's child?"

"Why would Prince Henry allow his son to be named William Seymour? And why would Edward Archer insist in the chronicles that the child was Arbella and Seymour's son?"

"That I don't know yet. I'll go back and find out."

Very pleasantly," he said, "The deuce you will."

She stared at him. "I wish you had not broken the lamp. I think you are jesting, but I cannot tell for certain without seeing your eyes."

He rose, picking her up in his arms. Slowly, feeling his way with short, sliding steps, he carried her toward the study.

"Stanmore, put me down."

"Hold still, lest you wish to see us both sprawled on the floor."

"But I can walk."

"Carrying you is the only way I know to keep a hold on you. I held your hand when we twisted the boss and opened the door, but you slipped away."

"I merely wanted to relieve you of the lamp. Your wrist looked sore."

His foot encountered wall, and he stopped.

"But I told you that it is only a bee sting."

"How could you get stung by a bee?"

"When I rode back from Rothamstead, I took the shortcut through the park to warn the housekeeper and Silas that my great-aunt's butler would arrive presently. And even though it was dark and only March, one of the bees found me. One always does. They know I don't like them, and they certainly don't like me."

He moved to the right and found the doorway to the study. The panel had swung partially shut. Nudging it with his elbow, he crossed the threshold into the study.

"Now you can put me down," said Thea. "I can see the hallway door."

"Not until we are far from the chapel." He quickened his pace. "When we opened the hidden door, I knew I should hold on to you. Something told me—warned me—not to let go of you. But you got away. When you swooned—dash it, Thea! Those few moments when you were unconscious—I was never more frightened in my life."

She hugged his neck. "Nothing will happen now. I don't feel the force tugging at me."

"It stopped as you started to pitch forward." He entered the hallway, where a lamp at the foot of the stairs diffused the darkness. "Believe me, if afterward I had felt the slightest sign of warmth, the merest hint of the power's presence, I would have snatched you out of the chapel even before I was assured that you were alive."

"Alive! Surely you did not think me dead!"

"I found no pulse at first. No heartbeat."

She knew him so well now, the very quietness of his voice and manner told her just how very frightened he had been.

"Thea, please stay away from the chapel."

"We're so close to having all the answers. I feel I ought to try once more to go back . . . to go back in time and become Thea Wortley."

They had reached the stairs, and he mounted them swiftly,

as though she were no burden at all. On the first-floor landing, he put her down, his face grim.

"I no longer care about answers. I no longer wish to solve the mystery of my ancestor's birth. I believed that I must prove our chronicles false lest my father have an apoplexy over my desire to break with Archer traditions. I was wrong."

A chill came over her. "Then you no longer need me."

"Not as a historian. But, Thea—I need you, I want you as my wife."

She was not aware of moving toward him. In fact, she was certain she had not done so but, nevertheless, found herself in his arms being soundly and most satisfactorily kissed until she was breathless.

His eyes held a gleam when he looked at her. "Please note that my aim improved with light. Also that I am keeping my word and am not pressing you for an answer. I am merely conducting my courtship."

"Courtship?" Struggling to regain her breath and composure, she failed dismally to sound as severe as the occasion demanded. "I am glad you explained. I might have regarded a kiss on the landing as the act of a libertine."

He frowned and lightly touched her brow. "You have a bruise. Scarcely noticeable, but it is there. Yet I am sure you did not strike your head when you swooned."

But she had struck her head when she tripped over the carved ship in Edward Archer's cottage.

"It must be a smudge. Good night, Stanmore."

"Good night, my love."

Hurrying to her room, she was aware that he followed her into the corridor and watched until the door shut behind her.

They did not meet again until late afternoon of the following day. Thea had finished her examination of the Archer Hall records and, with Silas Wilkins's able assistance, was returning every ledger and document to its proper place when Stanmore entered the muniment room.

"I'll help Miss Stone. Thank you, Silas."

The large man cocked a brow and looked from one to the other. "And, mayhap, I should stay to make certain you'll be thinking and speaking of the present and the future instead of a long dead past."

"I need no tutor to conduct my courtship, thank you very much," Stanmore said repressively.

Thea turned to the desk that had been hers for more than a month. One volume of the chronicles lay on the otherwise bare top. The last volume, opened to the last entry, the notation of a stillborn child and Charlotte Archer's death.

She had not placed the book there.

She heard Silas leaving, whistling softly, and was about to close the book when Stanmore spoke.

"The chronicles are one of the Archer traditions that will not be continued. When we marry, we shall start a family Bible—or, if you will permit, we shall add to yours. It would not be unfitting, would it? Since it appears that, although through different lines, we're both descended from Dorothea Wortley."

She faced him. "When we marry . . . how certain you sound. Do you wish to punish me by letting me know how much I will disappoint and hurt you if I choose Hochstein?"

"You will not choose Hochstein. I am certain of your love. And I am certain you will be released from your promise not to have that preposterous marriage annulled."

"How much I want to believe that!" She started to pace. "Stanmore, let us talk of something else. Your child, the one that was stillborn—"

"It was not my child."

She came to a halt and turned, facing him again.

"Charlotte and I had not lain together since Bella's conception. Charlotte had even left Archer Hall for a time."

"After the near drowning of the children. Silas told me."

His mouth tightened but, Thea felt sure, not because of Silas's indiscretion.

He said, "She fled to her father, and rightly so. I don't know what I would have done had she stayed. But some months later, her father brought her back. She was with child."

"And you let her stay. Because she was your wife."

"I had no choice then. I was caught in a trap of my own making. A trap dug by a misguided sense of duty and obligation. You see, I had seen to it that news of her misdeeds and the desertion was not spread. I let it be known she was caring for her ailing mother, because I felt I owed it to the children, to the Archer name."

"Perhaps you did."

"No." He stepped close to her and gave her a sudden smile. "I had a long discussion on the subject of children with your Miss Simmons this morning."

"And she told you that children are not the delicate creatures they seem. She recommended you deal with them truthfully."

He grimaced. "I felt a mere schoolboy myself when she was through with me. But I was restored to her good graces when I suggested that we accompany Bella and Charlie and Mr. Locke to a history lesson in the chapel."

"Oh, have you done so already? I wish you had sent for me."

He shook his head. "You know why I would not ask you to the chapel. Thea—did you dream last night?"

"No." She looked around the muniment room. "I have finished in here. There is no reason why I should not leave Archer Hall."

"I agree."

How chill the room was, though she had not felt it until now. And why did the cold make her think of Thea Wortley and Prince Henry?

She became aware that Stanmore was speaking to someone, a footman, and she had not even heard his approach or that Stanmore had left her to go to the stairwell.

He turned to her when the footman retreated. " 'Tis Markham and Felicity. They have news they wish to share immediately."

"A country house?" In a charming sitting room which, like its neighbor, the breakfast parlor, had a large window bay jutting into the south lawn, Thea looked from Felicity to Markham. "That is . . . wonderful."

"Then why do you sound so doubtful?" asked Felicity.

"I'm surprised, but no wonder. You meant it as a surprise. This is what you were scheming with Lord Ravensbrook, is it not?"

With mock severity, Stanmore said, "And interrogating me about bailiffs on the sly. Shame! Could you not trust me with your secret?"

"No need to pick on Felicity." Markham's bespectacled boyish face had a sober look. "If I hadn't flaunted myself as a man of principles who'd languish in debtor's prison before touching a penny of his wife's blunt, she would have had no cause to be secretive."

"Principles are very well," said Felicity, sliding closer to Markham on the sofa. "But not when they cause marital squabbles and unhappiness."

Markham clasped his wife's hand. "Don't blame me, though, if we have to flee the country when I slay the first man who calls me a fortune hunter."

He was smiling and once more looked the good-natured cherub everyone knew, but beneath the cheerfulness lay a bit of sober truth. He would, indeed, mind very much if he were suspected of having married for riches. And he did not feel comfortable using his wife's money.

"Four hundred acres go with the house," said Markham. "And there's adjoining land I can purchase later. I'll be dashed if I don't make a go of being a successful farmer. And I'll pay you back every groat and nickel you spent, my love."

"Yes, you will." For once, Felicity looked grave. "But the money will go into a trust for the children."

There was more talk, but Thea no longer listened. She was thinking about something Vespera had said to her. Something about good principles and foolish ones. And something about a sacrifice not being worth the pain ensued if the pain also touched another person.

"Thea!" Felicity clapped her hands like a governess demanding attention. "Stop dreaming! I'm returning to town with John. We're leaving in the morning. So will you come and have dinner with us tonight?"

"You're leaving?" Thea's thoughts tumbled. "May I go with you? I have business to attend in town on Tuesday. And my work is finished here. All that remains to be done—"

She turned to Stanmore. "Is an exploration of Barnet House. Do I have your permission to look over the house in the Strand?"

He gave her a pensive look. "I'm going to London, too. I'll personally show you Barnet House. And I shall give myself the pleasure of accompanying you when you tend to that business on Tuesday."

Felicity's bright, inquisitive gaze flying from one to the other precluded argument. And, in truth, any objection Thea might have raised, had she been alone with Stanmore, would have carried little conviction. Her foolish heart delighted in the opportunity to spend more time with him.

Twenty-five

"Barnet House."

Having circled the church of St. Mary-le-Strand, Stanmore brought the curricle to a halt. He cast a quizzing look at Thea, who gazed in silence at the decaying splendor of the hundred-fifty-year-old mansion with its Italian-style front of pilasters and tall windows.

At last she said, "Do you realize that very likely this is, except for the Savoy Chapel and Northumberland House, the oldest building in the Strand?"

"And has the looks of it, too." Handing the reins to the groom, Stanmore helped her from the curricle. "Come back in an hour, Jenkins."

Thea said, "How clutch-fisted you are with your time all of a sudden. Can you not spare me another two hours at least?"

Stanmore nodded assent to Jenkins, then followed Thea, who hurried toward the arched entrance to escape the blustering March wind.

She said, "And if it was regard for my reputation that inspired your wish to cut my visit short, pray consider that it will make no difference whether I'm seen leaving your house after one hour or after two."

"How true. In either case, you will have to marry me."

"Not at all. But I shall never again be invited to speak or write for the Society of Antiquaries if one of the august members happens to see me."

He chuckled. "So that is the reason for the upturned collar

and this mad dash to the house. And I believed it was the cold."

"It is both." She looked to her right where, past Strand Lane, stood Somerset House with rooms in the north front for the Society of Antiquaries. "Let us in, Stanmore. Or must we knock?"

He opened the door. "I warned Belton and his wife that I would bring a visitor. If we're fortunate, we may be served a dish of tea to warm us."

"Why must we be fortunate?"

"Because this morning when I left, the kitchen stove was belching smoke. And there was no sign of the sweep, who was supposed to have come last week."

"Then let us hope—" She broke off, staring at the dust coating the marble of a once magnificent entrance hall.

"Stanmore, this is a disgrace. I know you said the caretaker is old and plagued by arthritis, but can you not employ some help to maintain at least a semblance of order?"

"The house should be torn down."

"Oh, no! It was built by John Webb, was it not? A pupil of Inigo Jones. It ought to be restored . . . the woodwork replaced, floors and ceilings repaired. And, I daresay, the kitchens are antiquated. But, I vow, when you're done you will consider it money and effort well spent!"

He looked amused. "I shall ask my father to make you a gift of the house. A wedding gift. Then *you* may assume responsibility for the cleaning and renovation of the place."

She found it more and more difficult to reproach him when he spoke of their marriage as a settled fact and was glad to be absolved from the necessity by the caretaker's arrival.

Tall and gaunt, a muffler wound around his head and throat, the elderly man bowed stiffly. "There's a fire in the library, my lord. And the missus is asking if the lady would like a spot o' tea."

"How very kind," said Thea. "Perhaps I should see the house first, though."

"Nothing much to see, madam. Excepting dust and cobwebs. If you fancy a nice clean building, you should've stopped at Somerset House, which you passed as you drove up. I watched them tear down the old house and build the new one. That was before *your* time, madam. But you ought to go see it. And the exhibitions, too."

"I've been there. But I'm a strange creature, Belton. I would have preferred a look inside the *old* Somerset House."

"Doubt you would have been admitted, madam. 'Twas a palace then. Now, it's public offices and societies and such. But it's something splendid to look at. You go and see it again."

Knowing Belton's predilection for lengthy argumentation, Stanmore intervened. "Tell Mrs. Belton that we'll have tea in an hour."

"Aye, my lord."

Unfastening her pelisse, Thea watched the old man shuffle toward an archway covered by a length of dust-gray cloth that rippled and danced in a perpetual draft of cold air.

"I know," said Stanmore. "Belton ought to be pensioned off, but, like my great-aunts' butler, he is offended by the mere suggestion."

He placed his hands on her shoulders. "Don't remove your pelisse. You'll be more comfortable if you keep it on until we get to the library."

She stood quite still. If only he would not touch her. Every time he did, hard won resolve wavered. She wanted to consign duty and obligation to perdition and cast herself into his arms—to stay there forevermore.

At last she found the strength to move and to respond with suitable lightness. "Gracious. Are you saying the whole house is as cold as the entrance hall?"

"It is." He draped his caped driving coat over the back of a carved chair, a beautiful specimen of seventeenth-century artisanship. Alas, the wood was dry and cracked. "I feel sure you'll want to see the 'succession chamber' first, and it hasn't had the benefit of a fire since I was forced to abandon it on my last visit."

She started up the stairs. "So that is where the bed collapsed."

"The original four-poster bed commissioned by William Seymour Archer, First Earl Barnet."

"What a shame. He cannot have slept in it, though. He died shortly before the house was completed."

"You will have to be content to know that every succeeding earl slept in the bed. It is considered the master's bed, and the 'succession chamber' was originally referred to as the master's chamber."

"Francis slept in it. Or so I understood from your father. But then, your grandfather never stayed in town, did he? The master's chamber was not needed."

"My grandfather came to town once after his return from France. He attended the coronation, and thereafter left Archer Hall only to accompany my grandmother on visits to her beloved Paris."

Thea paused on the stairs, which, like the grand staircases at Archer Hall, was designed in the open well style.

Her eyes on the carved posts of the gallery rail above, she said, "In 1701, the third earl came to town when the Act of Succession was debated. He slept in the master's chamber on the night before he addressed the Lords and claimed precedence over Sophia of Hanover as successor to Queen Anne."

She looked over her shoulder at Stanmore. "And then he was killed on his way back to Archer Hall."

"If you have set your heart on finding the documents that supposedly disappeared at the time, I fear you will be disappointed."

"Disappointing or not, a search will give me something to do until Lord Wellesley returns from . . . wherever he is."

"Thea—little goose." His voice held warmth and a hint of laughter. "There is a more agreeable occupation to pass the time. A pasttime which *I*, at least, would consider much more delightful than a minute examination of dusty corners and cobweb-hung crannies."

How much she wanted to take him up on the audacious suggestion. His smile and the gleam in his eye—but, no. If she had lost her heart, she must at least keep her head.

She assumed a repressive look. "For shame, sir! You put me to the blush."

"Do I?"

"Indeed, you do. These are most improper advances under the present conditions."

His gaze lingered on her primmed mouth until, at last, she gave up the struggle for severity and, with a choke of laughter, turned and continued up the stairs.

He followed slowly, sorely tempted to tease her further and see her smile and hear her laugh again. And to win the embrace he craved. But if he persisted, he might, instead of a smile, elicit the look of pain that never failed to make him feel a cad.

He was certain that Thea loved him, but she considered herself bound by the pledge her father made over two decades ago on her behalf. And he knew she chafed at Lord Wellesley's absence, for he had accompanied her to the Foreign Office earlier that day so she might leave word that she was available for a meeting before Tuesday. Wellesley's aide informed them, however, that he could not pass the message on since his lordship had left for parts unknown. But he was expected on Tuesday.

Stanmore heard her voice, pensive, speculative—already she had returned to the past.

"The third earl . . . Henry Stuart Archer," she said. "How easy it would be to see significance in the name . . . how easy to assume he was named thus because he was the great-grandson of Henry Stuart, eldest son of James I."

"And is that not who he was?"

She did not reply immediately, but when they reached the first-floor gallery, she faced him.

"Do you believe it, Stanmore? Do you believe what I

dreamed? What I saw in the past—no, what I *lived* in the past? Or are you merely humoring me?"

"Since they are *your* dreams, I believe in them."

"And that time in the chapel, when you thought I swooned—"

"I still think it."

"No. You don't." Her look challenged him. "Or you would not refuse another visit to the chapel with me. And you know I cannot do it alone."

He ignored this, and Thea could not help but remember Lord Barnet's irritation at Stanmore's reserve. Indeed, she could almost sympathize with Barnet.

Stanmore said, "Why should I doubt your dreams when the entry in your family Bible supports them?"

" 'God bless the child born March 25, 1611. God have mercy on his mother.' "

"Do the words not make more sense if Dorothea was the mother?"

"Yes, they do." She frowned. "But it makes no sense at all that Edward Archer would not have known."

He smoothed her brow with his thumb. "If the Lady Arbella handed me an infant birthed in deepest secrecy, and asked me to take care of him, and even visited my cottage to kiss the child before making her escape, I would have good reason to draw the conclusion that I am raising Lady Arbella's child. Would I not, Miss Historian?"

"I suppose so."

She allowed herself to be ushered into a corridor whence another flight of stairs led to the second floor.

She started upward. "But I wish I knew more. I wish the dreams would come again. Or that I could return to the past once more."

"Mind the broken step."

They continued to the top of the stairs in silence. On the landing, she turned to him again, but before she could speak, he caught her in his arms.

"No, Thea. Don't ask. We will not visit the chapel again."

"I must go back. How else can we learn whether Dorothea took Henry's mother to see young William?"

"We know it already. She is the second lady visitor mentioned in the chronicles. Henry's mother. The queen consort, whom Edward Archer went to see at Greenwich, and who prevailed upon King James to confer a barony on a simple soldier and farmer, and to reward him with land and a purse. Because she wanted her grandson to be—"

He raised a brow. "Why do you look at me and smile like that?"

"Because you sound as if it were the sworn truth."

"Have *you* no faith in your dreams? Do you doubt William was James and Anne's grandson?"

She withdrew from his embrace. "I don't doubt it. But—Stanmore, among all the rumors recorded at the time there was never one of Henry fathering a child, or even connecting Henry's name with that of a lady."

"Except for Frances Howard."

He saw her moue of distaste, and smiled. "Just so. It is well documented that he referred to her as a worn glove."

"Do you see now why I must persist? It wasn't idle curiosity that kept me searching all these years. Something drove me, compelled me on this quest for truth. And still does."

"But perhaps your quest is over. The dreams have stopped, have they not?"

She faltered. It was true, there had been no dreams the last two nights at Archer Hall. Or the previous night in Upper Brook Street. But she was not yet willing to admit that he might be correct.

"Stanmore, which is the 'succession chamber'?"

If he had hoped she would pursue the previous topic, he did not show it but crossed the landing to the door behind her. He opened it and stood back to allow her to enter.

It was a large chamber, dominated by the bedstead in the center—the bedstead with its broken frame, three of the carved posts leaning drunkenly inward, the fourth snapped, and the drooping, tattered velvet of canopy and drapes as described by Stanmore the night they met at Felicity and Markham's house.

She walked around the bed to the window, which offered a splendid view of the river with its boats and barges, with Strand Bridge to her right, and the Southwark end of Blackfriars Bridge visible on her left. But she scarcely took note of the view. She was far too aware of Stanmore standing just inside the room. Aware of his silence.

She kept her eyes on the river. "Why do you think the dreams have stopped and the search may be over?"

"Because it was Dorothea compelling you. She was the hand of fate guiding you. It was not your quest you pursued, but hers."

She heard him come closer; still, she did not turn.

He said, "Dorothea and Henry's love was doomed. But she wanted their love to live on, and so she reached out through time and made it possible that you . . . descended from her, would meet me . . . descended from Henry. That we would love as she and Henry loved two centuries ago."

Her throat tightened. The view of the river misted over.

He took another step closer. "Dorothea's purpose is fulfilled, Thea. Now it lies in our hands to cherish the love we have found."

She did not dare turn. She mustn't show pain, mustn't indulge in tears, since her misery was of her own choosing.

Perhaps, if she could convince herself that she might, without loss of honor and esteem, disregard a promise . . . perhaps, if she could disregard the obligations inherent in her birth, her name, her very existence . . . but she did not know if she could.

At last, when she was certain her smile would not waver, she faced him again.

"What a lovely thought, Stanmore. Now, who is the romantic? Do you remember? 'Tis what you called me once."

He searched her face, then said abruptly, "If you still want to test the paneling for a hidden compartment, we had best get started."

And she knew that she had hurt him. She was doing what Vespera had decried. She was making a sacrifice that inflicted pain on another.

Twenty-six

Thea watched Stanmore tap the wall next to the fireplace, and the mantelpiece itself, but she did not join in the enterprise. For once, ancient lost documents held no allure.

Listless, she roamed the chamber. The 'succession chamber.' "Your father said he searched this room, indeed *every* room in the house, and found nothing."

Stanmore straightened from his examination of the lower wainscoting. His eyes rested keenly on her.

She said, "Besides, we have so little time before you must take me back to Upper Brook Street, it is hardly worth the effort getting started."

His face softened. "Now I know what ails you. You're in a miff! Because Vespera foiled your scheme to spend a night in this room."

"In a miff! How can you say so?"

He raised a brow and gave her such a quizzical look that she was hard put to keep a straight face. Alas, that he had been present when Vespera informed her that she would not accompany her to town.

"What an abominable creature you are! Telling me I'm in a miff, then trying to make me smile when I'm indignant. I was bowled over by Vespera's desertion, I admit. And how could I not be? After all these years, she plans to leave me."

"And you so dependent on her that you never take a step without her."

She ignored that. Trying to look her most severe, she joined him by the cold fireplace. "And *you!* I never expected to be dealt such a shabby trick."

"What was I to do? I was in desperate straits. The only applicant for the governess position wrote that she got married. And Miss Simmons offered her services."

"Indeed." Dryly. "You were quite innocent. Your hand was forced."

"You might say so. Bella was listening at the door. Her squeal left no doubt that she was pleased to have your Miss Simmons staying on."

"As was your father!"

"He never did enjoy playing cards with Higgins."

"And I suppose I am to be delighted that Vespera has proven such an admirable replacement!"

"What a ferocious scowl! But you do not deceive me, Thea. I see laughter dancing in your eyes."

He turned to the door, where a small, elderly woman in a gray stuff gown, apron, and shawl was clearing her throat.

"Good afternoon, Mrs. Belton. Have you come to summon us to tea? I did not realize it was so late."

"It hasn't been an hour, if that's what you mean, my lord. But there's scones, baked fresh, and Belton no longer any good at climbing stairs to tell you. And there's something I've been meaning to give you. But I plumb forgot yesterday and again this morning, until after you'd left."

"What is it?"

Coming closer, Mrs. Belton dipped a hand into a deep pouch dangling from her chatelaine. "I found it after your last visit, when I rescued the linen from the ruins of the bed here. Worm-eaten! That's what every stick of furniture is in this house. Good for nothing, excepting a bonfire down by the river."

"Yes, indeed. But what did you find? I don't recall missing anything."

"Can hardly miss what isn't yours, can you, my lord? And I doubt 'twas *you* who cut into the quilting of the canopy to hide old papers. No, I'm sure the misdeed was done before your time."

Thea and Stanmore exchanged a look.

Stanmore said, "Let me have the papers, if you please."

"But, didn't I just—" The caretaker's wife looked down, surprised to see her hand still inside the pouch. "Well, I'll never! Next I'll forget the head on my shoulders."

She withdrew her hand, along with a roll of papers tied with string.

Watching, Thea winced when fragments of yellow-brown paper fluttered to the floor. She drew a breath of relief when the scroll rested safely in Stanmore's hand.

He said, "This was in the bed, Mrs. Belton?"

"In the canopy. It's quilted velvet, and not a few of the stitches have come loose. But there was one spot—"

Moving with surprising sprightliness, Mrs. Belton pushed aside the tattered cloth that had once been a bed curtain and exposed a strip of thick quilting.

"Here, my lord. Where the post snapped, that's where the canopy tore off the frame. And here's the part where not just two or three stitches are loose but a good four inches of stitching. That's where the paper roll showed."

Thea wanted to examine the fabric, but when she touched the velvet, it started to shred in her fingers.

"It must be as old as the bed. Is that possible, Stanmore?"

"Quite possible." He undid the string around the scroll. "I doubt anything was ever replaced in this house."

"The drapes on the bed are new," said Mrs. Belton. "I remember when your grandmother had them made up. She was pleased that they matched the canopy, for 'twas fabric she brought back from France. But the quality wasn't a match to the older cloth. Thirty years or less, and already it's in tatters."

Stanmore started to unroll the paper. Dust danced in the air and more yellow-brown flakes drifted to the ground.

"Wait!" said Thea. "Don't try to straighten it. I'm afraid it'll crumble."

"There are three sheets, and one feels as ancient as the other. Like baked dust." He offered her the scroll. "In comparison, the string seems brand-new."

The string held no interest for Thea as she turned the loosely rolled sheets in her hands. It was very old paper, indeed.

"Stanmore, there are crease marks where the paper was folded at one time. Also, remnants of sealing wax."

"I scraped most of it off," said Mrs. Belton. "If you like, I'll take a hot iron and a scrap of blotting paper to the rest."

Dismay robbed Thea of speech.

Stanmore said, "Thank you, Mrs. Belton, that will be all."

The old woman tripped off but paused in the door, saying, "And if I don't mistake the young lady's intentions, she's set on reading those old papers. So you had best take her to the library, my lord. Else I can see the fire and the scones all go to waste."

"Those old papers" referred to by Mrs. Belton were a letter from William Seymour, Duke of Somerset, endorsed to William Seymour Archer, the Right Honorable the Earl Barnet.

The paper was discolored, the ink faded, and where the letter had been folded some words could only be guessed at. The first part of the date was smudged, leaving —ember, 1660.

"Which must be November," said Thea, voice and hands shaking, "It is the month he died. Just a few weeks after his restoration to the dukedom. Stanmore, if only you had examined the bed in February!"

He squinted at the spidery writing, and without comment lit every candle in the library, then fetched a pair of massive candelabrums from another room and placed them on tables near Thea's chair.

"You will either have to read the letter aloud or hand it over," he said, knowing full well what her decision would be.

She did not even glance up. Slowly, at times haltingly, she started to read, unrolling the brittle paper an inch at a time.

My honorable good friend, I have received your letter wherein you express your felicitations upon my restoration to the dukedom and yield you my heartfelt thanks. But you also expressed gratitude that I should have exerted my influence to gain you an earldom, and that gratitude I must humbly refuse to accept. It was your loyalty to the house of Stuart which caused honors to be conferred on you. I was but the instrument bringing your valor to His Majesty's notice.

My friend, having arrived at that point of my life when the physician shakes his head every time he enters my chamber, I must now discharge a duty I placed upon myself some time ago and confirmed this past May, upon the accession of our gracious majesty, King Charles II.

I doubt not that you remember as well as I do the occasion of our first meeting—the celebration after we took Bristol in the king's cause. You told me fate had destined that you and I sit side by side in the tavern because you had an inquiry. Then you spoke your name and asked if I am your father.

I told you nay, my honorable friend. Which is God's truth, I vow! And I believed that would be the end of the matter. But we met again some ten years later, and once more you spoke to me. You told the full tale of your birth as you knew it from your foster father, and again I told you nay, the Lady Arbella did not bear me a child. Again, God's truth.

Yet I might have told you who you are. And I spoke not. Silence was justified, I assured myself, because we were then in the second year of Oliver Cromwell's reign and none of your blood were safe. Your blood, my friend, is Stuart blood, though not through the Lady Arbella. You are the son of Henry Stuart, our most noble prince, whose untimely death was mourned by all Great Britain.

I had this from the Lady Arbella herself. She witnessed your birth and delivered you into the care of your foster father, Edward Archer, who was at the time a guard in service to the Bishop of Durham. Your mother was Mistress Dorothea Wortley, who exchanged vows with Prince Henry at Greenwich Palace that same morning of Friday, the twenty-second of June when the Lady Arbella and I were wed. I personally know not of the vows exchanged by the prince and his lady, but I did see him arrive at Greenwich on the Thursday at night, about twelve of the clock, when I myself arrived with two friends to await the minister who was to perform my marriage to the Lady Arbella.

And it please you, my good friend, I will show you the letter from the Lady Arbella in which she wrote of you after the funeral of our most beloved Prince Henry— though I did not receive the letter until my return to England, when it was presented to me by Lady Wortley, who was the mother of Mistress Dorothea, and who served my Lady Arbella until the end.

I crave your understanding for this ill written epistle. These days I suffer from a great tiredness and am therefore constrained to put down my pen every few moments.

Now I must inform you that it was the Lady Arbella's desire to have you named William Seymour, which honored me, and in my second marriage it pleased me to name a daughter Arbella.

I pray you not delay if you wish speech with me. I have not much time. And if we have no occasion to meet again, I beseech you to consider well what to do with the knowledge you now possess. I pray you to remember that someone deemed it wise to conceal your birth.

And so requesting you to maintain me in your favor,

I take my leave and commit you to the Lord's eternal protection.

> Your friend,
> William Seymour

The teapot was empty when Thea finished reading. The scones were eaten—by Stanmore. The fire had been replenished and was again burning low. And Belton had announced Jenkins's arrival with the curricle.

Across the tea tray, Stanmore met Thea's eyes. He did not speak, but there was no need.

"Yes," she admitted. "I should be able to let the matter rest now. Some questions have been answered. And others . . . I don't suppose they'll ever be."

"Others?" His voice held a teasing note. "Such as whether Francis forged the letter to make a point with his father?"

She gave him a startled look, then laughed. "Indeed! He would choose as the letter writer William Seymour, a man whose hand is well represented in the records at Oxford and in the state papers."

"Very well. Perhaps he did not forge. But I'd like to think it was Francis who supplied the string."

"The string has caught your fancy, has it not? But I admit, I rather think it, too. Francis must have seen that the paper was in danger of tearing at the folds, and therefore he rolled and tied it."

"What do you suppose happened to the letter from Lady Arbella to William Seymour—the Duke of Somerset?"

"I cannot begin to guess. He might have burned it on his deathbed. It might lie forgotten among other old papers. He might even have given it to his namesake, your ancestor."

She set the scroll beside Stanmore's teacup. "But this letter—if, in fact, Francis found it, why did he not take it to Archer Hall? Would it not have advanced his cause?"

"More questions without an answer. I wonder how *my* father will receive the news. He does not hold it against Felicity and her family that they're descended from an illegitimate son. But our own family . . . a bastard line?"

"And it can be nothing else. Even if Dorothea and Henry exchanged vows, even if the minister who married Arbella and Seymour also married Henry and Dorothea, the marriage would have been illegal since Henry needed his father's consent."

"No doubt about it, my father's pride will suffer a blow."

Thea remembered Lord Barnet's outburst when she questioned him about the bloodline. "Undoubtedly so—if William had turned out to be Lizzy Archer's illegitimate son. Yet I cannot help but think that your father may be pleased to claim descent from Henry, Prince of Wales."

"If you're right—" Stanmore groaned. "The prospect is daunting. Like my grandfather and the third earl, he may take it into his head that an Archer instead of a Guelph ought to sit on the throne."

She smiled. "A third Stuart uprising?"

"Not if I can help it. I've written the headmaster at Harrow—over my father's protest, needless to say—"

"Did you? How wonderful! Does Charlie know?"

"He does, and we're hoping to hear that he has been accepted for the fall term. A grandfather who incites rebellion would speedily put a period to that dream."

"I was jesting, Stanmore." She frowned. "Surely, you were, too . . . about your father and the Guelphs?"

"Not entirely."

He rose, picking up the scroll. In growing alarm Thea watched him stride to the fireplace.

"Stanmore, you wouldn't!"

He paused, looked at her, then at the embers in the hearth. Unholy glee lit his face.

"I'm sorely tempted. But, no, my little goose. I wouldn't do it."

She went to him. "Then what will you do with the letter?"

He lifted the lid off a large tarnished silver urn atop the

mantel and dropped the scroll in. Replacing the lid, he said, "It'll be safe here until I've spoken with my father."

"Judging by the depth of the tarnish, it is as good a hiding place as the canopy was."

"At least until you are mistress of Barnet House."

She turned abruptly. She did not speak. Could not speak.

Twenty-seven

"Thea. My love." Any vestige of lightheartedness had left Stanmore's voice. "I cause you pain. That was never my intent."

"I know."

She did not hear him move, but suddenly he stood before her. He looked pale, his eyes troubled.

He said, "You must think me insensitive to your dilemma. But I am not. I hoped, if I ignored it, I could sweep you off your feet."

"You do. That is what pains me so. All too often when I am with you, I forget that I am not free to love. I forget obligations, the promise I made. But oblivion does not last. And I feel an utter wretch."

"So I'm beginning to realize."

"And it is worse that I hurt *you* by behaving the way I do. Stanmore, I am very sorry."

"Don't apologize!" A flash of rare anger swept through him. He gripped her hands, drawing them to his chest. "I happen not to think much of the pledge your father made on your behalf. Or of the promise you gave the Foreign Secretary. But if *you* feel bound, then don't apologize for doing what you believe is right!"

She did not flinch or draw back. "I no longer know what is right."

Her quiet dignity doused the hot flame in him, and he gentled his hold on her hands.

"Thea, when Miss Simmons spoke to me about my children, she also spoke of you. She told me that she raised you as your parents would have wished it—because of the promise she gave your father in the Conciergerie."

Her eyes widened at the seeming switch of subject, but she made no comment. Neither did she try to free herself.

"You see, our upbringing was not dissimilar. *Duty, responsibility, obligation* might have served as motto for either of us. That is why I understand your scruples, even though I think them invalid."

"Stanmore, I do not care to discuss this any further." Her hands fluttered beneath his. "And we ought to go. We mustn't keep Jenkins and your horses standing in the wind."

For a moment longer, he held her hands. Then, reluctantly, he set her free.

"These are sad times when a man is slave to his cattle. But, indeed, we mustn't keep them waiting."

He fetched her pelisse, draped over a tapestry screen that was relegated into a corner of the library because of its tattered appearance. As he helped Thea into the pelisse and adjusted the wide fur collar, he was sorely tempted to kiss the slender neck, shown to advantage once more since she had reverted to her old hairstyle, the chignon. But, as if she sensed his intent, she drew away abruptly.

And, perhaps, it was better thus. He feared he would not have been content with one kiss—or to kiss her neck only. And a true kiss would have troubled her further. She felt so guilty already, he was beginning to fear that she would volunteer to go to Hochstein merely to appease her conscience.

Hard as it would be, he must see to it that she had no cause to make a rash decision before her meeting with Wellesley.

She faced him with the regality of bearing and the open gaze he had admired from the moment of their meeting.

"Shall we go?"

He grimaced ruefully. "Dash it, Thea! I was so certain I could convince you that our love is all-powerful if I simply pursued my courtship of you. Alas, I contributed to your misery."

"Untrue. You gifted me with your love and gave me precious moments of great happiness and joy."

"Mere moments are not enough. You're mine, Thea. I won't give you up."

She blanched. "Don't say that! 'Tis what Henry said to Dorothea. A month later, he was dead!"

"That is history. *We are now.* We shall be married. On the twenty-second of June. Two hundred years to the day Dorothea and Henry pledged their troth."

She was silent, and he feared he had hurt her again. Why the deuce did he not say what he meant to say and be done with it!

Suddenly, the ghost of a smile flitted across her face. "To the day, Stanmore? Have you forgotten the change of calendar, which jumped eleven days?"

"You're trying to provoke me, but you shan't succeed. As to the calendar—why should we worry about such a trifle? Dorothea did not, when she whispered in your ear to name the twenty-second of June your wedding day."

She started for the door, saying quietly, " 'Tis kind of you to blame Dorothea for my foolishness. But now, if you don't mind, I wish to speak no more of it."

"We won't." He hesitated for the span of a heartbeat. "Thea, 'tis best that we do not see each other again until Tuesday."

Not until Tuesday.

She could not afterward recall anything about the drive to Upper Brook Street, save for an aching tightness in her chest and the effort it cost to show a semblance of composure. But she must have conversed with Stanmore, for he had said, when he helped her from the curricle, "Then it is agreed that I shall call for you Tuesday morning at ten o'clock." She had not remembered agreeing, and yet she must have done so.

Tuesday morning was three days and four nights away. She would not see him again until it was time for her meeting with the Foreign Secretary, who might want to send her to Hochstein because Cousin Friedrich was dead.

Since Vespera delivered Lord Wellesley's message, Thea had given little thought to Hochstein, the country, or to Hochstein's people. She had left when she was four years old. She remembered the castle and the mountains—the Erzgebirge—but none of the towns and villages. She did not remember the people.

Perhaps they did not want her to return.

From her great-grandmother, she knew that the Hochsteiners had not been unhappy under Friedrich's rule. But then, the people of Hochstein would be content under the devil himself, Grandmother Augusta had written, as long as their menfolk were not expected to fight his battles.

Grandmother Augusta . . . Thea did not remember the old lady either but felt she knew her through her letters. If only there were a means of instant communication . . . or if Vespera or her foster father were in town . . . or if she could speak with Stanmore.

No, not with Stanmore. She had hurt him enough. It was for the best that she would not see him the next three days.

But if Stanmore gave an explanation why he would not see her before Tuesday, she had not heard it.

And if they did not meet, and on Tuesday she learned that she was needed in Hochstein—she wished she had told him that they must make the most of these three days while she did not know what would be required of her.

And she wished that he had stayed at Archer Hall and had not come to town at all.

Never ceasing, around and around, her thoughts tumbled—for how long, she did not know—until, all of a sudden, Felicity's voice, shrill with exasperation, broke through the wall of distraction.

"For heaven's sake, Thea! If you don't tell me this instant what Stuart did to you, I vow I'll throw my cup at you!"

The return from that otherworld of thought jarred. With growing astonishment Thea looked about her. She blinked and blinked again, but the scenario did not change. She was seated at the *breakfast table* with Felicity, glaring in outrage and poised to hurl one of her prized Worcester cups.

"Gracious!" Thea said weakly. "It is . . . Saturday?"

"Yes!" The glare intensified, but the cup was carefully returned to its saucer. "And if I did not know it was Stuart with whom you spent most of yesterday, I'd think you have suffered ravishment!"

"I beg your pardon?"

"What happened, Thea? You left in good spirits and returned—oh, I don't know how to describe it. You look ghastly. You've been oblivious to anyone and anything around you. Did the Foreign Office give you bad news?"

"No news at all. I shall have to wait for Lord Wellesley."

"Something happened at Barnet House, then. Dash it, Thea! We are friends. Tell me!"

"We found a letter from—"

"A pox on the letter!" Felicity drew several deep breaths. More calmly, she said, "I want to know what happened between you and Stuart. You're in love with each other. Even John noticed as soon as he saw you together. So why can you not resolve whatever problem lies between you?"

"If you are my friend, you will not press me for answers I do not have at present."

Felicity's irritation vanished and was replaced by concern.

"If you want a bit of advice—and even if you don't—listen to me, Thea. We've been taught to be quiet and patient and demure, and to allow the suitor to initiate conversation and to choose topics. We've been taught it is bold and unbecoming if we voice our feelings and opinions. *Don't you believe it.* Do you think I would be married if I had not shown some boldness? John would never have approached me if I hadn't made it impossible for him *not* to."

"Bold Felicity and timid Thea."

The wry comment elicited a giggle, but almost immediately Felicity was serious again. "No, I know you're not timid. Which means that your problem is not something that can be solved by a bit of frankness? By plain speaking?"

"It is not."

"Then it must be that preposterous marriage your father contracted for you."

Thea rose, and Felicity immediately followed suit.

"Now I've made you angry. I did not mean to, Thea. Will you help me pack? Molly has cut her hand and it had to be bandaged. She'll be too clumsy for a while to touch the crystal. And with just the two of us, you can talk to me anytime you wish."

Thea gladly assisted with the packing of delicate glasses and precious crystal. But she did not avail herself of the opportunity to talk. Indeed, now that she had pulled herself together, she could scarcely believe that she had longed to discuss her dilemma with Vespera or her foster father, or even with her great-grandmother.

Discussion would inevitably lead to a proffering of suggestions and advice that would not be of the least benefit to her. What she needed was news. The bare facts on the situation in Hochstein. And she could only pray that, on Tuesday, the Foreign Secretary would have more information than he disclosed in his note.

Tuesday morning. Three days and three nights.

It helped that she could be of assistance to Felicity, who hoped to move into the country house by the end of the month. Felicity possessed a great number of glasses—far too many for the modest dinners and musical evenings she had occasionally held in town—and there were also dinner services that required special care. Thus, Saturday night, Thea went to bed so tired that she fell asleep immediately.

But Sunday began inauspiciously when she awoke from a dream. Not a dream about Lady Arbella or Dorothea and

Prince Henry. But a dream showing her and Stanmore about to be married in the hidden chapel at Archer Hall. . . .

The minister saying, "If any man can show just cause, why they may not lawfully be joined together, let him now speak, or else hereafter for ever hold his peace."

And a tall, sullen-looking man rising in the last pew. "The woman, Theadora Evalina von Hochstein, is my wedded wife."

Upon which the minister turned to her, and she recognized him as her foster father, the Reverend Felix Simmons. "I require and charge ye, Theadora Evalina, as ye will answer at the dreadful day of judgment when the secrets of all hearts shall be disclosed, that if ye know any impediment, why ye may not be lawfully joined to this man, Stuart Seymour Archer, ye do now confess it."

She had awoken and lain in her bed, miserable and aching, until she heard the hall clock downstairs declare the hour of six. Until nine o'clock, when she could assume that Felicity and Markham had risen, she sorted through her trunks, which had been packed haphazardly and in a great hurry. And when she lifted the heavy tome of Tudor and Stuart history, out fell the note she had penned to Lord Wellesley to apprize him of her pending departure to Archer Hall.

Kneeling in front of the open trunk, she stared at the message. She had written it before Stanmore asked her to Archer Hall; when, in fact, it was still doubtful that she would be invited. How determined she had been to overcome Stanmore's reservations.

Had she pursued *her* quest? Or Dorothea's, as Stanmore suggested?

Crumpling the notice, she tossed it into the hearth. How simple it was to dispose of the written word. Would that she could banish thoughts with as little effort.

But it was impossible. She could not stop thinking of Stanmore and what he said about Dorothea reaching out through time so that her love and Henry's would live on.

When, on Monday, she sought out a jeweler and had the

ruby ring cleaned and examined, she was hardly surprised that he confirmed the day and month, 22 June, in the leaf arabesque etched to the left of the entwined T and H, and the year 1610 to the right of the initials.

Dorothea's ring. The ring given by Henry as a token of his troth.

Discovery of the date held no joy since she could not share the news with Stanmore. Lud! How she missed him. But she would not see him until the next morning, and then only as her escort to the Foreign Office.

And if she hurt with loneliness and longing for him after two days, how much worse she would hurt if she left for Hochstein. Without him.

Dorothea had traveled to Hochstein without her beloved Henry. And without her child.

God bless the child born March 25, 1611. God have mercy on his mother.

How Dorothea must have hurt.

And the Lady Arbella had languished and died in the Tower when she was separated from her love . . .

Leaving the jeweler and returning to Upper Brook Street, Thea hoped to give her thoughts a different direction with the tedious task of wrapping still more glassware and delicate china, only to find that Felicity had already finished the chore and as a result was tired, fretful, even lachrymose.

She greeted Thea with suspiciously red eyes. "I've just had the most horrid thought!"

"You may tell me all about it in a moment. But first put up your feet. Why do you think Markham bought the stool? Surely not because he adores the magenta- and violet-striped cover!"

But Felicity was not to be diverted. "Thea I'm beginning to *show!*"

"I believe it is a natural progression of your condition. But I did not think that you would mind."

"Well, I don't! That is . . . I do. Because I know that you

and Stuart will settle your differences, and in June I'll be eight months along, and I'll be so big—" Felicity blew her nose. "So big that you wouldn't possibly want me at the wedding!"

"You needn't worry about it." If Thea's voice sounded strained, it could be blamed on her bending and forcefully lifting Felicity's feet onto the stool.

"Truly? You promise to ask me to the wedding even if I'm as round as a tub?"

"If there is a wedding, you'll be the first to receive an invitation."

And that night, Thea once more dreamed of her marriage to Stanmore and the minister asking if there was just cause why they should not be joined together.

Twenty-eight

When Stanmore left Thea in Upper Brook Street, he was by no means certain that his decision not to see her again before the meeting at the Foreign Office had been the right one. She had been unnaturally calm and quiet during the drive, had scarcely responded when he explained his decision or when he told her he would fetch her on Tuesday morning and personally drive her to Whitehall. But it was done now, and he could only hope that instinct, telling him to stand back and allow her a brief breathing spell, had not misled him.

Meanwhile, he had three days at his disposal, and if he did not want to go out of his mind with missing Thea and worrying what decision she would make, he had best put the time to good use. He knew nothing about Hochstein, save what Thea had told him. He would try to fill that gap in his education.

He started with White's Club, always a font of information, and where he was a member—as was his father, as had been every Archer since the club's inception within the old White's Chocolate House in the days of the third earl. But although Stanmore spent the evening and a good part of the night at the club, dining and strolling from room to room, the only topic he heard discussed was the Peninsular campaign.

He left, knowing he had made a mistake. Since 1745, when his grandfather was exiled, the Archers had rarely come to town and had at best a nodding acquaintance with the lords, ladies, and gentlemen of the ton. None of the county families Stanmore knew were in town yet; thus, the faces at White's had been unfamiliar, the response cool to his attempts to turn the conversation to the German states. Perhaps he would not have been a stranger at the club had he attended Oxford or Cambridge—but he had not, and there was no point refining upon it.

On Saturday, Stanmore walked to Whitehall, the Foreign Office in Downing Street his first objective. Lord Wellesley had not yet returned, and neither were his aides available.

Not wanting to admit defeat, Stanmore went to the Admiralty. Lord Mulgrave, First Lord of Admiralty, had been the Foreign Secretary in '05 when Tushenko was supposed to have come for Thea but, instead, married Thea's cousin, Erika von Waldfrieden. It was Lord Mulgrave who had extracted Thea's promise not to have her marriage to Tushenko annulled.

The First Lord of Admiralty was in his office, and the name Thea Stone gained Stanmore admission.

Four hours later he left the Admiralty, his step slow, head bowed in thought. His distraction was deep, and he would not have noticed the young man passing him in the colonnade fronting the Admiralty had he not accidentally brushed his elbow against the other man. The contact was slight, but it roused him from his reverie, and a sharp expletive served further to bring him to his senses.

"My apologies, sir." Stanmore noticed the uniform, the sling cradling the right arm—the arm he had brushed with his elbow. And a thick bandage where the hand should have been. "I am *devilish* sorry. I'm a blundering fool. Never looked where I was going."

"No harm done, I think."

Rather white around the mouth, the young officer—a captain, perhaps, with one epaulette on his right shoulder—set down his cloak bag to adjust the sling beneath his forearm. There was something about him . . .

"Sir—"

Stanmore received an impatient stare. The man's face was thin and pale, the face of a stranger, yet teasingly familiar in its structure, the shape and set of the eyes, and the shock of flame-red hair showing beneath the high plumed cap.

"I'm Stanmore. I believe we may have met at some time, though I cannot, I fear, recall the occasion."

A sudden grin wiped out the look of impatience. "No, we haven't met. But if you're Stanmore, you've met my aunt—"

"Vespera Simmons!"

"Aye. Vespera, my father, and I are as alike as three peas in a pod. True Simmonses. One brother and one sister have my mother's dark coloring. The rest vary in shades between blond and brown."

"So you're one of Miss Stone's foster brothers."

"Miles Simmons." He extended his left hand. "Captain in the 52nd under General Craufurd. And you're the man who wants to marry our Thea."

Shaking hands, Stanmore said, "True. But how do you know of me and my intentions? It seems unlikely that Thea should have written."

"She didn't. I stopped at Archer Hall yesterday."

"Ah."

"And a good thing that I did. I meant to call on Thea in a sennight when I'm supposed to see a surgeon. But there's no bearing it at home with a dozen females smothering me with solicitude. And my father not much better. So I packed a bag hoping to find hospitality at Archer Hall."

"My father did not toss you out, did he?"

"No. Vespera did. Told me to make myself useful in Whitehall."

Stanmore looked at the building behind Simmons. "You were about to visit the Admiralty."

"And you just did."

Their eyes met. Stanmore said, "Perhaps we're on the same errand. Have you seen Thea yet?"

"I daren't until I've done Vespera's bidding."

"To find out more about the state of affairs in Hochstein?"

"Aye."

A corpulent gentleman on his way to the Admiralty glared at them. They stepped aside, Simmons nudging the cloak bag along with a booted foot.

"I've come from the Horse Guards. Lord Liverpool—Hawkesbury, then—was in the Foreign Office during the Addington administration. He never met Thea personally, but he did explain about Hochstein and the other German states which formed the coalition with France. And I thought I'd see Lord Mulgrave next."

"I just spent four hours with him. Perhaps we can save each other time by sharing the information we've gathered so far?"

Captain Simmons gave Stanmore a hard stare. "Vespera likes you . . . she's never been wrong yet. Yes, let us join forces. And if she's right about Wellesley wanting Thea to go to Hochstein—demme, I don't like it."

"Neither do I."

"Don't care to be a consort, do you?"

Rather startled, Stanmore said, "The possibility never occurred to me."

"You had better think about it if you want Thea. She's a wonderful girl, but between my father and Vespera she was fed a lot of rubbish about duty and obligation. There's no telling what she'll do if Lord Wellesley spouts off about responsibility to Hochstein and duty to England, and so forth."

"Wellesley needn't bother. Thea has already recalled her obligations. *And* the marriage that took place when she was four."

Simmons scoffed. "Surely you don't think that arrangement valid!"

"Never mind what I think. Thea believes herself pledged. That is what troubles me."

"Tell you what troubles *me.*" Simmons fell silent and waited for two naval officers to pass. "The last time Thea was supposed to return to Hochstein, she was attacked!"

"Attacked. . . . how? I don't understand. Thea said nothing—or Lord Mulgrave!"

"There was supposed to be a ceremony—with a priest and all—on her twenty-first birthday."

"But the groom never showed because he married Thea's cousin. I know that."

"This was before anyone knew he married Erika von Waldfrieden. My parents and Vespera accompanied Thea to the Foreign Office about a week before her birthday. There were details to be discussed—or whatever! Thea left Mulgrave's office. You know how she likes to pace! And a man from Hochstein accosted her in the hallway. He had a dagger."

Fear gripped Stanmore. What had happened once, could happen again. "Thea was certain the man came from Hochstein?"

"She said he introduced himself as a deputy sent by the Hochstein Council to apologize that they hadn't helped her father when Friedrich assaulted the castle. And suddenly he whipped out the dagger hidden in his coat."

Stanmore's mouth was dry. "Was Thea hurt?"

"No. Apparently she moved just as he was about to lunge. She screamed and fought him off, and Lord Mulgrave's aide shot him. Mulgrave had a notice printed in *The Times*, and he also sent messages abroad, that the Princess Theadora Evalina von Hochstein was dead."

"Why?"

"Because all they knew in Hochstein—and Tushenko, too— was that the Princess Theadora lived in England. But they didn't know she was Thea Stone of Ault Hucknall. They still don't."

Stanmore began to feel better. "So nothing has happened since?"

"No." Captain Simmons gripped the hilt of the sword on his right side. "And I'm dashed well going to see to it that nothing will happen."

The corpulent gentleman, leaving the Admiralty, glared at them again as he passed through the colonnade.

"Shall we walk in the park, Stanmore? I don't want to be

interrupted while we exchange information and decide what else we ought to do."

"I'm beginning to think that I must find a way to see Wellesley before Thea does."

"We can take turns watching the Foreign Office." Simmons picked up his cloak bag. "But for now, the park."

Stanmore frowned at the other man. "If you don't mind my saying so, you look a bit peaked and ought to be resting on your couch. Where are you staying?"

"I'll find a place after we've talked."

Stanmore took the cloak bag. "If you're not put off by furniture that collapses and stairs that crumble under your tread, you're welcome to a room at Barnet House. And on Tuesday, you can come with me to fetch Thea."

Thea looked at the watch pinned to her spencer. A quarter past ten. And no sign of Stanmore. Surely he would not allow himself to be detained by a mishap at Barnet House. Not today.

She paced in front of the windows in the downstairs sitting room, which was hardly ever used since the upstairs drawing room was more comfortable and elegant. But from here it was a mere step to the front door. And if Stanmore did not arrive within the next five minutes, she would walk out that front door and look for a hackney coach.

Over the past three days, the feeling that she would be asked to return to Hochstein had increased . . . as had fear that she would have no choice but to consent . . . and fear that she would lack the fortitude to do what was right. She could not bear the waiting any longer.

A distant rattle drew her to the nearest window. Surely this was Stanmore. How breathless she was suddenly—and not because he would take her to Lord Wellesley. She had not seen him in three days . . .

A curricle swept into view and pulled up. Stanmore. She should join him immediately. But she did not move, merely gazed at the beloved face. He nodded to a companion, then smiled—the bright, vivid flash of a grin that had given her a first glimpse of his lighter side.

Two closed coaches had followed the curricle and were rolling to a halt behind it. She paid them no heed; her eyes had moved on . . . to the man beside Stanmore.

Picking up her skirts, she ran outside. "Miles!"

Her brother had descended from the curricle and caught her in his good arm. "Have a care, my girl, or you'll send us sprawling in the gutter."

Careful not to show how his haggard looks affected her, she kissed his cheek. "What are you doing here? I believed you laid up in bed and cosseted by Mother Simmons and Gussy."

"I was. But when Father and all *seven* of Mama's young ladies also started bathing my brow, I escaped."

"Was that wise?" Gently, she touched the sling.

He laughed. "Probably not. Stanmore—he was kind enough to offer me shelter, but I'm afraid he's not much better than the lot at the vicarage. Fussing like an old mother hen."

Her eyes flew to Stanmore's face. Thank you, her look told him.

The smile he gave her in reply made her heart turn over.

She said, "I can't think how you two encountered each other, but there's no time for questions, save one. Miles, are you coming with us to the Foreign Office?"

"No, love." He indicated the first of the two coaches behind the curricle. The passengers were just alighting. "The Foreign Office has come to you."

"Let us go inside," said Stanmore. "There are some introductions that should not take place in the street."

Bemused, she led the way to the sitting room she had left in such a hurry that the door still stood open. She knew the Marquis Wellesley, of course, and believed she recognized one of his aides. But she did not know the third man . . . and there was also a child.

In the sitting room, Stanmore and Miles remained near the

door. Thea proceeded to the center of the room, then turned and faced Wellesley and his companions.

Lord Wellesley said, "Miss Stone, allow me to present the Count Sergei Tushenko."

She felt hot, then cold, and thought she would fall down in a swoon.

But she was Theadora Evalina von Hochstein, and she inclined her head as she had been taught. "Tushenko."

He bowed deeply, the man who should by rights be her husband.

Her heart was beating wildly as she looked at the grave face. She knew him to be thirty-six or thirty-seven years of age, but streaks of gray in his dark hair and deep lines etched into his forehead and along the corners of his mouth made him appear older. The child, a boy of about three, clutched his hand.

"And Tushenko's son," said Wellesley. After an almost imperceptible pause, he added, "Count August Sergeievich Tushenko."

The boy, dressed like Tushenko in a blue coat, breeches, and Hessian boots, let go of his father's hand. He bowed to Thea, speaking in English. "I am also Prince August von Hochstein."

His eyes were blue; wide, innocent eyes.

Bending toward him, she held out her hand. "And I am your cousin Thea. Welcome to England, August."

Gravely, he shook hands, then leaned against his father's leg. His head barely reached the tall man's thigh.

Thea looked to Lord Wellesley to conduct the meeting, but he had stepped aside and was engaged in a low-voiced conference with his aide, whose name, she suddenly remembered, was Mr. Featherlight. What a time her mind had chosen to concern itself with a name.

She met Stanmore's eyes but could not read their expression. Yet she took comfort from his presence. And Miles—it was good to have him here, though she worried that he looked far from well.

And there was Tushenko looking at her.

Instinctively, she stiffened already perfectly straight shoulders and back and held her head just a fraction higher.

"Gentlemen, I did not expect a gathering of this magnitude when Lord Wellesley requested a meeting. In truth, I am at a loss as to its purpose. Pray enlighten me."

Nodding to Mr. Featherlight, who promptly left the room, Wellesley addressed her.

"When I wrote, I had no notion that the proposed meeting would involve anyone but you and me. I should have sent a message—I knew you always stay with Lady Felicity. My apologies, Miss Stone. Also for descending on you unannounced."

"I left word at your office that I would call."

"So I was told when my guests and I arrived in Whitehall this morning. But I also found your foster brother and Lord Stanmore waiting on my doorstep. They were most anxious that you should not appear at my office, where others might be on the watch for you."

Her eyes flew to Stanmore. Even at a distance she had no difficulty seeing the lift of a dark brow, but whether it signaled apology for his high-handed action or something else, she did not know.

Wellesley said, "Miss Stone, Count Tushenko has requested the opportunity to address you."

She forced her attention back to Tushenko, who once more held his son's hand. How solemn they both were. Her heart went out to the child. If his father meant to stay on after he'd had his say, she would take August upstairs to Felicity.

"I hope Erika is well. Did she accompany you?"

"Erika is dead. August and I have come to fetch you. To take you to Hochstein with us."

Twenty-nine

How still it was in the room. She could hear the blood pulsing in her ears. Could hear little August's breathing. Could still hear the echo of Tushenko's words . . . Erika dead . . . have come to take you to Hochstein.

Fate had caught up with her at last.

She looked past Tushenko at Stanmore. Their eyes met and held, and with a start she realized that she knew his mind once more.

You're mine, Thea. I won't give you up.

In her heart, she answered him. *My love is yours. Forever.*

The harsh accent of Tushenko's voice drew her attention.

He said, "Toward the middle of May, five years ago, I set out to fetch you, as agreed. An Englishman intercepted me in Saxony. He had letters of passport, also papers identifying him as an agent of the Foreign Office. He said you had died and I was to return to St. Petersburg."

Miles, resting a shoulder against the door jamb, scoffed. "A likely tale!"

Tushenko turned to him briefly but made no retort.

Wellesley said, "Miss Stone, I explained to Count Tushenko that the man was an imposter. The messengers Mulgrave sent abroad with false news of your death did not leave London until the twenty-second of June, the day Tushenko was supposed to have met you at the Foreign Office. And they had instructions, should they encounter him, to speed him on to London."

"Discussion of the past can be to no purpose, sir. I would rather be informed about the present."

"It shall be as you wish," said Tushenko. "But the present, without the past, is not easily explained."

How could she deny that . . . Thea Stone, the historian. But she felt strangely disoriented, as if she was in a dream that had taken her into another time, a time to which she had no key—no Dorothea to lend her perspective.

She had expected a summary of the situation in Hochstein after Friedrich's death. Had even expected a request from Lord Wellesley—possibly, a demand—to go to Hochstein. But never had she considered the possibility that Tushenko would come to fetch her.

She set out on an agitated turn about the room but collected herself after a few steps and faced Tushenko and his small son again.

"August should not be here. Will you let me take him upstairs? My friend, Lady Felicity Markham, will look after him."

Tushenko hesitated. "Since his mother died he does not like to leave me."

Moving quietly, Stanmore fetched a pack of cards from the mantel. "August, do you know how to build a house of cards?"

Nodding, the boy took a tentative step toward Stanmore, then stopped and looked up at his father with questioning eyes.

"I will be here," Tushenko said gravely.

A few moments later, August and Stanmore both knelt on the rug Stanmore had pulled close to the hearth of cold, smooth marble. But while the child was totally engrossed in building the house of cards, Stanmore's eyes moved constantly from the cards to Thea and Tushenko standing alone in the middle of the room. Lord Wellesley had retreated to a window. Watch in hand, he was gazing out into the street.

Thea said, "Pray accept my condolences on the loss of your wife."

Tushenko bowed.

"I did not know," said Thea. "I was told only that Cousin Friedrich died."

"And I did not know until after the death of Friedrich—and neither did Erika—that she was not lawfully my wife. Theadora, you must believe me. Erika and I would not have wittingly wronged you. Now I have come to make amends, to honor the contract of matrimony existing between us."

If she had ever had a slim chance to choose her own destiny, it had escaped her clasp. Her breath caught, and she looked for Stanmore by the fireplace. Only August was there. For an instant, she knew fear that Stanmore had left.

Then she sensed his presence behind her. She felt it so clearly, it was as if he touched her, embracing her with his strength and support.

"You do not speak, Theadora." For the first time, Tushenko's voice betrayed uncertainty. His gaze flicked past her but returned to her almost immediately. "I was assured you were still waiting for me—did not have the marriage annulled."

Her eyes widened. *"Waiting!* I daresay you expected to find me wearing the willow."

"Wearing a willow? I fear I do not understand."

"It was a foolish comment. I beg your pardon." The feeling of unreality had passed. Crisply, she said, "Let me assure you that you need not feel obliged to make amends of any kind."

"On the contrary. I am legally and morally obligated."

Pocketing his watch, Wellesley joined them. "Count Tushenko will also honor his pledge—given ten years ago through the offices of his representative—to restore you to the throne of Hochstein."

Behind her, Stanmore moved. Determinedly, she kept her eyes on Tushenko.

"Why? If I return, your son will no longer be Prince von Hochstein. Not even Hereditary Prince. Nor will you be Regent."

"How can you ask why? We are pledged! Erika . . . she understood that I was in honor bound—"

A commotion could be heard in the street, but Thea wondered if that was, indeed, the reason Tushenko broke off. When he mentioned Erika, his eyes had darkened. With pain? Anger? Or some other strong emotion?

She wanted to ask how Erika had died, but somewhere nearby, perhaps outside the front door, perhaps as close as the entrance hall, an argument erupted. Lord Wellesley nodded to Miles, who opened the sitting room door.

Tushenko turned away from Thea, toward the noise, and Stanmore grasped the opportunity to step close to her.

"You're mine," he whispered, then moved aside.

Caught in the spell of the haunting words, Thea watched the arguing parties enter the room. The three gentlemen, one of whom was Mr. Featherlight, fell silent. The lady, thin and bent, dressed all in black, and walking with a cane, did not.

Advancing on Lord Wellesley, she said querulously, "I will not be kept outside a moment longer. Not in the company of oafs! And if Tushenko hasn't made use of his time and pled his case, then he doesn't deserve to be heard."

Thea was staring at the cane of thick carved ebony wood, topped by a golden dragon. Somewhere, sometime, she had seen such a cane.

The woman turned. Pale gray-blue eyes in an ancient, wrinkled face measured Thea with astonishing sharpness.

"So you're Theadora. You don't look anything like I imagined."

Joyful certainty warred with disbelief. "Grandmother Augusta?"

"Who else would be fool enough at my age—and don't ask me what it is—to cross the Channel in March? In a Dutch sloop of all things, hidden next to casks of smuggled rum! Well, don't stand there! Come here, child. Give me a kiss."

When Thea had hugged and kissed the matriarch of the von Waldfrieden family, she found young August at her side, his wide eyes fixed unblinkingly on her.

"That is *my* grandmother."

"Yes, she is. But we are cousins, August. That makes her mine, too."

"My house got blown over when the door opened."

"What house?" asked Augusta von Waldfrieden and allowed the boy to lead her to the fireplace.

For a moment, Thea stood alone. Her joy at seeing the one relative who had been close to her parents' hearts was submerged in a renewed sense of unreality. And she was gripped by a sudden chill. Grandmother Augusta would not have left home without a powerful reason.

A warm hand briefly closed over her cold one. Stanmore, passing her. No. Joining her. For once, she did not know whether his closeness made her feel better or worse.

She kept her voice light. "Quite a family gathering. But I wish Miles would sit down. He does not look at all well."

"No matter how ill he feels, he will hardly take his ease in a chair while you and your great-grandmother are standing. You never told me that she is English."

"Does it matter?"

"Yes. I want to know everything about you and your family."

"She has no family left here in England." Thea looked away, toward the window. "Who are the two gentlemen in conference with Tushenko and Lord Wellesley and his aide?"

"Don't ask me for names. I have forgotten. All I know is that they're members of the Hochstein Council."

Glad, after all, that he was near, she gave him a wry little smile. *"Not* a family gathering."

He did not speak. There was no need. She saw her own apprehensions mirrored in his eyes, and there was the occasional twitch of his left eyelid, which she had noticed on her first night at Archer Hall when he kept a tight check on his emotions over an outburst from Charlie.

He said, "I wonder how your cousin Erika died."

"Were you not told?"

"Miles and I were told nothing. There was no time, save for introductions."

"I confess that briefly I wondered whether Tushenko—" Embarrassed, she broke off.

Stanmore raised a brow. "Killed her?"

"Foolish of me, I know."

"Why?"

"Because it is impossible. He seems . . . *is* too much like you in character. Driven by a strong sense of honor, duty, and obligation."

Quietly, he said, "A man may kill to protect what he perceives as his honor."

She did not argue; she knew it to be true. She glanced at Miles, still standing by the door. How pale he was.

High and thin, yet imperious, Baroness von Waldfrieden's voice drew immediate attention. "Gadzooks! This room is as cold as the carriage. Theadora, order a fire lit immediately!"

"Stanmore will do it." With an apologetic look, Thea said softly, "You don't mind, do you? I want no interruptions now. And please get Miles away from the door. Have *him* build a house of cards with the boy."

But she need not have worried about Miles . . . or anyone. Her great-grandmother, seeing her first command obeyed, allowed Lord Wellesley to usher her to a sofa not too far from the fireplace but facing the door, and from there proceeded to direct all arrangements.

"August, give Captain Simmons your arm and take him to this ugly striped chair beside me. You've seen French soldiers at Hochstein. Let Captain Simmons tell you about the *British* army, and at the same time he can make himself useful and serve as a fire screen for me."

Next, she pointed a gnarled finger at Mr. Featherlight. "Young man, you won't be needed for a while. Come back in an hour. And bring wine!"

Then Thea was summoned so that the two members of the Hochstein Council could be presented. Baron von Feldhausen was of an age with the Marquis Wellesley, even looked a bit like the Foreign Secretary with his long, aquiline nose, the high forehead and balding pate. Herr Johann Huss was scarcely older than Thea, and his thick fair hair, curling wildly, must have been the envy of many a female.

"Your Highness." Baron von Feldhausen bowed deeply. "I represent a party of the Council wishing to see you installed as ruler of Hochstein—*without* Count Tushenko."

Before she could respond, or even react to the disclosure, Johann Huss stepped forward to state his case.

"Miss Stone—this is how Lord Wellesley said we should address you, but the Baron von Feldhausen has forgotten. I am sent to ask you to come to Hochstein at any cost—with or without Count Tushenko—for the reason that we wish to break away from French rule."

"I support that move," said Tushenko, joining them.

Huss nodded. "That is so, Miss Stone. It is one of the reasons we do not reject the count as consort."

"A *bigamist*." Baron von Feldhausen made it sound as if he spat.

Tushenko paled. Lightning quick, his arm cocked, the hand opening as if in preparation for a slap.

"Tushenko!" said Thea at the same time as Stanmore stepped between the two men.

"Your son needs you," Stanmore said quietly.

For an instant, it seemed as if Tushenko had not heard. Then he dropped his hand, bowed stiffly, and joined August and Miles.

Immediately, Johann Huss seized Thea's attention again.

"Miss Stone, we must consider Count Tushenko's connection with the court of St. Petersburg. It would not be in our interest to alienate Tsar Alexander, who, we are certain, will once more join the English in the fight against France."

"You're a fool, Huss!" Baron von Feldhausen raised a quizzing glass to his eye. "Green and ignorant and dangerous."

Huss ignored him. "By now, the Archduchess Marie-Louise will be on her way to France—"

"Precisely," von Feldhausen cut in. "Which means that next

time Austria invades Hochstein and Saxony, no French General will come to our aid."

"*You* are the fool, Herr Baron! When Austria signed the treaty with France, she became our ally as well."

"Then I advise you to remember that."

Huss looked taken aback.

The baron said softly, "You're not only a young fool, but a deceitful, seditious blunderer. Permitting the Bohemian rabble who plot secession from Austria to meet at your house!"

Huss turned crimson. "And *you,* Baron, are a cowardly traitor! You and your friends looked the other way when Miss Stone's father was dethroned. You have forfeited the right to criticize."

"If I have no right, I have a duty! And not only to criticize but to interfere. I swear I will stop you and others like you! You shall not destroy Hochstein!"

At some point during the argument the men had switched to German, though Thea, if asked, would not have been able to say when precisely the switch had taken place—or when precisely she had joined her great-grandmother on the sofa. Her mind was spinning with all she heard.

Bohemia, Hochstein's neighbor to the south, was part of the Austrian Empire. The majority of the population spoke Czech, as did many of the families living in the mountainous region of Hochstein, which adjoined Bohemia . . . and Huss was a Czech name. It seemed, political intrigue in her birthplace had not died with Cousin Friedrich, and now she was to have a choice after all. Three choices.

She felt the familiar tickle of wry laughter that had so often helped her in difficult times. But it would hardly help now.

She glanced at her great-grandmother. The old lady seemed oblivious to the anger simmering between the two men from Hochstein and was talking about Portugal with Miles and Lord Wellesley, whose younger brother, Arthur, was commanding the Peninsular campaign and had been created Viscount Wellington of Talavera.

Thea's gaze moved on to Tushenko. She could not see his face to judge how much of the rapid German he understood, for he had settled his son at a low table and was bending over him to demonstrate the laying out of cards in a game of solitaire.

And Stanmore—some time ago, she had seen him take the last pieces of wood from the basket and put them on the fire. Dusting off his hands, he had passed Miles's chair and walked around the back of the sofa. If she turned her head just a little, she would see him standing to her right. But she had looked once. That must suffice.

"Miss Stone—Highness!" Speaking English again, Johann Huss turned a heated face toward her. "Hochstein needs you. Say you will return!"

Baron von Feldhausen said sharply, "But not, I beg, to add to the unrest young firebrands like Huss are stirring."

"We must not be allied with France and Austria!" cried Huss. "I am speaking for Miss Stone, I am sure—"

Thea interrupted. "Do not presume, Mr. Huss. I will speak for myself."

All color drained from his face. "Highness! I was sent to convince you. I must not fail!"

When she did not immediately reply, he took an impetuous step toward her. He reached inside his coat—a gesture that sent a chill down her back, for she remembered it only too well from another time, five years earlier, at the Foreign Office.

But Johann Huss was not permitted to withdraw whatever he was reaching for. Stanmore leaped in front of Thea and clasped the young man's arm while Miles, kicking back his chair, thrust the point of his sword against Huss's neck.

"Guter Gott im Himmel!" The Hochsteiner did not move, only rolled his eyes.

Augusta von Waldfrieden tapped her cane sharply. "What is the meaning of this? Captain Simmons! Put down your sword immediately."

Stanmore said, "First we'll see what the gentleman has hidden away."

"A petition." Huss had recovered somewhat and tried to look around Stanmore at Thea. "Signed by the Czech speaking families in the Erzgebirge and south of it."

"The Ore Mountain region." She rose, feeling dazed. How fast Stanmore had acted! And Miles, too. "Stanmore, I believe Huss is speaking the truth."

"He has shown me such a document," said Wellesley.

And it was indeed a petition Stanmore drew from a pocket inside Huss's coat and handed to Thea. Miles sheathed his sword, and Stanmore let go of the young man's arm.

"A fine piece of knight-errantry," Stanmore said with a disarming grin. "My apologies."

He looked at Thea. "Only promise me not to tell Charlie or, heaven forbid, Silas about this!"

She could not help but smile, despite a wrench of pain at his assumption that she would see anyone at Archer Hall again. "Charlie is too well mannered to laugh. But how Silas would roast you!"

Tushenko approached, his grave eyes moving from Thea to Stanmore.

"Huss is not a man of deceit, Theadora. I would be sorry to think that you were frightened of him."

"There scarcely was time—and if I did suffer fear, it ceased the moment Stanmore stepped in front of me."

"Ah, yes. Your champion."

She looked at Stanmore. Her love.

"Theadora!" Augusta von Waldfrieden's voice was sharp. "Has Tushenko told you why he married Erika?"

Thirty

Slowly, Thea turned.

"It was my doing," said Augusta von Waldfrieden.

Baron von Feldhausen said, "Highness, if you permit, there is something I must explain. His Eminence, the Cardinal Archbishop—"

"Not now!" Augusta jabbed her cane at him. "If you don't have the decency to leave, at least stay out of sight and keep quiet. Huss, too."

When the two men had retreated with Lord Wellesley to a window, she turned fierce eyes on Thea.

"I had no traffic with Friedrich after he drove your father out of Hochstein. But I allowed Erika to visit me. And that is where she met Tushenko. At my house. He meant to return to St. Petersburg. But he stopped to share the news of your death."

Tushenko's mouth curled, giving him a sinister look. His voice, though, was gentle. "Babushka, do not trouble yourself. Theadora does not want to know about the past. I am beginning to think that, far from being the injured party, she is largely to blame for what has happened."

"Sir." Stanmore did not raise his voice, but it cut like finely honed steel. "You will take that back and apologize."

Tushenko's eyes blazed.

"Gentlemen." Thea did not raise her voice either; she stepped between them. "Before I am accused or defended, I would like to hear what else my grandmother has to say."

"As, indeed, you shall," said Augusta. "I have not traveled all this way for the pleasure of it."

Alert, knowing eyes moved from Tushenko to Stanmore, then came to rest on Thea. "Sergei and Erika fell in love—though she said that she loved him already when she was seven and watched him pledge his troth to you. But they hadn't seen each other since then; so I daresay that's a bit of nonsense."

And perhaps it wasn't. Thea knew well that present and future were seeded far in the past . . . in days of yore.

"Pay attention, child! Erika needed someone like Sergei—a strong yet gentle, honorable man. She was Friedrich's heir but not cut out to rule. So I encouraged them. And why not?" Augusta's voice held a defensive note. "I thought you were dead! By the time I received another letter from you, they had been married for almost a year."

"The letter," Thea said tonelessly, "in which I asked you not to let on that I was alive."

"And I didn't. I said nothing until after Friedrich's death. That was in early December, and on his deathbed he told Erika that it was he who sent a man to kill you. She was distraught. Christmas, Tushenko came to Waldfrieden and begged me to accompany him to Hochstein."

"Erika was with child," said Tushenko. "It was not good for her to be so unhappy. I believed a visit would help."

Augusta said, "I told Erika and Sergei that you are alive. It calmed Erika—or so I thought—even though it meant, of course, that her marriage was invalid. She was quiet . . . accepting of her fate. She insisted that Tushenko must honor the older pledge to you."

The silence following her great-grandmother's words filled Thea with apprehension. There was more to come . . . more, she had yet to be told. The silence seemed to speak to her, seemed intent on filling her mind with knowledge she did not want. . . .

There was a tower . . . a high, gray stone tower crowned with a battlement. She did not want to look. But some slight movement drew her, would not let her tear her eyes away. Something . . . in one of the crenels . . . light-blue cloth . . . a woman's cloak.

"It is Mama."

"No!" The ferocity of her own voice startled Thea and dispelled the vision. She was trembling, but no one seemed to notice. Tushenko was speaking softly to Augusta. Near the fireplace, Stanmore and Miles had their heads together.

But there was young August, standing before her, staring at her with bewildered, hurt eyes.

"Indeed it is! It is Mama." He offered a locket on a fob chain. "She fell off the Adlerturm."

The Eagle Tower. One hundred and twenty-six steps of wicked spiral stairs, so Vespera had described the north tower of Castle Hochstein.

Thea looked at the miniature in the locket. The young woman smiled at her—a warm, gentle smile—and her eyes were as wide and blue and trusting as August's.

She closed the locket and returned it to the boy. "Thank you for sharing it with me."

One hundred and twenty-six steps. And Erika with child.

August said, "I want go home. I want to see Mama. Is she better now?"

He was only three. And Thea felt woefully inadequate to explain death.

Tushenko relieved her of the task. He picked the boy up, settling him on his arm so that they were face to face.

"Soon we will go home. I promise. But Mama cannot be there. We miss her very much, do we not?"

Drawing a ragged breath, August pressed his face against his father's neck, but when his great-great-grandmother called him, he raised no objections to being set down.

Tushenko faced Thea. "Stanmore is correct. I must apologize to you. Erika and I married the day I should have been here in London—with you—to have the old promise of marriage solemnized. You are not to be blamed for my mistakes."

"Later, when I knew about you and Erika, I could have had that old contract voided."

Tushenko's face clouded.

Quickly, before she could reconsider, she said, "Erika's death—please tell me what happened. August mentioned the Adlerturm?"

His pain was a tangible thing. After a seemingly endless moment, he answered her.

"Erika enjoyed the view. But she had not gone up in months. Not since she learned she was with child. I do not know why she did that morning. Or why . . . she fell."

Thea could think of nothing to say, except that she was sorry. And that would not help at all.

Looking past Tushenko, she saw Stanmore hand a glass of wine to her great-grandmother, now in a chair close to the fire, and milk to August, on cushions at Augusta's feet. Was Stanmore a magician to procure drink from nowhere? She did not see Miles, or Wellesley and the two gentlemen from Hochstein. But it scarcely mattered as long as the smiling face in August's locket still haunted her.

With firm, purposeful steps, Stanmore joined her and Tushenko.

Tushenko asked, "Where is Lord Wellesley?"

"He returned to the Foreign Office with Huss and Baron von Feldhausen." Stanmore looked at Thea. "Miles decided to pay his respects to Felicity."

"Very proper of him." She recalled seeing Stanmore and Miles earlier with their heads together. No doubt, the departures were carefully arranged.

"And now," said Stanmore, "let us resolve this painful matter."

Tushenko's eyes narrowed. "You refer, I take it, to Princess Theadora's return to Hochstein. Have you a concern in this?"

"I have asked Miss Stone to be my wife."

"Theadora is not free to marry." Tushenko faced her. "You

did not have our contract annulled when I did not come for you. With good reason, I understand."

"It seemed so at the time."

"Lord Wellesley explained. Your consideration for Hochstein does you honor. I had no say when Friedrich decided to join Napoleon's Grand Empire. Now it is different. I am in agreement with Huss that we must separate from France, but we must wait for the right moment."

"Then I am not needed." Her pulse quickened. Could it be so simple? "You and Huss will play the role the Foreign Office intended for me. And I don't doubt that you, without prodding from me or anyone, will try to persuade Tsar Alexander to join forces with England."

Stanmore said, "The Tsar has already made overtures. I had it from the First Lord of Admiralty. No doubt, in his own good time, Wellesley will remember that such news is important to you."

How often Felicity had called her a pawn in the struggle for supremacy on the Continent. But anger at Wellesley's cavalier treatment would be wasted energy.

Tushenko said, "I do not understand. I believed you committed not only to Hochstein but also to the English government."

"Thea—" Stanmore's voice was calm, almost indifferent. "Forget governments. Forget the promise you made five years ago under vastly different circumstances. Give consideration to the people directly affected by the decision you must make now."

Tushenko raised a brow. "What decision is there? Theadora, we are pledged in marriage, and I gave my word to restore you to the throne of Hochstein. Now I have come to fetch you so that we may both fulfill our obligations."

She was keenly aware of the two men, not dissimilar in character or stature. Standing perhaps two paces apart, they faced her.

Tushenko said, "Erika understood that my obligation to you

must supercede my promise to her. She bore you no ill will, nor would she have been an embarrassment to you. She planned to remove with August to my estate in the Ukraine."

But Erika was dead. August, like Dorothea Wortley's son, was illegitimate. And there would have been a second child....

Thea looked toward the fireplace. August was once more playing with the deck of cards. Such a quiet little boy. Augusta von Waldfrieden appeared to be asleep, head resting against the cushioned back of the chair, face turned toward Thea and the two men. Ninety-two years old, she had traveled through war-ravaged German states and Holland, had crossed the Channel—not for the pleasure of it, she had assured Thea.

Augusta opened her eyes, looking straight at her great-granddaughter.

"Return with us. That's why I came. To ask you to come home. Erika hoped that you would adopt August. Make him your heir. Sergei—"

Tushenko's voice was harsh. "Theadora and I will make that decision when we are in Hochstein."

"Please! Don't have me making decisions in Hochstein when I have not said that I will go with you."

Struggling for composure, Thea started to pace. Had she truly believed, if only for an instant, that this would be a simple decision? It appeared, she need no longer feel obliged to honor the old promise of marriage for Hochstein's sake or England's. But now that she had seen Grandmother Augusta, had heard her plea, had met Tushenko and his son—

Tushenko said, "I have no fear that you will refuse to go with me. You would not consider the baron's proposal to return *without* me."

There was no need to deliberate. The throne of Hochstein in itself held no lure for her. "No. I would not."

"Then it is settled." Tushenko started toward her.

Stanmore's long stride took him past the other man. He clasped Thea's shoulders.

"You have heard Tushenko and your grandmother. You have

listened at great length to the baron and to Huss. Will you not accord me a few moments before you make a decision?"

His touch made her tremble. What could he say that she did not already know . . . that would not make the decision harder? Her love was his forever.

She saw Tushenko looking at her gravely, saw August cross the room and take his father's hand.

Stepping back, Stanmore released her. But then he spoke, and it was as if he had never let go.

"The moment I saw you, I was enchanted by your smile, your voice, the way you move and hold your head . . . your dedication and sincerity, your readiness to laugh at yourself and teach me to laugh . . . everything about you has captured my heart. Thea, what I want to say is—I love you."

She wanted to cast herself into his arms, wanted to hold him, never to let go.

"You're crying," said August.

Blindly, she turned. Somewhere ahead of her was a wall, windows . . . something to cling to. Her hand encountered velvet and clutched around a thick fold.

August. Erika's illegitimate son. Only three years old. If, five years ago, she had insisted on annulment of the old marriage contract, Tushenko and Erika could have repeated their vows, and August would have been born legitimate.

Instead, she had promised Lord Mulgrave not to have the marriage annulled. At the time, it had seemed a simple decision, the only possible decision in view of the rapid spread of Napoleon's Grand Empire. But she did not have to face a small boy then. Or her great-grandmother. Or the man whose eyes darkened with pain every time he spoke of Erika.

Present and future were seeded in the past. . . .

Her hand began to tingle and she loosened her clutch on the velvet drape. How quiet the sitting room was. Perhaps she was alone. But she did not turn to find out.

She thought of Erika, who had smiled at her from a locket. Who had loved Tushenko and married him because she believed her cousin Theodora dead. Erika, who had climbed to the top of the Adlerturm. And had hoped that August would be adopted.

Adoption, approved and sealed by the Hochstein Council, would grant August the right to succession.

Dorothea's son had been adopted. *God bless the child . . . God have mercy on his mother.*

Dorothea had left England to live in Hochstein—had she been happy?

For a moment, Thea rested her forehead against the cool window glass. To find love and happiness, was it not every man and woman's dream?

But she must reach a decision, not pursue a dream. She must take care to remember that present and future were seeded in the past. Before she drew another breath, this very moment would be the past. As soon as she would turn and speak, every word spoken would become past, with the power to touch and shape the future.

Taking a deep breath, she turned.

Only Stanmore and Tushenko were in the room, sentinals, one to either side of the fireplace where the remnants of a log glowed dully. But she had no need to see her great-grandmother and August to remember that they would be affected by her decision as much as the two men. As much as she herself would be. May God give her strength.

Stanmore and Tushenko moved in unison to meet her, neither attempting to outstrip the other. To Stanmore, each step taking him closer to Thea was a test of his strength as he watched the grave face and saw the look of pain in her eyes. He wanted to catch her in his arms and carry her off—and damn the consequences. But for that it was too late. He should have done it before she came to a decision. But he had not— just as he had not tried earlier to remove the two people who would most arouse her compassion and appeal to her sense of duty and obligation.

He did not look at Tushenko. If the man were a cur, despicable, loathsome, he could have dealt with him in an appropriate manner. But Tushenko was not. The only thing despicable about him was that he had a right to Thea.

She was looking at Tushenko. Stanmore's hands clenched. Was there a protocol? Did the lady first address the victor or the vanquished?

She said, "I am sorry. Very sorry. But I cannot go to Hochstein with you."

Stanmore's breath caught, and he, who had all his life abhorred an open display of emotion, found himself struggling against a shout of joy that would have put his father's best roar to shame. But he must neither shout nor catch his beloved in his arms and swing her high in a burst of sheer joy. Not in the presence of the pale man, who bowed stiffly in acceptance of Thea's decision.

"I shall not fight you." The look of defeat on Tushenko's face emphasized his words. "But tell me why. This is severe punishment, since August and I can hardly return without you. In past centuries, the boy's status might not have mattered. But today an illegitimate child holds no place in the succession."

As pale as Tushenko, Thea said, "I would not hesitate to adopt him, but I cannot be your wife. If I went with you to Hochstein, it would be with the greatest reluctance. And if the Council then refused approval of the adoption . . . Lud, Tushenko! I would have sacrificed my happiness and Stanmore's for nothing. Do you not think I would have learned to hate you?"

Quickly, Stanmore moved to her side. He could not flaunt his victory by taking her into his arms, but he would lend support by standing close. The smile she gave him caught at his heart. It left no doubt that she loved him, but it also betrayed a great sadness.

Turning back to Tushenko, she said quietly, "I believe you would have come to hate me, too. And to despise yourself. Much as you wish to remove the stigma of illegitimacy from your son, you want even more to clear Erika's name, do you not? By honoring the old contract with me, you would be doing just the opposite. August would grow up in a house of bitterness and hate."

"You need not justify your decision. I said I would not fight it. Pray hold me excused." Tushenko bowed. "Theadora—your servant. Stanmore—my congratulations."

Taking a step toward him, Thea placed a hand on his arm. "I wish I could undo the past. You and Erika married in good faith—believing me dead. Your vows were duly solemnized. Surely, if we put our heads together, we can find a way to restore August to his birthright."

Tushenko's mouth twisted. "Perhaps he shall, like his grandfather, take Hochstein by force and have himself proclaimed Prince of Hochstein."

"No need for sarcasm," Stanmore said absently, his mind on the small boy whose unfortunate situation gave Thea's beautiful eyes a haunted look. "These are halcyon days for the German states. But I doubt not that they are numbered. When war breaks out again next month or next year, new kings and princes will emerge."

Catching a glimpse of Thea's face, he hastily changed tack. "If Erika and Tushenko were lawfully wedded while the Princess Theadora Evalina was believed dead—"

"Of course!" A glow kindled in Thea's eyes. "The princess will remain dead. I have no need of the title. Tushenko, that would put everything to rights, would it not? Your and Erika's marriage. August's birth!"

"You are forgetting that others besides me have met you."

The sitting room door opened, helped along by a prod from Augusta von Waldfrieden's cane.

"It is settled, then? You will assume your duties in Hochstein, Theadora?"

Thea faltered, then crossed the room. "I am sorry, Grandmother Augusta. I will marry Stanmore."

Augusta's thin, bent shape seemed to shrink. She turned. "August and I are leaving. We're tired."

"Grandmother—"

Behind her, Tushenko said, "She *is* tired. Let her go. We left Lord Wellesley's country house at cock's crow, and she is accustomed to rest every two or three hours."

Her throat tight with unshed tears, Thea nodded.

"Lord Wellesley has put his apartments at our disposal. Come to the Foreign Office tomorrow. I will have explained by then."

"Thank you."

He bowed. *"Au revoir,* Theadora. And—I wish you well."

Their eyes met, one pair resigned, the other sad.

He stepped past her and out the door.

"Tushenko! Please wait."

Thea flew across the entrance hall and up the stairs. A few moments later she returned, breathless.

"Please give this to August." She offered a ring in the palm of her hand. "For his fob chain."

"Your father's signet."

"The signet of the Prince von Hochstein."

He hesitated only briefly. "On behalf of my son, I thank you."

Then, without a backward look, he strode off. Standing in the front door, Thea watched the carriage pull away just as a small face appeared at the window.

A hand, warm and firm, closed on her shoulder, turning her, propelling her into the sitting room. And before the door had shut, she was in Stanmore's arms.

He kissed her eyes and cheeks, wet with tears, then claimed her mouth. And Thea clung to him, returning his kiss with almost desperate fervor.

But the tears would not stop, and presently he drew her head onto his shoulder and let her cry. He made no attempt to stem the flow, only held her close, every now and then dropping a light kiss on her hair. When at last she raised her head, he offered his handkerchief.

"Thank you. What a watering pot I have become! I assure

you, though, the tears were an expression of happiness as much as they were of sadness."

He drew her to the sofa, settling her in the shelter of his arm. "We shall find a way to make August the Prince of Hochstein, I promise. Sadness shall not haunt you forever."

She smiled at him, and his pulse quickened, for it was the smile that had enchanted him from the moment he first saw it.

"I love you, Thea."

"And I love you. Stanmore, let us get married soon."

He clasped her more firmly. Holding her, breathing the delicate fragrance of her hair and skin, was intoxicating. How tempting it was to take her suggestion and marry her out of hand.

"When we are married, will you still call me Stanmore?"

Her eyes widened. "I believe I will. Stuart just does not sound right. Will you object?"

"No." He traced the delicate curve of her upper lip. "I like the way you say Stanmore. You make it sound . . . distinctive."

"Good. I feared that you would withdraw your offer if I refused to call you Stuart." She caught his hand, firmly keeping it away from her lips. "You did not answer me. About marrying soon."

"Thea, today would not be soon enough for me. But there is the small matter of getting an annulment."

A shadow crossed her face.

He said, "Leave it to me. I will arrange it with Tushenko, Wellesley, and the gentlemen of the Council. Meanwhile, I want you to return to your family in Ault Hucknall. I want to come calling and properly ask the Reverend Simmons for your hand."

Softly, she said, "You *are* a romantic."

"And we shall be married by your foster father on the twenty-second of June, in the chapel at Archer Hall. Two hundred years to the day Arbella married Seymour, and Prince Henry pledged his troth to Dorothea."

He thought she was about to refuse, but she asked, "You are not afraid that something will happen?"

"Dorothea has achieved her aim. She can have no cause to reach out to you again."

"You don't sound as certain as, perhaps, you wish to be. But you're right. We shall get married in the chapel. You must cast off that vestige of doubt I heard in your voice. And I—Stanmore, there was a dream."

"No more talk. We must make the most of our time before Felicity and Miles—"

There was no need to say more. Winding her arms around his neck, she offered her lips. Slowly, savoring the moment, he bent his head until his mouth touched hers.

Their kiss was promise, avowal of love. It was remembrance and discovery. It was a flame lit in days of yore, burning bright, never to darken.

Epilogue

June 22, 1810

Candlelight softened the starkness of fresh whitewash on the chapel walls. Above the fireplace and to either side of the crude mantel where once hung a collection of swords and guns, garlands of ivy, briar roses, harebells, bloodwort, and honeysuckle provided a touch of color. Late blooming lilacs and early roses decorated the altar and mingled their sweet scent with that of beeswax applied to the pews.

"Dearly beloved . . ."

As the Reverend Felix Simmons commenced the solemnization of matrimony, Thea stole a glance at the man beside her. Stanmore looked calm, but she did not miss the slight twitch of his eyelid. Perhaps he, too, was caught in the twin grip of breathless anticipation and sudden apprehension, the feeling of being hurled toward the unknown.

Their eyes met.

"I love you, Thea. Soon you will be mine."

"My love is yours forever."

"If any man can show just cause, why they may not lawfully be joined together, let him now speak, or else hereafter for ever hold his peace."

Her breath caught, even though she knew Tushenko did not sit in one of the pews to rise and claim her as his wife. Even if he were present, he would have no cause to speak. Two days ago, annulment of the old marriage contract had arrived from the Hochstein Council. Also a message of felicitation from Tushenko, who was taking August to St. Petersburg. Johann Huss, Tushenko wrote, was working on a scheme to reinstate August as Prince von Hochstein, but whether he would find support was questionable.

Her heart grew heavy, as always when she thought of the little boy. And of Grandmother Augusta. Not a word had come from Waldfrieden.

Thea had visited her great-grandmother daily at the Foreign Office in the hope of gaining Augusta's forgiveness. At last, when arrangements for the return journey were complete, Augusta had softened. She had hugged Thea tightly and imperiously told her to bring her husband to Waldfrieden for a visit. Surely, if she was in good health, she would have written.

Thea heard Stanmore's firm, "I will."

Her own response was a little shaky; she had almost missed her cue. Perhaps every bride had a hundred thousand thoughts and questions at the moment of marriage, despite the seemingly endless span of time leading up to the feverishly awaited day.

"Who giveth this woman to be married to this man?"

Miles stepped forward, together with Charlie, gravely bearing the ring. Ignoring Charlie's repressive frown, Bella accompanied her brother.

Throughout the exchange of vows Thea was aware of a stillness, an air of hushed expectancy in Stanmore. Each time they loosened their hands, she felt his reluctance to let go. When, at last, he placed the ring on her finger—the ruby Prince Henry had given to Dorothea—his hands were shaking. Did he not then believe what he had told her, that Dorothea no longer had reason to reach out through time and touch her life and his?

The ring slipped on the smooth silk of her glove. It had always been too large unless she wore it on her middle finger. Later, she would give it to Stanmore to wear. 'Twas only fitting that he should have Prince Henry's ring.

Once more her hand was joined with Stanmore's.

The Reverend Simmons said, "Those whom God hath joined together let no man put asunder."

Suddenly the familiar tingling warmth was there, increasing ever more and yet not burning. Stanmore's fingers closed painfully around hers as the chapel without windows slowly filled with bright sunlight.

In front of them, where the Reverend Simmons had stood at the altar table, was nothing but the bare floor of flagstones. By the fireplace stood a young couple gazing into each other's eyes, their hands entwined. At their feet, sitting on the hearth stone, a small boy was playing with carved farm animals.

"I love you, Thea."

"Henry . . . my love is yours. Forever."

As the couple embraced, the vision and the sunlight faded. Once more the chapel was lit only by candles on the altar and in wall brackets.

The Reverend Simmons said, ". . . and thereto have given and pledged their troth, each to the other, and have declared the same by giving and receiving a ring, and by joining hands; I pronounce that they are man and wife . . ."

Thea looked at Stanmore. He was pale, the hand that clasped hers, shaking. But the strange warmth no longer flowed between them, and after a moment he loosened the tight clasp on her fingers.

He leaned close. Softly, for her ear alone, he said, "I can no longer doubt that you journeyed into the past."

Just as softly, she replied, "And now my quest, and Dorothea's, is over."

There was no opportunity for further exchanges. The Reverend Simmons stepped forward to kiss his foster daughter and embrace his son-in-law. Lord Barnet, rugged and vigorous and not limping at all, approached from the first pew. He was followed by Vespera and Mary Simmons, both crying as befitted the bride's mothers. No one seemed at all perturbed or made a single reference to an inexplicable burst of shunshine in a chapel without windows.

Bella, looking important, gathered the train of Thea's gown, and they proceeded past the pews filled with a great number of Markhams and Simmonses. Silas Wilkins, a proprietary arm around his bride of two weeks, stood at the door opening into the great hall where the Archer Hall staff was waiting.

Bending, Silas whispered to Thea, "Look at him, will you! Dazed, he is. Didn't I tell you? When a man past thirty falls in love for the first time, he falls hard."

"Indeed. I don't need to turn my head, Silas. A look at you is quite sufficient."

In the great hall, Stanmore assisted Thea as she removed the myrtle coronet from her hair and, according to Hochstein tradition, presented it to the nearest unmarried female—Vespera Simmons. Then he took Thea into his arms and, according to Archer tradition, kissed the bride.

"Welcome, my love. To my house and to my heart."

1 - 800 - 52cp - 65 65
Instrumental Gold
3 Cassettes $17.95
4.00

Author's Note

Some time ago I happened to read a bit of history that instantly inspired the germ of a plot. It was the ancient rumor that Lady Arbella Stuart bore William Seymour a child during her stay at Barnet from the twenty-first of March, 1611, until the third of June, when she escaped.

Arbella and William Seymour were married on the twenty-second of June, 1610, and separated two weeks later, on the eighth of July. Arbella was placed in the custody of Sir Thomas Parry at Lambeth, and Seymour sent to the Tower. Historians make it clear that it was not impossible for Seymour to slip away from the Tower and row downriver for stolen meetings with Arbella, but I chose the twenty-fifth of March, 1611, as the birthday of my fictitious child since that was the day before Arbella was examined by the physician sent by King James, and it placed the date of conception within the two weeks Arbella and Seymour lived as husband and wife.

I used the original spelling—Arbella—since Thea Stone, my lady historian of Regency times, would certainly have done so. Throughout, I tried to be historically correct. I did take some liberties: by attributing an illegitimate son to the Master of Ruthven, younger brother of the Earl of Gowrie, and by making Dorothea Wortley's mother a cousin of the Earl of Gowrie, thereby creating a family connection between Lady Felicity and Thea Stone. And, of course, the greatest liberty of all: by creating a love relationship between Henry, Prince of Wales and the fictitious Dorothea Wortley.

Prince Henry died when he was only eighteen years old, but he had a maturity far beyond his years. He was an admirer and patron of the visual arts. He excelled in the martial arts in the tiltyard. Upon his creation of Prince of Wales at age sixteen, he set up his own court and was looked upon and saw himself as the conqueror who would vanquish England's enemies. Dreams of glory and a sense of destiny kept him from romantic dalliance, but he was precisely the kind of young man who, if he had fallen in love, might have given his troth in defiance of his father's wishes. He was called the glorious, the incomparable prince. The title of a contemporary elegy (William Basse, 1613), speaks for itself: *Great Brittaines svnnes-set, bewailed with a shower of teares.*

The principality of Hochstein is fictitious. When it joined Napoleon's Confederation of the Rhine, I merely allowed Hochstein to follow the example of Saxony and other German states.